DAUGHTER *of the* UNDERWORLD

DAUGHTER *of the* UNDERWORLD

KATHARINE & ELIZABETH CORR

CANDLEWICK PRESS

This is a work of fiction. Names, characters, places, and incidents are either products of the authors' imaginations or, if real, are used fictitiously.

Copyright © 2022 by Katharine and Elizabeth Corr

All rights reserved. No part of this book may be reproduced, transmitted, or stored in an information retrieval system in any form or by any means, graphic, electronic, or mechanical, including photocopying, taping, and recording, without prior written permission from the publisher. Additionally, no part of this book may be used or reproduced in any manner for the purpose of training artificial intelligence technologies or systems, nor for text and data mining.

First US edition 2025
First published by Hot Key Books (UK) 2022

Library of Congress Control Number: pending
ISBN 978-1-5362-4453-3

25 26 27 28 29 30 SHD 10 9 8 7 6 5 4 3 2 1

Printed in Chelsea, MI, USA

This book was typeset in Berling LT STD.

Candlewick Press
99 Dover Street
Somerville, Massachusetts 02144

www.candlewick.com

EU Authorized Representative: HackettFlynn Ltd, 36 Cloch Choirneal, Balrothery, Co. Dublin, K32 C942, Ireland.
EU@walkerpublishinggroup.com

A JUNIOR LIBRARY GUILD SELECTION

To everyone who has ever stood up to a tyrant

The Four Orders of Theodesmioi

Theodesmioi of the Order of ZEUS
king of the gods, ruler of the heavens and the earth

Battle Wagers ~ fight with beyond-human powers of speed and endurance

Weather Workers ~ control the clouds and wind

Theodesmioi of the Order of POSEIDON
god of the sea

Sea Singers ~ enhance the speed and strength of ships

Theodesmioi of the Order of HADES
god of the Underworld, ruler of the dead

Soul Severers ~ separate the soul from the body and send it on its journey

Theodesmioi of the Order of HEPHAESTUS
smith god and master of metals

Spell Casters ~ bind magic into metal

Note: Houses of the Orders of Zeus, Hades, and Poseidon are found in most cities. There are only two houses of the Order of Hephaestus, in Mycenae and Thebes.

Αἱ Μοῖραι προστάττουσι τοις πασιν θνητοῖς ἀποθνήσκειν
Οὕτως σε προσκαλέω τον ἀπαραιτήτους Θανατον.
Αἱ Μοῖραι προστάττουσι τοις πᾶσιν θνητοῖς πασχειν.
Οὕτως σε προσκαλέω τον ἀπαραιτήτους Θανατον.
ὅς, ὁ των θεών μόνος, ἡμας των ἡμετέρων Μοιρῶν ἄν ἐλευθεροῖ.

The Fates decree that all mortals should die.
Thus I call on you, pitiless Death.
The Fates decree that all mortals should suffer.
Thus I call on you, merciful Death,
Who alone of the gods
May free us from our fate.

Extract from "A Song of Severing,"
as recorded in the archives of the Order of Hades

Prologue

Sing, O muse...

That's how the old stories used to start. At least, that is how they used to start in Hellas, Greece—of all realms the most jealously guarded by its gods. A light-drenched land set in wine-dark waters, its craggy hillsides dense with pine, bright with acanthus, loud with the constant thrum of cicadas. Hillsides crowned with the cities of men: Mycenae, citadel of long-dead Agamemnon; warlike Sparta; rocky Aulis, where Iphigeneia died at her father's hand. Pylos of the golden sands, on which the palace of wise Nestor once stood, looking out across the Ionian Sea. And mightiest of all, Thebes, from where Orpheus the Tyrant sends out his armies, cutting down kingdom after kingdom.

Sing, O muse, a song of Death...

There's the city of Iolkos, high on its hill above the Gulf of Pagasae. Onetime home of Jason, second-rate hero, third-rate husband, and thief of the golden fleece. But the heroes—good and bad—dwindled and disappeared long ago. Now there are gods, and there are men, and there is Orpheus—a mortal who thinks he is a god. Iolkos is just a backwater, another place caught within his net. And there, in a granite-walled complex beyond the boundaries of the city, in a small lamplit room with its windows open to admit moonlight and the scent of rosemary from the garden beyond, lies a girl who is dying.

Sing, O muse, a song of Death and the maiden . . .

Sickness stalks the broad streets of Iolkos, and Death follows in its wake. After all, he is everywhere, in all living things: their beginnings, their endings, and each moment of existence between. Built into every atom of the space they inhabit. He is only, and always, to be expected. Whether through disease or violence or the swift-footed passage of the years, all life eventually falls beneath the shadow of his wings.

A plague has left fresh scars on this girl's cheeks. Her eyes are mismatched—one dark brown, one gray green—and half veiled by fever-fluttered lids. And there's a symbol on her forehead. She's one of the Theodesmioi, the god-marked. Marked by Zeus, king of the heavens and the earth, or by Poseidon, lord of the seas, or by Hephaestus, hammer-wielding master of metals, or, in this girl's case, by Hades, ruler of the Underworld. Serving the city in Hades's name and drawing a fraction of the god's power in return. A very small fraction. Not enough to save herself.

Death tightens his grip on his sword. Swings back the blade, ready to sever her lifeline and unship her soul from its earthly vessel. The movement brings him closer to her face.

Her unseeing eyes open. For the first time in more centuries than he can remember, Death hesitates.

A ring of gold has burst into being around the pupil of the girl's dark brown eye like the sudden unfolding of a sunflower. She gasps with pain and sinks back into oblivion. His sharp-edged blade is still ready. He knows he ought to use it.

And yet . . .

And yet, who's to say she can't survive? She's strong. A fighter. Perhaps there's something she wants very badly. A reason for her to try to stay alive. Death sheathes his sword, doing his best to ignore the voice he thought he'd long since silenced, the insidious whispering of hope.

What if she could be the one?

The girl's existence hangs by a fraying thread, fine as spider's silk, brittle as old bone but not quite broken. Death lingers, warming himself at the flickering embers of her life. She can't see him. She can't hear him. Still, he murmurs two words into the darkness.

Fight harder.

1

Iolkos, two years later

Hope, Deina decided, was a terrible thing.

From where she was standing in the shady, stone-paved portico of the megaron—the labyrinthine palace that sat at the heart of Iolkos's citadel—she couldn't see the guilty man. He hadn't yet been brought up from the cells. She could hear him well enough, though. Pleading with the guards. Begging, over and over. Bargaining. He'd been sentenced to what was generally held to be a fate worse than death. But apparently, despite all evidence to the contrary, he still hoped for mercy. Maybe even a miracle.

The gods alone knew why. In Deina's experience, neither they nor the city's rulers dealt in either. After all, the man had been condemned to undergo the Punishment Rite. The ritual stripped a soul from its human housing and trapped it forever in the Threshold—a space that functioned most of the time as a transition between life and death, a staging post between the mortal world and the Underworld, but which was transformed by this particular rite into an eternal prison. Of all the functions carried out by the Soul Severers—the Theodesmioi of the Order of Hades—the Punishment Rite was the most terrible, inflicted only for the worst crimes. So terrible that years might elapse between performances. No wonder so many had come to watch.

The dead heat of midsummer wrapped the city like a shroud, and even the buzzing clouds of fat black flies seemed drowsy. Still, people were crammed into the huge colonnaded courtyard that extended outward from the front of the megaron. More were huddled precariously on top of the massive ceremonial gateway that gave access to the palace complex. Some silent. Some gossiping. Some, enterprising, moving among the throng and trying to sell refreshments to anyone who could afford them. There weren't a lot of young men in the crowd, all told. So many had been conscripted into the Dominion's armies; so few had returned.

But there at the front of the crowd stood Aster, one of Deina's fellow Severers. Despite the press of people, there was a little space around him. Partly because of *what* he was, partly, Deina suspected, because no one wanted to accidentally jostle someone with such large and obvious muscles. As Aster frowned up at the portico, running a hand impatiently through his auburn curls, his lips were pursed like he'd eaten some particularly sour grapes. She'd heard him complaining—for days—that the rite should have been performed by him, or, at a push, Theron. They'd both been adepts for half a year longer than Deina; they were skilled; they were men. Deina gave him a cheery wave. Too bad Theron wasn't also here to witness her victory.

Deina's gaze drifted to the proclamation pinned to one of the gilded columns making up the front and sides of the portico. She could read a little of it. A sentence with the condemned man's name, Dionys, and his crimes: murder, treason. And the word *eupatridae*—the wellborn. Dionys either was a member of the nobility or the warrior class or had killed one. But the rest of the text was still beyond her. She had a lesson later—unofficially, of course. Perhaps she could somehow take the proclamation with her . . .

Her mouth was parched. Heat radiated off the stone altar, ready and waiting on the top step. Various priests, all nobles, were huddled into the deeper shade on the other side of the portico, fanning themselves and wilting. Deina's mentor, Anteïs, a red-robed elder of the Order of Hades, was standing nearby, eyes closed in meditation. Shouts from the crowd signaled the beginning of a fight. But the rite couldn't start without the presence of the archon, the highest rank in the city now that Iolkos was ruled from Thebes and had no king of its own. Perhaps the archon was still counting the gold for the quarterly tribute; the Theban collection ships were overdue. More likely, he was working out how much he could siphon off for himself while his city grew more and more impoverished.

There were two other Theodesmioi flanking the doorway to the megaron. The thunderbolt sigils on their foreheads marked them as members of the Order of Zeus, the god who held sway over the heavens and the earth. Part of the palace guard, so most likely Battle Wagers—Theodesmioi gifted with more-than-human reflexes and stamina, reflecting the earthly side of Zeus's remit. Only a few of their Order had the much rarer gift of influencing the winds and rains with their minds. If the archon had a Weather Worker in his employment, he would have boasted about it for all the city to hear. Still, Deina hissed at the nearest of them.

"Hey, can't you summon up some clouds?"

The man scowled at her, but before he could answer, the archon—heavily perfumed, ruddy faced, robes flapping—hurried through the doorway.

"Bring up the condemned," he ordered.

Struggling, still appealing for mercy, the man Dionys was dragged into the daylight. He was younger than Deina had expected. Naked, with bloody lacerations crisscrossing his skin from some earlier flogging. She'd seen bodies in a worse state. But the way he screamed when the guards bound him to the hot surface of the stone altar made her wince.

The archon cleared his throat. "People of Iolkos, this man, Dionys of the clan Diminae, has been found guilty of patricide and of plotting treason against the city." He dabbed the sweat from his forehead. "In accordance with the wise commands of our master, Orpheus, sovereign ruler of the Theban Dominion, he is to be handed over to the Soul Severers of the Order of Hades for punishment."

The archon wasn't telling the people anything they didn't know already. Still, the noise level in the courtyard rose.

Until one of the palace servants struck the huge bronze gong that stood nearby. The sound rippled through the air, leaving silence in its wake.

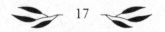

Deina came forward to stand next to the altar. The crowd stared at her, faces tilted upward, squinting in the noon sun. Even the blank stone eyes of the leaping dolphins that formed the gateway's arch seemed to be fixed on her. For once, she was grateful for the too-thick ceremonial robes and the veil that concealed her pockmarked face. Black linen for an adept, edged with scarlet—the sigil of Hades repeated in unending loops of woven flame.

But the people had the right to see the sign of her authority. Deina took a deep breath and folded back her veil to reveal the sigil on her forehead. The same symbol that scarred the forehead of Anteïs and that of every other Severer. Three stylized lines representing a scepter, topped by the upswept wings of a bird.

"Why don't you just kill me? My father deserved the death I gave him!" The condemned man was writhing, trying to break free. He twisted his head toward the archon. "You deserve it, too! All of you, standing by while Orpheus takes our lands and birthright, forcing us to fight over what's left—" He raised his eyes to Deina, standing by his head. "Please, I beg you . . ."

The bronze torc Deina had to wear was heavy against her collarbone. Ignoring the thumping of her heart, she deliberately turned away from Dionys as he was gagged. Doubt—of her choices, of her abilities—was a luxury she couldn't afford if she wanted any chance of being free. And what were the squabbles of the nobility to her? The wellborn knew nothing of what the Theodesmioi suffered, and they cared even less. In any case, if she'd turned down this opportunity, Theron would have taken it. Him, or Aster, or another Severer. Punish the criminal and earn a year's freedom—an entire twelve months struck from the forty-year period of her indenture—or watch someone else do it. An easy-enough choice.

As the archon and his retinue withdrew beyond the limits of the sacred circle, Deina tried to remember everything she'd been taught, everything she'd practiced, all the advice that Anteïs had given her.

The first time is always difficult. It's hard enough to draw a soul from a body that's not ready to leave. Harder still to resist the pleading—and there is always pleading. Remember, they are condemned by the king and by the city, not by us. We don't have to judge. We just have to act . . .

That's why the older woman was here: to lend a hand. Not that Deina planned on needing any help.

Deina's tools were already laid out on the table next to her: a sharp-bladed knife carved from bone, a small bowl of white poplar wood, dried herbs, and roots. And a vial of ashes, taken from the burned remains of the man's victim. She murmured the opening lines of the Song for this rite, the words that gave shape and purpose to the power that dwelled within her. Gripping her knife tightly, she focused on sliding the blade across the man's wrist to open the vein. His skin split exactly like the ripe figs Deina had practiced on, his blood flowing easily into the bowl. So far, so good. Ignoring his stifled screams, still chanting, she sprinkled the blood with a pinch of pungent mint, beloved of Hades, and one of rosemary, for memory. Added some shavings of dried asphodel root. Finally, she tipped in some of the ashes and mashed everything together with her knife.

Deina passed the bowl to Anteïs, keeping hold of the knife. She dipped her forefinger into the mixture, leaned forward, and

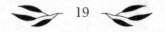

spoke the final lines of this part of the rite as she pressed her fingertip against the man's breastbone, then against Anteïs's, then against her own, staining the skin.

"Heart to measure."

The bright afternoon sunshine faded. Shadows began to gather and grow at the edges of the circle. Deina dipped her finger again.

"Touch to find." Forcing Dionys's hands open, she smeared the mixture on his palms. Then on Anteïs's, then on her own. The hair on Deina's arms stood up as the air within the circle cooled.

"Tongue to summon." His lips first, then Anteïs's, then hers. The noise of the crowd in the courtyard faded until Deina could hear nothing but the man's sobs and the slowing beat of her own heart.

"Blood to bind." She pressed her damp fingertips to Anteïs's brow and tipped what was left in the bowl onto the man's forehead. Placed her free hand gently on the side of his face as Anteïs gripped her shoulder tightly. Dionys had finally stopped struggling; no hope left now.

The sigil of Hades bound into Deina's skin was pulsing. Not pain exactly, but something so close to it that she had to grit her teeth and force herself to breathe evenly. She bent over until her forehead was just above Dionys's. Waited, until the light had almost gone, until she could feel frost forming on her skin, until she couldn't bear to resist a moment longer.

Finally, she let her head drop. The bloody mixture staining Dionys's forehead came into contact with her sigil. Darkness fell like an ax.

* * *

Sensation crept back. Deina became aware of the weight of Anteïs's hand on her shoulder. The cool solidity of the knife hilt in her palm. As the light returned, so did her sight.

She knew where she was: the Threshold. She'd been here before. A place constructed centuries ago by the first Soul Severers, drawing on the power of the Underworld but separate from it, and accessible only to those bearing the sigil of Hades. The Threshold was both familiar and strange. Always the same, but always different. Reconstructed each time according to the type of rite and the power of the Severer who had summoned it. A few days ago, Deina had carried out a Severing Rite, releasing the soul of a child from her badly burned body and setting her on the first step of her journey into and through the Underworld. An act of mercy that was the most common of the rites they were called on to conduct. The Threshold then had been welcoming—a small garden, bright with flowers. But this version of the Threshold was bleak and angular. A flat expanse of lifeless rock, dull gray sky above, surrounded by dense, unmoving clouds. It was almost like being marooned on the peak of a high mountain, with no visible means of descent. And looming over the space, conjured by Deina's will and the Punishment Rite, stood the Deathless Trees. Every detail from the Song, all exactly as she'd practiced: blackened bark, gnarled trunk, branches drooping like so much lank hair. Bones for roots, poking up out of the ground. Menace leaked from their rotting hearts like sap.

The man, Dionys, was standing nearby. His lifeline encircled his body—a faint silvery thread that also looped around

Deina's waist and around Anteïs's. It would fade soon, but until then, the lifeline tethered them all to the mortal world. But Dionys didn't seem to see it. Instead, he was staring at the unblemished skin on his wrist.

Deina cleared her throat, drawing his attention. His eyes widened in recognition, and he took off, sprinting full tilt toward the wall of mist surrounding the space, glancing over his shoulder at Deina while his lifeline unspooled behind him—until he slammed into the mist and flew backward. With one finger, Deina carefully prodded the fluffy edges of a nearby cloud—as solid and as sharp as glass.

Dionys still wasn't giving up. Back on his feet, he began running back and forth around the boundary, testing it, hurling himself against it in growing desperation.

Deina looked away and thought about the sketch of a ship pinned to the wall of her room. The kind of ship she hoped might one day take her somewhere. Anywhere, as long as it was far, far away from Iolkos.

"Deina." Anteïs nodded toward the man, one eyebrow raised. "Get on with it."

"Right." Deina ran her tongue over her dry lips, recalling the next part of the rite: the fettering. She took a deep breath and held up her arms.

"Deep-rooted Guardians of the Threshold, I call on thee. Deathless, lifeless, keep this accursed villain in your tender embrace and subject his soul to everlasting chastisement."

The roots and the branches of the two trees began to quiver, growing and slithering toward their prey, seeking blindly. When Dionys realized what was happening, he flung his hands up, mouth open in a silent scream. But there was no escape. With a mesmerizing inevitability, the trees embraced him, weaving themselves around him—arms, legs, body, head—until he was caught fast. The last tendrils latched on to his eyelids and forced them open.

Next, the summoning. Dionys bore the imprint of Deina's sigil on his forehead. At her words, something like smoke spilled from the mark, billowing and shifting until it became a full-size image: a living, moving memory, built out of the smoke itself. There was Dionys, a cup in his hand, approaching an old man who was lying propped up in a bed. Holding the cup to his father's lips and making him drain the contents. Standing there and watching as the other began to thrash about. The air within the Threshold grew rank with the stink of death and excrement, strong enough to make Deina gag. She could hear everything, too: the horrible gurgling of the old man choking, trying to breathe through the blood gushing from his mouth and nose. Until Dionys stood over his father's corpse, spattered with blood, an expression of triumph on his face.

As soon as it finished, the scene replayed from the beginning. Over and over. That was the point: for the murderer to experience the horror of what he had done. For eternity.

Anteïs was leaning heavily on Deina now, her eyes closed, her face drained of color, her breathing fast and shallow.

"Are you all right?"

"Yes, yes . . ." Anteïs sniffed and straightened up. "Hurry. The severing."

Deina nodded, tightened her grip on the knife, and picked her way across the floor of the Threshold—Anteïs following

closely, still gripping her shoulder—to where Dionys hung, immobile. Reaching the trees, Deina chanted the final prayer to Hades to end the rite as she drove her knife into a crack in one of the black branches and widened it. She gathered up the glimmering thread of Dionys's life and looped it tightly around the branch, making sure the lifeline was stuck fast into the crack, trapping him there, inside the Threshold. She shifted her hold on the knife to cut the other end of the cord, to send her and Anteïs back before it was too late.

Paused.

He was there . . .

Long hair, dark as jet, framing a young man's face. What looked to be old scars spiraling up and around the bare flesh of his arms. He wore a black tunic with a silver sword belt and seemed wrapped in a cloak of darkness, though his eyes glittered all the more brightly for that, like sapphires held up to the sun.

Deina lowered the knife as her grip on the hilt slackened.

Two years had passed since she'd first noticed him; every time one of the Severers' rites had led her beyond the boundaries of the mortal world into the Threshold, there he had been, watching her at a distance, as motionless as a beautifully crafted statue. Silent, too; he'd never spoken. Only his gaze had suggested he had some interest in her.

Questions crowded her mind: Who was he? What was he? Some Underworld creature that had breached the other side of the Threshold, even though all Deina had been taught told her that shouldn't be possible? A tremor of fear—of the creature, of what his appearance might mean—unsettled her breath.

He—it—moved. Cocked his head to one side, locked eyes with her, smiled, and began sauntering toward her.

A bolt of pain shot from Deina's left temple into her eye. She gasped. The creature drew closer, and the pain intensified until she was gritting her teeth. What was he doing to her?

"Deina, the knife!" Anteïs's voice jerked Deina back to the rite. To Dionys's lifeline, rapidly fading from existence. Before Deina could do more than swear at the danger her loss of concentration had placed them in, the elder snatched the blade and sliced through their end of the lifeline. Just in time. The Threshold spun away from them, and they were dragged back into the mortal world with a suddenness that took Deina's breath away.

They were standing on the top step of the portico. Dionys's body, now no more than an empty shell, was still bound to the altar.

Deina caught Anteïs as the older woman slumped. A servant hurried forward, and together they began to lead her back into the megaron.

"Fire . . ." Anteïs barely breathed the word, her eyelids fluttering.

Deina glanced over her shoulder at the archon, still loitering outside the circle. "It's done. You can burn what's left." No long rest for Dionys within the silent enclosure of the city's tombs. By the time she got Anteïs inside and the doors were shut behind them, kindling had been spread on top of his body, and the flames were already eating into his flesh.

The servant led them to one of the small rooms that made up the bulk of the megaron, helped Deina settle Anteïs on a

couch, and made his escape. Olives, bread, a jug of water, and another of vinegary wine had been left there in readiness; Deina poured herself a drink, picked at the refreshments, and watched her mentor's face. Anteïs was undergoing the Toll, the side effects that almost inevitably followed performance of any of the rites. The exercise of power exacted a varying price, depending on the strength of the Severer and the difficulty of the rite: headaches; vomiting; bleeding from nose, ears, or pores; temporary blindness; stomach cramps; seizures. Death, if you were inadequately prepared, weak, or unlucky.

Deina fretted a piece of bread into crumbs. She had carried out the whole rite, apart from cutting the lifeline at the end. Would it be enough? Would she receive the reward for the rite, or would Anteïs? Deina didn't feel tired or unwell, but then she very rarely did; for whatever reason, the Toll was mostly something that happened to other people. She lifted the neck of her tunic and gazed at her torso. Like that of all Soul Severers, her skin bore a record of her deeds. Rite-seals, they were called. Every severing, every laying, every hallowing—every time she'd wielded Hades's power in the service of the city—was imprinted on her flesh. A different symbol for each rite. Like one-half of a balance sheet, they showed how much time she had earned from her work, to set against the term of her indenture. The rite-seals began above one's heart; Deina's first, curving around her left breast, had already begun to fade to a paler scar. There was no sign yet of any new imprint, though sometimes they took a while to appear . . .

Anteïs opened her eyes, groaning.

"Hades, I'm getting too old for this." Her gaze focused on Deina. "What happened?"

"Don't you remember?"

"Oh, I remember. I remember having to take your knife and free us before the lifeline faded. Damn." Anteïs wiped away a trickle of blood from her nose. "So I'm going to ask you again: What happened?"

Deina hesitated. Going into details about the dark-haired boy would raise all sorts of questions. And she didn't have any answers. "I lost my nerve. That's all."

Anteïs pushed herself up on her elbows, eyebrows raised. "You lost your nerve."

The words, generously salted with disbelief, hung in the air. Deina would have to offer an edited version of events.

"I thought . . . I thought I saw something. Something in the Threshold that didn't belong there, that I hadn't called into being. I was mistaken, obviously. But it made me lose my concentration and I got a headache." She touched her temple. "The Toll, I suppose." Thinking about it, perhaps she *had* created the dark-haired boy, unintentionally. Those Severers who survived the physical demands of the rites often ended up losing their minds instead. Deina tipped back her head and drained the wine in her goblet.

"The Toll, before the completion of the rite? Hmm." Anteïs lay back on the couch. "Well, it's unfortunate." The elder pushed the fabric of her tunic up above her elbow, revealing a fresh abrasion on her bicep. "You lost your nerve, and I completed the rite, so I benefit from what should have been yours." She gave Deina's hand a quick pat. "I'm sorry, child."

Deina stared at the puckered red skin around the new rite-seal. A year off the term of her indenture. That's what she would have earned, if that mark had currently been burning its way into *her* skin. An entire year. There were no symbols yet on her own arms; they hadn't reached that far. She'd been earning rite-seals for four years, but of the forty years of service due under her indenture, she'd only worked off three.

Hot rage pounded through Deina's skull—but she couldn't give in to it. Not here. She wanted to slam the silver goblet she held over and over against the archon's elaborately painted walls. Instead, she gripped it until her fingers ached. Forced herself to breathe slowly until the fury ebbed. All she could do was keep playing the game, and play it even better.

A cart took them from the megaron back to the House. Anteïs slept while Deina brooded, listening to the bustle of the city and the gossip passing between their servant and the cart driver. The men discussed the weather, the price of bread, the latest war Orpheus was waging to push the boundaries of the Theban Dominion even farther. There'd been fresh news in the marketplaces that morning: a battle won in the west, twenty thousand of the enemy dead, more captured. Some of Orpheus's own soldiers, a cohort from Athens, slaughtered for objecting to the scale of the bloodshed. The walls of the defeated city pulled down and its fields plowed with salt because it had dared to resist. Rome, the driver called it. As the cart passed through Iolkos's main gates, into the short stretch of countryside that lay between the city and the House of Hades, Deina rolled the strange name around her mouth, almost like a prayer. Orpheus never lost. The people of that city had never stood a chance.

The heavy bronze gates of the House rumbled closed behind them. Even blindfolded, she would have known where she was. High stone walls sealed them in and shut out the rest of the world. Here, all was order. Bells, used to start and end the constant competition bouts in the training grounds—running, wrestling, archery, and bladework—formed a counterpoint to the chanting of the apprentices and novices as they learned the Severers' ancient Songs and rites. There *were* children here. Every winter solstice more arrived, those on whose foreheads the sigil had appeared that year, rounded up and taken from their parents. Most had seen no more than five summers, some were even younger, but their childhood ended as they entered the House; there was no sound of play.

Deina couldn't properly remember her life before the House, or how old she'd been when she'd come here. She'd long since stopped trying. She didn't even recall her real name; the House gave you a new one. In theory, it was to protect you against ghosts and sorcery—it was harder to work evil magic against someone without knowing their true name. In reality, it helped the Order suppress any sense of identity that didn't relate to being a Severer. The House named you, fed you, clothed you, and you owed it everything.

Singing and chimes and the clash of weapons and the scent of the rosemary that edged every path—this had become home to her.

And she couldn't wait to escape.

2

Brown-robed servants were hovering in the front courtyard of the House. Deina waved away their offers of help and went straight inside, hurrying along the cool stone cloisters that led to the women's quarters and her own room. She didn't linger, staying just long enough to change from the ceremonial robes into a plain tunic and to stick her larger, everyday knife into her belt. Out of habit, she tested the point of the blade against the pad of her finger: good and sharp. Every city in the Dominion had at least three Houses of Theodesmioi, usually from the Orders of Zeus, Poseidon, and Hades. In theory, the god-marked could be called upon to fight for whichever god they served, should the gods prefer to play out their power struggles on a mortal battlefield. In practice, it had never happened. Still, the possibility remained.

Deina smiled to herself; no *point* in being unprepared. She snatched up a shawl and retraced her steps toward the cool shadows of the entrance hall.

"Deina!" Chryse was hurrying toward her, footsteps ringing on the polished marble tiles. "Did you carry out the rite?"

"Yes. No." Deina shrugged one shoulder. "Not exactly."

Chryse gazed up into Deina's face, her forehead creased. "You're unhappy. Was it so horrible, the rite? Or is it the Toll?"

"Neither—I just need some fresh air and some quiet." Deina gestured to the front doors, kept shut against the heat. "I'm going down to the shore."

"I'll come with you, then. I was waiting for you to get back, so I've not been out today."

"Are you sure? You look tired." There were shadows beneath Chryse's large blue eyes, dark as bruises. "How long ago was your last severing?" Deina demanded. "Shouldn't you be resting?"

Chryse shook her head, impatient.

"I've been in bed for the last three days. Not that I could sleep." She swallowed, bringing her fingers to her temple. "It was an elderly nobleman. He passed through the Threshold and into the Underworld easily enough—he was happy to leave behind the pain, I think—but his memories . . . They were difficult. I promise, though, I feel much better today. And look"—Chryse brightened up—"the family gave me a brooch." She lifted the folds of her tunic to display the trinket pinned there: copper set with carnelian. Pretty enough, but of little value—unlike the fee the man's death must have brought into the House treasury. Deina tried to calculate it in her head. A man, and a member of the eupatridae—that would be at least one gold ingot. More, if one of his family members had held the archonship. And then Chryse was charged out at the highest rate, the same as the male Severers of her grade;

apparently people preferred it if the last living face they saw was breathtakingly beautiful. Deina didn't blame them; she loved looking at Chryse, too. Her friend had the kind of beauty that might make Aphrodite jealous: dewy skin, plump lips, lustrous clouds of golden hair. The Orders tried to erase the identity of the Theodesmioi as much as possible, but how a person looked was one thing they couldn't control. Chryse knew nothing of her parents—none of them did—but it was obvious that one of them must have been a northern barbarian. Just as it was easy to guess from Deina's dark brown hair and the warmer tone of her skin that her parents were probably both from the territory around Iolkos, like most of those in the House, and to guess that Theron's black hair and darker skin were due to a parent or grandparent who had perhaps come from the great Phoenician city of Carthage, which even Deina had heard of. Not that such guessing helped. The sigil marking them as Theodesmioi was all that mattered, and ranking within the House was based partly on age but mostly on talent. Chryse wasn't strong enough to carry out frequent severings and spent most of her time hired out, less lucratively, as a professional mourner. Still, her good looks made her popular with clients, which was enough to lead the elders to treat her with some indulgence.

Chryse linked her arm through Deina's, squeezing tightly, and glanced up at her. "*Please* let me come with you. You've been so busy preparing for the rite. I've missed you."

Deina smiled.

"I've missed you, too. Let's go."

They gave their names to the gatekeeper—only one outing allowed a day, unless you had a token to prove you were on official business—and headed down the scrub-covered hillside, still dotted with the fading blooms of white lilies that grew among the rocks. Before they reached the city, Deina rearranged her shawl so that it veiled her head, covering her sigil and shadowing her scarred cheeks and odd-colored eyes. Chryse mimicked her action. Their torcs would pass, at least under casual inspection, as the kind of jewelry that many people wore. For a little while, they could be ordinary.

Beneath the watchful scrutiny of the city guards, they passed through the gates into Apollo's Quarter, home to the city's artisans: potters, carpenters, smiths. Though the dusty streets were quiet, with furnaces banked against the heat of the afternoon, the occupants were still busy; the tap of hammer against metal, the repetitive whisper of wood being planed, sounded from open doorways. But other houses were abandoned. Beautiful things tended to be costly, and in Iolkos there were fewer and fewer who could afford them.

"So, tell me, then." Chryse, her arm still linked with Deina's, spoke low. "The rite. Was it difficult? It must have been hard to watch what he'd done. I've heard the others talking about the way he murdered his father." She shuddered. "But at least it's finished. And you've worked off a whole year."

"Except that I didn't. Right at the end, I got distracted. I—" The word *failed* stuck in Deina's throat like an olive stone. All that practicing, not to mention a hefty bribe slipped to the archon's steward to ensure she'd be chosen for the Punishment

Rite instead of Theron, and for nothing. "I didn't earn any time for today." She glanced at Chryse. "It didn't exactly go to plan."

Deina's plan had started as a barely formed dream while she was still an apprentice. It had grown in detail once she'd become a novice. And finally, a year or so ago, the day she reached the rank of adept, she'd sworn to herself that her dream would become reality. Deina—stronger, far better suited to the life they'd both been born into—was going to work off her indenture faster than any Soul Severer ever. What she couldn't earn, she was going to steal. And then, once she was free, she was going to accumulate enough to buy Chryse's freedom, too—Chryse was the person she cared most about in the world, and Deina owed her. And then, she'd buy passage for them both on a fast ship, and then . . .

The open horizon. Freedom. To go wherever, to be whatever they wanted. Not that she'd shared her plan with Chryse. Better for it to be a wonderful surprise rather than have Chryse counting the days until Deina was able to purchase the rest of her indenture.

Chryse patted her hand.

"You fret too much. It's not as though we have a bad life here. We've got a roof over our heads, and the food's good and there's plenty of it . . ." She trailed off. "And a special place in Elysium when we die. That's something. More than most have to look forward to."

Deina shrugged. Guaranteed bliss in the afterlife was all very well, but she wanted a life this side of the veil, too—a better life than this. Forbidden to marry or have a family. Told where to go and what to do for the entirety of an indenture that virtually none of the Theodesmioi ever earned out because most didn't live long enough. The Battle Wagers of the Order of Zeus died in wars, and the Sea Singers of the Order of Poseidon went down with their ships, and the Soul Severers of the Order of Hades lost their minds, trapped in the memories of the dying ones they'd been summoned to help. Deina had only ever met a handful of Spell Casters from the Order of Hephaestus; they were all taken to Mycenae or Thebes, and were only sent to other cities when the Theodesmioi of the other Orders needed new torcs fitted. But they probably died young, too. Human frames weren't meant to channel the power of a god.

"It's hot," Deina muttered. "Let's rest."

They climbed a set of steps leading to the shaded portico of a temple. As the thin, inhuman scream of an animal being sacrificed echoed from open doors behind them, causing Chryse to wince and murmur a protest, Deina picked a daisy from a crack in the stonework and began plucking off its petals. The dark-haired boy who'd watched her in the Threshold . . . was he human? *Pluck.* Or a monster from the Underworld? *Pluck.* Or a sign of the insanity that every Severer feared? *Pluck.* Over and over, until every petal lay on the floor at her feet.

A young servant slouched out of the temple doors and headed toward the animals penned up nearby. He had golden bracelets about his wrists—more gold, Deina thought sourly, than most of the worshippers within the temple courtyard would be able to earn in several lifetimes. The boy selected a piglet for slaughter, bound its legs, and slung the squealing bundle over his shoulders. When he noticed Deina, the sullen frown on the boy's face deepened—did he take her for a beggar?

she wondered—until he saw Chryse. The frown became a leer. "You . . . I can show you somewhere more comfortable to rest, if you like. Somewhere private."

As Chryse, oblivious, began to thank him, Deina drew back her shawl.

It took the boy a moment: to focus on the sigil on her forehead, to work out which of the Houses she came from. When he gasped and stepped back, fumbling to retain his grip on the squirming piglet, Deina smiled.

"I didn't mean to offend," he muttered. "Forgive me, merciful one . . ."

His attempt at a deferential expression didn't quite mask the distaste and fear in his eyes. Still, as names went, it was better than "death vulture." As a child, Deina hadn't understood why Severers were considered bad luck. Why the House of Zeus and the House of Poseidon were within the city walls, but the House of Hades wasn't. After all, severing, the most common of the rites they performed, *was* merciful. For a price, the House would send a Severer to the bedside of anyone in the city who was dying, to ease the soul from the suffering body and accompany it into the Threshold, so it wouldn't have to start its journey to the Underworld alone. But as she'd grown, Deina realized why healthy people didn't want a Severer around. No one wanted to think about dying or about what might happen next. And then there were the rumors, not exactly discouraged by the House, that a Severer could alter a soul's destiny. No wonder people avoided them until death was inevitable. Deina replaced the shawl, nodding a dismissal, and the boy turned to leave.

"Wait"—she held out her hand—"why another sacrifice, so soon?"

He shrugged. "The priest saw something he didn't like in the entrails of the last one."

As the servant retreated into the darkness of the temple, Chryse made a gesture, a swift bringing together of thumb and middle fingers that was meant to turn away the evil eye.

"I agree," Deina observed. "He was definitely evil."

"Not him." Chryse seemed to look through Deina, her eyes unfocused. "Something else. Something's coming. A storm."

"But the sky's clear . . ."

Chryse shook herself, closed her eyes, and tilted her face up to the sun, as if she were one of the flowers that bore its name. "You're right. It's the wrong time of year for storms. And nothing unexpected *ever* happens in Iolkos. I'm tired still, I suppose."

From inside the temple, the squealing and the invocation started up again. "Immortal gods of Olympus, hear me. Poseidon, lord of the sea, bless me . . ." Piglet and priest together, louder and louder. Until the knife fell, and relative silence with it.

"Immortal gods be damned," Deina muttered through gritted teeth. If gods could be killed, she'd know what to do with her freedom once she'd earned it: hunt them down and slit their throats, and smile while she was doing it. "D'you hear me, Poseidon?" They were in his quarter now, in a straggling street that ran down toward the harbor. She slammed the side of her fist into one of the temple's brightly painted wooden pillars. "I'd like to chop you up and feed you to your own fish."

"Deina, don't. What if he does hear you?" Chryse glanced up and down the street, as if the god himself might suddenly manifest: angry, vengeful, garlanded with seaweed.

"Relax. I'm sure Poseidon has better things to do than come after us." They both knew the gods existed. But unlike Chryse, Deina didn't care what they thought.

Her gaze drifted to the tavern opposite. Almost deserted now, apart from a man sitting at a table outside, shoveling down a mound of what looked like roasted lamb. The boulder-built citadel, topped by the enormous complex of the megaron, loomed in the distance. Nearer at hand were racks of fish, laid out to dry in front of tiny, dark-windowed houses. The stink of last night's catch had risen with the heat.

This was a place of fishermen and sailors, a few of whom—too drunk to stagger home—were still slumped on the tavern steps. But the man at the table didn't look like either. His body was soft—dimpled and rounded, like bread that had been left to rise but not yet baked. He was a ship owner, more likely. A trader in wine or olives, still doing well enough—despite the ever-increasing taxes and tributes imposed by Orpheus—to wear a fine linen tunic and gorge himself on meat. Or—Deina caught sight of what looked like a badge of office pinned in the folds of his cloak—a tax collector. Perhaps there was a way to salvage something useful from the day after all.

"Chryse, I think you should head back to the House."

"Why?" She followed Deina's gaze. "Oh." A long, slow exhale, shaking her head. "You know, one of these days, you're going to get caught."

"I never get caught. And if I did . . ." Deina shrugged. "I earn plenty for the House, and enough of that finds its way into the city treasury." She thought back over the last week. On a single day, a good day, she'd reduced her indenture by a day and three-quarters: severing a soul (half a day), laying a ghost (an entire day), and hallowing the house of a nobleman—expensive for him, even though she'd only earned a quarter of a day. Trickery, really. The House recommended an annual hallowing ceremony to keep ghosts at bay, preferring not to tell people that ghosts generally didn't linger in the mortal world. Like Chryse's beauty, Deina's capacity for work added enough extra silver to the House's coffers to gain her a certain amount of indulgence.

She nodded toward the tax collector, who was now mopping up the last juices of his meal, his jowls glistening with smeared oil and spice. "You know I don't like to pass up a good opportunity. And if I steal a bit from him, what's he going to do about it?"

"Report you. Identify you. And if he makes enough of a fuss, they'll have to do something. You'll be charged with bringing the House into disrepute. They'll stop you from working and add five years on to your time." Chryse shook her head. "I don't understand why you keep taking these kinds of risks."

"Yes, you do." They'd had this conversation before. Deina stole because she wanted something that was just hers. Something that didn't belong to the House. Or the gods. Or this damn city. Even if it was no more than a couple of bronze coins. And of course, she had her plan to think of.

"Well, maybe I do," Chryse conceded. "But I still wish you

wouldn't. I worry about you. Do come back with me. Or let's just walk to the shore as we planned. Or let me stay and help. I could—"

"Definitely not." Deina sighed and raised one eyebrow in the direction of the tax collector. "I can't look after you and deal with him at the same time."

Chryse pouted a little. She was fiddling with the tassels of an embroidered belt, bright with blue flowers; Deina gestured to the needlework.

"You finished it. Very pretty."

Her friend nodded. "It is, isn't it. Though I've not finished the one I'm embroidering for you. Or the hem of my tunic. I've run out of thread." Her fingers stilled, and she glanced up at Deina. "I suppose, if you stole from that man, you could give me a little to buy some more . . ."

"Exactly."

Chryse grinned. "Then, thank you." She stood up. "I mean it, though: Be careful."

"I'm always careful. But my potential victim's had two skinfuls of wine, at least, and the way he eats, I'd be willing to bet that the only part of him used to running is his bowels." Deina winked. "I think I can handle him." As the other girl turned away, Deina added, "Cover for me, if Mistress Kalistra asks where I am. And go straight back to the House."

Deina watched Chryse to the end of the street before drawing her shawl farther over her head and shuffling back into the shadows of the temple portico. She didn't have to wait long; the tax collector soon pushed his chair back from the table, tossed a few coins to the tavern keeper, and staggered off down the street.

Deina followed.

Her target led her through the nearest marketplace, which would have been useful if she'd had the opportunity to rob him earlier in the day. Plenty of distractions. Fishmongers, butchers, and bakers all plying their trades, filling the air with their cries. But the only noise now was the squawk of crows squabbling over dusty scraps of smoked fish and fly-blown meat. The stallholders had packed up for the day, driven home by the heat to courtyard gardens or shady balconies. The little square was almost deserted. Almost, but not entirely: There were three beggars still huddled by the water trough. There were beggars on most corners, even though things weren't quite as bad now as they had been last winter, when the bulk of Iolkos's grain had been sent as tribute to Thebes and famine stalked the city's streets, hollowing out its homes.

A woman wearing a frayed tunic was hawking glass beads from a tray.

"Pretty trinkets, best Egyptian glass! Blessed by Aphrodite herself, guaranteed to get you a good match!" As Deina slipped past, the woman's sales pitch rose to a litany of complaints: she'd sold nothing all morning, she was behind with her rent.

Deina didn't slow down. She carried no coins, and everyone had their problems. But if her theft was successful, she'd come back this way. Or think about it, at least.

The tax collector left the square and passed into a network of narrow lanes, mostly empty. Outside one house, there were a few children playing five-stones in the dirt. The man watching them gave her a disinterested glance and went back to mending his fishing net. She clung to the shadows and gripped her knife tightly. Her target slowed. But instead of entering a doorway, he turned to face the nearest house, lifted his tunic, and began pissing loudly against the wall, sighing with relief.

A woman's head emerged screeching from the window above. "Get away from there, you filthy, stinking sack of wine!"

As the tax collector started to tell the woman exactly what she could do with herself, Deina darted forward—dodging the damp patch of earth—cut the money pouch from his belt, and ran.

There was a bellow of anger from her victim, a shout of laughter from the outraged householder, followed by a yell. "Run faster!"

Deina glanced over her shoulder and saw why: The man was pelting after her, a blade in his hand, neither quite as drunk nor quite as unfit as she'd believed. She cursed and switched directions, leaving Poseidon's Quarter for Demeter's.

The street widened to a crossroads. Her pursuer slowed, panting and purple-faced. Deina slowed, too. To one side, a wall enclosed a small orchard. She jogged away from the wall, then turned, ran, and leaped and dragged herself, grunting, up onto the top. A moment to catch her breath, and she was off again. Brushing past the twisted fingers of olive trees, she flew along the flat tops of the stones, cheered on by a deafening chorus of cicadas. The road itself veered away once it reached the bulk of a grain store up ahead; anyone following it would have to take a detour to catch up. By that time, she'd be long gone.

It was a good plan. Until a snake dropped from the branch

of a tree onto the wall directly in front of her. The creature reared up, hissing, and Deina jumped to avoid it. Lost her footing. Teetered for a moment on the very edge of the wall, flailing her arms, trying to regain her balance—

Pain blinded her. Once she'd blinked it away, the pattern of stones in front of her resolved into the base of the wall. There was dirt beneath her hands and on her right cheek. Something worse than dirt, too; she took a breath and gagged, pushing herself onto her knees—*everything* hurt—grabbing the purse from where she'd dropped it and her knife from her belt as heavy footsteps thudded nearer.

"Why, you thieving cutpurse, I'll make you wish you'd—" The man she'd robbed stopped, mouth open, fist clutching a larger knife than hers, poised to strike. But the blow never fell. He blanched. Pulled an amulet out from beneath his tunic and held it up, hand shaking, his eyes flitting between Deina's forehead and her mismatched eyes. A trickle of sweat ran from his temple to his jaw.

"Give me back my money." He brought his knife nearer. "Or . . . or I'll make you pay. I swear."

"No." Deina raised her own knife and tightened her grip on the money bag. They had an audience: two men carrying sacks of grain, and a young boy leading a donkey. All three were looking on with interest. None of them seemed inclined to intervene. She got slowly to her feet. "You might need our services one day. Consider this a prepayment." Edging closer, she slashed her knife in the tax collector's direction. "Or you might end up leaving Iolkos for the Underworld sooner than you'd like."

The man spat out a stream of curses, but as Deina backed away, he made no move to pursue her. When she reached the corner of the grain store, she ran. Ran through a maze of small streets and the nearest city gate. Kept running through the groves beyond, just for the pleasure of speed and the wind in her face.

Until the sea lay before her. She sank onto the sand-washed turf. Closed her eyes and listened to the rhythm of the waves. Breathed deeply. Pine resin, thyme, the scent of seaweed carried on the breeze . . . overlaid by the stench of whatever she'd fallen into. Grimacing, Deina ripped a handful of thyme from the ground and tried to clean herself off, inventorying her injuries along the way. One swollen ankle. Two grazed palms. More cuts and bruises elsewhere than she cared to count.

Time to see if it was worth it.

The contents of the money bag glinted, heavy in her palm. It was a good haul. As well as the usual pieces of bronze, bearing the marks of the cities that minted them, there were a few stamped disks of Persian silver and one delicate Minoan bull. Held between finger and thumb, the small circle of gold gleamed in the sunlight. Definitely worth it. Deina grinned as she unpinned one shoulder of her tunic and stashed the loose coins beneath the linen band that bound her breasts. The weight of them against her skin was pleasing—little bits of freedom, held close to her heart.

The tide mark was just below. She walked down there carefully, the tip of one finger beneath the heavy torc that encircled her neck. It was made of spell-cast bronze, created by the Theodesmioi of Hephaestus. The sea itself was beyond her reach, but Deina knew how far to go, exactly how close to the waves she could edge, before the torc would start to tighten. To choke her. To remind her of another of the limits the city had placed on her freedom.

There were stories about Theodesmioi—Severers, and those from other Orders—who had ended their lives this way. An escape. A final choice that even the city couldn't take away, if the day came . . .

But this particular day had redeemed itself. Deina began sorting through the washed-up pebbles, looking for small, flattish stones to refill the money pouch. By the time she was done, her injured ankle was throbbing; she tore a strip from her tunic and bound the ankle tightly. Only when she'd completed this task did she stand up and stretch her stiff shoulders and look out across the bay.

Five black-sailed galleys. Warships, with many banks of oars and battering rams attached to their prows. Theban ships, come to collect the quarterly tribute.

Deina shook her head and turned to go, but a flash of gold and red caught her attention. The wind had unfurled the flag planted in the prow of the largest ship, and it was fluttering brightly in the afternoon sunshine.

A chill clawed its way out of the pit of Deina's stomach.

The flag was the King's Standard, and it signified only one thing.

Orpheus the Tyrant had come to Iolkos.

3

The ships drew closer, sails billowing in the stiffening breeze. A few more moments and the breeze bore sounds: the chants of the men at the oars, the shouts of the captains, the clash of metal as the heavily armed hoplites assembled in the prows. Why was Orpheus here? If he was bothering to visit a backwater like Iolkos in person, then the king must want something in addition to the quarterly tribute.

Fear cooled Deina's flesh.

Everyone knew the official version of events; the tale formed part of the customary prayers on the major feast days. Eighty years ago, or maybe more, Thebes was a decaying city with a dying king, living on borrowed time and dreams of squandered glory. Orpheus had arrived from out of nowhere and led the city to victory against the tide of northern barbarians that was threatening to overwhelm it. He'd been rewarded, shortly after, with the city's throne, and a wife: Eurydice, a member of the royal family. Gradually, over the following decades, the other kings of Greece, moved by the wisdom of Orpheus's rule, had abdicated and handed their cities over to be governed from Thebes: Aulis, Athens, Mycenae, Argos, Sparta, Pylos, Knossos, Iolkos. And now all were united within the benevolent embrace of the Theban Dominion.

Military hero, devoted husband, lover of music, blessed by the gods with the enduring vigor that enabled him to keep ruling, year after year—Orpheus claimed to be all these things. Maybe he believed his own myth. Maybe so, too, did his queen, Eurydice, and the people of Thebes. But as far as Deina could see, the poverty on the streets of Iolkos, the constant draining of wealth and resources to fund the Dominion's endless wars—that told a different story.

The harsh bray of a trumpet made Deina jump and sent her hobbling as fast as she could manage back toward the city. The House was the safest place to be.

Rumor traveled faster than fire along the city's streets. By the time Deina limped into Demeter's Quarter, the news was drawing people from their houses in spite of the heat. Some had climbed onto rooftops, shielding their eyes against the searing sun as they stared out to sea. A few were hurrying down to the harbor. Others, not waiting for confirmation or detail, were shuttering their windows and piling belongings into sacks. Heading for the hills, and whatever safety distance might grant. Gossip about the Tyrant's motives was fast turning speculation into fact. He was here to double the tribute. Or he had come to select men from Iolkos for his Iron Guard, the creatures born of metal and flesh and dark magic that served him as soldiers. Or Iolkos's archon had done something to arouse the Tyrant's ire.

The outer walls of the citadel were ahead of her now. Armed

men were gathering on the ramparts. The Battle Wagers of the Order of Zeus, who formed the elite core of the palace garrison, with their bronze body armor, boar-tusk helmets, and slim-waisted shields, were hurriedly forming into a guard of honor. Messengers were rushing along the broad streets that led to the upper reaches of the citadel, the site of the megaron and the city's most important temples.

Orpheus's arrival was like a burning brand dropped into an ants' nest.

"Ow!" Deina toppled backward as a man collided with her. He stopped and held out a hand to help her up.

"I'm so sorry. Are you hurt? I didn't—" The concern bled from the man's face. "Oh. It's you. Perhaps you should watch where you're going."

Aster. Deina grimaced as she let him pull her back onto her feet.

"I was. You ran into me, remember?" There was another Severer hovering nearby—Lysias, still only an apprentice even though he was at least two years older than Aster. The gossip in the women's quarters was that he'd been entered into the lottery every year for the last five years; it was only luck that he'd never won. Every House ran a lottery and entered the weakest of their Theodesmioi into it; the prize was being ritually slaughtered at the winter solstice to honor the god you served. Deina shivered, remembering the stifled sobs of the girl who'd been chosen to die last winter. She acknowledged Lysias with a nod. "If you're returning to the House, you're heading in the wrong direction."

"Let others panic." Aster gestured toward the chaotic crowds filling the streets. "I count myself honored that Iolkos is receiving a visit from the king. I'm sure Lord Orpheus must finally intend to confer some great benefit on the city for our sacrifice and service. The people should be rejoicing."

He sounded as if he actually believed it. Deina almost laughed.

"If you say so. Where are you going in such a hurry, then?"

"Lysias has a severing to perform in the citadel. I'm going with him to supervise." Aster smiled at the apprentice, slapping him so forcefully on the back that he was knocked off-balance. "It's going to go well this time, isn't it?"

"Of course." Lysias returned the smile, but Deina saw the desperation in his eyes. Lines of exhaustion were etched deep in his face. She wondered how long he'd had to recover since the last death he attended. Whether he was still reliving that person's life, their anguish, their guilt, every time he closed his eyes.

"May Hades go with you," Deina offered. Lysias looked as if he'd need some kind of divine intervention. She began to walk away.

"Wait," Aster called after her. "Is it true, what they're saying back at the House? Did you fail to complete the Punishment Rite? Serves them right, in my opinion."

For giving the job to a woman? Or to her specifically? She wasn't surprised Aster already knew of her humiliation. Severers kept secrets as well as gods kept marriage vows.

"Go to the crows, Aster." An old insult, implying that you wished your enemy dead and his corpse picked clean by scavenging birds; she didn't have the energy to think of anything original. Turning her back on him, Deina continued on her way. Through Poseidon's Quarter, keeping an eye out for the tax collector. Out of the city through the gate in Apollo's Quarter that she and Chryse had used earlier. Past the site of the half-built theater; the city had run out of funds with which to complete it, and the wooden stage, supposedly destined for recitals of the great epic poems, was already rotting. Finally, up onto the path that led into the shadow of the hills, where the House of Hades sat in lonely grandeur: a complex of low buildings, overlooked by a tall bell tower, all built of black marble and rough, dark gray rock hewn from the mountains farther inland. There were other Severers on the path with her, hurrying to regain the relative safety of the high walls. A queue formed at the main gate as the doorkeeper, sweating over his clay tablet, laboriously marked everyone back in.

"Name and grade?"

"Deina, adept. Did Chryse return yet?"

"Yes." The doorkeeper didn't look up from his work; everyone knew Chryse. "A while back." Deina nodded her thanks and entered the crowded courtyard. The large bell that hung in the tower was still silent; no gathering summoned. Hopefully there wouldn't be. She needed some time: hide the money, take a bath—dirt and sweat had stuck her tunic to her back—check on Chryse, go to the herbarium to get something for her ankle, meet Drex for her reading lesson—

A strong hand closed around her wrist as a voice whispered in her ear.

"Just keep walking. You and I have something to discuss."

Theron.

Deina clenched her free hand into a fist. "Give me one good reason why I shouldn't hit you?" she murmured, staring straight ahead. "It wouldn't be the first time I've beaten you in a fight, and no one would care." The House encouraged competition of any and every kind between its younger members, both organized and spontaneous. To fail to compete was to risk appearing weak. To risk entry into the lottery. Personally, Deina enjoyed the rivalry, and she was one of the best at hand-to-hand combat. Not that Theron would admit it.

"You only ever beat me because I pulled my punches, and you know it," he muttered. "And I know what you did this afternoon."

Deina glanced over her shoulder.

"I don't know what you're talking about."

Theron grinned, though the dazzling smile didn't meet his eyes. "We'll go to the maze garden, I think."

Automatically, Deina turned away from the grand entrance hall onto a smaller path leading to the gardens and exercise grounds that lay to the rear of the complex. No one followed. Deina tried to yank her arm free, but Theron was as strong as she was and one of the few Severers who was taller than her; his grip was too tight. He chuckled.

"Not far now."

The maze garden lay just ahead. It wasn't really a maze; more a collection of meandering paths, lined with dark green cypresses and lavender bushes, some ending in secluded seating areas, others looping around open spaces of different sizes. Deina could just hear a group of apprentices chanting somewhere within the garden's cool green enclosures, repeating

after their teacher lines from one of the ancient Songs: the Strychomphe, the Severing Rite to be used when someone was dying from a slow poison.

"Here." Theron steered her down a narrower path that ended in a small domed building, heavily draped in ivy. He let go of her wrist to push her inside.

Deina turned on him.

"What in Hades's name do you think you're doing?"

"Getting my own back." He was standing in a patch of sunlight that burnished his skin but hid the exact expression in his eyes. "Did you really think I wouldn't find out that you bribed your way into getting selected for the Punishment Rite instead of me? You're not the only one who wants out of here, Deina. You're not the only one with a dream. And that rite should have been mine. I should have been the one earning a year's freedom and—"

"Why? Because you're a man?" Deina laughed. "You shouldn't believe your own publicity. The House may plan to give men all the best jobs, they may claim you're somehow superior—"

"Because we are."

"—and they may have even convinced the idiots in Iolkos to pay more for your services, but you know I'm better than you."

"Really? Then why did you fail?" He came closer, moving with the same easy grace with which he did everything, fury glittering in his dark brown eyes. "Yes, I found out. Much good it did you, bribing the archon's servant. It's about time you learned your place, Deina. Women are too weak, too irrational to carry out major rites. That's why there is only one female Guardian of the House—because everyone knows women should only be severing the souls of other women and children. That's all you're fit for. That and cemetery duty."

"Cemetery duty wouldn't even count toward my indenture—"

"I. Don't. Care." Theron spat the words at her. "I only care that you wasted a chance that should have been mine. And now you owe me."

Deina stiffened and crossed her arms in front of her body. "Owe you what?"

"The money you stole this afternoon. I'd like to say it was good planning on my part, but really it was luck. I had a severing in Demeter's Quarter. A wine merchant who'd been half crushed by some of his own barrels. I left his house just in time to see your altercation with that tax collector. When you took off, I followed him. I know where he lives."

"So? It's your word against mine."

"Not really. Not if I persuade him to make a complaint. To accuse you of stealing the city's tax money."

Deina closed up the gap between them, one hand going to the hilt of her knife. "I'm not an idiot. It was his own money pouch I took, not one of those bags with the city seal stamped on it."

Theron shrugged and ran one hand through his dark curls.

"Your word against his. I'm sure I can persuade him to make the accusation. Promise him that he won't suffer for it." He flashed a smile. "Stealing tax money is a serious crime, against the city and the Dominion. Against Lord Orpheus himself. Who knows if the House would try to protect you? You might even get a death sentence. Or worse." Theron leaned down to whisper in Deina's ear, his lips almost grazing her cheek.

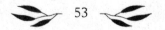

"Maybe I'll be selected to perform the Punishment Rite."

"Bastard." He knew they wouldn't use the Punishment Rite for theft. But they might still hang her. The hilt of her blade was hard and solid in her hand. This close, Theron wouldn't stand a chance. No one had seen them come in here; she could silence him easily enough. Let him lie here, bleeding out in the shadows, and walk away.

But she'd cared about him once. And she might be a thief, but she wasn't—yet—a murderer. Deina pulled the knife out, cut the stolen money pouch from her belt, and tossed it to Theron. "Happy now?" She tried to walk past him.

He stepped in front of her. "Not so fast." It took only a moment for him to open the pouch, tip the stones into his hand, and throw them down. They scattered and rattled across the paving stones as he shook his head. "Nice try. Where is it?"

She lifted her chin. "I spent it."

"Liar." Theron grabbed her upper arms and pulled her close, glaring, his eyes scanning her face.

Deina held his gaze, her body taut even as her mind was racing. Would he actually try to search her? Would he dare?

Abruptly, Theron let go of her and backed away. "This isn't over. But in the meantime, I've got boundary duty at sunset."

"I heard. One too many times abandoning the apprentice you're supposed to be supervising to do something more fun?" The best Severers usually got excused from things like boundary duty; Theron must have really irritated one of the elders if he'd not been able to escape it.

He scowled. "Now you're going to do it for me."

Deina shook her head. "No."

"Yes. You're doing it, and you'd better not even think about trying to get out of it." He sniffed, making a face. "Take a bath, too. You stink."

Deina's hand connected with his cheek hard enough to send him stumbling backward. "I hate you."

Theron was massaging his jaw, but he still managed a grin. "I know." He turned on his heel and was quickly lost among the trees.

She stooped to snatch the empty money pouch from the ground, then turned and drove her knife as hard as she could into the wooden post next to her. It didn't help; she was still furious, with herself as well as Theron.

Next time, Deina, maybe just stab him.

Deina went to find Drex first. She spotted him by the vegetable beds in the far corner of the grounds, sitting on a bench near the end of a row of feathery fennel; the gardeners had packed up hours ago. He was bent over, clutching what looked like a long pin in one hand, poking at something small that was balanced on his knee. At the sound of her sandals crunching over the gravel path, he leaped up and hid his hands behind his back, squinting.

"Who's there?"

"It's only me."

Drex's face relaxed into a tentative smile. He couldn't see well; except for the fact that he'd been brought to the House about three years later than he should have, that was almost the only thing Deina knew about him. His world was a blur, apart from whatever bit of it was right in front of his face at

that moment. Drex was still a novice after others his age had become adepts, and the elders might have started entering him into the lottery by now if he hadn't been able to read. It was a rare skill, valued by the House; presumably, Deina mused, a skill he'd acquired during those extra three years of freedom. "You're early. I—I managed to slip something out of the archives today." He nodded to a small, fragile-looking roll of papyrus on the bench. "Better to practice with."

Brave of him to take such a risk.

"I hope you'll be able to return it safely. I can't stay." Deina took a deep breath, smoothing the anger from her voice. No doubt Theron would soon be crowing about his victory over her in the men's quarters, if he wasn't already, but she preferred to hold on to her dignity for a little longer. "There's something else I have to do."

She was standing close enough now that even Drex would be able to see something of the dirt caked into her clothes and skin, but he just nodded and said, "Of course."

He looked disappointed; perhaps he'd been counting on the money. The House provided for all basic physical needs, but if you wanted anything extra, any little luxuries, you had to find a way of acquiring them yourself. Deina's decision to learn to read—part of her plan for when she was free of the House—had probably been a godsend for Drex. She doubted he had any other source of income.

On impulse, she said, "Close your eyes and hold out your hand."

Drex hesitated, staring at her as if trying to read her intentions in the depths of her eyes. A reasonable reaction; they were both Severers, so they were hardly likely to trust each other. Deina could have told him what she was going to do. But once you started explaining, started justifying your actions, people took it as an invitation to point out what you'd done wrong. She stared back at him until he swallowed nervously and did as she'd asked. Deina fished out one of the bronze coins from where it was pressed against her skin and dropped it into his palm. Drex brought his hand close and peered at the metal disk.

"It's warm."

"It's a down payment. For the next lesson. I'll let you know when."

Back in the women's quarters, she went to Chryse's room first, opening the door quietly when her knock went unanswered. Chryse was asleep, breathing softly, her golden hair fanned out across the pillow. Deina pushed back a stray tress that was lying across the other girl's cheek. At least she wasn't caught up in this mess.

Reaching the safety of her own room, Deina barred the door. She unpinned her stained and torn tunic, unbound her breasts, and let the remaining stolen coins fall onto the bed. The golden bull and the silver shimmered in the late-afternoon sunlight that filtered around the edges of the shutters. For a moment, Deina let her fingertips caress the coins, before lifting her hand to flatten her palm against a sketch pinned to the wall. A crude drawing of a ship, its sails bellied out by the wind, riding wild waves; just a few lines of charcoal on a square of animal hide. Eyes closed, she allowed herself to dream, to imagine the sanded boards of a deck beneath her feet, sea spray on her face, no torc around her neck. The open horizon before her. Freedom. To go wherever, to be whatever she wanted.

"One day," Deina murmured. Half to the ship, half to herself. She replaced her stolen treasure in the tax collector's pouch, dragged the bedclothes and mattress off the bed, and tipped the wooden frame on its side. The pins that held the legs in place were wobbly; not enough for the frame to collapse, but enough that she'd realized, many years ago, that the legs could be taken off and put back on again. It had been simple enough after that to gradually hollow out each one a little at the top. She had other hiding places in the room—a gap behind a loose stone in the wall, a crevice in the beam that ran across the ceiling—but the bed frame was reserved for her most valuable acquisitions: a little gold and some silver, increased by what she'd acquired this afternoon. The foundations of a new life for her and Chryse.

One day . . .

Deina took a deep breath and grimaced. Theron had been right about one thing—she did stink. Beneath the makeshift bandage, her ankle was turning an unattractive shade of purple, and the heavy bronze torc had chafed her neck. They were not designed for running in. Once the bed was back to rights, she unpinned her hair and shook out the thick dark waves. A spark of vanity warmed her for a moment; the plague had scarred her face, and her eyes had earned her strange looks all her life, but her hair was still beautiful. She took a loose robe from the cedar chest in the corner of the room and set off for the baths. A quick soak, dinner, and then Theron's tedious boundary duty. At least she'd be clean.

* * *

It had been a while since she'd had to perform boundary duty. Deina had not forgotten, though, that curious mixture of boredom and tension. Hurrying around the entire boundary, stopping at each marker to recite the complex incantation, half of which was in a language so archaic, its meaning had long since blurred, like an image carved in old limestone. The entire thing had to be word-perfect and completed between the start of sunset and the end of twilight. By the time it was done, she was sweating—so much for the bath—and her ankle was sending sharp pulses of pain up through her leg. The ritual had to be performed every new moon; it prevented anyone who didn't bear the sigil of Hades from entering the grounds of the House uninvited. Though who knew whether it would really work against someone like Orpheus, who was said to possess a dark magic of his own. Deina patted the cooling stone of the final boundary marker, still glowing faintly from the power of the incantation.

Offering moral support to a lump of rock. Just as well no one else is around.

She took her sandals off and hobbled back slowly through the gardens, enjoying the roughness of the springy grass beneath her feet. Past the training grounds, silent now apart from the cicadas and the owls, calling to each other from the night-wrapped pine trees. Starlight and familiarity were enough to guide her safely back inside, desperate to lose herself in sleep. Surely tomorrow would be better. Maybe in the morning, Orpheus and his warships would be gone. And once she was rested, she'd be able to figure out how to finesse her way into another major

rite. And what to do about Theron. And maybe—

The door of her room was half open. She pushed it open farther, groping for the flint and lamp kept on a shelf by the entrance. The third spark caught, and the oil-soaked wick flamed into life.

"Oh, Hades . . ." Deina's hand went to her mouth. It was chaos. Her clothes dragged out of their chest. Bed linen in a twisted heap, half concealing the broken shards of the vase that had stood upon the table. The table itself, the chair, and the bed frame, upended. Her mattress had been gutted; clumps of wool lay scattered across the floor like snow in a thaw.

She shut the door behind her and barred it. The mess didn't matter. But her treasures . . .

The legs were still on the bed. Deina unpinned one, hands shaking. The gold and silver were still there. Relief drenched her in cold sweat; she paused and closed her eyes, taking a deep breath. Calm and methodical—that was the way. The beam next. Setting the chair upright, she felt for the shallow depression in the top of the beam. Her stash of bronze and copper was still there. So was the second, smaller stash concealed behind a loose stone below the window. Perhaps Theron—who else could it be?—hadn't found anything. That would explain the mess. The thought of his futile anger sent a fierce thrill through her core. There was only one place left to check. Deina heaved the cedar chest upright and began throwing her possessions back inside, searching for her doll.

As soon as her hand closed around the rag figure, she knew. The doll had been split open, its stuffing pulled out. The gold ring, the little copper brooch, and the broken string of carnelian beads were gone.

Deina threw the doll on the floor and flew out of the room. If she let this go unchallenged, Theron would believe he could do whatever he liked—that he could treat her however he liked. She ignored the puzzled looks she got as she limped hurriedly through the women's quarters. Ignored Chryse, who called to her as she passed the doors to the women's hall. She didn't know where Theron's room was, but this time of the evening he would likely be holding court in the men's hall. This part of the House was reserved for novices and adepts; the children and the apprentices had their own, more tightly controlled spaces, and the elders lived around the central courtyard behind the great hall.

But even if all the elders had been there, forming an audience to watch her as she broke one of the primary rules of the House by forcing her way into the men's quarters, it wouldn't have stopped her.

She'd taken enough risks already today. What was one more?

4

Deina slowed as she neared the men's quarters. Cold calculation was more useful than hot rage—Anteïs had taught her that. Neither her determination nor her intention wavered, but, as satisfying as a dramatic entrance would be, choosing her moment might give her revenge some teeth. She paused and studied her surroundings. A window at the end of the corridor to her right overlooked the courtyard garden that formed part of the men's quarters. Deina switched direction and hurried past a door that led to the herbarium. Jamming her toes into the gaps in the stonework and ignoring her sore ankle, she pulled herself up onto the windowsill and dropped silently down into the lavender bed that lay on the other side of the wall.

The men's hall was now on her left, forming one side of the courtyard; the male sleeping quarters formed another side. Five tall windows, shutters thrown open, connected the brightly lit hall to the garden; music and laughter spilled into the darkness. Deina crept nearer, staying close to the wall until she was concealed behind the nearest shutter. She pressed her eye to the gap between the shutter and the stonework.

The generosity of the men's space was no surprise, but the extra layer of luxury was: more tapestries on the walls, more oil lamps, more tables laden with platters of food. Lion skins on the floor instead of just rushes. Most of the Severers she could see were either playing or betting on games of chance, proving the point of the old saying: Seal two Severers in a tomb and they'd still find a way to make it into a competition. Some were chatting. Some, out of her view, were singing, accompanied by the soft resonance of a lyre. There was Aster, lying with his head in the lap of Melos, a lithe, raven-haired novice who was clearly the current object of Aster's devotion. Melos was feeding Aster grapes. They were lucky. Relationships between male and female Severers were forbidden, and pregnancy was punishable by death; Deina supposed the elders, almost all of whom were men, didn't want the more valuable male Severers getting distracted. They certainly didn't want to pay for upkeep of any children who weren't Theodesmioi. But what went on within the confines of the men's and women's quarters was another story. Deina shifted position slightly. Where was Theron? Drex she could see. He was just on the other side of the window, his wavy golden-brown hair falling forward as he bent over some small object. But Theron . . .

A sudden movement revealed him lounging on a fur-covered couch, holding court, just as she'd expected.

"So I made her come with me into the maze garden and then I told her." Theron passed his wine cup to someone to

refill. "I knew she'd offered something to the archon's servant to get selected for the Punishment Rite ahead of me, and I was going to inform the elders."

"And what did she do?" A novice Deina didn't recognize. One of Theron's starry-eyed admirers no doubt, nasal and overeager.

"Deina? She fell to her knees, weeping. Clung to my legs, begging me not to turn her in." A pause. Theron clutched his hands together. "'Oh, please, dear Theron, I implore you! I'll do anything!'" Theron's high-pitched impression made Deina scowl, even as it elicited a roar of laughter from those around him. Gods, she wanted to wipe that smirk off his face. "And that was how she ended up doing boundary duty this evening instead of me."

"I bet I can guess what kind of bribe she offered the archon's servant." The nasal novice again. "I wonder how many times she had to do it with him? I wonder if he made her keep her veil on, so he didn't have to look at the pockmarks on her face or those unnatural eyes."

Deina gasped as she flinched away from the shutter. The boy's words sent a hot tide of shame across her skin. Stupid—stupid to care what he thought, especially when it wasn't even true. She knew that. So why was she trembling?

She waited for Theron to say something in her defense. These men, these boys—whatever she said, they would never believe her. She was a woman and her word carried little weight. That was just how the world worked. But Theron knew her—had known her—well enough to know that she would never . . .

His silence spoke for him.

Deina jumped over the low sill. She caught Drex's eye; he

quickly looked away, turning his shoulder toward her. Keen to keep his head down, literally. Fair enough; neither of them had any particular desire to acknowledge their relationship—such as it was. Instead, she began striding across the pelt-covered floor toward Theron. Murmurs of shock rippled in her wake.

Theron's jaw tightened, but he did not get up. When Deina came to a halt in front of him, he lifted his gaze unhurriedly.

"Are you lost?"

Smug bastard. She clenched her fists and leaned toward him.

"You are a liar. And a thief. And I want what you stole from me."

He raised an eyebrow. "I've no idea what you're talking about. I'm no thief. Unlike some people."

"More lies, just like the nonsense you've been spouting to these idiots. I know you broke into my room and ransacked it while I was doing your boundary duty." She turned on the nasal-voiced novice who was sitting next to him. "Did you help him?"

A look of exasperation flashed across Theron's face as the boy blushed and began to stammer excuses. Deina spoke over him.

"Really, Theron? Maybe next time you pick an accomplice, you should choose one with a brain."

"Hold your tongue, Isaeus," Theron hissed. He rose from the couch to stand in front of Deina. "I don't know what you thought you were going to gain by coming here, but you should go back to where you belong. You're making a scene."

The room had grown very still; the other adepts and novices had stopped whatever they were doing to watch. Gradually

they drifted closer, forming a loose ring around the unexpected entertainment. One or two were staring at Deina with a faintly calculating expression in their eyes.

Deina's hand went to her belt, and found only the empty space where her knife should have been.

Damn.

She settled for crossing her arms and lifting her chin. "Are you threatening me?"

"Of course not." Theron smiled and glanced around at the other novices. "I'm advising you." His words drew a ripple of laughter from the onlookers.

Deina gritted her teeth. "You fat-headed, gutter-spawned *whelp*—" She seized a wine jug from the nearby table and hurled its contents at Theron.

The wine splashed over his face and head and the front of his tunic.

"For Hades's sake, Deina!" He staggered back, spluttering, and dragged the linen cloth from a nearby table to dry himself off.

There was another smattering of laughter.

Deina shoved him. "Give me my things, Theron. Or I'll tell the elders you broke into my room."

"And I'll tell them what you've done." Theron pushed her back. "I'll tell them everything. Gods, I don't know what you're so upset about anyway. A couple of old bits of jewelry. It's not like they're worth anything."

"They're mine."

"You mean you stole them."

"No, I didn't. They were given to me. They belonged to—" Deina bit off her words. "They're mine."

"Right," Theron said scornfully. "Of course they are."

Aster pushed his way through the crowd. "Enough of this. She's broken the rules by being here, Theron. And she's insulted what little honor you possess, which means—"

Theron rolled his eyes. "Here we go. Honor, glory, destiny . . ."

"Which means," Aster shouted, "she's insulted the honor of all of us."

There were murmurs of agreement from some of the Severers gathering behind Aster, while others voiced their support for Theron. No one, Deina noted without surprise, seemed to be on her side. A couple of younger novices started chanting: "Fight. Fight. Fight . . ."

Aster nodded at the chanting Severers, drawing himself up. "If you won't deal with her, Theron . . ." He made a grab for Deina's wrist.

Deina aimed a kick. Too late: Theron shoved Aster hard enough to make him stumble back. "Stay out of this."

Aster snarled and turned on Theron. Some of the onlookers cheered as they began scuffling, upending a table and scattering olives across the floor.

"Forgive me for interrupting . . ." It was Drex. He was hanging back, fiddling with what looked like a small stone, turning it over and over in his fingers.

"What?" Theron barked at the novice.

"Well"—Drex gulped—"perhaps this isn't a good idea? Theron, you've already been in trouble with the elders this week. Aster, the person who's hired you as a mourner tomorrow may prefer your face unblemished. And for a woman to be found in the men's quarters . . . the elders could add five years

to your time. I . . . It's just a thought." He ducked his head and turned away, carefully not looking at Deina, but murmuring as he passed her, "I don't like people shouting."

Aster and Theron, reaching some unspoken agreement, backed away from each other. Aster jabbed a finger at Deina.

"Get rid of her." He grabbed Melos's hand and stalked away.

Theron jerked his head toward the door. "Go, Deina. Before someone does tell the elders you're here."

Theron had a narrow leather cord around his neck in addition to the torc. The charm hanging from the cord was concealed beneath his tunic, but Deina guessed what it was: a tiny butterfly crafted from copper. The charm he'd torn from Deina's own neck when they'd fought each other in the spring games. The charm he'd made for her—before their relationship had dissolved into bad blood and rivalry—kept to taunt her with. She could demand that, in return for what he'd stolen . . .

But the charm was a symbol of his victory; he wouldn't hand it over willingly. And Drex was right. If she stayed here any longer, it wasn't going to end well.

"This isn't over."

Deina swung away from Theron. But the men surrounding her didn't seem inclined to make way. Some seemed curious. A few looked as if they would happily kill her, judging from the venom in their gaze. Deina wondered what exactly she'd done to deserve such hostility.

So be it. As she clenched her fists, ready to fight her way through the crowd, Theron said loudly, "I suppose I'd better make sure you don't get lost again." He fell into step beside her. The others, after a moment's hesitation, drifted away, resuming the conversations and games Deina's entrance had interrupted.

Theron accompanied her as far as the door that led to the men's quarters.

"You'll be safe now." Did he expect her to thank him? She kept walking. "The beads and the ring"—he called after her—"where did you really get them? Who gave them to you?"

Deina ignored him. But as soon as she turned the corner and was out of Theron's sight, she sagged against the wall, eyes closed, grateful for the cold solidity of the stonework against her shoulder blades. She was a Severer, and a valuable one at that. She probably hadn't been in any real danger.

Careless, though, to have gone there without a knife.

Deina waited as her breathing slowed. Leida—that was the answer to Theron's question. It was years since she'd allowed herself to think about her. Leida was already a novice when Deina was brought to the House. Grown-up, beautiful, talented. Whereas Deina, from what she could recall of that first year, hadn't exactly been endearing. She remembered being scared. Using her anger and her fists as a shield to hide behind. And yet, after finding her alone and crying in the gardens one evening, Leida had taken the time to comfort her and teach her. To befriend her, even when the children in her dormitory had mostly given up. Had she been trying to mother her? Hard to say—Deina had no recollection of her own mother, no sense of what an actual mother might do. Still, to be like Leida had become Deina's sole ambition. Until one night, less than two years into Deina's indenture, before she was even an apprentice, Leida crept into the children's dormitory and knelt by the bed. She tucked a small pouch into Deina's hands and placed

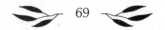

her finger against Deina's lips. *Keep these for me, little one. I'm summoned to Thebes tomorrow. But when I come back, I'll be free, and I'll take you away from here. I promise.* There'd been such hope, such excitement in her dark eyes.

So Deina waited. Prayed. But Leida never came back. And in time, Deina had cut open her doll and sewn the trinkets Leida had given her inside, trying to believe she was burying the pain of it all at the same time.

She could have shared that memory with Theron. It might have changed things between them. Then again, the way he'd looked at her when she confronted him—as if she were of no more value than the broken string of beads he'd taken—

A sickening wave of pain from her injured ankle, forgotten in the heat of her anger, almost pitched her onto her knees. The herbarium was nearby. Clinging to the wall with one hand, she limped on toward the rooms that formed the heart of the House: the refectory, the herbarium—with its associated garden—and the great hall. If she was lucky, the herbarium would be deserted; she could get something for the pain and go to bed.

Of course, given the kind of day it had been, she wasn't lucky. There were more than the usual number of oil lamps burning, and someone was sitting at one of the large tables in the main room, stripping leaves off a branch and dropping them into a basin of steaming water. But at least the someone was Anteïs. She looked Deina up and down and raised an eyebrow.

"What have you done to yourself this time?"

"My ankle. I think I twisted it when I was . . . out."

"Not racing the boys again, were you? You promised me, after the last time I had to patch you up—"

"No." Deina shook her head. "Definitely not racing." She sat down in the chair Anteïs indicated and took a deep breath, savoring the scent of the herbs hanging from the drying racks above. Not that they should really blame her, if she had been racing. What did the elders expect? As soon as they arrived at the House, Severers were taught that competition was good, and that winning was the best. Girls and boys competed together, and Deina absorbed the lessons she thought she was meant to learn. Grow strong and prove your strength. Beat the boys, even if they didn't like it. And then they became novices, and suddenly it was wrong for girls and boys to train together, wrong for women to compete with men. Oh, there were still training and races, but Deina always won too easily. There was no thrill in it. When she raced someone like Aster—secretly, with only a handful of other Severers watching and betting on the outcome—she felt alive.

The tall shelves that lined the room were filled with terra-cotta urns, all identical, marked with symbols that neither of them could read but that Anteïs knew by heart; the elder had been going from urn to urn, gathering ingredients to add to a large marble mortar. Now she was mashing them together.

"Hold out your leg."

Deina obeyed, wincing as Anteïs crouched and ran her fingers over her swollen ankle. "At least it's not broken." She smeared the bruised skin with the grassy-smelling contents of the mortar and wrapped a fresh bandage around it. "All done. Now get some sleep. You look as if you need it. And tomorrow—" Anteïs broke off, coloring faintly. "Well, I expect tomorrow will bring its own challenges."

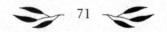

Deina stood, testing to see if the bandaged ankle could take her weight. "It already feels better. Thank you, Anteïs."

The elder grunted in acknowledgment, waving a dismissal.

"Anteïs . . . do you remember Leida?" Deina rushed the question out before she could change her mind.

The older woman froze. Carefully finished setting the jar she was holding in its space on the shelf. "Why do you ask?"

"I was thinking about her earlier." Deina pressed a hand to her stomach, suddenly queasy. "Do you know what happened to her?"

Anteïs was still facing the shelves; Deina waited. What answer was she hoping for? That Leida had broken her promise and was free? Or that she was dead?

Anteïs turned slowly. "I don't recall. So many of us fall by the wayside, for one reason or another. That's why we're not supposed to get attached." She took a deep breath and straightened up. "Bed."

Deina bowed and walked haltingly back to her room. It was still a mess, but her body ached and her eyes were stinging with tiredness. She pulled off her clothes, dragged the tangled heap of bedclothes over herself, and fell right to sleep.

Deep, echoing chimes rolled from the bell tower into Deina's dreams, and drove her to consciousness. She blinked and rubbed her eyes, squinting in the pale light that spilled from behind the shutters. Not long after dawn, by the looks of it, and yet they were ringing the bell to summon a gathering . . . Deina struggled out of bed, wincing at a grumble of pain from her ankle, drew a blanket around her body, and stuck her head out into the wide cloister. Other adepts were also looking out of their rooms or hovering nearby. Chryse—yawning, also wrapped in a blanket—wandered over.

"Do you know what's happening?"

Deina shook her head. But it had to be something to do with Orpheus; yesterday's altercations with Theron had driven the Tyrant from her head. "I suppose we'll find out. Let's go."

Together, they joined the adepts and novices heading toward the women's hall. No fire had been lit yet in the central hearth, and the large space was cold. They curled up next to each other on a couch. Before long, the doors that connected the hall to the rest of the House swung open to admit Anteïs and three of the other women elders. They waited for the novices to fall silent.

Kalistra, the hall mistress—sour-faced and sour-tempered—stepped forward.

"The House is to be honored with a visit from Lord Orpheus at noon. All Severers above the rank of apprentice are ordered to attend. You will be ready, clean, and in your ceremonial robes but unveiled. When in his presence, you will remain kneeling with your eyes downcast unless instructed otherwise. After bathing, you are to remain in your rooms until the time comes to gather in the great hall. Questions?"

Kalistra's tone made it clear that she didn't expect any response. Still, one of the novices slowly raised her hand.

"Honorable Sister, what of our work? I was to attend a dying woman this morning."

"Canceled. Messengers have been sent to those who

requested our services. The city will have to do without us today." She drew herself up. "We hold ourselves in readiness for the king's commands."

Kalistra left the room, two other elders following in her wake. But Anteïs lingered.

"Deina, wait there. I want to check your ankle."

As the other adepts and novices dispersed, talking in low voices, Chryse—a favorite with all the elders—stayed where she was.

Anteïs knelt and bent over Deina's ankle, pulling down the edge of the bandage. "The swelling has reduced."

"It feels much better. Thank you."

The last group of Severers left the hall. Anteïs sat back on her heels. "You asked me what happened to Leida yesterday; what I told you wasn't entirely true. I was an adept, at the time. I don't know what happened to her, but I do remember her. And I remember that she and some others were summoned to Thebes by the Tyrant. None of them returned."

"Do you know why he's here?"

"Because he wants something, I imagine. Some treasure the House has laid up. Its gold, or its people. So be careful, both of you. Stay out of sight if you can." She pushed herself up, resting one hand briefly on Deina's shoulder. "You're talented, Deina, but sometimes you draw far too much attention to yourself. A little more discretion, and you'll live longer."

Deina dropped her gaze.

"Yes, Anteïs."

As the elder strode away, Chryse yawned.

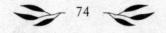

"Whatever Orpheus wants, I hope he gets it and goes away again quickly. Or Anteïs could be wrong—perhaps he wants to give the House a gift, to honor Hades. Perhaps he'll pay for us to have a feast."

"Perhaps," Deina murmured doubtfully.

"The elder is right, though," Chryse added. "You do dangerous things that make you stand out, and it scares me. I wish you wouldn't."

They wandered toward the baths. Theron's comment about making a scene echoed through Deina's memory. Was that what everyone thought she should do: stay in the shadows, rule abiding, until death or madness claimed her? No risk, but no freedom, either.

That wasn't living.

That was just dying slowly.

It didn't take long to bathe and dress, and noon seemed in no hurry to arrive. Deina's window overlooked an interior courtyard—a shady garden planted with flowers and olive trees; even with the shutters open, all she could hear of the preparations was the occasional shouted order and—once—a metallic crash, as if someone had dropped an armful of silverware. Mostly she sat and listened to the drone of the bees visiting the lavender bushes, trying not to fall asleep. Her old doll lay on the table nearby. Chryse had offered to mend it—and to stick a needle into Theron for good measure—but there didn't really seem much point in stitching the torn fabric back together.

Finally, the deep-throated bell began to toll again. Deina hurried from her room and joined the others streaming through the corridors.

The communal areas of the House were as they had been yesterday, but when they reached the colonnades that linked the rest of the House to the great hall, Deina saw that the sandstone pillars had been hung with garlands of laurel leaves into which sprigs of yellow-flowered immortelle had been woven.

Chryse caught up with her and slipped her hand into Deina's. Together, they passed through the tall doors, carved from some ancient tree and inlaid with the sigil of Hades in pale marble. The symbol glowed bone white against the dark wood. Within the hall, the bronze lamps set in niches around the walls were all aflame, gilding the forest of black marble columns that held up the roof. A richly colored carpet, glowing with deep reds and bright blues, had been rolled out to cover the tiled floor between the double doors and the dais. The Guardians of the House, eight men and one woman—Anteïs—chosen from among the elders, were already there; their plain wooden chairs had been shunted aside to make space for a golden throne set beneath a gem-studded cloth-of-gold canopy.

The adepts, novices, and other elders were soon assembled, women to the left of the dais, men to the right. Hard on their heels came priests from the Temple of Hades, who inevitably turned up to important events whether they'd been invited or not. The priests swaggered in, noses in the air, the lamplight glinting from their jeweled headdresses and capes. They headed to a place of honor next to the dais. Watching the priests, Deina noticed Theron. He was standing to the other side of the dais, his face strangely blank, his hands clasped tightly together.

Everyone was in place: scarlet-robed elders, black-robed adepts, and novices in gray. Silence spread, broken only by the shuffling of feet and the occasional cough.

The harsh bray of a trumpet rang out. The Severers sank as one to their knees as the first members of the Tyrant's entourage stepped onto the jewel-colored carpet. From her place behind the row of elders, Deina risked the briefest of glances before bowing her head. Enough of a glance to make her wonder whether Anteïs was right about staying out of sight. Iron Guards led Orpheus's procession; at least, that's what Deina guessed they were. She'd heard of them, though she'd never seen them before. Men taken from among the guards of the Dominion's cities, or from its armies. Selected by Orpheus to be sealed forever into metal bodies, enchanted with dark magic to become silent creatures of immense strength that needed neither food nor water nor rest. An honor, it was called.

Deina shivered and sank lower.

The heavy tread of the Iron Guards was followed by a repetitive clanging sound, like a bell with a muffled tongue, and the hall filled with the heady aroma of incense; Orpheus had brought his own censers with him. The lamplight seemed to dim, swallowed by the thick clouds of scented smoke. More footsteps. The creak of wood as someone ascended the dais.

Deina stared at the soles of the sandals of the woman kneeling in front of her. Silence fell again. And in the silence, someone started to sing.

Theron. So much for not drawing attention to yourself. He was singing an anthem, an ancient Song of praise to Hades that was sometimes performed on the great feast days of the Order. The sound rippled through the gloom like liquid silver and sent a shiver down Deina's spine. Theron was a conniving, selfish piece of work who needed to be put in his place sooner rather than later. But when he sang . . . that, surely, was a gift from the gods.

The echo of the final note died away.

"Welcome, mighty ruler." That was Neidius, white-haired Leader of the House. "Welcome to our House, the home of those fortunate enough to have been marked by Lord Hades for his service. We hold ourselves ready to assist you."

"We thank you for your welcome." A reedy, rough-toned voice. Deina frowned; it wasn't how she expected the Tyrant to sound. "We have heard much of Iolkos's worth, and of the abilities of its Severers. His Majesty has long desired to visit the city." *Not* Orpheus, then. "And now that his wish has been fulfilled, His Majesty requires the assistance of a few of your Severers for a task he would have them perform."

"We are here to serve." Neidius didn't sound as nervous as Deina would have expected. "The House is ready to hear your commands."

"Severers of Iolkos, I am Aristaeus. I am the voice of the king. When I speak, Lord Orpheus speaks. When I listen, Lord Orpheus listens." A pause. "We require volunteers: adepts or novices. From those who put themselves forward, His Majesty will personally make his choice. Only at that point will the details of the task be revealed." The wooden dais creaked, as if Aristaeus was pacing its length. "I am authorized to tell you that the task is dangerous, and there is no guarantee that anyone who attempts it will survive. However, for every Severer who dies, the House will be compensated by His Majesty for loss of income. To every Severer who succeeds, His Majesty will be equally generous. I have here a box of gold that will be given into the safekeeping of your Guardians. More importantly, His Majesty will purchase your freedom."

Freedom.

The last word reverberated inside Deina's head as her mind raced. A chance to wipe out her indenture. To escape Iolkos and the House while she was still young. It was an opportunity of which she'd never even dared to dream.

"As His Majesty wishes, of course," Neidius murmured. "I am sure there are many here who would consider themselves blessed to sacrifice themselves for Lord Orpheus and the honor of the Theban Dominion."

Deina almost smiled. Neidius would be hard-pressed to find anyone in the room who would choose to die for Orpheus, or for such an insubstantial and unrewarding idol as honor—with the possible exception of Aster. But for *freedom* . . . there were plenty here, surely, who would be willing to risk everything for such a prize.

Aristaeus continued. "Let those who wish to volunteer stand, keeping their gaze fixed to the ground. To look upon His Majesty without permission is death."

Before Deina could get to her feet, Chryse anticipated the movement and gripped her hand, trying to stop her from volunteering. Despite the fear bubbling in the pit of Deina's stomach, despite the long list of reasons why it might be better to stay exactly where she was, how could she not seize this offer? Chryse would understand, eventually. Gently, Deina prized Chryse's fingers from her wrist and stood up.

Was she the first? Hard to tell without looking around. The only certainty was that Chryse and the woman to her right were both still kneeling. Deina strained her ears for the slightest movement. Surely, she couldn't be the only volunteer? If she was, they'd have to pick her. She'd have a chance to win—the gold and her freedom. She should *want* to be the only choice. So why were her palms sweating? Why did the thought of standing in front of Orpheus alone make her feel so horribly sick? Wait—Aristaeus hadn't said this competition was only open to men, had he? She thought not, but when he'd dangled the possibility of freedom in front of her, she'd been distracted . . .

"Is that all?" Aristaeus asked. Deina waited, but there was no rebuke. No one questioned her right to volunteer. "Very well.

Now, those who have not volunteered, you may make your obeisance before His Majesty and then leave. Your services will no longer be required. Neidius, you and one of the other Guardians may remain."

A barely audible murmur, as if almost everyone in the room had just exhaled in relief. When it came to her turn to leave, Chryse tugged on Deina's hand, trying to pull Deina out of the hall with her. Deina resisted. She didn't dare look up to bid Chryse farewell. She just kept staring at the floor while the numbers in the great hall gradually diminished. It seemed to take ages, drawn out by Aristaeus's command that each Severer should bow to Orpheus before leaving. The longer she stood there, the harder Deina had to fight the temptation to look up, or to run after the others. She studied the tile that lay directly beneath her feet: an asphodel bloom cut from white marble, set in a polished black marble pentagon. The edge of the pentagon was highlighted with an undulating line of deep blue lapis lazuli, representing the rivers of the Underworld. The same pattern repeated across the whole floor. It was almost like standing on a field of flowers. She let her gaze follow the flowing blue lapis, trying to slow her breathing, to still the trembling of her hands. Until, finally, the massive doors slammed shut with a bang that echoed around the room. The air grew colder.

"Now you may look up." Aristaeus's voice again. Deina raised her head slowly.

The golden throne was empty, but directly in front of the dais stood four of the Iron Guards—Deina looked hurriedly away from their mouthless metal faces—bearing on their shoulders a litter, curtained with white silk. Neidius and Anteïs were still on the dais, next to a stocky gray-haired man who had to be Aristaeus. He smirked, as if he was enjoying their fear. "You will be wondering what is required. All will soon be made clear, to those who are selected. But the selection process itself must first be endured. Come, line up here." He pointed to a space in front of the litter. They hurried to obey. Twenty or so, as far as Deina could tell from a quick glance, more adepts than novices. Far fewer than she'd expected. Only two other women beside herself, both adepts. And among the men—

Theron. A spasm of annoyance left a sour taste in her mouth. What did she have to do to get away from him? Even volunteering for almost certain death didn't seem to be enough.

Aristaeus struck his staff on the floor and a servant approached, straining under the weight of the wooden box that filled his arms. He set it down and backed away.

The box shuddered. Whatever was inside wanted to get out.

Stooping, Aristaeus unfastened the clasp of the lock.

"You know we have a House belonging to the Order of Hephaestus in Thebes, the only one outside Mycenae. It is truly a blessing: Those marked with the sigil of Hephaestus have constructed many wondrous mechanisms for His Majesty. Weapons that can fire a spear faster than any man. A metal mole of gigantic proportions that can burrow through a city's wall in a day. But I think these might be my favorite." Stepping back, he opened the lid just a crack and stuck the end of his staff inside. When he withdrew it, there were things clinging to it. Scorpions, each one as large as a man's hand. Or what scorpions might look like if they'd been constructed by a master smith: burnished copper carapaces studded with some sort of brown crystal, with legs, tails, and pincers made of gold. At the tip of each tail, a curved, thornlike needle gleamed a dull red. The scorpions started to clamber stiffly up the staff. Deina couldn't drag her gaze away.

"Only those who are the most determined are likely to survive what will be required of you." Aristaeus laughed softly. "The most determined, or perhaps the most desperate." Carefully, he picked up one of the scorpions by its tail and shook the others back into the box. The creature's legs kept moving, making its body jerk from side to side in a horrifying dance. "This will determine whether you are sufficient for His Majesty's requirements. I've experimented with a number of poisons: hellebore, hemlock, the secretions of a curious black-and-red beetle from the island of Makaria. But it is the combination of my blend of poisons with the copper in the body of the scorpion that makes this so effective."

"What does it do, Lord?" The question came from Theron. Possibly brave. Possibly stupid. Possibly just another sign that Theron believed himself to be invincible.

But Aristaeus, if anything, seemed pleased by the interruption.

"It inflicts pain, through the creation of an illusion. Pain of such intensity that, even though the poison does not cause actual physical harm, most are not strong enough to survive the experience. The human mind is so easily deceived." He closed his eyes briefly, smiling as if recalling a pleasant memory, then dropped the scorpion back into the box. "If any of you are regretting your decision, you may leave."

Most left the line, hurrying toward the door. But Theron, curse him, was still there. So was Aster, standing a little apart, one hand on the hilt of his knife, gripping it tightly enough that his knuckles showed white. Lysias, too, though the gods alone knew why. He was pale and sweating and looked about to pass out. On Deina's other side stood Xenia, an older female adept who had hoped—and failed—to become an elder this year, her lips moving in silent prayer. The only novice remaining, to Deina's surprise, was Drex. He was frowning, his large eyes unfocused, hands loose at his side, almost as if he were only still here because he'd forgotten to leave.

"Six left," Aristaeus observed. "More than enough scorpions to go around. I hope for your sakes you are strong."

Deina's heart hammered so hard, it made her feel sick. But she just had to get through this. Survive, and she'd have the chance to convince Orpheus that she was the best choice for the task. Whatever it turned out to be.

Aristaeus had beckoned two servants forward, both of whom were wearing gauntlets of leather covered with copper plates. They lifted the box between them and carried it to where Drex was standing. "Now," Aristaeus ordered, "when I lift the lid, put your hand inside."

Drex flinched, suddenly seeming to become aware of Aristaeus. As the lid was raised, he lifted his hand. His fingers were curled into a fist; he had to stretch them out to slide them into the dark gap. Nothing happened. Until Drex moaned softly and one of the jeweled scorpions appeared, crawling out of the box and up the bare skin of his arm. As the box was moved along the line to Lysias, Deina watched the scorpion disappear beneath the shoulder of Drex's tunic. He was staring straight ahead, the tendons on his hands and neck standing out, sweat trickling from his temple down the side of his face.

His head went back and he shrieked. Over and over. Dropped to his knees as Lysias, next to him, collapsed and began convulsing on the floor.

Her turn. Aristaeus and his servants were waiting. Automatically, Deina reached out her hand; it was trembling, and her knuckles scraped against the edge of the lid as she slipped her fingers into the darkness. The first needlelike touch of the cold metal claws made her gasp. The creature emerged from the box and started lurching its way up her forearm. Deina clenched her other hand into a tight fist, fighting the urge to sweep the scorpion away. Onward it came, past her elbow, onto the soft flesh of her upper arm, the thornlike stinger at the end of its tail twitching. She screwed her eyes shut, but she could still feel its claws as they dug into her shoulder, her back, her neck, her spine.

The scorpion stopped moving. Tightened its grip. Deina held her breath as it stung, injecting its poison into the base of her skull—

The great hall erupted in flames. Everything was burning—ceiling, walls—and she couldn't move, couldn't escape. Closer and closer the fire came, surrounding her, until she heard nothing but its roar and crackle. Saw nothing but the dancing gold and orange flames that licked at her clothes. Ate away the fabric. Crept up her legs and across her torso, blistering the flesh and charring the bone and withering her hands into claws as waves of agony ripped scream after scream from her throat.

An illusion—that's what he'd said. It wasn't real. Deina tried to make herself believe it. To stop screaming long enough to form the words. *Not real. Not—*

But the flames burned away her lips, crawled down her throat, and silenced her. They took her breath as they spread to her lungs, shriveled her eyeballs, boiled the blood in her veins, and melted the fat from beneath her skin until it ran in rivulets and pooled on the black-and-white marble tiles, until she was begging any god who would listen for death—

The tiles. She could still feel them. They were still there, cold and hard beneath her hands. The tiles were real. White marble asphodel blooms, and rivers of blue lapis streaked with gold, flowing, flowing . . .

Deina winced as pain darted through her left temple. For a moment, the flames were veiled by a mass of swirling darkness, like black smoke billowing. But instead of choking her, the enveloping shadow cooled her tortured skin. She took a sharp breath inward, catching the faint taste of winter at the back of her throat, the fleeting impression of black-feathered wings, an almost familiar presence . . .

Gradually, both the fire and the darkness faded. So did the pain. Deina blinked until the world came back into focus, until the tiles once again filled her vision, stretching away from her across the hall. She was on her hands and knees. Shaking, sweating, but whole. Uninjured. Reaching up to the sore spot on the back of her neck, she wrenched the metal scorpion away from her skin. Dashed it as hard as she could to the floor. It wriggled once, its claws rattling against the marble, and was still. Her stomach heaved and she clapped a hand to her mouth.

"Here—drink." Anteïs stooped to offer her a cup of water. There was a fierce expression in the older woman's eyes. Deina sat on the floor and sipped the water, looking to see what had become of the other volunteers.

Drex was on his knees, holding his head in his hands. He'd been sick, too. Theron was sprawled on the floor, groaning, as was Aster. Xenia wasn't moving. Neidius was crouched next to her, holding a bronze mirror to her mouth to check her breathing. And Lysias—

Lysias was rigid, his face contorted into a rictus of agony, his eyes open, staring blankly upward. A pool of blood was seeping from beneath his body, soaking into the fabric of his tunic.

Anteïs leaned over and closed his eyes.

"The power of the mind." Aristaeus nudged Lysias's corpse with his foot. "Truly, a wondrous thing."

"I thought—I thought I was drowning." Drex's voice was a rough whisper, and he winced as he spoke. "I couldn't breathe."

Aristaeus looked smug. "Pain takes many forms. As does fear. Back into line now. Quickly."

Deina moved swiftly to obey, forcing herself onto her feet and hurrying into place in front of the silk-shrouded litter. The only woman left—to even have a chance at being chosen, she'd have to beat Theron, Drex, and Aster convincingly in whatever test they were given next. Anteïs had already placed a cloak over Lysias's body; from the corner of her eye, as she waited for the others to line up, Deina saw the same office performed for Xenia. She was dead, too, then.

At that moment, the Iron Guards bearing the litter carried it away, revealing the now-occupied throne.

A golden mask gleamed from the shadows beneath the canopy: the face of a man. The gold had been molded to show eyebrows; a mustache; a narrow, pointed beard. Full lips, partly open, the gap between them filled with gold filigree. There was a crown, too, an ornate band running across the forehead. And just the suggestion of a pair of eyes somewhere behind the dark, empty eyeholes.

Orpheus?

He looked like a statue, sitting upright and square on the throne, both hands on his knees. One palm down, the other palm up, fingers clutched around a polished sphere of crystal.

"The survivors, Majesty." Aristaeus bowed, indicating with a click of his fingers that the Severers should do the same.

Orpheus rose smoothly and stepped down from the throne. The rich purple silk of his robe, fastened with a gold belt and a brooch at each shoulder, shimmered. His long hair—dark, with just a hint of gray at the temples—was braided with gold thread. Even the straps of his sandals were jeweled.

"Only four, out of the six? I am grieved for your losses." Kind words, though there was too little emotion in his tone to be convincing. He sounded strangely detached. "Be assured that the final test involves no suffering. The seeing stone merely reveals the truth of your nature." He moved to stand in front of Aster and held the crystal up to the eye socket of the mask, tilting his head. "A warrior."

He moved on to Drex, then Theron, peering at them in turn through the crystal. "A thinker. And a bard, of course. We were moved by the beauty of your voice."

A bard? Surely, he had to be out of the running; compared

with strength and brains, a talent for singing wasn't much of a qualification for a dangerous mission. Theron murmured his thanks. But Deina could hear the disappointment in his voice, and when he caught her watching him, she saw the flash of fury in his eyes.

And now the Tyrant was directly in front of her. Her nostrils filled with the sickly sweet perfumes that clung to him. She stared into the crystal as he held it up between them, its shifting, rainbow-streaked interior like rain clouds lit from behind by the sun. Orpheus drew back, lowering the crystal. Shook it and tried again. What would he see? Speed, hopefully. Or mental strength—that had to be as important as Aster's muscles. He lowered the crystal again.

"Hmm. A thief."

A thief? Deina dug her fingernails into her palms. She wanted to object, to tell him it wasn't fair—that she was so much more than just a thief. That a lump of magical crystal couldn't possibly reveal the full measure of a person, any more than Aristaeus's scorpions. But Orpheus had already passed the crystal to a servant and resumed his seat on the throne.

Aristaeus barked an order. All the servants—apart from the guards carrying the litter—filed out of the hall. At least they took the box of scorpions with them.

"Well . . ." The golden mask was still. But Deina could feel the Tyrant's gaze resting on her briefly. He was going to choose either Drex or Aster—that much seemed certain. At least it wasn't likely to be Theron.

Please, don't let it be Theron . . .

"Well," Orpheus repeated. "I believe you have sufficient capabilities between you to embark upon this quest with at least some possibility of success. We have our company of adventurers. Continue, Aristaeus."

A *company*? Deina glanced sideways at Theron and the others. Drex was standing with eyes closed and his head bowed; she couldn't tell whether he was full of regret or relief. Aster, on the other hand, looked stunned. She didn't blame him. He probably hated the idea of being forced to be part of a team as much as she did. But at least she—and Theron, unfortunately—were still in the game.

Aristaeus beat his staff on the floor.

"Oaths are all very well, but I believe threats are a better way to ensure your secrecy. What we are about to discuss is never to be mentioned to anyone other than those already in this room. If I find any reason to believe that one of you has disobeyed me, then a tenth of the people of Iolkos, adults and children, will be selected at random and publicly executed. They will suffer grievously. Do I make myself clear?"

Everyone voiced their agreement.

Aristaeus nodded approvingly. "So. You will not be aware that His Majesty's wife, Queen Eurydice, died at midsummer."

Neidius bowed. "Your grief is our grief, Majesty."

"Indeed." Aristaeus's voice was dry. "However, the king does not wish to grieve any longer. He wishes you to bring the queen back."

Deina looked to Neidius, expecting the elder to exclaim—to object—to say something, instead of remaining silent.

Perhaps Anteïs expected the same; she was still gazing

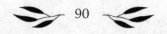

doubtfully at Neidius as she asked, "By 'back,' Lord, you mean . . . ?"

"I mean alive. Back here. Flesh and blood and bone, just as she was before."

Was that even possible? There were stories, of course. Ancient legends, of those who had journeyed to the Underworld and returned. Of people rescued from death. But mostly, they were rescued by heroes.

Deina looked at Aster and Theron and Drex. Not a hero among them, herself included.

"Clearly, the queen meant a great deal to His Majesty." Neidius bowed to the Tyrant.

The golden mask stared back. "She is life itself to me."

He spoke in exactly the same tone in which he'd complimented Theron's singing. But perhaps that just reflected the depths of his grief. Deina could barely remember her life before the House. Only fragments. Frayed remnants of memory, as fragile as gossamer. A phrase of a song with most of the words missing. The worn surface of a wooden toy beneath her fingers. The flavor of what she thought might have been her favorite dish, though she could no longer remember its name. Of her parents, she recalled even less. But there was just enough, all told, to make her think she must have been happy. And she remembered the agony of separation clearly enough. The way she'd tried to skim over it, to keep her thoughts on the surface of things, because the pain of the loss, if touched, was too much to bear. The way it had sat like a lump in the center of her chest until she'd covered it with enough layers not to feel it anymore.

Anteïs was asking another question. "Forgive me, Lord

Aristaeus, but—why Iolkos? Surely the Severers in Thebes—"

"As I said," Aristaeus replied, "word of the prowess of your Severers has reached us."

From whom? Deina wondered. Iolkos was small for a city. If she'd been looking for the widest pool of talent, she'd have looked elsewhere.

Aster, of course, was nodding in agreement.

Aristaeus looked Deina in the eyes.

"I didn't say this would be easy. But if it were easy, His Majesty wouldn't be offering such rewards as freedom. And this gold to be shared among those who return." He pointed to a small, heavily carved chest that had been set down by the throne. "All you have to do is succeed. And survive."

"I grow weary," Orpheus murmured.

Aristaeus clapped his hands, and the Iron Guards approached with the litter.

"Your elders will explain to you what is necessary. We leave at dawn in five days' time."

Orpheus stepped into the litter, and Aristaeus drew the silken curtains closed. He grinned at them as he followed the litter out of the hall. For the first time, Deina noticed the unusually sharp points of his teeth.

6

Outside the great hall, there were Severers everywhere—huddled together, discussing what had happened, speculating. Even keeping her eyes fixed on the back of Anteïs's head, Deina felt the curious stares. Heard the way conversations paused as she and the others approached, only to resume with more energy after they'd passed. It was a relief to reach the herbarium and have the door shut behind them.

"Anteïs will prepare a draft to help you recover from your ordeal," Neidius said. "I have a few matters to arrange, and I imagine you all need some rest. However, we are short of time, so I will begin your instruction this evening. From now on, you will stay together in the elders' quarters. You will eat there. Sleep there." Neidius hesitated, frowning at Deina. "You'll have to sleep in Anteïs's room. Stay here until you're sent for."

Neidius trudged out. The room sank into silence, apart from the scrape of Anteïs's pestle and mortar and the clicking of Aster's knuckles. The mixture of excitement, fear, and excruciating pain left Deina feeling as if she'd just outrun a volcanic eruption. The others looked as if they felt the same.

She was roused by Anteïs handing her a horn cup. Deina sniffed the dark liquid: sage, mingled with another scent—bitter, earthy—that made her nose wrinkle.

Anteïs sighed. "Just drink it."

She took a sip. "You'll be teaching me, won't you? And Neidius will teach the others."

Anteïs shook her head. "The most ancient of our Songs were never passed on to me."

"But I thought all the Guardians of the House—"

"Only the men. I was not deemed worthy." Anteïs shrugged one shoulder. "Drink." Deina obeyed and returned the empty cup to Anteïs. "Good. I'll go and see about some food; no doubt Neidius is far too elevated to have thought of something so basic."

As the echo of Anteïs's footsteps died away, Deina stared at the herbarium door and wondered. Was Chryse upset—angry, even—that Deina had resisted her attempts to stop her from volunteering? She'd assumed they would all be returning to their quarters afterward. That she'd have a chance to talk to Chryse. To explain. As it was, she hadn't even thought to ask Anteïs to take a message for her. Deina jumped up from where she'd been sitting and began to pace the length of the room. What had she gotten herself into? There was a chance for freedom, yes. But to get the most out of freedom, to actually enjoy it, you needed to be alive. And even though she was in no immediate danger, she was still stuck in a room with two people she'd happily punch in the face and a third who—

"For Hades's sake, will you sit down and be still?" Aster exclaimed, startling her. "You're prowling up and down like . . . like a dog that's forgotten where it's hidden its bone. I'm trying to think."

"How can anyone think over the noise of you pulling your fingers out of their sockets? It's disgusting."

"I'm hungry!"

"We're all hungry." Deina kept walking back and forth. Orpheus's quest had seemed relatively straightforward in the great hall. But now . . . "Severers work in the Threshold. The Threshold was created by the first elders for that very purpose: to allow us to use our power as a—a bridge, between the mortal world and the Underworld. But we don't go *into* the Underworld. Not for any of the rites. So how could we possibly do what Orpheus demands?" She shook her head. "Drex, what do you think?"

"Me?" Drex looked up from where he'd been carving a line into the table with his thumbnail. "Well, I—"

"The old stories," Aster interrupted. "The journeys of Herakles and Theseus and Odysseus. They tell us that living mortals—not even Severers—*are* able to journey into the Underworld if they are strong enough. Brave enough. We need to look to the tales of heroism."

"Tall tales," Theron scoffed. "Tales for children."

"Heroes were real, once. A hero can enter the Underworld, and a hero can bring someone else back." Aster nodded, agreeing with himself. "That's obviously why I was chosen. Though I'm not sure why the rest of you are here. Particularly you, *bard*."

Theron colored. "Me? I'm as strong as you, and I'm good with a bow. Better than good." He waved a hand in Drex's direction. "He can't even see what target to aim at."

Drex didn't react. Was he too used to being insulted? Deina came to a halt in front of Theron. "He can read. It means he has a brain, unlike you."

Aster folded his hands behind his head. "He was brave enough to volunteer, and at least he's a man. I was surprised any women were allowed to participate, even one who's quick on her feet."

Would Drex back her up? No. Too busy carving up the table. Last time she'd leap to his defense.

"And then," Aster continued, "to find out she's a thief, that I'm expected to ally with someone without honor—I very nearly withdrew."

"I wish you had," Deina retorted. "It would have spared the rest of us from listening to you."

Aster smiled. "I am honor bound to compete. Clearly, I'll be the one to survive and to restore the queen to life. Lord Orpheus is a mighty king, and no doubt he is an honorable man. As well as the gold, he'll probably make me a captain in the army. Perhaps even a general . . ."

The door opened and a servant looked in. "You're to follow me to the elders' hall. There's some food waiting."

Deina, already on her feet, was the first out of the room. She threw Aster a look of disdain, a look that hopefully said, *Yes, I'm quick on my feet, therefore I'm going to get to the food before you.*

She was going to need all the energy she could muster. It looked like it was going to be a very long day.

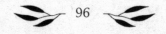

***

Each of the next four days was long. Lonely, too. Theron and Aster ignored her, and even Drex—pleased, she guessed, to be treated as something approaching an equal by two of the most popular male adepts—barely spoke to her. Every waking moment was spent with Neidius, secluded from the rest of the House. In the cool of the morning, they went to a corner of the training ground to practice bladework and wrestling, the idea being to help them fight as a team if—when—they were attacked. Hopeless, really; Drex was outmatched, and Deina knew that she and the others were more intent on winning than on working out any kind of joint strategy. Each afternoon they sat in the archives, trying to absorb as much information and guidance as Neidius could offer. He taught them new Songs—Songs that had last been sung in a time so distant as to be more myth than history. The words and actions of the particular rites and sacrifices that would have to be performed before they could enter the Underworld, and the rite that would get them back out again—*if* they had the queen's ghost. The chants they would have to use to bind her and to restore her to physical life, re-forming her body, layer by layer—blood, bones, organs, skin—until ghost became flesh. The unfamiliar phrases, sung over and over each day, threaded their way each night through Deina's dreams. As well as the Songs themselves, there were stories. Descriptions of the Underworld and its inhabitants: daimons, gods, and monsters of infinite variety. And if they didn't kill you, the Underworld itself almost certainly would. It was a place that couldn't be mapped, couldn't be reduced to some measurement of height or breadth or depth.

A landscape in constant flux, obeying no rule that anyone had ever been able to determine, that would try to drive out those who weren't supposed to be there. You couldn't eat anything that grew there, you couldn't drink from its rivers. And if you strayed too far from whatever path you attempted to follow, you might never find it again.

After she got back to Anteïs's room each night, Deina was too tired for conversation. Too tired even to wonder why, after she'd asked Anteïs to get a message to Chryse, her friend hadn't tried to reply.

By the afternoon of the third day, Deina understood: They might well succeed in getting into the Underworld. But the odds were against them ever getting out again. Perhaps that was why Orpheus had come to Iolkos seeking volunteers for this madness. Iolkos wasn't important enough for anyone to care what happened there. She and the others were expendable.

There was to be a banquet later. A way of honoring the volunteers, supposedly. But their bodies were to be anointed and robed in the finest garments the House had to offer, so it felt more like a funeral. Before the time came to get ready, Deina slipped away to the temple that lay within the grounds of the House. A fire was burning on the altar as usual. She drew her knife and cut off a lock of her hair and dropped it into the flames. Kneeling, she offered up a prayer. Not to Hades but to Hecate—one of the old gods, a deity of the Underworld, of thresholds, of ghosts and magic.

I've never asked you for anything. I've never dared. The gifts of the gods are always double-edged and seldom worth having. But if this is a game, I pray that the Underworld at least gives us a real chance to play . . .

There was no answer. She hadn't really expected one.

The banquet was in full swing. Deina leaned closer to Chryse, shouting into her ear to be heard above the din of drums and pipes and voices.

"The others are taking bets."

Chryse shouted back, "On what? None of us are allowed to know what you're doing."

"It's a safe assumption that we're going off to do something dangerous, so they're betting on which out of the four of us will survive." Deina shrugged. "On how we might die, too, from what I've heard."

Chryse threw Deina a sympathetic glance. "That's horrible. I wish everything here didn't have to be turned into a competition."

They fell silent, and Chryse was soon absorbed by watching the dancing: feet tapping, upper body swaying slightly in time to the music. Deina studied her profile. As soon as she'd left the temple, she'd gone to find her. Anteïs had already told Chryse that Deina and the others would be leaving very soon to undertake a task for the Tyrant. Deina had expected to find Chryse distressed and demanding answers. Instead, she'd been met with calm; Chryse had claimed to understand Deina's choice, but when Deina had tried to talk about her longing for freedom, to finally explain her plan and how—if she won—she would use Orpheus's gold to buy Chryse her freedom, too, Chryse had stopped her. "I was wrong. Things are changing, and the future's uncertain. You might not come back. I might not still be here if you do. Please, let's just try to enjoy this evening." They'd embraced. And that had been that.

Since then, Chryse had been as affectionate as usual. There was nothing in her manner that had changed. Deina decided the faint unease she felt when she looked at her friend was nothing more than her own anxiety over what was to come. She took a deep breath, sipped her wine, and surveyed their surroundings.

The refectory had been transformed. The bare stone walls were enlivened by embroidered hangings and dense garlands of scented, multicolored flowers. And the couches, which had been set out in a place of honor for her and the others to recline upon, had been draped with silk and piled with cushions. The elders of the house were waiting upon them, and all the delicacies the kitchens and cellars could offer had been brought to tempt them. Roasted goat stuffed with figs, sheep's cheese drizzled with herbs and honey, a rich stew of tomatoes and eggplant, preserved olives, flatbreads and pomegranates and a dozen or more other dishes. Deina picked at her food, remembering the animals she'd seen only five days ago, the ones penned up next to that little temple of Poseidon. No doubt they were also fattened up before being sacrificed.

Still—she'd *chosen* this. She was going to see it through.

With a little luck, she might even survive.

The music increased in tempo, its rhythm intoxicating. But

Deina didn't feel like joining in. All four volunteers were wearing old-fashioned robes usually reserved for holy days. But while the men's tunics, apart from their bright colors and decorated necklines, were not that different from their normal clothes, she'd been laced into an outfit that somehow managed to be both restricting and exposing: a long skirt, made from tiered layers of fabric, and a tight-waisted, short-sleeved bodice that was open at the front from collarbone to navel. Everything dyed in brilliant, clashing colors that were giving her a headache—not helped by the way her hair had been pinned and teased into elaborate curls. The heavy gold earrings pulled on her earlobes, and the heeled boots pinched her toes. The outfit's only concession to practicality was the dagger Deina had insisted on wedging into the waistband.

Chryse's fingers were tapping out the beat of the music. Deina nudged her.

"You should go and dance."

"But what about you?"

"I'll be fine." As Chryse hesitated, Deina added, "You know what I always say—"

"Don't pass up an opportunity?" Chryse finished the sentence for her as she leaned forward and put her arms around Deina's neck, hugging her tightly. "I know. I remembered."

"You'll come and see us off tomorrow morning? I don't want to leave without saying goodbye."

"Of course." Chryse stood. Perhaps it was just a trick of the torchlight, but Deina could have sworn there was something mischievous in her expression. "I'll be there. Don't worry. And don't stay up too late. You look tired." She smiled and moved to join the throng of dancers.

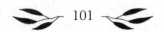

Deina watched her until she disappeared in the crowd.

"More wine?" Anteïs was holding out an earthenware ewer.

"No, thank you. Am I allowed to leave?"

"Of course. You can sleep in your own room tonight, if you wish, and I'll wake you in the morning. We're to be at the harbor by dawn, and it won't do to keep His Majesty waiting." She smiled very slightly. "Your last night. I hope you get some sleep."

Her last night. She should be happy; she'd been planning her escape from this place for long enough. And whatever Theron thought, she was the best Severer the House had to offer, at least among the adepts. She just had to convince herself that her best was going to be good enough.

Standing on tiptoe, Deina scanned the room for Chryse, but it was impossible to see her amid the press of bodies. She turned and bumped straight into Theron.

He stopped humming and raised his hands. "Careful."

"Don't touch me."

"I wasn't about to." He stepped back, his eyes widening.

"And don't look at me." Deina tugged at the bodice, cursing.

Theron muttered something under his breath, but he stared carefully over her shoulder at the crowded room. "The others are enjoying themselves."

"Good for them. I'm going to bed."

"Not having second thoughts, are you?"

"Why would I be?" Deina looked him in the eye; she'd jump in the Styx before she let Theron see the anxiety that had stolen her appetite. "I'm going to win. The queen's ghost, and then my freedom."

"*You're* going to win? We're meant to be doing this as a

team. I know you treat everything like it's a competition, but this isn't."

If he really believed that, he was a fool. Even if they all helped return Eurydice, if they all survived and were all set free, there was only one box of gold. The purchase of Chryse's freedom, two passages on a fast ship, plus enough left to set up a new life somewhere for them both—that was going to be expensive.

Theron leaned in, one hand on her shoulder, and spoke into her ear. "Since we're being honest, consider this a warning: I intend to make sure our *team* succeeds. And you're definitely the weakest member. Being handy with a knife is no match for my skill with the bow, or Aster's skill with the spear, or Drex's skill with . . ." A pause. "I'm sure his ability to read will turn out to be useful somehow. But if you can't keep up, if you hold us back, I swear I'll put an arrow in you without even—" He gasped.

They were standing almost cheek to cheek. Close enough for Deina to feel the way his body had suddenly become rigid. She smiled.

"The point of my blade, as you're aware, Theron, is positioned against a part of your anatomy I'm sure you'd hate to see damaged. Sometimes being handy with a knife is all one needs. You're lucky this room is too full of witnesses for me to slit you open like the pig you are."

An elder walked past; Deina concealed her knife in her skirts as Theron stepped back. Anger blazed briefly in his eyes, but then he gave her one of the lopsided grins that seemed to reduce so many adepts and novices—men and women both—to lust-befuddled idiots.

"As enjoyable as this has been, you'll have to excuse me; I found a buyer for a gold ring I recently acquired."

The ring that Leida had given her. The one he'd stolen, the bastard.

Deina scowled. "Just stay out of my way." She pushed past him.

"I will," Theron called out, "if you stay out of mine. That bodice was a great choice, by the way. Anything that makes you blush at least stands a chance of letting you pass for a human, rather than the stone-fleshed, stone-hearted daughter of some gods-forsaken . . ."

Deina lost the end of the insult. But she'd heard enough. Stuck together in the Underworld, for who knew how long? She'd end up killing him, if nothing else did.

Deina returned to her room, undressed, and collapsed into bed. But the rest she needed evaded her. Instead, she lay awake, reliving the past few days and trying not to think about the future. When sleep finally came, her dreams were dark and confusing. She seemed to be trapped in some version of the Threshold. No sunlit garden but the Threshold as it might be conjured by the words of the Punishment Rite: inhospitable, desolate, joyless.

Deina walked in silence across scorched red earth, beneath copper-tinted clouds. There was nothing green or living here. Just a flat expanse of dust, stretching off in every direction, without even the occasional rock to relieve the monotony. Though there was something on the horizon, moving toward her. She stopped. Squinted. Flinched at a sudden stab of pain in her left eye. When she'd blinked it away, she could see that the something was a young man—tall and well-built with jet-black hair. *The* young man. The one who'd been haunting her in the Threshold these past two years.

Deina shivered and rubbed her arms; it was getting colder. The coppery clouds were darkening to slate gray, and there was a weight to the air as if a storm was coming. No shelter here; nowhere to hide. And when she put her hand to her belt, her knife was missing.

Am I still dreaming? If so, this seems like a really good time to wake up . . .

He came to a halt a little distance away. Tendrils of fine black mist rose from the ground, curling around him like a shadow, winging back from his broad shoulders like a cloak.

Breathing deeply, Deina drew herself up to her full height. Braced herself to meet an attack if one came.

"It's you. *Again.*"

He smiled, his cheeks dimpling. "So it would seem."

"Well? What do you want?"

The shadows around him deepened. "Isn't it obvious? I'm here to help you." A few flakes of white snow drifted toward the ground.

"Help me to do what, exactly?"

"To survive, for one thing. To reach your potential, for another." He took a step toward her. The swirling darkness moved with him. An angry clap of thunder sounded in the distance. Deina backed away.

"What *are* you?"

Irritation flitted across his features, quickly suppressed.

"Think of me as a friend." He held out his hand to her. "Come. I've much to show you."

Lightning flared across the sky. For an instant, the face before her vanished, and in its place was a skull: skin and hair and bright blue eyes replaced by gleaming white, empty-socketed bone. Deina gasped and turned her head away.

"Look at me."

Something compelled her to obey.

He was as he had been. Pale, unfathomably handsome, but human—at least in appearance.

"What are you?" Deina demanded.

"I've told you: I'm the only one who can help you." He began to stride forward, hand stretched out toward her. "Come!"

Deina ran. Intent on putting as much distance as possible between her and whatever he really was, she thudded across the dead earth, sending clouds of dust up into the air, until her foot went through something, pitching her forward onto her knees. The ground was breaking apart. Skeletons were clawing their way up through the widening gaps. Deina cried out in horror and pushed herself back to her feet, jumping across chasm after chasm, trying to stay upright, to avoid the bony, clutching fingers. Another jump—not enough. She slipped, her nails scrabbling for purchase in the dirt as she slid toward the abyss below.

Sapphire eyes gazing down at her. An arrogant smile. He held out his hand.

No. Deina let go. Screaming, she tumbled through the darkness, falling and falling . . .

***

"Deina, come on. We've not much time." Anteïs's voice. "Hades, it's like waking the dead . . ." Something poked Deina hard in the shoulder.

"Ow!" Groaning, Deina opened one eye: lamplight, bright enough to make her squint. She pushed herself up as Anteïs threw open the shutters and let in a rush of cold air. It was still dark, but the blue-black of the sky beyond the window was touched with the warmth of dawn.

"Hurry up." Anteïs passed Deina a bundle of black linen. "Official robes, since you're working. And I've prepared some food for you to take with you. There's no time for breakfast. You have your bag ready? Your tools? Your knives?"

"Yes. Um . . ." Deina, dazed with sleep and struggling into her tunic, ran over in her mind the list of things she'd thrown into her bag yesterday. "Yes."

"Good." Anteïs gathered up the cast-off skirt and bodice from last night. "I'll wait at the main gate."

As the elder left, Deina sucked in her breath at a sudden stab of pain. A spot of blood was beading on the pad of her thumb—she'd pricked herself with the pin of her brooch. *Clumsy.* She stuck her thumb in her mouth and sucked the blood away. An accident or an omen? Either way, it was too late to change her mind. The Tyrant was expecting her, and she'd heard the rumors of what happened to those who disappointed him. She grabbed her bag, slung it over her shoulder, and headed for the main gate without a backward glance.

Anteïs was already there. So was Neidius, with Theron, Drex, and Aster.

And so was Chryse—dressed just as Deina was, in her official robes, a bag clutched in her hands.

"Chryse? What's going on? Where are you going?"

"I'm coming with you." She grinned. "Oh, not to wherever it is you're going. Unless you happen to be going to Thebes."

"What? Why—"

"Enough! There's no time for this," Neidius said, fretting. "We're leaving. Now."

The guards drew back the bolts. Together, Deina and Chryse followed the others from the gloom of the porch into the morning twilight. The clang of the gates swinging shut behind them sent a flock of starlings squawking into the sky in a whir of wings. But apart from the birds, the hills and the paths leading down to Iolkos were empty. Even once they'd entered the city, admitted through the nearest gate by a single sentry, there was no one, except for the beggars huddled in doorways, to observe their silent passage through the deserted streets.

They approached the harbor as dawn broke. Deina knew times were hard, but she'd expected some amount of noise and bustle, even this early in the day—fishermen returning with the night's catch, or a few merchant ships being loaded at the quayside. There should have been gossip and haggling. But today, the fishing boats lay unheeded on the shore, the shops and taverns that lined the waterfront were still shuttered, and the gulls feasted undisturbed in the shallows farther along the bay. While the Tyrant's warships remained, no one wanted to draw attention to themselves.

The torc around Deina's neck started to warm and tighten. She halted; they'd reached the limits of movement allowed to them by the spell-cast bronze. As the Severers waited for instructions from Aristaeus, currently surrounded by a knot of sailors and Iron Guards, she hissed at Chryse.

"Are you being forced? Did Orpheus threaten you?" Grabbing Chryse's arm, she began checking the skin for signs of injury. Not that there weren't plenty of ways to hurt someone without it showing. Chryse exclaimed and pulled away.

"Stop that. There's nothing wrong with me. I'm here because—"

"Deina . . ." Anteïs was beckoning to her. Unwillingly, she left Chryse.

"Yes, Anteïs?"

"Here." The elder handed her a small bag. "A tincture, to stop your monthly bleed. A healing salve. And a bronze charm of the goddess." Anteïs meant Hecate, the goddess who had helped lead Persephone out of the Underworld. The only god who counted, for most female Severers. "Remember what I've taught you. Remember that you represent our House. And remember to be careful. I'll miss you, Deina." Anteïs sighed, stepped forward, and embraced her.

Deina stiffened. She couldn't help it—she hadn't known Anteïs had such gentleness in her.

"Anteïs. Deina." Neidius's voice shattered the moment.

Anteïs turned away quickly. Deina trailed behind her.

Aristaeus, flanked by two of the Iron Guards, was stalking toward them.

Neidius bowed. "They are ready, my lord, but in order to proceed . . ." He gestured to the torcs. Aristaeus said something to one of the guards in a language Deina didn't understand.

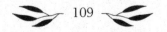

The creature stomped over to Aster, grasped the two ends of the torc—ignoring Aster's protests—and wrenched it from his neck. The bronze splintered as if it were made of rotting wood. Aster stumbled, cursing, rubbing the chafed skin that had been beneath the torc. But there was wonder in his eyes.

When the iron creature approached Deina, she had to force herself not to shrink from its mouthless face, to focus instead on the human eyes just visible behind the metal eye sockets. A moment of panic, as its fingers scraped against her skin, and it was done. Her first torc had been fitted when she became an apprentice, more than eleven years ago. The spell-cast bronze had pinned her in place—reminded her of her place—every moment of every day. Only now that it had been removed did she realize how heavy was the weight she'd been bearing.

Chryse was freed next—confounding Deina's hope that her friend's presence was a mistake or a joke. Yet the removal of her own torc ignited a spark of hope in Deina's chest, despite the misgivings that had begun to plague her yesterday. When she turned to bid Anteïs farewell, there was something that might have been jealousy in the older woman's face, vying with the affection Deina had only just understood.

The volunteers followed Aristaeus toward the ship. Deina was the farthest she'd been from the House since she'd been taken there, so many years ago. She was leaving behind the only home she knew.

The torc was gone, but something inside still tugged at her.

7

As soon as they'd climbed the rope ladder that led to the deck of the flagship, Aristaeus told them to keep out of the way and ordered them to the prow, a small empty space at the front of the ship, hemmed in by coiled ropes and folded sailcloth. As gulls screeched overhead, Deina watched the sailors hurrying to finish their tasks before the ship launched. There were some Theodesmioi among them—Sea Singers of the Order of Poseidon, she guessed, though they weren't close enough for her to make out what sigil they bore on their foreheads. They wore the same type of spell-cast torcs around their necks from which Deina and the others had just been freed.

There was a catapult bolted to the deck of the prow. Theron and Aster were standing next to it, both resting one hand on the mechanism while carefully ignoring each other. Maybe they hoped proximity to a large weapon would make them look more manly or at least less nervous. Drex was hovering near them, even though neither one was paying him any attention.

Deina supposed she should feel sorry for him, but no one was forcing him to stand there. Chryse had sat down on one of the coils of rope and was looking back toward Iolkos. She pointed to the city as Deina wriggled in next to her.

"It looks different from here. Smaller."

"We've never seen it from this distance. Or from this far above the sea." The flagship was huge, towering over the smaller triremes that made up the convoy. Deina lowered her voice. "Are you going to tell me what's going on? Why in the name of all that's sacred are you going to Thebes? How could Neidius and Anteïs allow it?"

Chryse sighed. "I knew you'd be like this. I'm not a child, Deina. And you're not an elder."

The unexpected antagonism of Chryse's voice and words silenced Deina for a moment. "I know that," she said eventually, trying to speak gently. "But I'd like to understand how it happened."

"The king asked to see me; I suppose he noticed me in the great hall." Chryse glanced at the other Severers and bent her head closer to Deina. "He said I reminded him of the queen. Then he invited me to Thebes. To visit the city and wait there, just until you come back. And I said yes." She straightened up again. "I saw a good opportunity and I took it. How is that different from what you did?"

"It just is." Deina thought back to what she'd heard about the terrible retribution inflicted upon the city of Rome for daring to resist. The Tyrant took what he wanted and crushed those who refused. What if he wanted Chryse in his bed? She clasped Chryse's hand. "If we don't survive, you could be stranded in Thebes. Or he might refuse to let you go even if—when—we return. You should have stayed safely in Iolkos until—"

"Stay on my own in Iolkos, in the House?" Chryse pulled her hand free. "I'd rather be in a palace in Thebes. Besides, I'll have to return to the House eventually, because you will come back, Deina. You're fast and strong and fearless, and like you said, you never get caught. You were born lucky. And I don't want to talk about this—or the House, or the future—anymore." She jumped up and strode across the deck to stand next to Aster, her back to Deina.

Deina rubbed one hand over her face. It almost sounded as if Chryse was jealous of her, which was ridiculous. They were the same grade. And even though Deina was stronger, she reckoned, in the normal course of things, it would take her twenty years or more to earn out her indenture. *If* she was able to keep working at the same rate, and *if* she didn't end up dying—like she almost had already—from one of the plagues that frequently swept through the city. Twenty years . . . such a stretch of time. Yet Chryse was angry that Deina had volunteered; that much was obvious. Had she agreed to go to Thebes to punish her, to give her another thing to worry about while she was pursuing Orpheus's quest?

Deina frowned at her friend's back. Many years had passed since Theron had set her up—had tried to make it look as if she, not he, had stolen food from the storerooms. Chryse had pitied her. She'd taken the blame and the punishment: a week of bread and water, for a first offense. Deina, frequently in trouble and not yet earning the House enough for the elders to turn a blind eye, would have been whipped and had an extra six months added on to her time. Ever since then, they'd looked out for each other, and they rarely argued. She didn't know how to deal with Chryse being resentful.

But perhaps she wouldn't have to. They'd be apart soon enough, no doubt. And maybe Chryse was right, and she would be safe in Thebes. Then, when Deina came back and was given the gold and used it to buy out Chryse's indenture, all this would be forgotten. Things between them would go back to how they were before. Except they'd both be free.

Deina got up and went to stand with her back against the bulwark, closing her eyes and lifting her face to the sun and trying to forget about the argument by focusing on the different smells carried on the breeze: seaweed, wood shavings, paint, salt water. Until she became aware of someone next to her. Drex was turning a small stone over and over in his fingers as he squinted at the activity on deck. When he realized she was watching him, he tucked the stone into his fist and smiled slightly.

"What do you think of the ship?"

"Well . . ." She looked about them. "It's big."

Drex leaned closer, as if about to impart a secret. "I think it must be a quinquereme, at the very least. Probably even heavier."

A trireme had three banks of oars. So a quinquereme had to have five, surely? Deina shook her head.

"No. I counted when we came up the side. Only three banks of oars, the same as the smaller ships."

Drex laughed.

"Three banks of oars, but the oars on the lowest level

have one rower per oar, those on the upper two levels each have two rowers per oar. Five."

"Oh." Deina tilted her head, studying Drex more closely. "How do you know about ships?"

His smile faded. "Why do you ask?"

"I'm curious." True enough, as far as it went. It had never occurred to her to question Drex about himself before now because she hadn't needed to know. But things had changed. Having some extra information about her . . . associates, for want of a better word, might help her win. "And Theron says we're meant to be a team."

"Hmm." Drex didn't sound convinced by Theron's team-building claims. But he continued, "You probably know I came to the House three years late; I was eight, or thereabouts. I spent some of that time in Tyre." When Deina didn't react, he raised his eyebrows. "It's a Phoenician city. It's where the best ships come from. You haven't heard of it?"

His tone made her feel stupid.

"If Orpheus hadn't come, we would never have left Iolkos. Not much point in learning the names of all the places you'll never visit." She ran her fingers over the calluses left by her torc, as Drex clamped his mouth shut and crossed his arms tightly over his chest. The movement made the neck of his tunic gape; the edge of a rite-seal, low on his breastbone, was just visible beneath the gray fabric. From a Severing, as far as she could make out, and recent; the skin was still not fully healed. Even as a novice, Deina's rite-seals had extended farther across her torso than that. Now they flowed over her breasts and abdomen and around her waist. The last one she'd earned—before the failure of the Punishment Rite—just brushed her collarbone. It looked as if Drex had hardly earned any time to set against his indenture. No wonder he'd been desperate enough to volunteer.

But he knew about ships, and that might also be useful. Deina gestured to the wooden structure that stood on the deck just behind the prow.

"So why does a ship need a house on it? Is it a cabin? A storeroom for something important?"

"It's not a house. It's a forecastle. It's designed to give extra height, as a place of attack." He waved a hand toward the catapult. "This ship's heavily armored. I bet it's carrying marines. And there's probably a ram attached to the bow." He edged past Deina to lean over the front of the ship, peering down. "Yes, there's definitely a . . ."

Something in Drex's silence as he stood there, gripping the rail at the top of the bulwark, made the hair on Deina's arms stand up.

"What is it?"

"Um . . . I'm not sure. I can't quite see—" His voice was taut.

Deina came to stand next to him and looked over the side.

"Oh, gods . . ." Her hand went to her mouth. There were people, gagged and bound, lying on the beach in the path of the ship. It was to be launched over them. People from Iolkos, from her city—arrested on some made-up charge? Or picked at random and told, like Theodesmioi entered into the lottery, that they should be honored to die for whatever cause this was supposed to be? "Why?"

"An old Phoenician custom." Drex had turned away from the

scene, though he still clung on to the rail, the tendons of his hands rigid beneath the flesh. "Meant to ensure a safe voyage. They believed the spirit of the ship would see the sacrifice and be sated."

For the first time, Deina noticed an enormous eye painted on the exterior of the ship just below them, below the elongated, iron-tipped bow. Was that why Aristaeus had told them to wait here—because he'd wanted them to see this? She glanced over her shoulder. Aristaeus was watching them. Smiling.

Chryse wandered toward them. "What are you looking at?"

Deina held her at arm's length. "Don't."

As Aster and Theron joined them, the ship shuddered.

Drex murmured a prayer beneath his breath. "They're about to launch."

A forward jerk sent Theron stumbling. Muffled shrieks split the air as the ship slowly slid into the sea. Deina covered her ears with her hands. They all did. But it didn't block out the agonized groans of the dying.

Their journey had begun in blood.

The convoy passed slowly enough through the Gulf of Pagasae, but still too quickly for Theron, Aster, and Chryse, all of whom were clinging to the bulwarks and heaving the contents of their stomachs into the water before they'd traveled any distance from Iolkos. While Deina rubbed Chryse's back and murmured words of comfort, she didn't feel remotely sorry for the other two. She was the only one still on deck to witness the moment when the city shrank from sight and finally disappeared behind the southern peaks of Pelion. Anteïs

had told them once that the centaur Chiron lived there. A great healer, she'd said, though his pupils were best known for other things. Jason, Herakles, Theseus, Achilles. Names from the distant past, when humans had heroes, not just gods. As the flagship passed beneath the densely wooded slopes, Deina looked up and breathed in the scent of pine and wondered what secrets the trees might still conceal. Whether she might get the chance, one day, to return here and find out. She caught her first glimpse of the Aegean Sea, sparkling in the sunlight, soon after. But the morning's sunshine was followed by rain and then by a gale that threatened to rip the sails away. There was a Weather Worker bound to the ship, one of the rarer of the Theodesmioi of the Order of Zeus. The sailors lashed him to the highest masthead, from where he flung his arms wide and chanted his incantations into the strengthening wind to draw its sting. But even calmed by the Weather Worker's Songs, the wind remained fierce enough that the fleet fled southeast down the coast of Euboea as if harried by the hounds of the goddess Artemis herself. When the storm finally broke above them, Deina clung to the prow and watched the water foam and rage as the iron-tipped ram drove through it like a blade. She hung over the stern to catch a glimpse of the dolphins leaping in their wake. And for a few brief moments, before the captain saw her and threatened to have her locked below, she climbed into the rigging and braced herself there, grinning into the teeth of the tempest as the ship plunged down one wave and was borne up upon the crest of another.

Gradually the wind failed, until it was no more than a whisper. The sails fell limp and the oars were brought out. Deina settled into the point of the prow. A Sea Singer, bearing the trident sigil of Poseidon, began to work nearby. She was chanting a Song to help with the repair of one of the sails that had been damaged in the storm. Deina listened to the unfamiliar words and watched the woman's sure, spare movements until her gaze drew the Singer's notice; Deina gave her a quick smile and turned her attention to the ragged clouds drifting across the sky. Their lower edges were flushed with the warm rose-gold of sunset.

"You look . . . windswept."

It was Chryse, pale and slightly gray, but upright.

"How are you feeling?" Deina asked.

She shrugged. "It's no worse than the Toll. They've brought some food to our cabin. I'm not hungry, but I thought you might be." She held out her hand to help Deina to her feet. "What were you thinking of just now? You looked"—Chryse tilted her head and scrunched up her face—"sad, almost."

Was she right? Deina had thought she knew what exhilaration felt like, and what made her feel that way: winning a challenging race, or pulling off a successful theft, or cheating Theron out of the Punishment Rite. But those experiences faded into pale unreality compared to what she'd just been through. She couldn't swim; if she'd fallen, or been swept overboard, she'd have drowned. So perhaps it *was* sadness. Because if she had to court death to feel truly alive, she wasn't likely to live very long. She shook her head.

"Just hungry. And in need of a bath." Her skin was sticky with salt spray. "Show me where this cabin is."

* * *

There was no excitement to equal that of the storm over the next few days. By night, they were locked up below in two tiny makeshift cabins. By day they were allowed onto the deck, but there was little to do other than stare at the sea—mostly empty, apart from the occasional fishing vessel hugging the coastline and the other four ships keeping pace at a distance—and avoid getting in the way of the sailors. Often, the five of them ended up back in the empty space at the prow, though increasingly Chryse was summoned to Orpheus's side, where he apparently plied her with sweetmeats and dazzled her with visions of her visit to Thebes. Deina made one ill-received attempt to temper her friend's enthusiasm, then gave up and hoped Chryse was right: that Orpheus, childless, saw her more as a daughter than anything else. Without Chryse, Deina was left with Theron, Aster, and Drex. But it could have been worse. Her fellow Soul Severers were at least somewhat familiar. Nothing else on this black-sailed ship was. The Iron Guards, with their shadowy human eyes staring out of immobile metal faces, made her flesh crawl.

    Deina spent some of the time chanting the Songs Neidius had taught them, going over and over the words and actions. When Chryse was present, she listened and compared and tried to offer useful comments, though there wasn't much she could say. Deina was used to learning Songs, and she learned fast; the extra practice wasn't necessary. She kept repeating the exercise just the same; it gave an illusion of control. They didn't know which of the legendary entrances to the Underworld Orpheus had selected or how long it would take to get there; the answer, when Theron asked, was that questions would get them locked belowdecks for the rest of the voyage.

By the end of their seventh day at sea, Chryse refused to listen to any more repetitions of the Songs. Deina was muttering the words to herself, staring across the open sea, when something made her pause. She went to lean against the bulwark, shading her eyes to see more clearly.

"I wonder if we're coming into a port." She half turned her head, addressing whichever of the others cared to listen. They were all nearby, standing or sitting on the deck or perched on the chest of sharp-tipped bolts that had been piled in readiness next to the catapult. "The land looks closer." The other ships were, too—much closer than they'd been since leaving Iolkos. A woman dressed in black was leaning against the bulwark of the nearest ship. As the setting sun gleamed from beneath the bank of clouds, Deina caught a glimpse of red along the edge of her tunic. Another Severer? She raised her hand in greeting. A small gesture. The woman looked over her shoulder, then did the same.

Theron came to stand next to her. "What are you doing?"

"There's a woman over there—" Deina pointed. But the woman had gone. "Oh."

"Seeing things?" Theron raised an eyebrow. "First sign of madness."

Deina smiled as sweetly as she could. "Go drown yourself."

"I'd love to oblige," he said loudly, "but I'm invited to sing before the king this evening."

How long had he been waiting to let slip that piece of information?

"Just you?" Chryse asked plaintively. "What about the rest of us?"

Theron turned and crossed his arms.

"Can anyone else here sing?" When no one answered, he grinned. "Thought not."

"Your voice *is* wonderful," replied Deina. "And at least when you're singing, it's other people's words that are coming out of your mouth, not the usual nonsense."

Aster laughed, and the smirk slipped from Theron's face. He stomped away along the deck.

Deina glanced back at the other ship, but there was no sign of the Severer she thought she'd seen.

With luck, the woman was a ghost. Better to be haunted than mad.

Before long, Deina saw she was right about them nearing port. The ships shifted course and were rowed into a wide bay, at the far end of which was a harbor with a city climbing up the slopes that lay behind it. She and the others were sent below and shut into their windowless cabins before they got close enough for her to see exactly what kind of place it was. Soon after came the rumble of the anchor being dropped. Other noises followed: Thumps, as if smaller boats were being brought alongside the ship. Shouted orders about storage and guards. Snatches of conversation. She heard the words *tribute* and *treasure*. And in the distance, a high-pitched crying. Despite Chryse's fears that someone, somehow, would see, Deina went on tiptoe and pressed one eye against a knothole in the side of the ship. She could just make out one of the smaller triremes, drawn up on the sand. People with manacles around their wrists were being herded on board. Children as well as adults; one young boy was sobbing wordlessly, reaching toward a woman who'd collapsed on the beach even as he was dragged onto the ship.

"Stop!" Deina smacked her hands as hard as she could against the planks as she yelled. "Stop it!"

No one could hear her. It wouldn't have made any difference if they could. She sank onto the straw-stuffed mattress, straining her ears as the boy's cries faded.

"What was it?" Chryse asked, her voice trembling a little.

"They're taking people as slaves. Part of the quarterly tribute, I suppose."

Chryse didn't respond. Deina wondered if she, too, was thinking back to when she'd been taken by the House as a child, trying to remember—or trying to forget. The Theodesmioi were clearly not slaves. Still, the agony in the boy's cries had threatened to unearth something that Deina wanted very much to keep buried.

"Chryse—"

"It's late—too late to talk." Chryse lay down on the other mattress. "I'll see you in the morning."

Chryse fell asleep at some point, but even after the ship got underway again, Deina couldn't rest. She listened to the surge of the tide and the creak of the timbers and the Songs of the Sea Singers, who spent the night watches whispering spells for speed and safety to the wood, rope, and canvas in their care. She stared at the planks above her head as the air grew hotter and the cabin closed in. When she couldn't stand it any longer, she got up and pushed against the door.

Locked, and no handle on this side. But she'd paid attention;

the only thing keeping it shut was a short metal latch. One of her long hairpins forced through the narrow gap at the edge of the door soon dealt with that obstacle.

The sound of snoring filtered down from the rowing decks above, but otherwise the ship was quiet. There was no sign of any Iron Guards. Barefoot, wrapped in her dark cloak, Deina slipped silently through the shadows. A cool breeze brushed her skin; the ladder that led up to the top deck was just ahead. She set her foot on the bottom rung, noticing at the same time a sliver of light spilling from a doorway farther on.

Deina left the ladder and crept forward.

The door was ajar. Holding her breath, she peered through the crack into the small room beyond. Empty. A slight push, and the door swung open. A lamp was burning on the table, as if someone had been called away in the middle of a task.

Deina stifled a gasp as her gaze fell upon a pile of gold coins, glinting at her through the partially open neck of a sack that barely contained them. There was no one to see her. So much wealth, just there for the taking . . . She licked her lips in anticipation, took a deep breath to steady her nerves, then quickly scooped up a handful of coins and tipped them into the pouch hanging from her belt. Easy—she smiled to herself. Opened another sack. Loose garnets, ropes of amber, bracelets studded with emeralds, rich blue lapis lazuli inlaid in silver rings, all jumbled together. Enough to buy her freedom ten times over. She added to her pouch a long gold chain, each link of which was set with a brightly colored gemstone. The room was crammed with boxes and bags, and there was treasure in every one. More jewels.

More coins. Bolts of some soft fabric that shimmered when she stroked it. Strands of vermilion saffron in a scented cedarwood box.

Next to the burning lamp lay two large heaps of polished amethysts; she picked a gem off each pile. There was a square of parchment with writing on it: a list of numbers, as if someone had started reckoning up the value of the stones, and a word Drex had taught her to read—*Iolkos*. Had some of this wealth come from her city? She returned to one of the sacks of gold. There on the side was the city crest, the same as she'd seen on the tax collector's bag the other morning in Poseidon's Quarter.

Anteïs had tried to explain it once. The Tyrant demanded a quarterly tribute. The nobles paid some of it, contributing jewels, silks, rare spices. But the bulk of it came from the people, in the form of taxes and grain. Every year, the Tyrant demanded more. Every year, the people had less to give. No wonder there were so many beggars on the streets of Iolkos. Deina's fists clenched. Her city was slowly starving—

No. Iolkos wasn't *her* city. She forced herself to relax, reminding herself that she didn't know where she'd been taken from; the city was her master, not her home. She didn't owe Iolkos anything.

As she was about to leave, something on one of the shelves caught her eye: an intricately carved box, half buried beneath tangled ropes of carnelian beads. Deina lifted it down and opened it, revealing a dagger unlike anything she'd ever seen. The hilt—no wood or stone that she recognized—was the color of cream, light and warm to the touch and wound about with ruby-studded gold filigree. The blade seemed to be made from crystal, with silver letters somehow set into it. After a moment's hesitation, biting her lip, she stuck the dagger in her belt, retrieved a silver knife that she'd spotted in one of the sacks, put that in the box, and shoved the whole thing quickly back onto the shelf, hiding it again beneath the snarled necklaces.

Not a moment too soon—the sound of voices sent her heart pounding. She peered around the door. Two men were standing by the ladder that led to the upper decks, blocking her path back to the cabin. One of them—scrawny, with a stoop—she didn't recognize. The other, the one holding a lantern, was Aristaeus.

". . . will be back on board any moment. Should I tell him you abandoned your task only half done? Or did you wish to join the expedition to the Underworld? They can't have gone far. Or there are other ways I can send you there, if you're so anxious."

Deina wondered about who *they* were, but the other man didn't seem confused.

"Forgive me, my lord! I only wanted a little air . . ."

As the man continued to plead, Deina scoured the shadows of the corridor for somewhere to hide. There was a group of barrels standing nearby; she'd have to come into the open to reach them, but it was that or use the burning lamp to start a fire as a distraction. Even to her, that seemed unnecessarily risky. Aristaeus still had his back to her. She took a deep breath, pulled her hood forward, and slid from the room, melting into the darkness between the barrels and crouching as low as she could.

Aristaeus broke off his conversation. His footsteps grew louder. "Did you see something?"

"No, Lord, nothing. May I continue my work? I'm anxious to make up the brief amount of time I've lost and—"

"Go. And think yourself lucky. If I find you abandoning your post again, the consequences will be severe."

The door to the treasure room closed. But the light from Aristaeus's lantern grew brighter. He was searching near the barrels. Deina held her breath. *Hecate, goddess, if you can hear me, hide me . . .* More footsteps. Retreating this time, as Aristaeus walked away and then climbed up the ladder. The light from the lantern faded and disappeared.

Deina waited for a few more minutes, staring into the darkness above. But there was no sign of movement. She wiggled out from between the barrels, edged slowly back past the ladder—just in case he was lingering at the top—then ran the rest of the way back to the cabin. Opened the door a crack, slid inside, and closed it behind her. Shook the door a little, until the latch on the outside dropped back into place. She was trembling now. But she had the gold, the amethysts, and the dagger. They would be worth something. A little insurance in case Orpheus's promises proved to be empty.

Deina wrapped her stolen treasure in her cloak, tucked the bundle beneath her pillow, and tried to lose herself in the rhythm of the waves. It wasn't easy. Somehow, she could still hear the sobs of the boy who'd been taken from his mother. As sleep finally came, his cries changed to a question.

You wish to flee Iolkos. But if all cities are like Iolkos, if all cities are starving and enslaved, then where can you go to be free? Where can you run to, Soul Severer of Hades? Over and over the question was repeated. But there was never any answer.

8

By the time Deina reached the top deck the next morning, the wind had shifted, and the black sails, straining full-bellied against the rigging, were driving them north. Chryse and Drex were standing together on the landward side of the prow. He was talking about the countryside slipping by, just visible through the low cloud that was slowly lifting from the shoreline. From what Deina could hear of his words, Drex—who could read the names on the map pinned next to the steering oar—believed they were sailing up the west coast of the Peloponnese, the territory once divided between the cities of Sparta and Pylos but now belonging to the Theban Dominion, and to Orpheus. Drex's gaze was fixed on Chryse's face. His eyes were wide, his lips slightly parted—the same expression of rapture Deina had seen on the faces of others who'd fallen beneath her friend's spell.

Deina edged around Aster to where Theron was lounging against the seaward bulwark.

"You're still alive. The evening with Orpheus went well, then?" At her question, Theron turned toward her, revealing a faint bruise discoloring one of his perfect cheekbones. "Or maybe not."

"My performance was good enough, if that's what you mean. Though I don't know why he asked for it. He showed no interest in the music. After I'd sung twice, he made me stand there while he walked around me. Then he questioned me about my parentage. About these." Theron held out his wrists, both of which were encircled by old scars. "Questions to which I had no answer." He shuddered and leaned on the bulwark, gazing out at sea. "It was like he was inspecting me. As if he wanted to make sure I knew my place, to remind me that even without my torc, my life isn't my own. That I belong to Hades, to the Order, and now to him."

There was a blemish on the back of Theron's neck that looked different from the welts caused by the torc. A birthmark, perhaps, that had always been hidden beneath the circle of spell-cast bronze. Deina wondered whether Theron even knew it was there.

"Still," he continued, "I'm not scheduled to be executed, as far as I know." His gaze met hers, and he smiled faintly. "Sorry to disappoint you."

Deina stared back into his eyes until, irritated with herself, she forced herself to look away. Theron certainly was handsome. And he knew it. She gestured to the bruise on his cheek.

"So how did you end up with that?" Theron didn't reply. But glancing back at Aster, who was still running a stone over the blade of his knife, Deina noticed that his bottom lip was cut and swollen. "Oh. A quarrel? Did you fall out over who's got the biggest—"

"You'll hold your tongue," Theron retorted, "if you know what's good for you."

Deina smiled. Theron's angry flush told her all she needed to know. No doubt he and Aster had been fighting over who was going to lead this little expedition. All the better; as far as she could judge right now, it would be preferable to have her teammates wary of one another than ganging up together.

Theron was glaring at her. "If we're dishing out insults, Deina, you look terrible. Why?"

"I didn't sleep well."

He narrowed his eyes. "What have you done?"

"What makes you think I've done anything? What's there to do here, other than wait?"

Theron's scowl deepened as he lowered his voice. "If you've done something that's going to put the rest of us at risk—"

"I've done nothing." She bristled and turned her back on Theron. How dare he accuse her, even if it was true? Suddenly conscious of Aster standing close by, she frowned at him. "What?"

He held out one of the spears he favored as a weapon: an ash shaft with a bronze leaf-shaped blade at one end and an iron spike on the other.

"I need you to bang this on the deck to keep time for me."

"Why?"

Theron groaned. "Not this again . . ." He tried to push the spear away.

"No one touches my spears," Aster growled. "Not unless I allow them to." He nodded at Deina. "I've got to stay strong. Strength is what's going to matter in the Underworld. So I need you to keep time while I jump."

There was no hint of a joke; apparently Aster really did expect her to stand there as he leaped up and down and sweated over them all. She was about to tell him exactly where he could jump when she realized that agreeing would drive even more of a wedge between him and Theron.

"Very well."

Aster bowed his thanks, handed her the spear—with a scowl at Theron—and retreated a few steps. Bent his knees and glanced at Deina.

"Ready?"

Before Deina could reply, Theron hurried to the point of the prow.

"Look." He turned back toward her, pointing. "We're coming into shore."

He was right. The sails were being lowered, and the oarsmen were maneuvering the ship into the mouth of a wide, deeply curved bay. At the far end lay a long, pale stretch of sand, but they seemed to be making for a smaller beach. The dark entrance to a cave gaped in the rocky hills above it.

"Severers!"

Aristaeus's voice. He was flanked by four Iron Guards. Theron shot her a look of alarm.

"You will come with me. Now."

Deina exchanged a brief glance with Chryse as they followed Aristaeus toward the far end of the ship, where

Orpheus's chambers were built into the stern of the vessel. The guards fell into place around them, their heavy tread a counterpoint to Deina's racing thoughts. Why had they been sent for? Had Aristaeus discovered the theft of the dagger? She stared at his back as if it might give her some clues. The dagger was beneath her tunic, lashed to her waist with a strip of fabric torn from the bottom of her cloak, but its weight against her skin felt like an accusation. The amethysts and other treasure she'd stolen were still wrapped up in her cloak down in the cabin.

"Here." Aristaeus gestured to the door ahead of them. "His Majesty is waiting for you."

There were guards on either side of the door, in addition to those escorting them. No possibility of escape. Deina took a deep breath and followed the others into the chamber. The door swung shut behind her.

Aster and Theron were already on their knees. Deina followed suit, sinking into a thick carpet woven in shades of blue and gray. Orpheus was reclining on a couch at the end of the room, three more Iron Guards standing to attention behind him. No mask this time. The quick glance Deina stole before lowering her eyes showed a middle-aged man. Gaunt and dark-eyed, with deep lines bracketing his mouth and more gray in his hair than she remembered from the great hall. Still, she could hardly believe it was the face of one who'd ruled Thebes and its empire for so many decades. He should have looked older. Much older.

"Welcome, Severers of Iolkos." The same soft voice. It *was* Orpheus. "It will soon be time for you to begin your work. We are approaching the mouth of the Caves of Diros." Neidius had told them about it: one of a handful of places in the mortal world that gave physical access to the Underworld, at least according to the legends. "I have one final instruction to give you: When you have recovered the queen, use the rite and return with her immediately. From what I have been told, your safety will lie in your swiftness." Nothing new there. Deina already knew she would only be able to eat and drink what she carried with her; their rations would run out soon enough. "Remember, you must have the queen's ghost for the returning rite to work. And the quicker you return, the quicker you will gain your freedom."

The word hung in the air; Deina could almost taste it.

"Aster, you will remain here for a moment. The rest of you have my leave to go and prepare for your departure. Aristaeus tells me that some items have gone missing, including two valuable amethysts, so I have had your possessions searched."

Deina froze. Next to her, Chryse gasped softly. But she and Theron and Drex were already getting to their feet.

Move, Deina. You have to move.

Instinct took over. Somehow, she stood, bowed her head, and left the cabin. Aristaeus and his guards were waiting outside. Deina couldn't meet his eye. What would he do to her if the amethysts had been found? Throw her overboard? Too quick. Too merciful. He was more likely to get out the box of scorpions. Or turn her into an Iron Guard. She forced herself to keep walking as they descended the ladders that gave access to the interior of the ship, to stay ahead of the unconsciousness already clouding the edge of her vision.

There was a Sea Singer waiting outside the cabins. The same woman whom Deina had watched repairing a sail that first day on the ship.

"Well?"

All Deina could think of was the Iron Guard standing next to her. Its terrible stillness. The dull metal sheen of its mouthless face.

The Sea Singer shook her head.

"No amethysts, Lord Aristaeus. I found nothing that shouldn't be there."

Aristaeus lunged forward and grabbed the Singer by her neck, setting his hands above her bronze torc and forcing her head back and up. He stared down into her eyes. Deina's heart beat louder.

"If I find you are lying to me . . ."

The Sea Singer said nothing. Did nothing. Aristaeus released her.

"Suitable clothing has been laid out in your cabins. You"—he gestured at one of the Iron Guards—"stay here. Watch." Followed by the remaining guards, he stalked away. Deina waited just long enough to be sure he'd gone. Just long enough that it wouldn't look as if she was desperate. She opened the cabin door and closed it again behind Chryse.

No way of keeping the door shut, not from this side. But she had to know.

"Help me look," she whispered. "Quickly." Together, they searched bags, bedding—everything. Even in the dim light provided by a single oil lamp and the knothole high up in the timbers, it didn't take long. The amethysts, the necklace, and the gold were gone. Deina slumped onto the thin straw-stuffed mattress. "Why didn't she tell him?"

"She is Theodesmioi, as we are," Chryse replied, speaking softly. "Perhaps that was enough for her to wish to save your life. And mine, maybe." She shuddered, her eyes wide. "Deina, to take such a risk . . . What if Aristaeus had blamed me, too? He might have thought we were working together. He might have persuaded the king to—"

The door opened a little. Aster appeared. "Chryse, you're to go to the king's quarters."

Chryse and Deina looked at each other. It was hard to tell in the gloom, but Deina thought that tears had sprung into her friend's eyes.

"Don't be scared."

"I'm not. But what if you leave the ship before he lets me return here? What if we're not allowed to say goodbye?"

Deina pulled Chryse into a hug. "Then I'll just have to make sure I get back again even quicker."

Chryse tightened her arms around Deina, clutching her. Another moment and she was gone.

Aster was still standing in the doorway.

"What?" Deina threw up her hands. Aster scowled and slammed the door behind him.

What Chryse had said, about the risk she'd taken . . . Deina hadn't thought about the others when she'd stolen those things last night. Not even about Chryse. But thinking wouldn't set them free. Actions—risks—were necessary. And Chryse knew that, deep down—why else had she said yes to Orpheus?

With a sigh, Deina turned to the heap of clothes they'd

swept onto the floor and began sorting through it. There was a knee-length tunic pinned at the shoulders by a pair of bronze brooches embossed with dolphins, the symbol of Iolkos. The tunic was woven of some dark fabric that she couldn't identify. Warm when she put it on but light, too; when secured around her waist by a leather belt, its soft drapes fit her much better than the voluminous adept's robes. The belt had scabbards for her knives. There was also a pair of tall leather boots and a cloak, of the same fabric as the tunic but lined with fine fur. The cloak was too heavy to wear now; she rolled it up and stuffed it into the bag she'd been given, which already contained a flint and two full waterskins. To these, Deina added the vial and the ointment Anteïs had given her and her Severer's tools. Finally, she wrapped the stolen dagger in her veil and placed that in the bag. The Hecate charm, Anteïs's other gift, was strung from a leather cord; Deina hung the charm around her neck, brushed and braided her hair. After that, there was nothing to do but eat as much as she could stomach of the food that had been left out from breakfast, and wait.

It was difficult to keep track of time in the lamplit shadows. They'd stopped moving—that was the only thing she was sure of. The ship rocked with the swell of the waves, but the drum used to keep the oarsmen in time was silent. All she could hear, other than the creak of the ship's timbers, were the murmurs of Theron, Aster, and Drex in the adjoining cabin.

Deina dragged the mattresses to one side and began to pace the tiny space that was left. Finally, the door opened, but it was a servant, not Chryse—the Sea Singer who had searched their rooms.

Deina's hand crept nearer to the hilt of her dagger.

"I've brought your provisions," the woman said loudly as she shut the door. "Dried meat, dried fruit, plenty of flatbreads." In a lower voice, she murmured, "You've nothing to fear."

Wondering, Deina took the food and stowed it in her bag. It seemed little enough for the journey they were expected to undertake.

The woman was also holding out a small pouch. Deina opened the neck; gold glinted back at her. The amethysts were there, too. And the necklace.

Why hadn't the woman kept all of it, or even some of it? She must want something in return. Everyone did.

As if reading her thoughts, the Sea Singer placed a finger to her lips, leaned forward, and whispered in Deina's ear.

"This torc binds me to the ship and to the sea that immediately surrounds it. I was brought on board as a child, and I'll die here. If the ship sinks, I'll be dragged down with it. I've no use for gemstones or coins. But an opportunity to help you take something back from the Tyrant, or to put a hole in Aristaeus's sails—that's something I've wanted for a long time." She paused. "Sometimes defiance is worth almost any price."

And Deina had thought Iolkos was a small-enough prison. Horror turned her stomach.

"What can I do?"

"Remember. And if you're going to risk your life, do it for something more valuable than gold." She straightened up. "Hurry. Bring your bag. And your friend's things, as well."

Deina quickly swung her bag onto her back, scooped Chryse's

tools and her knife from the floor, and followed the Sea Singer up into the blinding late-afternoon sunlight. The other Severers were already waiting on the deck. Aster had four short-shafted spears strapped to his back, Theron had his bow and arrows in a quiver, and Chryse—

Chryse was dressed in the same style of tunic and boots that Deina wore. As she held out her hands for her tools, she forced a smile.

"Wonderful news, Deina. I'm going with you. His Majesty realized I would not wish to be separated from you. His honor is matched only by his kindness." There was a too-bright, brittle tone to her voice. Her hands, as she slid her knife into the sheath, were trembling.

Deina's chest tightened. Honor, kindness—Deina doubted the Tyrant had much of either. What had he done to her? She studied Chryse's face for some sign, but Aristaeus was nearby, and they were surrounded by guards and servants. The truth would have to wait. Together, they clambered down the ladder that was hanging from the ship's bulwark and splashed through the shallow water of the bay toward the beach. A small boat was landing the supplies that would be needed for the sacrifice; Orpheus's litter and his guards were already waiting on the sand.

The procession set off toward the cave in the cliffs. The sun was hot against the exposed skin of Deina's neck, and her tunic soon started to stick to her back. But as they walked farther up the sand, the air grew colder. Dank, almost. As if the cave was exuding a chilly miasma from its dark interior.

Chryse shivered. "Did you hear that?"

"Hear what?" Deina murmured, aware of the Iron Guard just behind them.

"Voices, on the breeze."

Deina strained her ears as a gust of wind from the hills above tugged at their clothes and swirled the sand around their feet. The breeze bore nothing but the faint cries of seabirds and the steady rhythm of the tide against the shore.

"You're imagining things. It's just nerves." Hardly surprising, given what they were about to attempt.

The guards ahead of them, carrying Orpheus's litter, came to a halt. They drew the curtains aside to reveal the Tyrant himself, golden mask and all, seated on an ornately carved chair.

"We have reached the Caves of Diros, one of the ancient entrances to the Underworld. You know your quest. Begin."

Deina stared into the gaping mouth of the cave.

The black sheep—the one they were to sacrifice to Hades—began bleating. Aster and Theron eyed each other, no doubt weighing up how best to take control. Deina stepped forward.

"We all know our parts. Chryse"—her friend was hanging back, twisting her hands together—"just stand next to me."

Servants had already dragged logs into a pile and started a fire. The Severers formed a ring around the flames. Deina retrieved the white poplar bowl from her bag, took a sack of wine from a servant, and tried to breathe steadily, grateful that it was Drex who'd gotten the job of reciting the prayers, wishing they'd had more time to practice this bit of the rite before leaving Iolkos.

"Is everyone ready?"

Nods, murmurs of assent.

"Very well."

Approaching the black sheep and the lamb that were tied to a stake next to the fire, Deina sprinkled wine on their brows. The creatures tossed their heads, giving the illusion of assent and free will—about as much free will as anyone had when the gods were involved. As Drex began intoning the start of the prayer, she cut off some of the wine-stained wool from each animal and threw it onto the fire.

Aster was up next. He straddled the sheep. Held it steady, murmuring words of comfort—a picture that might have made Deina smile in different circumstances—as Theron bent back his bow and loosed an arrow straight into the animal's head. It dropped instantly.

Deina felt herself sag with relief. But there was no time to waste—Aster was already cutting the dead sheep's throat. She darted forward to catch the blood in her bowl. Dipped her thumb into the blood and smeared some of the red liquid over the sigil of Hades on Aster's forehead. Made the same mark on Theron, Drex—still reciting the prayers—Chryse, and herself. Theron and Aster between them heaved the sheep's carcass onto the fire.

Drex paused, tipped some water into his mouth, and began a new prayer. This was to Hermes, the first to guide the souls of the dead into the Underworld. And, Deina reminded herself, the god of thieves. She offered her own quick prayer to the god—*One thief to another, Lord Hermes, I'm asking you to get me through this*. Then as Theron slew the lamb, Aster slit its throat, and she added its blood to their foreheads.

The dead lamb was consigned to the flames. Drex chanted the final line of the prayers. It was done.

"Let us hope the gods accept your sacrifice," Orpheus murmured. "Let us hope, for all our sakes, they allow you to bring my Eurydice back to where she belongs. My Iron Guards will wait for your return."

Aster lit a torch from the fire as Deina rinsed her bowl clean in the sea and stowed it away. Together with the others, they climbed up the slope that led to the cave mouth, Iron Guards standing on either side of them, silent and watchful and motionless as so many metal pillars. Would they rust if the tide rose to cover them? Would they die? Deina dragged her attention back to the cave, its rocky walls now directly ahead. It was colder still up here; she rubbed her arms, glad of the warmth of the tunic. Aster raised the torch and led them forward into the gloom. Just beyond the entrance, if the ancient Songs were correct, they would find the beginning of the waterway that would carry them into the Underworld. The sand beneath her feet gave way to moss-covered stone as the darkness deepened. Deina found herself peering down, testing each step before she trusted it; she felt as if she might lose her footing at any moment. As if she was about to lose everything that anchored her to the mortal world. Down, down, and the path became steps cut into a rocky wall, and the light from Aster's torch caught the ripple of water far below. Deina paused and looked behind her. One more step, and the mouth of the cave would be out of sight. The last glimmer of daylight would vanish soon after. She remembered, with a sudden pang of dismay, the drawing of the ship, still on the wall of her old room back at the House. Closing her eyes, she tried to fix their sea journey in her memory—the wind whistling past her ears, the salt spray cold against her skin, the smooth wood of the ship beneath her hands. To conjure up an image of the horizon that it offered her: freedom, possibility, happiness.

But the exhilaration had gone, turned to ashes in her mouth. Would she ever see daylight or the sea again?

"Deina, hurry up!" Theron's voice, the exasperation tinged with fear.

Deina resumed her descent, and the darkness swallowed her.

9

"What in Hades's name is taking you so long?"

Theron was lingering at the bottom of the steep flight of stairs. The ruddy flames of the torch gave just enough light for her to see his breath, frozen into tiny clouds in this sudden winter into which they'd been plunged. That, and the look of exasperation on his face.

"I didn't ask you to wait for me." Drex and Aster had already come to a halt up ahead. Chryse, arms wrapped tight around her body, was hovering just behind them. All three were staring at what looked to Deina like an immense underground sea, its dark waters rolling away as far as she could see before disappearing into the shadows. There was no hint of another shore. And yet, this was a river: Oceanus, the first, and the greatest, of the six rivers of the Underworld. The river that encircled Hades's kingdom.

Deina shivered as she and Theron drew closer. The top of a post became visible. Then a shallow but spacious rowboat, tethered to the post and drawn up onto the sand at the river's edge. Aster had already strolled down to the boat and was peering inside, holding the torch high.

"We may have a problem," he called out. "There are no oars." His voice echoed loud in the still air.

"But there must be," Theron replied. He and Aster started walking the rocky bank in both directions, scanning the ground. Did they really think the oars would just be scattered about? Or perhaps they were searching for some handy pieces of driftwood that might be cunningly repurposed. Drex was kneeling on the sand by the prow of the boat. Deina crouched down behind him.

"What are you looking at?"

"Oh—well, I think—I mean, this is an inscription." His finger traced the outline of lines carved deep into the wood. Deina squinted. Some of them *might* form letters . . .

"It's just the name of the boat," Aster snapped. "Stop wasting time, you two. Get up and help us look. And you, Chryse."

Chryse stared at Aster, snorted, and sat down on a boulder with her arms crossed.

Drex's eyebrows went up. He glanced at Deina—she nodded at him—then he swallowed hard and said, "It's not just the name, it's an inscription." Another gulp. "Perhaps you would like me to read it to you? Since you can't read it yourself . . ." His voice shook a little, but there was no mistaking the edge to it.

The surprise on Aster's face almost made Deina laugh.

"What does it say, Drex?"

Drex beckoned to Aster.

"I need more light. Aster, would—would you bring the torch? Please?"

Aster muttered something beneath his breath, but he stomped over to the boat, followed by Theron, and held the torch near to the prow.

"This script is very old. Ancient, I suppose." Drex straightened up again and ran one hand through his hair, frowning. "But as far as I can tell, it says . . . *If worthy, into the jaws of the gates of death I shall bear thee.*"

The silence went on for a long time.

"Well, that's comforting," Theron murmured eventually, to no one in particular.

"It means we don't need oars," replied Deina. "The boat will take us to the gates of the Underworld. Assuming we're all sufficiently *worthy*." She looked up; a glance showed her that everyone else was also weighing the likelihood of meeting that condition.

Aster grunted, then threw his pack into the boat.

"The women aren't likely to be considered worthy. They're weak by nature, and not brave enough; I always said it was a mistake to allow them to volunteer." He turned his back on Deina. "I'd advise them to wait here until we return."

"What?" Chryse leaped up. "No. We've got to stay together."

As Chryse darted toward the boat, Deina pushed Aster's shoulder, forcing him to face her.

"I know male Severers have little concern for the lives— or deaths—of women, but ignorance doesn't excuse this blind arrogance." She prodded him in the shoulder again. "You think you know what courage is, Aster? You think it's something only possessed by men? I've seen bravery among the women of Iolkos that you couldn't even aspire to. So when you've borne children, when you've watched your sister or daughter die in childbirth, when you've sold your body to keep yourself and your family from starving, then you can talk to me about the weakness of women." Ignoring Aster's furious scowl, Deina joined Drex and Chryse in the boat.

A moment later, Aster brushed past her and clambered into the prow. "Theron, push us off."

"You're not our leader, Aster," Theron said, and cursed. Still, he dropped his bags into the bottom of the vessel and untied the rope. Gripping the stern, he began pushing the boat down into the water. "And if you keep ordering me around, I swear to Hades that I'll—"

Theron's rebuke ended in a startled yelp and a splash; the boat slid into the river as if one of the more vicious sea nymphs had grabbed it by the prow, pitching him into the water. Deina was drenched with icy droplets as he scrambled to his feet and threw himself into the stern.

Not a moment too soon—the vessel gathered speed. By the time Theron had stopped spluttering, it was being drawn swiftly through the shadowy cavern, either by the current or by some unseen force. The five of them were cocooned in the dim circle of light cast by Aster's torch, reflected in the glassy surface of the water, while the riverbank and the cave entrance behind them were swallowed by darkness. Onward and onward the boat carried them. Eventually it was as if the beach and Orpheus's ship had never existed.

In the silence, Deina took stock of the company. Aster was in the prow. She could see his back, straight as a column, and the rigid angle of his arm, bicep bulging, as he held the torch aloft.

Drex was just behind Aster. He was holding something small between his fingers, tipping it to catch the torchlight—that pebble she'd seen him fiddling with before? It might be worth her while to find out its significance. Chryse was next to her, hunched onto the bench that spanned the boat, twisting a gold ring around and around on her finger—another recent gift from the family of a wealthy client, Deina guessed. Theron was behind them in the stern. She glanced over her shoulder.

When she met his gaze, Theron looked uncomfortable. He'd been staring at her.

"What?"

"Nothing." He began digging around in his bag and pulled out his cloak.

It was getting colder. Deina retrieved her own cloak, shrugging off the echo of the dream she'd had the night before they left Iolkos: the dark-haired boy with his long hair and scarred arms and the white snow falling around him. The warmth of the fur-lined fabric was welcome.

"Chryse, do you want your cloak?"

There was no reply. Chryse was staring unblinkingly at the dark water as if she'd never seen a river before and didn't much like the look of it. Deina found Chryse's cloak and draped it around her shoulders.

"Oh—thank you."

"You're welcome." Deina shifted closer and lowered her voice—not that there was really much hope of privacy here. "What happened? Why would he not take you to Thebes?"

"Because you were right. When he summoned me, it was to invite me into his bed. I refused. He . . ."

"He hurt you, the bastard—"

"No. He—he just said that, in that case, I had better go with you." Chryse sniffed. "It wasn't what I was expecting."

Deina studied Chryse's face, but her friend wouldn't look her in the eyes. What was she feeling? Upset? Scared? Angry? All of those things? Maybe that was why she was not more obviously distressed—a faint crease between her brows, but nothing else. The horror and fear were too much for her. There were no bruises, as far as Deina could see. No scratches. Aside from the sigil and her rite-marks, Chryse's skin appeared to be as unblemished and perfect as it always had been. Still, Deina was sure that there was something her friend wasn't telling her.

"Chryse—"

Chryse flung up one hand and slid farther along the bench. "Enough, Deina. I don't want to talk about it." There was an edge of agitation in her voice. "Tell me something useful instead. I haven't prepared for this. I don't know the Songs . . ."

"But I do—just stay with me." Deina paused, thinking how best to sum up the myths and stories and scraps of history Neidius had shared with them. "Legend says that any mortal who succeeds in entering the Underworld through one of the gateways will find a path. The paths are numerous and not easy to follow, but they all intersect the rivers of the Underworld. You can only cross each river in one place, and to cross the Styx, you have to collect the leaves of a golden-boughed oak that grows nearby. But all the paths, supposedly, will lead you through the different regions of the Underworld to Hades's palace. To whatever reward or punishment might await you there."

"We have to face the god?" Chryse gasped.

"No. We only need to follow the path until we find the region where the queen's soul wanders. Then we have a rite to bind her ghost, and that will allow us to use another rite to bring us back here." It sounded almost straightforward. "The trick is going to be surviving until that point. We can't drink any water that flows through the Underworld, and we can't eat anything that grows there. And if we stray too far from our chosen path, we might never find it again."

"And what if you can't find the queen's ghost?" Chryse asked. "How will you get out?"

"Don't worry. She's there somewhere. We will find her." They had to.

There was a sudden twanging noise from behind. Deina drew her knife and swung around, making the boat tip drunkenly from side to side.

Theron had his bow out. With the point of Deina's knife hovering just in front of him, he nodded toward it.

"Just testing the bowstring, that's all. Isn't it a little early in our journey for you to be pulling a dagger on one of your teammates?" There was the hint of a smile on his lips.

But Deina had been caught by a smile like that before. Whether running from the elders or breaking into the bell tower, it meant trouble.

"As far as *you're* concerned, it's never too early." Sheathing her knife, she settled with her back against the side of the boat, one foot up on the bench—the better to keep all her *teammates* in sight—and clutched her cloak tighter. Gods, she'd never known cold like it! Even Aster had given in; he let Drex hold the torch while he swathed himself in his own cloak, then huddled in the prow, gripping the torch with one hand and warming the other at the flame.

"You'd better not drop our only source of heat and light into the river," Theron called out. Aster grunted, but didn't offer any other response. "By the way, what did Orpheus want with you? When he kept you behind and sent the rest of us away—was he inviting you into his bed, too?"

One advantage of long legs: Deina was close enough to kick Theron hard in the shin.

"Ow! What was that for? It was a joke."

"It's not a laughing matter. Idiot." She glanced at Aster, who was now looking out across the water and away from them. "It's a fair-enough question, though, Aster. What did Orpheus want?"

"Nothing."

"Nothing. Really?"

"He wanted to give me the queen's spindle, the token to which we may bind her soul once we find her. That was all."

The queen's spindle. That was how that rite was supposed to work: You had to bind the soul to something it had used daily in life in order to carry it back out of the Underworld. Deina had guessed that Orpheus must have given it to one of the boys for safekeeping. Clearly the king had already decided which Severer he was going to bet his box of gold on. She chewed on her bottom lip. She would just have to make him realize that he'd bet wrong. Aster shoved the torch into Drex's hands and drew from his bag a rope—Deina noted that she hadn't been given one of those—followed by a cloth-wrapped parcel. "The king also entrusted me with these." He peeled back the cloth to reveal a small basket of cakes. "Drugged honey cakes, for the hound Cerberus, if we should be so unfortunate as to draw its attention." He put his face near the cakes and drew a deep breath, sighing with pleasure. "They smell so delicious . . ."

"Be careful," Drex urged. "Even the fumes of the poppy seed can have dangerous effects. To consume just a morsel of one of those cakes might be fatal." He looked back toward the others. "I—I read it in a scroll in the archives."

"Better beware, O mighty leader," Theron muttered. "I'm not dragging your unconscious body through the—"

"Deina . . ." Chryse pointed into the river. The dark surface of the water was covered with chunks of ice that were bumping against the side of the boat. The torch flickered, plunging them briefly into darkness. "What's happening?" She reached for Deina's hand.

Aster was peering at the torch.

"The cold, I think." Aster's voice echoed around them. "The torch isn't going to last much longer." He leaned forward over the prow, peering into the river. "We've stopped."

"What now?" Drex asked. As if in response to his question, a breeze sprang up. It swirled around them, plucking at their clothing, ruffling their hair. Behind the sharp chill Deina detected something else: a hint of earthiness and decay. The breeze caressed her face, and the sigil on her forehead, still crusted with dried blood, throbbed with pain. Next to her, Chryse drew in her breath sharply and pressed one hand to her forehead.

"Aster," Theron murmured, "hold the torch higher." He paused as Aster complied. "What in Hades is that?"

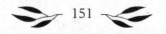

The boat had stopped in front of what looked like part of a natural arch of rock spanning the river, though Deina couldn't see what was holding it up. A huge image was carved into the stone. At first, she thought it was the outline of a wheel: five spokes radiating from a central hub out to a rim formed from two concentric circles. But the edges of the lines and the circles were wavy. On their own, they reminded her of—

"Rivers. It's showing the rivers of the Underworld." The rivers were woven into the lore and fabric of the Order of Hades, from the words of the Song to summon up the Threshold that was part of the most basic Severing Rite, to the tiles on the floor of the great hall back at the House in Iolkos. Deina drew a circle in the air with one finger. "The rim of the circle is what we're on now: the great river, the water that divides the Underworld from the mortal world, Oceanus." As she spoke the name, the rim of the wheel lit up with brilliant golden light. In its glow, Deina could just see the far bank of the river. It wasn't too distant now, but the boat was still held fast, caught in some invisible net. "I think—I think we need to name them all."

Drex cleared his throat.

"Well, I'll name the river of pain, that which carries away the suffering of mortals. Acheron." One of the spokes began to glow red.

In the prow, Aster straightened up.

"I name the river of rage, that pours the poison of unending hate into Tartarus, the place of punishment. Phlegethon." Another spoke lit up with orange fire.

"I name the river of oblivion, the water that washes away all memories." Theron's voice. In the darkness it seemed to Deina that his words were tinged with some emotion, though whether it was regret or longing, she couldn't tell. "Lethe." Pale green light spilled from another of the wheel's spokes.

Chryse took a deep breath.

"I name the river of lamentation, that which bears the many sorrows of the mortal world. Cocytus." The fourth spoke suddenly shone deep blue.

There was one river left. After this, Deina was sure that something would happen. They'd be found worthy, and allowed to proceed . . . or they'd be found unworthy, and then . . . She squared her shoulders.

"I name the river that all mortal souls must cross, the water that bears the dead upon its waves. Styx." Purple light spilled from the final spoke of the wheel, and the boat began to slide forward once more. As they passed beneath the arch of rock with its glowing symbol, Deina was seized with a deep cold that bit into her bones, so intense that it made her cry out in agony. But the pain faded as quickly as it had magnified. The cold waned, too.

Aster turned toward them, holding out the torch.

"Look." His voice was hoarse. "Look at the flames." It was as if they'd been frozen in place, radiating light but unmoving, unchanging. "Why aren't they burning?"

"Because"—Drex pressed one hand to his chest—"because there's no time here in which they can burn."

They weren't in the mortal world any longer. How much time did they have in this place with no time until their lungs and hearts, the things that kept them alive—each breath, each

pulse of blood—grew as fixed and unyielding as the flames they were all watching? Deina took a deep breath, pushing away the tide of panic that was threatening to rise within her.

The boat moved slowly forward, until it finally ran aground on a narrow strip of sand. They'd crossed Oceanus and had reached the other shore. Protrusions of rock glittered from the shadows above. They dangled from the stony ceiling like twisted, elongated icicles. Or, perhaps, Deina thought with a shudder, like questing fingers reaching down for them. Ahead was a sheer stone wall carved with another symbol. She recognized it immediately: the sigil of Hades. The same sign she bore on her forehead.

Aster jumped out of the boat, wedged the unburning torch upright in the sand, and struck what he no doubt thought was a heroic pose—hands on hips, one foot on the sand and one up on the bank. He surveyed the rest of them.

"We have reached the Underworld." Aster gestured to the cliff wall, the confidence of his action at odds with the slight tremor in his voice. "Our quest may begin."

For once, not even Theron had a sarcastic comment.

One by one, they followed Aster out of the boat and climbed up the bank to the rock wall.

Chryse stood close to Deina. "What do we have to do now? We've been allowed this far . . ."

Deina stared at the huge symbol. There were only two things that Neidius and the old Songs had been completely clear about: the possibility of drugging Cerberus and the importance of the blood sacrifice they'd offered on the beach before descending into the cave. She could still feel how the skin of her forehead was pulled tight by the dried blood smeared across her sigil. Just like in the Punishment Rite, when she'd rested her forehead against that of the condemned man, it so often seemed to come down to blood and symbols . . .

Could it be that simple?

Slinging her bag onto her back, Deina climbed up until she was right in front of the cliff face. After a couple of deep breaths to steady herself, she leaned forward and pressed her forehead against the very center of the carved image.

"Deina," Theron called from below, "what are you doing? We can't just—"

His words were swallowed by a wrenching, grinding roar from high up on the cliff wall. Somehow, the rock was . . . was splitting down the center line of the sigil, coming apart as if an invisible hand were dragging a giant knife down the layers of stone. Shock sent Deina stumbling backward. The noise went on and on, louder and louder, forcing her to cover her ears—until there was a narrow fissure between the two halves of the cliff. A fissure just wide enough for a person to walk through. And beyond, darkness.

Their path into the rest of the Underworld, or a trap? Deina stared into the shadowed crevasse as the others gathered near her. If they walked in, and there was no way out at the other end—if the rock came back together—they'd be killed. Or worse, sealed inside the stone, buried alive. Her gaze went to the unburning torch, its frozen flames throwing a strange, steady light across the scene. Alive, and never dying. Indecision sapped her strength.

The shadows rippled. A hand appeared within the darkness.

A hand, and a muscled arm with pale scars crisscrossing the skin. A face surrounded by dark, flowing locks that mingled with the shadows. Just the suggestion of a denser darkness at his back.

The boy from the Threshold, the one she'd dreamed of, held out his hand to her.

"Come, Deina. Your path lies this way." He smiled. "If you're going to trust me, you'd better do it soon. The gate will not be open for much longer."

Deina glanced to either side. The others were staring into the darkness of the fissure just as she had been doing.

"Can you see—" She broke off, unsure how to describe her vision. Or unwilling. "Can you see anything through the gap?"

"Just darkness," Theron answered. "What shall we do?"

The boy in the shadows answered. "Prove your worthiness. Follow me." He glanced up toward the top of the cliff. "Now."

If she gave up, what would she have? A lifetime of regret. Tensing every muscle, digging her nails hard into the palms of her hands, she walked into the darkness.

Light blazed in front of her, so bright she had to throw up her hands to shield her eyes. Another step and another, eyes half closed against the radiance. The ground beneath her fell away. As pain stabbed from her left eyeball up into her skull, she tumbled forward and landed face-first on a hard surface.

Grass. Deina could feel its rough prickle beneath her cheek. Head swimming, she forced herself to her feet. The gash in the rocks was above her now. She could see through it clearly from here. Could see the dim torchlight and the shadows of the others still hesitating on the other side.

"I'm here. Come through!" A thunderous crash drew her gaze higher still. The fissure in the rock was closing up. "Quickly!" Could they hear her? "You have to hurry!"

Aster appeared. He fell onto the grass, just as she had done. Theron followed on his heels, landing on top of Aster and making him groan. Chryse was through, too, as the rocks just above her head slammed together. But where was Drex?

"Drex," Deina yelled, "now!"

At the last moment, Drex squeezed himself out. Before he'd even hit the ground, the final section of rock crashed together and all trace of the gap in the cliff vanished. The cliff face was smooth and seamless—there was no sigil carved into the stone on this side. Deina swung around, searching for the dark-haired boy.

He was gone, too.

She dropped to her knees and sank her head in her hands, her heart slamming against the inside of her rib cage as if mirroring the violence of the rocks.

They were sealed within the Underworld. One of the new rites they'd learned would return them to the place they'd entered the Underworld, but it wouldn't work unless they'd first recovered Eurydice. To reach her, they needed to follow the path deeper into the Underworld. If they could find it.

Deina forced herself to lower her hands. To open her eyes and look around. They seemed to be in a broad valley that sloped down from the towering cliff face, edged at a distance by gently undulating green-gray hills. The tops of the hills were dusted with snow. The pale shoots of newly emerging flowers poked up through the grass that clad the valley floor, though when Deina bent to examine them, she found the buds to be frostbitten—cankerous and malformed. This might look like a place on the brink of spring, but it was a spring that would never bloom. She shivered. The air was chill and dry, faintly scented with some herb she couldn't identify. And—she frowned, looking around and then up—there were no shadows. No sun, either. An even, muted light came from the unbroken cloud above, bleeding color and detail from their surroundings, flattening everything out. The scene was more like a child's drawing of a place than somewhere real. The only brightness came from a smear of red on the rock face nearby.

Blood.

"Did someone cut themselves?"

Drex held up his arm.

"I took the skin off my elbow on the way down." He peered at the wound. "It's stopped bleeding."

Something about the blood on the rock was making Deina anxious. It looked wrong—too garish, too obvious—in this bleached and bloodless landscape. She tore up a handful of grass and tried to rub it away. But the stain was set. Even splashing a very little of her precious water supply over it didn't help. It seemed to glow, a slash of scarlet against the dull stone. As good a way of advertising their presence as any she could think of.

"Deina, Aster thinks he's found the start of the path." Theron had come to stand next to her. He frowned at the smear of blood before dragging his gaze back to her face. "How did you know that it would be safe to pass through the rocks?"

"I didn't. I—" Deina broke off with a shudder. She glanced back toward the cliff, half expecting the dark-haired boy with his cloak of shadows to be lounging against the rock, smiling at her. Creature, not boy. Not man. He wasn't human, whatever else he was. "I took a chance, that was all."

Theron raised his eyebrows in acknowledgment. "You always did trust your instincts." He looked for a moment as if he was going to say something more, but instead he jerked his head toward the others and turned away.

You might not be saying that, Theron, if either of us knew exactly what it was I trusted.

She hurried after Theron, wishing the empty sky above didn't seem so watchful.

10

Deina had lost track of how much time they'd spent walking. The path, no more than two parallel lines of small boulders set in the grass, unfolded endlessly toward the horizon ahead. The cliff through which they'd entered had long since disappeared from view, and the land and sky were so monotone and unvarying that they might as well not have been moving at all. It was only her aching legs that hinted at the distance they'd covered. No signs of life—or what might pass for life here in the Underworld, the realm of the dead. Empty sky. Empty ground below. So why did it feel as though they were being examined? The path was wide and there was plenty of space. Still, despite their antipathy, the five of them were huddled together in its center. Aster had made sure he was at the front, of course. Yet from her position at the rear, Deina could see him glancing up at the sky from time to time, or looking over his shoulder, or flinching as if startled by some sudden noise. The others, too. It wasn't just her.

Drex was immediately ahead of her. Was it worse for him?

she wondered. Though there was little to see, he could see even less of it than the rest of them. He had that small stone in his right hand again, turning it over with his fingers. She increased her pace to draw level with him.

"Is that a good-luck charm, Drex?" The vast silence around them somehow compelled her to whisper. "You had it on the boat, too, didn't you?"

Drex's fist clenched around the stone. "It's nothing."

"He's allowed a secret," Theron chimed in. "You keep enough. Like, what happened to the things you stole on the ship? The amethysts, and whatever else it was that Orpheus wouldn't mention." His tone was jeering. Different from the way he'd spoken to her before at the cliff face. The same old double-dealing Theron. Deina rested a hand on the hilt of one of her knives.

"I have no idea what you're talking about." She'd have to be careful if they were down here long enough to need to rest. The dagger she'd stolen was probably even more valuable than the amethysts. Even if Aster decided it was dishonorable, Theron definitely wouldn't hesitate to root around in her bag while she was asleep.

Perhaps Theron read her thoughts. He shook his head. "I wouldn't trust you further than I'd trust Drex here with a spear."

"You trusted me enough to follow me in here."

Drex had changed color. "I—I'm not that bad. If the target's not too far away, and the light's good, and—"

"No one cares," Aster growled from up ahead. Drex instantly muttered an apology, which Aster ignored. "Now is not the time for idle gossip." He glared at Deina over his shoulder.

"This isn't the women's quarters back at the House."

"We don't have time for gossip in the women's quarters," Deina replied. "We're too busy plotting the destruction of all men. Isn't that right, Chryse?"

Chryse didn't answer—in her thoughts, at least, she was clearly somewhere else—and Aster just scowled. But there was a hint of doubt in his eyes. He wasn't, Deina noted with pleasure, completely certain that she was lying.

Her gaze drifted back to her friend. She'd been so quiet since they left Orpheus's ship. So preoccupied. It had to be something Orpheus had done to her, whatever she said about the king simply accepting her refusal. Something he'd done, or something he'd said . . .

Theron stopped walking so quickly, Deina almost ran into him. "What's that?"

He was pointing toward the hills that rose in the distance to the left of the path.

"Where?" Deina squinted in the direction he was indicating. "I don't see anything."

"On the top of that ridge. I thought I saw something moving." Everyone was staring at the hilltop now. Theron sighed. "No. It's gone."

"Or it was never there." Aster stomped onward.

Deina couldn't resist. Brushing close to Theron, she murmured in his ear, "Seeing things? First sign of madness." She hurried to catch up with Chryse before he could reply.

They marched on in silence. But within a few strides, with a rapidity that reminded Deina that—despite the stunted grass and the snow that appeared to dust the hills—they were not in the mortal world, the landscape changed around them. Although the boulders marking the path continued on, the grass stopped abruptly and was replaced by coarse, pale sand. The hills on either side were suddenly closer, their bare, rocky slopes looming over them. The group's pace slowed as the menace of the hills dragged at their feet. Bones appeared, scattered across the sand. Fragments initially, mingled with what looked like teeth. Then larger bones: hips and thighs and ribs and skulls, obscuring the path in places and forcing them to pick their way more carefully. The skeletal remains not just of people and animals—dogs, goats, horses—but of creatures Deina knew had no counterpart in the mortal world. Claw-tipped wing bones, that reminded her chillingly of the descriptions of harpies from the old stories, lay next to a huge skeleton that looked almost human, apart from the horned bull's skull at its top. Beyond them, she could see the remains of what could only be the hydra, its many necks spread out across the sand like a fan. And through all the other litter of bones looped the long spine of an enormous serpent.

Was this the place that myths came to die?

Drex was hurrying ahead to where the serpent's skull lay halfway across the path. Reaching his goal, he bent to examine it before beginning to pull something away.

"What are you doing, Drex?" Chryse muttered as Aster yelled the same question.

The answer came back: "Teeth."

When Deina and Chryse reached him, Drex held out his hand. In his palm lay several long, daggerlike teeth with sharp points and serrated edges. Carefully, Drex tipped them into

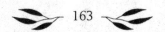

the pouch hanging from his belt and set about cautiously loosening another tooth from the serpent's jaw.

"Is this a game to you?" Aster blustered.

"Leave him alone," Theron began. "It's not as if—"

"No." Aster pushed Drex back, snatching the tooth from his hand. "Unlike the rest of us, you're only a novice. That means you do as I say—" The sentence ended in a sharp intake of breath and a yelp of pain. Aster dropped the tooth. Blood was welling from a gash across his palm. "Argh! Why didn't you tell me they were sharp?"

"Well, they're teeth . . ." Drex began.

"You didn't give him any chance to tell you," Theron observed. As he and Aster began arguing, Deina knelt to examine the scarlet splashes accumulating on the ground beneath Aster's outstretched hand. It was the same garish, painfully bright color as the bloodstain Drex had left on the cliff.

Chryse had crouched down next to her and was running her fingertips over the pale sand, frowning. "This sand doesn't feel normal. It doesn't feel . . . *real*."

Deina scooped some into her palm and let it trickle out again. Chryse was right. Whatever it was, it lacked the weight of sand, and the texture was wrong. It was more like dust. Very fine, creamy-white dust, mixed with some larger fragments, a little like shell, but—

"Oh, gods." Deina jumped to her feet, brushing her palms against her clothes. "It's not sand. It's bone, all of it. Ground-up bones." There was no time for her to listen to the others' exclamations of horror or disbelief. Ripples, like those on the surface of a lake, were spreading outward from the patch of bloodstained ground. Deina grabbed Chryse's hand. All five of them backed away. A sudden intense gust of wind surrounded them, driving the bone dust up into the air, into their mouths and eyes. But instead of dispersing or falling back to the ground, the pale powder seemed to coalesce. Choking, Deina squinted into the swirling dust.

There was something sweeping toward them.

Skeletons. Some picked clean, some half clad in rotting flesh, all bearing weapons. Spears and swords and huge, long-handled hammers formed out of jagged slivers of bone. A green light shone from the creatures' empty eye sockets, and as they stalked nearer to the Severers, they screeched: a loud, keening wail that made Deina want to cover her ears. Chryse screamed. Hands shaking, Deina dragged her knives from their scabbards. One of Theron's arrows sang past her and thudded into the grinning skull of the nearest creature, its bones partially covered by tattered ribbons of skin and the remnants of some scarlet fabric. When the creature disintegrated, Deina's heart leaped. She ducked and swiped through the legs of another. Watched as it turned back into a pile of bony fragments before raising her blades to face another of the monsters. But the blow never fell—her path was blocked by the creature Theron had destroyed. It had, impossibly, re-formed. Leering at her, it swung the massive hammer it carried toward her head. She ducked just as another gust of wind blew more dust into her eyes. Blinded, she felt the creature grab her arm, blinked her vision clear in time to see its wide-open jaws lunging toward her. The stench of decay made her gag. At the last moment, she twisted and drove one of her knives into the putrid flesh clinging to the monster's rib cage, causing it to crumble again. But there were more nearby, and the mound of bones and dust at her feet was already re-forming.

"Run!" Theron's voice. He pushed her away from the skeletons and along the path. Chryse, Aster, and Drex were already ahead of them. Aster flung out his arm, pointing to the hills.

"A cave," he panted. "Shall we—shall we hide?"

The cave was some distance from the path. Too far to risk it. "We can't!" Deina yelled back.

Theron looked over his shoulder. "What in Hades's name are those things? They're still after us. Keep going!"

Deina forced herself to remember the skeletal creature that had nearly overwhelmed her. There was something important—some detail that was nagging at her memory . . . She shook her head and gave up.

"I think—I think it was the blood that summoned them. The ground—it was crawling, where Aster had been bleeding on it."

"And whose fault was that?" Aster gasped. "If Drex had been concentrating on the plan instead of collecting souvenirs—"

A long, low growl interrupted him. The sound echoed around the hills and went on and on.

Chryse slowed, clutching her side. "It's coming from the cave." She glanced behind her. "Those things have fallen back."

There was no time for relief. Emerging from the cave and stalking toward them was by far the biggest living animal Deina had ever set eyes on. It was at least four times the size of a horse, with thick, muscular legs and a whiplike tail that had the head of a vicious, fanged serpent at its end. It had not one but three massive-jawed heads, each surrounded by a thick mane. But instead of fur or hair, the manes were formed from hissing snakes that waved back and forth, twisting frenziedly around one another. The eyes of these snakes were filmy white. The creature's own six eyes glowed a flickering, fiery red, and its coat was the color of midnight.

Cerberus. The legendary hound of Hades, whose task it was to prevent the souls of the dead from escaping the Underworld, and to stop the living from entering it. In essence, a dog, though never had a word seemed so entirely inadequate.

"Seriously?" Theron groaned. "I suppose that's why they stopped chasing us."

"At least we've got the honey cakes," Deina replied. She nudged Aster. "Now would be a good time."

"Yes. Of course!" Aster pulled his bag off his shoulder and began frantically searching through it. His face paled. "I can't find them."

"What?" Deina hissed. "But you had them on the boat."

"I—I think I left them there . . ."

Theron threw Aster a withering glance, retrieved his bow from his back, and fitted an arrow to the string. Aster slid one of his beloved spears into his hand and leveled it at the approaching monster.

Deina shook her head in disbelief, silently cursing Aster's carelessness, even as she drew her knives and crouched to meet the hound's advance. Chryse and Drex, both armed with short swords, copied her movement. There was no time for anything else.

The creature came to a halt only a few strides away. Even from here, Deina could feel and smell the animal's hot, putrid breath. She gagged and tried to edge away, but her movement was met by a low growl that reverberated through her entire body. Standing still seemed a better option.

"What shall we do?" Chryse whispered.

"We . . . we fight!" cried Aster somewhat hesitantly. He hurled his spear at the creature. The gleaming, bronze-tipped weapon flew straight toward its target, but at the last moment the hound leaped forward, caught the spear between the teeth of its middle head, and bit clean through the wooden shaft. The ground shook as it landed.

Deina's pulse raced as her muscles braced for the inevitable attack. Cerberus batted away the remains of the spear with its huge front paws, growling. The fierce gaze of the nearest head was fixed on her.

"Theron," Aster murmured, "shoot it."

"Have you seen the size of it? Shooting it will just make it angry."

"Then we'll have to make a run for it," Aster replied.

"There's nowhere to run to, even if we could outrun it. The slowest of us would be ripped apart. Or is that the plan: to sacrifice Chryse for the greater good?"

As Chryse gasped, Deina slowly moved her arm so that one of her knives was pointed at Aster.

"If either of you tries that, I'll kill you myself."

Aster didn't answer. Deina could hear Chryse's rapid breaths. She tried to edge toward her, but as soon as she moved, the hound began barking and snapping its jaws. All three heads were now turned in her direction. It took a step toward her. Deina froze. What did it want with her? What was it waiting for? She tried to stare the creature down, glaring at it defiantly. Tried not to imagine what it was going to feel like when its three sets of fangs, glistening with ropes of drool, tore into her.

"We need . . . we need to find another way to pacify it," Drex said slowly.

"What are you suggesting?" Theron replied. "Tell it a bedtime story?"

"Lullaby," Drex blurted out. "Sing to it."

A lullaby? A word from Deina's past. Someone had sung her to sleep, once. A low, gentle voice—Leida? Or someone else, someone from before the House claimed her? The sliver of memory faded as quickly as it had appeared. But it had felt real.

"It seems to have fixed on Deina as the most edible," Aster muttered. "The rest of us could probably walk away." As if to test his theory, he backed away a little. Cerberus didn't seem to care. All three heads were still focused on Deina.

"But—but—" Chryse was looking from Aster to Deina and back again.

"Honestly," Drex murmured, "I think the singing might work." But he, too, was edging away.

Theron didn't reply. Did he want her to beg? Well, she wasn't going to. Drex was probably wrong, and Deina refused to have her last words be a supplication to Theron. Cerberus lowered its heads and hunched its shoulders, pawing the ground and growling even more loudly; whatever doubt it seemed to have had about eating her had clearly evaporated. Deina gripped her knives more tightly. So be it. An ache grew in her chest. She hadn't thought she'd be betrayed this quickly.

She hadn't thought her dreams of freedom would be turned to ashes this easily. But at least, as one of the Theodesmioi, she had her place in Elysium. And before that, if Cerberus was about to take her life, she was going to make sure the creature paid dearly for it.

"Go then, all of you. Run."

Cerberus crouched lower, its bunched muscles coiled, ready to spring.

Deina bared her teeth and planted her feet more firmly—

Theron's voice broke across the unreal landscape with the sudden splendor of dawn, his music flowing through her veins like wine.

Deina had never heard Theron sing with so much passion before, with so much emotion in his voice—every note caressed, every shade of nostalgic melancholy wrung from the lyrics. The hound's tensed muscles relaxed, and one by one, the three enormous heads swiveled in Theron's direction, until the animal's focus was entirely on him.

Theron's voice trembled and his eyes widened in panic. Deina prayed that this was a song he knew well—hoped he didn't have to concentrate too hard to remember the words.

One of the hound's heads swung back toward her. Theron sang a fraction louder, reclaiming the creature's attention. Cerberus shook itself, two of the three heads yawning widely, and padded over to Theron. Its huge ears were flattened back against the sides of its heads. Utterly mesmerized by the sound of Theron's voice, it didn't seem to mind that he'd now sung the lullaby three times over. As he kept singing, the head on the right began to nod, its eyelids drooping. The animal let out a low, appreciative-sounding rumble and settled itself on the grass. The eyes of the middle head grew glassy with sleep. The left head yawned and rested on one of the giant paws. The snakes that formed the creature's mane went limp.

Carefully, barely daring to move, Theron glanced sideways at Aster and raised one eyebrow.

Aster gave a tiny nod. He tapped Drex on the shoulder and began walking stealthily around the dozing dog and away along the path. Drex and Chryse tiptoed after him. Deina stayed. Theron had saved her life. She didn't want to think about why, but she did want to pay off the debt sooner rather than later, by making sure he got out of this alive, too.

One of Cerberus's heads was snoring now. Theron began to back away, very slowly. Deina walked softly next to him, scanning the ground carefully. She didn't trust this place. It would be so easy for a skull to suddenly appear and trip Theron up, or for a particularly brittle bone to materialize beneath his foot. A quick glance at the hound showed all three heads now dozing contentedly. A little farther on, the path curved away through the hills. If they could get to that point, they'd be out of sight of Hades's guard dog; out of sight and hopefully out of mind. Not much farther. Theron's voice grew quieter still. His song was almost swallowed by the surrounding silence.

Deina saw the avalanche a fraction before she heard it.

"No!" The clamor of rocks tumbling down the scree slope of the nearest hill filled the valley with thunder. With astonishing speed, Cerberus leaped to its feet, snarling. Theron swore, took a deep breath, and opened his mouth as if he were actually about to start singing again. Deina dragged him around to face her. "Run, you idiot!" She threw herself forward, glanced backward once, and saw that Theron was fleeing along the path at her heels. But Cerberus was closing in on them. She could hear the thud of its feet. Could almost feel its panting breath against her back. Ahead, the others were running, too. And beyond them, a vast shadow had appeared. More of those skeletal monsters? No—a forest. A forest that hadn't been there a moment before. Tall, dark-leaved elm trees, crowded together like a row of hoplites in tight formation, shutting out most of the light; dusk lay beneath the dense canopy of their branches. But there was nowhere else to hide. And no worse terror, surely, to scare the hound away. Drex, Aster, and Chryse had already plunged into the gloom that marked the boundary of the forest. Cerberus was so close now. Deina grabbed Theron's hand, pulling him behind her. The sudden rush of memory almost made her stumble: one of the last times, up in the hills, Theron's hand warm in hers, their feet bruising the wild thyme as they ran—

No.

She sped up, making a final effort as her heart pounded against the inside of her ribs, dragging him with her, plunging between the close-set trunks and into the welcoming shadow of the trees. On and on, with Cerberus whining in impotent fury behind them.

Deina glanced over her shoulder at Theron and grinned. "He's too big to follow us. He—"

She tripped and landed heavily on hands and knees at the edge of a muddy puddle. Her reflection stared back at her:

mismatched eyes, dark hair coming loose from its bonds, the sigil of Hades like a fresh scar on her forehead.

The skeleton creatures, she remembered.

"Theron—"

Pain erupted in her head.

There was dirt in her mouth.

Deina pushed herself onto her hands and knees and spat it out, keeping her gaze fixed on the ground—dead leaves, more dirt—until the world stopped spinning. Gods, her head ached. Had someone hit her? She reached up gingerly and touched the back of her skull, expecting to find her fingertips stained with blood. But there wasn't even a bump, and the skin seemed unbroken. Perhaps the denizens of the Underworld didn't actually need to hit you with a big stick to make you feel like they had.

Trees, all around her. If she stretched out her arms, she could touch the trunks of three of them without even moving. She was crouching in a hollow formed by their roots, which were poking up out of the ground like the hinges of huge spiders' legs. Somewhere in the far distance, Cerberus was whining. A pitiful sound; it reminded her of the stray dogs begging for scraps on the streets of Iolkos. She felt a faint tremor of regret for the comfort and familiarity of the House; shook herself to banish it. Iolkos was in her past. The important thing now was to survive the present.

Trees. But no Theron, as far as she could see. Deina got cautiously to her feet and climbed out of the hollow.

"Aster? Chryse? Drex?" She called their names as loudly

as she dared, aware of the monstrous presence still patroling the boundary of the forest. No one answered. "Theron?" He at least should be here. He'd been just behind her, and then—

There'd been a puddle, hadn't there? She'd seen—something. Groaning, she closed her eyes and pressed her fists to her forehead. What had happened? Why couldn't she remember? And where were the others? Lost, like she was, wandering somewhere in the woods?

Doubt stuck its cold claw into her mind. Unless they were together but thought her dead. Or wished she was. Unless they'd decided to go on without her.

Deina took a deep breath. Wriggled her shoulders, trying to shake the doubt away. She still had her bag. Her knives were still in their scabbards. She brushed her fingertips across the leather, drawing comfort from their solidity. Something dependable in the gauzy unreality of the Underworld.

Staying where she was wouldn't help. She peered into the shadowy heart of the woods. The path was nowhere in sight, and there was no indication of which way she should go, but away from Cerberus seemed like the best choice of direction. She set off, clambering over tree roots and beneath branches, pausing every so often to call out to the others. No one responded. In fact, apart from the crunch of her boots on dead leaves, the forest was swathed in silence. Soon, she couldn't hear Cerberus anymore. There was no birdsong. No insects buzzing. No breeze rustling gently through the canopy. No life anywhere. Just the watchful trees, and the remnants of their slow decay.

Deina shivered and thought about being shut inside a tomb.

Her pace slowed. There seemed to be no end to this forest. Though for all she knew, she might be walking around in circles. In the gloom, the trees were all starting to look the same.

"Chryse? Theron?"

Voices, just on the edge of hearing.

"Aster?"

There was no reply. Deina hurried to follow the faint noise before she lost it again. Two male voices, she guessed as she drew closer. She was about to call out again when a laugh rang out. Were they Severers, or could someone else be wandering in these woods? She crept closer until she was certain. Theron, and Aster with him. Scrambling to catch up, she burst into a clearing.

"Theron, wait!"

He turned. The smile faded from his face. "Not dead? How very unfortunate."

11

The statement hung in the air as Deina's heart thumped against her ribs.

"I don't understand."

Theron sighed and glanced at Aster. "How to make it clear to her?" Vaulting gracefully over a fallen tree that was barring his way, he took a few steps toward her and raised his voice. "I hit you on the head. Clearly, not hard enough. I should have checked."

Deina's hand went to the back of her skull.

"Why? Why save me from Cerberus only to—"

"Oh, Deina." Theron's smile returned. "I wasn't trying to save you. I was saving myself. Cerberus might have toyed with you, or he might have killed you quickly and come after the rest of us. That was why I sang. But once we'd gained the safety of the forest, leaving you as a sacrifice for the hound, should it find a way to pursue us . . ." He shrugged. "It just made sense."

Theron's eyes were bloodshot. And perhaps it was just the lack of light in this cursed place, but Aster's skin had a gray cast to it that made him look ill.

Deina drew one of her knives. "I don't believe you. There's something wrong with you both. Where's Chryse? Where's Drex?"

"He was slowing us down." Chryse's voice, coming from just behind her. Deina swung around. Chryse reached out and cupped Deina's cheek briefly; her touch was warm and real enough. "He got tangled up among some brambles, so we left him there. Just like we left you."

Chryse's cheeks had the same ashen tint as Aster's, but there was no trace of distress in her face. She looked as she used to back at the House, when she'd just been given another pretty trinket by the family of one of her wealthy clients.

"You're lying." Shock graveled Deina's voice.

"I watched you learn to live on rivalry. To thrive on it. I'm a Severer, too." Chryse tilted her head. "You think I couldn't do it? That I couldn't choose myself over Drex—or even over you—if I had to?"

Deina opened her mouth. She wanted to say, *This is different. This is leaving someone to die, not trying to win a race.*

Chryse raised an eyebrow.

"Perhaps." Deina forced the word out. "Perhaps you could. But you'd feel it more than this."

Chryse seemed to consider for a moment. Then tears welled up in her eyes and spilled across her cheeks. She wiped them away.

"Of course I feel it. But you would have done the same, Deina. I had to do what was best for me." She shrugged. "You always do."

Deina swallowed hard. "That's not true."

But Chryse was already picking her way through the undergrowth. She came to a halt next to Theron.

Deina's breathing had grown shallow. Trying to slow it down, she tightened her grip on the hilt of her knife. Something was wrong here. Yes, they were Severers, and, yes, this was a contest, whatever Theron had claimed. But this . . . It didn't make sense.

"Why Chryse, Aster? She wasn't chosen for this quest. You know she's not as strong as me. Not as fast. So if you were looking for a sacrifice, why pick me?"

Aster smirked. "Theron chose. He persuaded me that Chryse had more feminine skills. More appropriate skills."

Before Aster had even finished speaking, Theron pulled Chryse into his arms and bent his head to kiss her hungrily.

"No—" Deina's protest died on her lips. Chryse had wound her fingers into Theron's dark curls; as Deina watched, she hooked one leg around Theron's hips, drawing him tight against her.

Aster tapped Theron on the shoulder. "Hey, there'll be time for that after we've found the queen and claimed the prize. Come on." He began walking away, forcing a path through the trees. Theron and Chryse broke apart. They smiled at Deina.

"You were never going to be free, Deina. It was just a foolish dream." Chryse raised one hand in farewell. "I'm sorry."

"Don't try to follow us, Deina, or next time . . ." Theron drew one finger slowly across his neck, winked at Deina, took Chryse's hand, and pulled her after Aster. Within a few moments, all three had disappeared from view.

Deina took two steps after them. Stopped. What was the point? Something—someone—was controlling them, or poisoning them, or—or—

"Chryse..." Deina barely murmured the word. She refused to believe it. Chryse wouldn't have willingly left her. They cared for each other. And even Theron...

She'd studied Theron as an enemy for almost as long as she'd counted him a friend. But perhaps that wasn't enough, after all this time, for her to truly know him. Perhaps she no longer knew him at all.

A rattling sound drew her attention. It was the blade of her knife, knocking against a jutting boulder. Her hand was trembling. Carefully, Deina put the knife down on the boulder. She swung her bag off her back, found her waterskin, and allowed herself a few mouthfuls of the precious liquid. Sat on the boulder and murmured the prayer to Demeter, goddess of the harvest, that was said at the start of each meal at the House, and forced herself to eat some bread and a couple of pieces of dried fruit. The food tasted like dust in her mouth. Rooting around in the undergrowth until she found a flattish stone, she began sharpening the blades of both her knives.

Time and a few repetitive, everyday actions—they helped a little. With a degree of calm came clarity. She didn't have to work out the reason for the others' behavior. She just had to decide how to deal with the consequences.

Follow them, that was the obvious choice. Whatever Theron

threatened, she was quiet enough and quick enough to keep up without being seen. Follow them, wait for the right moment to steal Eurydice's spindle from Aster's bag, and get to the queen before them. Hopefully find a way to get Chryse away from the other two as well. Or she could try to find Drex. An ally might be useful, and she didn't like the idea of leaving him trapped here to die of thirst. Deina shivered and stared up into the silence of the dense canopy above. Where was he, though? A long search for him would make it virtually impossible to catch up to the others. She might search and find him already dead, or never find him at all, and without the spindle . . .

Her shoulders were aching. Closing her eyes, Deina reached back to massage the tight muscles at the base of her neck.

"I wish you were here, Anteïs. I wish you could tell me what to do."

"Perhaps I can help?"

Deina yelped and jumped up, stumbling backward. The boy from the Threshold, the one with the pale scars who'd convinced her to step through the fissure in the rock, the one she'd dreamed about that last night at the House—he was standing only a couple of strides away.

"You." Deina was about to add, *Are you real?*—but given their location, it seemed like a stupid question. The terms *real* and *unreal* scarcely had any application in the Underworld.

The boy spread his arms wide and bowed. "As you see." He grinned, dimples leaping into his cheeks. "And please don't ask me what I want again. I think we've been through that."

A slate-gray sky with the first soft flakes of snow drifting on the wind, and him, telling her he was there to help . . .

"But that was a nightmare."

"A nightmare?" His eyebrows went up. "That's harsh. Personally, I don't sleep, but I'd have thought the appearance of a devastatingly handsome man—"

"Creature," Deina interrupted. Her knives were still lying on the boulder. She edged a little closer. "Men sleep."

He rolled his eyes. "—of a devastatingly handsome *individual* offering you his aid would have counted as a rather enjoyable dream."

"Enjoyable?" Deina sidled a little nearer the boulder. The knives were almost within lunging distance. "Did you miss the bit with the skeletons and the falling?"

"That bit was conjured by your own mind and had absolutely nothing to do with me. Now, would you like to tell me why—"

In one quick movement, Deina grabbed the nearest knife and sent it flashing through the air toward the boy's chest.

He caught the blade in the palm of one hand. Still smiling, he tossed it up and caught it again, this time by the hilt.

"That was uncalled for. Here." He spun the knife gently back to Deina. Automatically, she caught it—no trace of blood on the blade—and slid it back into its sheath.

The boy strolled toward her. She could hear the crunch of dead leaves beneath his feet. He seemed far more real here than he had before. Taller, too, she realized, when he stopped in front of her. He picked up the other knife, still on the boulder, and handed it to her.

"Tell me what's happened."

There was that irresistible note of command in his

voice—the same as she'd felt in the dream. Without even meaning to, Deina found she was telling him everything that had occurred since they'd entered the Underworld: marching through the empty landscape, the pursuit by the half-rotten corpses, the attack by Cerberus, the betrayal by Chryse. By the end, a tear was tracking its way across her cheek. She sniffed and dashed it away. "Damn."

"There's no call for tears. No call for you to linger here, either. The others have made their choice. Let them wander among the shades and face the trials of the rivers." The boy deftly slipped one arm around Deina's shoulder, picked up her bag with his other hand, and began guiding her out of the clearing. "Who needs them? Not you. Because you and I are going to—"

"No." Deina ducked out from under his arm and grabbed her bag. "I'm not going anywhere with you." She tried to recall the words of the Song for laying ghosts to rest; he didn't sleep, and he couldn't be injured by a knife, so despite his apparent solidity, that's what he had to be. Besides, she couldn't think of anything else that might work. "You say you want to help me, but I have no idea who or what you are." She paused, looking up into bright blue eyes fringed with long black lashes and set beneath thick dark brows. Eyes that contained both amusement and more than a hint of exasperation. "Do you even have a name?"

"A name?"

Deina waited.

"Nat. You can call me Nat."

The single syllable fell oddly on her ears. What kind of a

name was Nat? But at least he'd told her. Knowing the name of the ghost made the rite so much easier. Deina held up her hand and began to chant the opening words of the Song. "Lord Hades hear me, boundaries of the Underworld answer me—"

The boy—Nat—burst into a shout of laughter that echoed through the lowering trees.

"I'm sorry, but that isn't going to work. Severers' rites are for the mortal world and, by extension, the Threshold that the one performing the rite creates." His laughter died, and the faintest note of menace colored his voice. "I am not some mere spirit to be bound and dismissed at your pleasure." For a moment, Deina had a vision: her, human and frail, standing before something of immense, incomprehensible power. She blinked and it was gone. Nat was smiling again. "But even though you tried"—he wagged an admonishing finger at her—"I'm still going to help you." He frowned. "The others—why won't you abandon them as they have abandoned you?"

"Because I don't believe it, that's why. Chryse wouldn't abandon me. And none of them were behaving normally."

"Are they normally so perfect, then?"

"Of course not. We're Severers. Theron is a devious, cheating liar. Aster's a condescending, overly muscled bastard. Drex has no spine, and even Chryse"— Deina hesitated—"even Chryse can be selfish."

"And yet you *don't* believe they would have left you . . ."

Deina crossed her arms. "I'm telling you, there was something wrong." A flash of anger in Nat's eyes made her flinch. She backed away. "I have to find Chryse. I can't waste any more time."

"Wait."

Unwillingly, Deina paused.

"I might know what's happening to your comrades." He held out his hand, just as he had done in her dream and when guiding her through the cleft in the rock. "I promise: I'll take you to where they are."

Stuck here on her own, with no obvious way forward—what did she have to lose? Deina looked into his eyes again. There was no anger there now. They were wide, guileless, warm. She slipped her hand into his, gasping a little at how cold his skin was.

Nat smiled. "So the third time *is* the charm. Hold on."

Tendrils of dark mist rose from the ground, twining around their feet, legs, hips—higher and higher, enveloping them both. The mist began to swirl, faster and faster, until Deina felt as if she were standing at the center of a whirlwind. The rushing shadows roared in her ears, plucked at her hair and clothes, and stung her eyes until she screwed them shut and lowered her head, leaning into the shelter of Nat's shoulder. Louder and louder still, holding on to Nat's hand so tightly, her knuckles ached, until she thought the noise must surely crush her skull—

Silence. Deina lifted her head and looked around. They were deeper in the forest, beneath the dense and spreading boughs of a tree bearing large purple flowers. There was no trail of destruction from the whirlwind that had carried them there.

Nat was watching her.

"What are you?" Deina yanked her fingers free, ignoring the small part of her that, for some unfathomable reason, thought it would be a better idea to keep holding his hand. "A god?"

Scorn twisted Nat's mouth. "One of those who dwell on

Mount Olympus? No. I'm not Hades, either. You should call your teammates. They're not far."

Deina eased one of her knives from its sheath and left the shelter of the tree.

"Chryse? Theron? Aster?"

As though they'd been waiting for her, the three Severers came hurrying through the trees.

"I warned you not to follow us, Deina," Theron called out, unslinging his bow and fitting an arrow to the string as Aster leveled one of his spears at her.

Chryse clapped her hands together excitedly. "Tie her to a tree! Use her for target practice!"

Theron drew the bowstring and took aim.

Deina raised her arm, ready to throw her knife. "Theron, wait—"

She felt Nat's hands on her shoulders. He was standing behind her. The other Severers stopped abruptly.

"Nooo . . ." Theron drew the word out into a whine. Aster and Chryse took up the chorus, "No, no, no . . ." over and over.

"What's happened to them?" Deina whispered.

"These are no humans."

Theron's frame sagged and stooped as if suddenly bowed by old age. "No," he wheezed. "Why are you here? You—"

"Enough." Nat snapped the word out. The Severers—or whatever they were—fell silent. "Do you wish to see them in their true form?"

Deina wasn't sure she did, but she nodded her head.

Nat plucked one of the purple flowers from the nearest branch and crushed it between his fingers.

"Close your eyes." Deina obeyed. She felt Nat's cold fingertips smoothing something across her eyelids. "Now look."

The forest had vanished, reduced to a grove of tall trees hung with dark, trailing vines that swathed the space beneath the boughs in shadows; Deina could see the path, still edged with stones, running nearby. The forms of the other Severers had vanished, too. The stoop-shouldered creatures that stood in their place were roughly human in shape, but that was where the resemblance ended. They were covered in silvery fur, from the tips of the pointed ears that sat, catlike, on top of their heads to the ends of their three-clawed toes. Instead of fingers, their hands also had three claws, and between their overlong, muscular arms and their bodies hung black, bat-like wings. Large dark eyes sat above dagger-sharp beaks, and the creatures' hooting voices reminded Deina of dusk and the calling of owls in the gardens of the House. All three leaped into the air and flapped upward, disappearing into the treetops.

"What are they?"

"Some of the Oneiroi. They're also called the Dream Children; they live in the elm tree that grows at the center of this grove. The gods send them as dreams or nightmares to sleeping humans. They can take the shape of your memories, and they draw on your hopes and terrors to either soothe or torment. They must have separated you from the others after you fled Cerberus, entered your mind, and discovered what you're most afraid of." Nat touched a finger to Deina's temple. "Being bested. Being abandoned. Being trapped."

Deina knocked Nat's hand away. "Why did they do it? Because a god told them to?"

Nat shrugged. "Because they were bored, probably. They're nothing if not mischievous." He began to stroll toward the path.

Deina started after him. Stopped, tore a handful of the purple flowers from the tree, slipped them into the pouch that hung from her belt, then hurried to catch up.

"And what about the others? Where are they really?"

"There." He pointed. Chryse, Theron, Aster, and Drex were standing on the path where the trees thinned. She could hear them, calling her.

"They didn't leave me."

"Oh, please, they've hardly waited any time at all," Nat said petulantly. "From their perspective, your adventure with the Oneiroi took up mere moments, I imagine." He stopped walking. "So now you've seen them. They're safe. Let them carry on with this mighty quest." The sarcasm dragged his voice down a pitch. "You should be on a different path—a path I can show you." Gripping her shoulders lightly, he leaned closer. "Come with me. I told you before, I want to help you fulfill your potential. Your destiny."

Other than the name he'd given himself, she didn't know anything about him. What he was, where he'd come from, how he knew about her. It would be insanity to go with him. Still, Deina couldn't deny that part of her was tempted. There was something about this boy, and it wasn't just his heart-stopping good looks. Perhaps it was the intensity she could feel radiating from him. He wanted something, and whatever it was, he wanted it as badly as she wanted to be free. Could she use that? Would he help her, if she helped him?

Not "him." Not really. You have no idea what you're dealing

with, but you know he's not human. A daimon, maybe.

She shook her head. "Destiny is for heroes, not thieves."

Nat's mouth tightened, his fingers digging into her flesh as a gust of cold, snow-laden air whipped Deina's hair back from her neck and stung her skin. But the next moment, he released her.

"As you wish." That confident smile again. "The blood hunters that pursued you through the valley of bones will be back. Once blood has been spilled and awakened their thirst, they will find you wherever you go." The smile faded as Nat lifted a hand toward her face. "They are terrible, and relentless in their pursuit."

"Blood hunters? What in Hades are—"

Chryse's voice, calling her. Deina turned to see her friend approaching, beckoning to her. When she looked back, Nat had vanished.

"Deina, finally! I was so worried. Theron said the mist came down so suddenly it was as if you'd vanished." Chryse tugged on her arm. "Deina? What are you looking for?"

"Honestly, I don't know." Deina shivered, wondering whether the Oneiroi were still lurking among the shadowed branches, watching. "Nothing. Let's get out of here."

The others were lingering on the path just beyond the glade of trees. Deina thought about passing on Nat's warning about the blood hunters, or whatever he'd called them, but it might only raise questions she didn't know how to answer. Better to thank them for waiting for her.

"We didn't wait for long," Theron replied. "You'd have done the same." He shrugged one shoulder. "Probably." As they fell into step behind Aster, he added in a lower voice, "Thank you for not running off when Cerberus was chasing me. I thought I was dog food." The back of his hand grazed against hers. "I don't think I'd have made it if you hadn't pulled me along. It was almost like old times."

Like the old times before Theron had gone and ruined everything. But for once, Deina didn't feel like reminding him of that.

"You're welcome. Thank you for singing. I'm still going to try to win your share of Orpheus's gold, but I'm glad you didn't let Cerberus eat me."

The corner of Theron's mouth quirked upward. They followed the path onward.

The sky remained the same—a pall of gray clouds filtering a pale, even light that seemed to have no particular source—but it grew warm. Sticky, like the air cooked by the stone pavements of Iolkos on a summer day. The landscape changed, too. The rocky plain beyond the grove of elm trees had become a downward slope and then, as the slope grew steeper, a mountainside. The path twisted its way toward the valley below, cutting between overhanging crags that cast stunted shadows across the scorched ground. The *main* path, Deina corrected herself; in this area of the Underworld, the path splintered, with several smaller paths branching off and curving away into the distance. Every so often, they'd had to stop—had argued, for more time than she cared to remember, about which way to take.

Ahead, Aster slipped on the scree that was tumbled across the path.

"Gods damn it!" Regaining his balance, he slapped angrily at one of the tiny red-bodied flies that hung around them in clouds. "This is meant to be the Underworld. Whose blood do they suck the rest of the time?"

"Maybe we're—ow!" Drex flapped his hands around, momentarily dispersing the flies that were tormenting him. They returned as soon as he stopped. "Maybe we're lost—perhaps we should have taken a left at the fork back there. Maybe this is Tartarus, and we're being punished."

"Condemned to spend eternity with the rest of you?" Theron replied. "The gods wouldn't be so cruel. Though if Aster's lost the path, it wouldn't be the first thing he's lost—"

"We're on the path," Aster yelled, stamping one foot on the ground. "This is the path. And if you keep going on about those honey cakes—"

"Could you stop talking about food!" Chryse's voice was fretful, though Deina was relieved that at least she'd said something. Since they'd left the trees behind, Chryse had grown quieter and quieter, walking as if wrapped in her own thoughts, twisting the golden ring around and around on her finger. "Deina, do something!"

What could she do? Aster and Theron fought. They always had, they always would, and the temperature wasn't helping; strange how a sunless sky could shed such fierce heat. Theron's hand was on his sword hilt; any moment now, she just knew that Aster would reach for a spear. But she was too tired and sweaty and parched to intervene. Or even to care that much.

If the blood hunters do show up again, they might well be too late. We'll have already killed one another...

Perhaps she should have gone with Nat, whatever he was.

Drex sat down and started unpacking the rations from his bag. When he noticed Deina's questioning glance, he shrugged one shoulder awkwardly.

"I'm hungry."

Aster stopped shouting and gazed at the apple Drex was devouring. He licked his lips.

"*Gods.* I'm hungry, too." He looked from the apple to Theron and back again. Swore, shrugged his gear off his back, and settled next to Drex. "Food first. I fight better on a full stomach."

Theron stared at Aster in disbelief, then shook his head and lowered his sword. "If you say so." He sat down, too. So did Chryse and Deina.

"Drex, you're a genius," Chryse murmured. Deina was inclined to agree.

The meal, such as it was, didn't take long. They sat in silence, no easy camaraderie here. Deina closed her eyes, imagining an evening in the women's hall back at the House: music, games of chance, gossip, and other, more intimate exchanges. The sudden pang of longing surprised her. Here, now, having walked willingly into the very jaws of death itself, she missed the relative safety of the House. Deina opened her eyes and glanced at Chryse, to ask whether she felt the same. But Chryse was watching Drex, who had taken out one of the serpent's teeth he'd collected, and the small stone he carried, and was holding both close to his eyes. He seemed to be using the one to mark the other.

"What are you doing?" Deina asked.

He blinked at her, shrugged, and held out the stone. "It's not finished. I'm thinking of adding a fallen comrade at the swordsman's feet."

The stone was a small oval of agate, about half the length of Deina's middle finger. There was something engraved on it. Deina tilted the agate's polished surface back and forth to catch the light. The movement revealed a delicate, detailed carving, one of the most perfect and beautiful things she had ever seen. An engraving of two men engaged in combat—though they were so closely entwined, it might almost have been an embrace. One man, partially protected by a shield, was thrusting a spear with an outstretched arm. The other, leaning against his competitor, was stabbing downward with a sword. Every muscle, every lock of hair, every item of armor or decoration was carefully and precisely brought to life by impossibly small incisions.

"This is . . ." Deina shook her head in wonder. "This is glorious. You made it, Drex?"

"Yes, I did." Drex's voice was warm with pleasure.

"But how? To carve something like this on something so small—it's impossible."

"Not for me. There are many things my sight makes more difficult, but I can focus easily on things very close in front of me. All I need then is a sharp-enough blade." He held up the tooth.

The agate was passed around. With every word of praise, Drex seemed to grow more upright.

Finally, Aster held the stone up, squinting at it. "This one with the spear . . . Is that me?"

Drex smiled. "Based on you. You're the best in the House with a spear. I wanted to get the stance completely right. Did you never wonder why I spent so much time watching you train?"

"No." Aster studied the stone further. "And the one with the sword is based on Theron?"

"You two are constantly fighting. It made sense."

For the first time Deina could remember, Aster looked a little self-conscious as he returned the stone.

"It's fine work. If you survive, I'll commission you to make me one. Once I win Orpheus's gold, I'll be more than rich enough."

When *he* won it . . . Deina could feel the fragile thaw, begun by the shared appreciation of Drex's work, shrink back into ice.

Chryse's head snapped around. "Did you hear that?" She pointed toward a smaller path that curved up over a nearby outcrop of rocks. "Voices."

Deina strained her ears and caught the sounds of conversation. The voices were getting nearer. As everyone stood and reached for their weapons, two figures clambered over the crest of the steep path. Both Severers—they were close enough for Hades's sigil to be clearly visible. A young man and a woman.

Deina recognized her.

12

It was the woman Deina had glimpsed standing at the prow of one of the other ships in Orpheus's convoy, that evening when Theron had been ordered to sing for him. The one she thought might have been a ghost. Deina remembered that moment of connection, the ships drawing close enough together for each of them to see the other, to raise a hand in silent acknowledgment. Now that they were closer, Deina could see she was as beautiful as Chryse: dark-skinned, with a mass of hair the same golden brown as oak leaves in autumn. Nothing like her companion, whose long gray hair fell incongruously around a young, pale face with narrow eyes and high cheekbones.

But what were either of them doing here?

The newcomers had raised their weapons. Whom did the odds favor? They had the advantage of the higher ground, the Iolkosans had the numbers. Neither stranger carried a spear or a bow, but the woman had a battle-ax. Deina wondered how far and how accurately it could be thrown.

"I know you," Deina called out. "From the ship. Did Orpheus send you after us?"

The woman muttered something to her companion, and they both edged nearer.

"Orpheus sent us. But not after you." She tilted her head, studying Deina. "Why are you here?"

The man—boy—took another step forward. "Do you know how to get out?" He sounded panicked. "There's nothing to sacrifice here—do you know how to open the gates? We've lost the—"

"Argys!" The woman grabbed the boy's wrist. "Be silent!"

"Why, Dendris?" He yanked his arm free. "We're trapped here. We're going to die. The quest is over."

Quest?

Deina glanced at Theron and saw the alarm suddenly churning her stomach mirrored in his eyes.

"We were sent here by Orpheus to retrieve the soul of Queen Eurydice so she might be returned to life. We were given a spindle to which to bind the queen's ghost." Deina hesitated, not wanting to have her fears confirmed. "You were sent for the same purpose, weren't you?"

The woman lowered her ax. Nodded. "He gave us her mirror."

They'd been lied to.

"No, no, no." Aster was shaking his head. "You're wrong. His Majesty sent us, no one else. He specifically said he'd chosen our House because he'd heard how skilled its Severers are. Why would the king lie to us? It doesn't make sense."

Deina remembered the treasure she'd seen on the ship, the

boy on the shore who'd been torn from his mother, the starving people in Iolkos. The kind of bastard who would take a city's food and enslave its children would hardly balk at lying.

"It makes sense for him. The more people looking for the queen, the quicker he gets her back. But he might not have gotten so many volunteers if he'd told us the truth about the odds we were facing." There was no escape from the Underworld without the queen's ghost. And if this other team had found her first . . . Deina turned her attention back to the newcomers. "Where are the rest of you?"

They looked at each other and stowed their weapons in unspoken agreement before descending the rest of the path and coming to stand in front of Deina and the others.

"Two of the men argued over who was leading us," the woman began. "They agreed to settle the dispute through single combat, but almost as soon as the first blood was spilled, these creatures appeared from nowhere. Half bone, half rotting flesh. We managed to escape, but—"

"They fell upon the others." There were tears in the boy's eyes. "Tore them limb from limb. Began to feast upon them before they were even dead . . ." The boy screwed his eyes shut and pressed one hand to his mouth. Chryse gripped his shoulder, a small gesture of sympathy that reminded Deina why she loved her.

The woman sighed. "We had to leave them there, unburied. We had to leave the queen's mirror, too." She inclined her head to Deina. "I am Dendris. This is Argys. We are from the House of Hades in Mycenae."

"Deina. Iolkos." As the others introduced themselves—grudgingly, in Aster's case—Deina thought quickly. They'd been on Orpheus's flagship. The Mycenaeans had been on a second ship. But there had been another three vessels in the convoy. Her provisions were still on the ground where they'd been sitting; she hurried to repack them into her bag. "We have to go. Now."

"Why are you suddenly rushing?" Aster asked. "We have to decide what to do with the Mycenaeans. Or do you have some devious purpose of your own?"

Deina gave way to her temper.

"Aster, if I had a devious purpose, I'd currently be slamming it point first into your stupid head. Five ships, idiot. That means he could have sent out five teams of Severers. And the rite to get out of here only works if we have the queen's ghost." The group of Severers who found Eurydice would get to go home. Would get to be free. But the others . . .

Her words acted like a spark on summer-dry scrub. Everyone rushed to gather their things.

"But what about the Mycenaeans?" Aster persisted.

"Better to keep them with us," Deina suggested. "Better to have your competition ahead of you at knifepoint than behind you with a knife." She glanced at Theron. "Isn't that right?"

Down, down into a narrow chasm that lay at the foot of the mountainside. The path here was lined with pine trees, all dead. Only a few brown, withered needles still clung to their drooping branches. The heat grew and grew until Deina felt as if her skin might shrivel and peel from her bones, leaving her as naked as one of the drought-stricken trees. But relief—perhaps—was in sight. Ahead, the overhanging walls of the chasm met to form a huge archway. The cavern beyond was lit by a brilliant glow, and there was a noise like rushing water. A waterfall, probably. Deina ran her tongue across her parched lips and tried not to think about how thirsty she was.

Aster had stopped a little way inside the cavern. Deina saw why: The path here split in two. One branch of the path veered sharply left. They all turned toward the right-hand path, the source of the noise and the ruddy light.

She'd never seen anything like it. Not a waterfall but a firefall. Ribbons of flame twisted and tumbled in an endless, fiery torrent—a crimson cascade that plunged from high above them down into a glowing chasm.

"Phlegethon." Drex, who had come to a halt at Deina's shoulder, shouted over the thunder of the flames. "The river of fire."

The river that poured down into Tartarus, the place of unending punishment. The thought of being plunged into the searing heat of the firefall made Deina squirm with horror. And who were the gods to assign mortals to such torment? Murderers, adulterers, cheats—there was no crime committed by a human, no act of wickedness, that hadn't already been conceived of and accomplished by a god.

The gods show us the way, and condemn us for following in their footsteps . . .

She held up one hand, trying to ward off the heat and the

brilliant light. The path, as far as she could see, wound around the flames, which threw a constant shower of sparks right across it. They'd be incinerated before they even got close. Blinded, too, probably; her eyes were watering, and she could feel the hair on her arms beginning to crisp. The left-hand path seemed attractive in comparison. In unspoken agreement, they followed that path to where it disappeared over the lip of a cliff. The air was cooler here, tainted with a slight metallic tang that caught at the back of her throat.

Chryse, standing well back, picked up a stone and threw it over the edge of the cliff. It landed—eventually—with a sullen splash. She glanced at Deina.

"Another river? Or a lake?"

Deina edged forward. In the shadows at the bottom of the gorge was another river, wide, dark, and sluggish in its bed. The light from the firefall was still bright enough to reveal the crumbling steps, cut into the side of the cliff, that led down to the water's edge. The river looked to be much shallower at this point, as if a ford had been constructed to allow one to cross to the far bank or to the wooden platform built in the middle of the river. Three boats were tied up alongside the platform, and there were empty spaces where others might have been. She nudged Chryse.

"Ready?"

Chryse shook her head and backed away, her bottom lip caught in her teeth. "You know I don't like heights."

Theron—keeping Dendris ahead of him—had already begun to descend. The others were following. Aster, last in line, glanced over his shoulder as he navigated the first few steps.

"Hurry. We can't afford to wait for you."

Chryse stamped her foot. "I hate you, Aster." He shrugged and disappeared below the line of the cliff.

"Come on." Deina held out her hand. Her friend hesitated, twisting her fingers together. "Chryse . . ."

"You're going to leave me, aren't you?"

"What? Of course not. When have I ever left you?"

"You would have left me in Iolkos while you came here."

"That's different." Did they have to talk about this now? Deina peered over the cliff edge, trying to keep an eye on the others. "You know why I volunteered: so I can be free and—"

"And leave the House. And Iolkos. And me."

"No. I mean, yes—but not forever. Only for as long as it would have taken me to free you, too. I was always going to come back."

Though Leida hadn't. The name echoed through the silence between them. Deina cut a ragged strip from her tunic and knotted one end to the back of her belt, the other to the front of Chryse's belt. "There. I won't let you fall. And you won't get left behind. We'll do this together."

As Deina turned away, Chryse clutched at her shoulder. Was this it? Was this the moment that Chryse would explain her uncharacteristic silences, would share what Orpheus had really done to her?

Apparently not. Deina sighed and patted her friend's hand.

"Come on. We'll be down there before you know it."

The descent was slow, but Chryse was concentrating too hard to talk. Either that, or she was too scared. The steps made

Deina nervous enough. Some had crumbled half away; some were missing entirely. Coaxing Chryse down, telling her where to put her feet, where to hold on, took all of Deina's reserves of patience. But finally, Chryse jumped from the last step onto the strip of dark sand that fringed the river.

If it *was* sand this time, and not more bone dust—the air down here was rank enough to make Deina gag. She and Chryse joined the others at the water's edge. Dendris was surveying the river.

"The current looks weak. It should be easy enough to wade across to the boats. Though this doesn't look like water to me." She picked a stick off the shore, dipped it into the river, and gingerly sniffed the liquid that was dripping from it. "Ugh!" Her face twisted with disgust. "Blood. Old, I'd say—it stinks of decay. That might explain why those creatures aren't here."

As one, they turned to stare at the river crawling along by their feet.

"Cocytus," Chryse murmured. "The river of lamentation, which carries the sorrows of the mortal world."

They all knew the story. Gaia, goddess of the Earth, had made the Cocytus—weeping a single, bloody teardrop for every grief that tore at the hearts of her human children. From what Deina had seen, there was enough grief in Iolkos alone that someone might cry a river of tears at the injustice of it all. She was surprised the smoothly flowing crimson wasn't a raging torrent.

"Let's get on with it." Aster stretched and cracked his

knuckles. "I'm not afraid of a bit of blood." He pulled off his boots and stepped into the river.

Violent screams erupted from the Cocytus, echoing around the cavern and sending Deina reeling backward, gasping, her lower arms clamped over her ears. Through half-shut eyes, she identified the source of the shrieking: heads, formed from the blood of the river itself, featureless apart from a mouth, rising out of the stinking liquid on twisting necks for just enough time to emit a piercing wail before dissolving back into the murk. Over and over, more of them than she could possibly count, filling the river from bank to bank. Chryse was curled into a ball next to her. Argys was thrashing around nearby. She couldn't see Theron or Dendris or Drex, and Aster—

Aster was kneeling in the bloody water, clutching his head, shaking.

Deina forced herself to her feet and staggered to where Aster was crouched. Although she could hardly believe it was possible, the shrieking was even louder here.

"Aster!"

He couldn't hear her. She couldn't even hear herself. Every sense was consumed by the terrible, shattering screams. The force of them beat against her, wave after wave of overpowering, agonizing noise. But even though it meant uncovering her ears, she had to get him out of the river.

Bracing herself, she snatched at the straps of the harness that held Aster's spears against his body and dragged him back onto the bank. They fell, tangled together.

The screams cut off. The heads collapsed back into the river with a splash. Apart from the distant roar of Phlegethon, muffled groans from Aster, and her own rapid breathing, the cavern was quiet again. She pushed herself up onto her elbows—the others were all nearby, sitting with their heads in their hands or struggling to their feet—and pulled her legs free from Aster's bulk. The movement seemed to wake him, and he sat up.

"What . . ." He shook his head and groaned again. "What happened?"

"When you touched the water—blood—whatever it is, the screaming started. I reasoned that pulling you out might make it stop."

"The noise would have torn me apart. I could feel it beginning, but I couldn't move. I couldn't do anything but wait for death." He turned his head to look at her. "You saved me."

"I guessed right. I often do." Deina fixed him with a stare, challenging him. "Stealing and sprinting aren't my only skills."

For the first time, as far as she could remember, Aster smiled at her.

"Evidently." He nodded. "You have my gratitude."

"Unfortunately," Theron said loudly, "saving Aster doesn't get us any closer to our goal." He walked past her to the edge of the bank. "The boats aren't that far. But to reach one of them, untie it, and pull or row it back here, all with that gods-awful shrieking going on—we'll all end up dead."

Deina chewed her bottom lip. The cacophony was worse closer to the river, judging by her own experience and Aster's description of what he felt. If they could just find a way to protect one person, to stop up their ears somehow so they could wade through the blood . . .

Sliding her bag off her shoulders, she began searching for

the two vials that Anteïs had given her that last morning in Iolkos: a healing salve and a tincture to stop the monthly bleed. She couldn't think where in her cycle she was. It was hard to calculate in a place without day and night—without any time, if they'd understood the frozen torch flames correctly. Both vials were sealed with thick wax stoppers. Taking the smaller of her knives, she carefully pared as much wax as she could from each of them without breaking the seals, catching the shavings in the palm of her hand. Even down here they could feel the fierce heat of Phlegethon, so it didn't take long to mold the wax into two soft lumps. The others were watching her. Deina went to push the lumps into her own ears—but hesitated.

They might get only one attempt at this, and Aster was the strongest.

"Can we trust you, Aster?"

"Of course." He nodded. "There's no honor in abandoning you to a slow death. If I wished to be rid of you, I'd simply challenge you to combat and kill you. Besides, I owe you a life debt now."

Theron muttered something beneath his breath. Deina ignored him.

As the others got ready—getting as far as possible from the river and wrapping their fur-lined cloaks around their heads—Deina cut some more fabric from the jagged hem of her tunic. She beckoned Aster nearer.

"If you're lying to me, if you do abandon us and we die, I *will* find a way of coming back to haunt you. If you abandon us and we don't die, I'll hunt you down and kill you instead. Either way, you won't enjoy it."

Another small smile. "I don't expect I would. I'll be as quick as I can." He pushed the fabric into his ears, and Deina sealed them shut with the wax. As Aster walked toward the river, she hurried to protect herself from the onslaught, wrapping her cloak around her head and stuffing as much of it as possible into her ears. Next to her, Chryse had her eyes shut tight. But Deina couldn't drag her gaze away from Aster's form. He was bouncing up and down on his tiptoes at the edge of the river. No hesitancy this time; he crouched as if at the start of a sprint. Straightened his back leg. Ran.

13

The screams were endless. Deina couldn't keep her eyes open. Despite the added protection of the cloak, the shrieks began to penetrate deeper and deeper into her body, driving through skin, muscle, and bone, piercing her as sharply as any spear. They skewered her brain, fragmenting thought and memory, until she was no longer capable of any response—couldn't even wish for it to be over, or wonder whether she would survive. All she could do was clutch her head and endure.

The screams were endless—until, suddenly, they weren't.

Deina let the cloak fall away from her head. Aster was at the riverbank, on his hands and knees, vomiting. The boat lay next to him, pulled up onto the dry ground.

He'd done it.

Up close, the boat was neither as sturdy nor as large as Deina would have liked. It was flat-bottomed with shallow sides, and some of the wood around the rim had rotted away. But there was at least a pair of oars and something that Drex said was a steering paddle in the bottom. With everyone in, Aster and Theron used the oars to push the boat into the river without any of them touching the surface of the stinking liquid. The current was slow. They drifted on it as Theron and Aster, working from their observations while on Orpheus's ship and the little that Drex could add from his childhood memories, got to grips with rowing. The strength expected and rewarded by the House meant that they were soon pushing the boat along as fast as possible. Deina took charge of the steering paddle, holding it steady to keep to the middle of the channel where the river was deepest, hoping she'd be able to use it correctly to guide them to shore. The other four sat in silence, Dendris and Chryse looking out from the prow, Drex in the middle of the boat with Argys hunched next to him, his arms wrapped around his legs, looking as if he was too nervous to move; with seven of them in it, the boat was very low in the water. The glow of the firefall gradually faded, but as they emerged from the cavern, the light grew. Soon, they were back beneath the same clouded gray sky that had been above them before they entered the cavern, a pearlescent strip bordered by featureless stone walls on either side.

On and on the river flowed, between the smooth rock walls toward a hazy horizon. It was easier to breathe here; the sharp, metallic tang of the blood had dissipated, softened by open space and the faint sweetness of mint. Not that Deina could see any plants, or any hint of green; the landscape was so unvarying it was hard to judge what progress they were making. No sign of any other Severers, either, but she was sure Orpheus must have gathered teams of volunteers from more cities than just

Mycenae and Iolkos. The worst thing was that if someone else had already claimed the queen's ghost, the Iolkosans would never know. They'd just wander down here until death found them. It wasn't how Deina had imagined her story ending.

"It's unfortunate Aristaeus won't allow us to talk about what we're doing. Otherwise, someone might write the tale of this adventure one day," Drex murmured. "The story of Orpheus and the quest to retrieve his queen from the Underworld."

"What do you mean 'write'?" Theron asked, panting, all his effort focused on driving his oar through the river. "Stories are composed and then they're sung. That's what keeps them alive. That's what bards are for. Writing is just for—for making lists. For clerks. It'll never be used for art."

Drex, the set of his jaw surprisingly stubborn, didn't reply.

A written-down story? It would be more interesting to learn to read using something like that than the House records and inventories Drex had found for her to practice with. Deina remembered the stolen knife, its blade set with silver letters.

"Drex, look in my bag; there's a dagger wrapped up in my veil. Can you read the inscription on it?"

Carefully, Drex fished the swaddled dagger out of the bag. When he unwrapped it, he wasn't the only one who exclaimed.

"Where did you get that?" Chryse asked. "It's beautiful."

Theron glanced over his shoulder at the dagger.

"It's Orpheus's. Stolen." He glared at Deina.

"Stealing is dishonorable," Aster rumbled. "Especially stealing from a king."

"Orpheus steals from entire cities and calls it tribute. You know he does," Deina replied. "What does it say, Drex?"

While Argys commented on how he wished he could read, Drex squinted at the dagger, turning it back and forth to examine both sides of the blade.

"It says, *I am death and I am light, taking life and giving sight.*" As the words died on his lips, a steady white light shone out from the blade. Drex gasped, fumbled the object, and dropped it. The light went out immediately. "What in Hades's name was that?"

Theron and Aster both stopped rowing. Ignoring their stares, Deina reached between them and retrieved the dagger—torch—whatever it was. No light.

"Strange." She repeated the words Drex had said, and the light blazed out again. "Well . . . we don't have to worry about torches anymore."

"But what else does it do?" Dendris asked. "You must have seen Aristaeus's scorpions and his Iron Guards—what if he made it? It could be dangerous."

"She's right," said Chryse. "You should throw it in the river."

"No." Deina passed the dagger to Drex. "Put it away." The dagger looked even more valuable than she remembered. If they found the queen—if they were able to escape the Underworld—she might still need some insurance: something to offer the House to reduce her indenture. Her fingers drifted to her throat and the scars left by the torc. They knew Orpheus had already lied to them. His promises of freedom and gold might prove to be less reliable than she hoped.

Something thumped against the bottom of the boat.

"What was that?" Argys exclaimed.

Deina peered into the murky depths. "I can't see anything.

Must have been a boulder." She tried to feel lucky that the unseen obstacle hadn't torn a hole in their frail craft, but the growing unease in the pit of her stomach crowded out every other sensation. There was no talking now. Only the rhythmic swish of the oars disturbed the watchful silence. Onward and onward along the never-ending, unbending river, and maybe just a hint in the distance of a shift in the landscape . . .

Chryse, in the prow, knelt up and raised a trembling arm, pointing back the way they had come.

"Look . . ."

Unwillingly, Deina turned just in time to see two jagged spires of wood breaching the surface of the river, one behind the other. Higher and higher they rose, followed by a fretwork of stained and slime-covered wooden beams that extended in front of and behind the spires, with slender poles extending to either side, almost like the legs of a beetle—

She blinked, and the image resolved itself into something recognizable. Masts, not spires. Oars, not poles. The thing behind them was the rotting carcass of a ship.

And it was crewed. Blood hunters clung to the remnants of the prow, corrupted skulls grinning down at her, spears clutched in bony hands. The ship's oars, controlled by some invisible force, began to dip in and out of the river.

"Row!" Even as Deina yelled the word, Aster and Theron were scrambling to find their rhythm, to drive the fragile boat forward. The other four crouched down in the prow, hanging on, shielding their faces from the bloody spray flung up by the oars. Their increased speed and the ripple of waves from the pursuing ship almost twisted the steering paddle from Deina's hands; as she flung her body across it, fighting against the drag of the river, she risked a backward glance.

The skeletal ship was gaining on them. The iron-tipped ram at its bow, red with rust or blood or both, was only a boat's length away; it would smash through their vessel like a hammer through honeycomb. One of the blood hunters, tattered lumps of mottled flesh still clinging to its limbs, shrieked and brandished a corroded sword before skittering spiderlike down the prow of the ship. It hung there for a moment, crouched down, and Deina realized it was about to leap.

"Faster!" She drew one of her knives as she screamed at Theron and Aster, twisted, and slashed desperately at the creature as it launched itself forward and caught hold of the steering oar, almost dragging Deina out of the boat. "No!" Raking her knife backhanded through the blood hunter's ribs, they were for an instant face-to-face. Deina gasped. There was something on the monster's forehead. Some faded brand that looked almost like a sigil. Her gaze flicked lower. An eroded circle of metal clung to its neck.

No. It isn't possible.

Deina hacked at the bony arms that were still gripping her, channeling all her hate, all her despair into destroying this—this *thing* that seemed to be mocking what she was, because it couldn't be true, it couldn't be.

The blood hunter fell apart, and Deina tumbled backward into the boat. The vessel bucked and twisted until she grabbed for the steering oar. There were more blood hunters swarming down the prow of the skeleton ship. Theron and Aster were sweating from the effort of thrusting the boat forward, yet

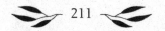

they were only just staying ahead of the ship's ram. They had to get off the river.

The stone cliffs ended abruptly. To the left was a dense forest of twisted pines. Deina decided to steer the boat to the right, toward what looked like a green plain, with a bank of dark clouds in the distance.

"Ugh—" The boat lurched and something yanked her backward. Another blood hunter had grabbed the end of the steering oar. "No, damn you!"

The rim of the boat burst into life. Tendrils shot up from the rotten wood, whiplike branches that thrashed wildly, sweeping the nearest blood hunters into the river. Someone was chanting in a language Deina didn't understand; she looked over her shoulder to see Dendris on her knees, arms outstretched, eyes closed as she shouted the strange-sounding syllables. Aster and Theron were both gasping for breath, but the shore was drawing closer.

"We're nearly there. Keep going!" The blood hunters' ship was dropping behind—the river was growing too shallow for it—though they were still within the reach of the creatures' weapons; a spear thudded into the stern only a palm's width from Deina's arm. Yet the shore was near enough now that she could see a gap in the rocks, a place where the boat could be beached, if its timbers would only hold together long enough. She pulled on the steering oar, swinging the frail vessel farther away from the main channel of the river. "We're going to make it!"

Too late, she saw the blood hunter alongside the boat, clinging on to one of the long, sinuous branches Dendris had somehow summoned into existence. More rotting corpse than skeleton, it gave her a worm-eaten grin as it pulled itself up and reached toward Theron. Horror pinned her in place for a heartbeat—Theron's yelp of terror jolted her free. The monstrous thing couldn't have him. Wrenching loose the spear that was still stuck in the stern, she drove it into the creature's chest. The force of the blow knocked it farther into the river. As it scrabbled to keep its grip, it seized hold of Argys, who was bracing himself on the edge of the boat, and pulled the Mycenaean into the river.

"No!" Dendris's cry was cut off, overwhelmed by the cacophony of shrieking as the bloody, wailing heads erupted once more from the river. Deina collapsed into the stern of the boat, cradling her head in her hands, capable only of wishing for the noise and the agony to stop. It did—but someone was still screaming. Pulling herself onto her knees, Deina saw that the blood hunters had dragged Argys onto their ship. They were biting and clawing at him, tearing his flesh in bloody chunks from his body. Unable to look away, she watched them eat his eyes, rip open his abdomen, and pull out his intestines as he squealed and writhed in agony.

"Help him," Dendris begged, sobbing, "please . . ."

"Deina—the steering oar. Drex, Aster, start rowing." Theron's tense voice cut through the horror. Deina dragged the steering oar back into the right position, and the boat resumed its course toward the shore. Theron quickly fitted an arrow to his bowstring. The bow sung, and the arrow soared toward Argys.

The screaming stopped, and Argys's body went limp. Dendris

clapped both hands over her mouth as the blood hunters sent up a furious wail.

The bottom of the boat scraped onto sand. Deina stumbled after the others onto solid ground and drew her blades, forcing herself to stay on her feet, to be ready for another attack. But the blood hunters had stopped. They were still screaming in defiance and shaking their weapons, some on the ship, some in the river a couple of strides beyond the tip of the ram—but it looked as if they couldn't come any farther. Something was holding them back.

The skeletal ship began to sink back into the river. As if bound to it by invisible chains, the blood hunters were dragged beneath the surface.

Dendris, stunned and silent, was clutching Argys's bag. Chryse led her away. Slowly, the others followed, turning from the river and trudging up onto the ridge of higher land that lay beyond the shore, until only Deina was left, still staring at the crimson tide of Cocytus. She slumped onto the sand.

She knew—she thought she knew—why the blood hunters hadn't been able to pursue them. The one she'd seen up close, with the mark on its forehead and the circle of metal around its neck—it was, or had been, one of the Theodesmioi. A Sea Singer, she guessed, bearing the sigil of Poseidon, wearing the same type of spell-cast torc that had for so many years sat heavy and unyielding around her own neck. And if one was a Sea Singer, why not all? A ship full of dead Theodesmioi, still bound in death to the carcass of the vessel that had been their prison in life.

She just didn't know how or why. Deina sighed, rubbing

away some of the dried spray that was stinging her skin. She would have liked to have asked Nat what he knew about the blood hunters. Right now, she would have welcomed his smile and his seemingly unflappable self-confidence, even though she knew he could turn out to be as dangerous as the things from which they'd just fled. More, perhaps. His sapphire eyes, strong jaw, and muscled arms might be no more than a mask, concealing whatever inhumanity lay beneath . . .

"Deina."

She glanced up. But the figure silhouetted against the pearl-gray sky was Theron, not Nat. He settled on the sand next to her. Sat in silence with her, for a little while.

"Why did you stay behind down here?"

"I wanted a moment to think. To be alone."

"It's too dangerous. None of us should be alone here—look at what happened to Argys." He swore and dropped his head into his hands for a moment. "May the gods have mercy on him."

Deina huffed. She doubted the gods knew the meaning of mercy.

"Argys wasn't alone. There were six of us there when he got pulled into the river, and we still couldn't save him." Theron was frowning at her, peering at her eyes. "What?"

"Nothing. Trick of the light. My point is, you shouldn't wander off. I was worried." He smiled a little and took her hand in his. The way his fingers interlaced with hers . . . She didn't want to remember how that had felt. He had no right to try to make her. Deina pulled her arm free.

"Your worry is your problem. And you don't get to tell me what to do. You're not an elder, Theron, and you're not in charge."

His smile faded as his gaze hardened. "I was going to thank you for steering the boat and for driving that monstrous thing away from me. I thought you might thank me for rowing. But I suppose that would require you to have some feeling of fellowship. Or any kind of feeling at all." He pushed himself back to his feet. "Your heart is as cold and withered as one of those creatures."

Deina scrambled upright to face him. "Is that so? Then I wonder what withered it?"

Theron rocked back on his heels, eyes wide, before erupting into a shout of mocking laughter.

"And that's why I'm going to win. Because I'm focused on the present, and you're still trapped in the past." His handsome face twisted into a sneer. "Aster's found the path. The others are ready to move on. I honestly don't care, but if you do want to join us, you'd better hurry." He turned on his heel and strode away.

Deina glared at his retreating back. One definite benefit of freedom would be never having to see Theron ever again.

When she reached the top of the bank, Deina found the others were gathered not far off. She took her cloak out of her bag—the air here was cool and damp—slung the bag across her shoulder, and went to join them.

Dendris, standing slightly apart from the Severers from Iolkos and gripping her ax as if her life depended on it, swung around to face her. "You mustn't tell, if we ever get out of here. You mustn't tell the Order. Promise."

"I don't understand . . ."

"Dendris believes she has dryad blood, from somewhere,"

Drex explained. "But no one from her House in Mycenae knows that she has"—he shrugged one shoulder—"magic."

"It's not magic," Dendris insisted. "It's a skill." She took a deep breath. "I don't know where it comes from. Don't have the right words, either. The House took them from me, like everything else. I remembered a little, though. Made up the rest. I could feel the power, you see." She tapped her chest. "I had to find a way to give it a voice."

"The power to do what?" Deina asked.

"To talk to trees. With persuasion, I can bend them to my will. Sometimes, it even works with things that merely remember being trees. Not often."

"Well, I'm glad it worked on the boat." Glancing briefly at Theron, Deina inclined her head to Dendris. "Thank you. And I promise not to say anything to your elders. If we survive."

Dendris nodded as a spasm of grief contorted her features. "Argys was kind. He didn't deserve to die like that."

"No one does," replied Aster; he sounded, to Deina, unusually thoughtful. "Let's get away from this place."

Two lines of boundary stones marked out the path, running roughly parallel into the distance across what Deina had taken to be a field. It became apparent, as soon as Aster took the first step, that it was in fact something altogether less substantial. His foot sank in up to the ankle. They'd reached the Stygian Marsh.

Crossing the marsh was slow work. Though squelchy, the ground was mostly firm enough to walk on. But every so often it would give way, tipping them onto hands and knees into the foul-smelling mud. The landscape was littered with broken

arches and fallen columns and the remnants of stone walls. There were even mosaic tiles, still bright, jumbled into formless splashes of color. Nothing could have been built here, on such precarious foundations; Deina wondered if these were the ruined shells of temples or palaces that had once existed in the mortal realm but were now not even memories.

The dark bank of clouds she'd seen from the boat still lay in the distance, though something golden seemed to flicker in front of it. Deina shivered. When she'd been an initiate, still sleeping in the nursery dormitory, one of the apprentices had terrified her and the others with a tale of ghostly creatures that lived in marshes, taking the form of glowing lights to lure unwary travelers to their deaths. Marsh vapor, Anteïs had said. Just a story. But maybe, down here, the story was true.

A whisper, just by her ear. Deina whipped around, but Drex, Chryse, and Dendris were all some way behind her, focusing on the marsh and their own steps. Aster and Theron were ahead. She kept walking.

There it was again. As if she were catching the echo of something said in another room.

Theron turned back to her. "Are you playing games?"

"No."

"But you just said something—"

"No! It wasn't me. I heard something, too, just now. Like someone was speaking to me, but I couldn't quite catch what they were saying . . ."

"Yes. Someone mumbling in my ear." He waved his hand as if he were batting a fly away from his head. "Ugh. Where's it coming from?"

There seemed to be more than one voice now. Louder, but still too indistinct for Deina to distinguish any words. She turned slowly, looking for the source.

The others caught up.

"Can you hear them?" Chryse asked, fearful. "They're calling for our help because they're—they're lost. Unburied. Unremembered."

Dendris flinched. None of the dead Mycenaeans had received burial.

"You can understand them, Chryse?" Deina asked.

A flicker of confusion crossed Chryse's face.

"Can't you? They are pleading with us."

"I can hear voices. I can't make out what they're saying." Deina drew one of her knives. There was no visible target, but she felt better with it in her hand. "Let's keep going."

They walked closer together now, hurrying as fast as they could across the uneven terrain. But with every step, the voices—still unintelligible to everyone but Chryse—grew in number and volume. The air thickened, until Deina, squinting into the clouds that seemed to cling to the edges of the path, almost thought she could make out ghostly bodies with indistinct features, packed together like the seeds inside a pomegranate. Chryse had her head down and her shoulders hunched, flinching away from the writhing mass of spectral forms. Deina had to focus on the ground ahead, trying to watch her friend's steps as well as her own.

"Stop!" Aster, who had come to a halt just ahead, threw his arms out and pushed her and Chryse back into the shelter of a nearby ruin. "I think we've found the tree with the golden bough. And more Severers." He jerked his head toward Deina. "She was right."

Deina peeked from behind the ruin. In another rapid and disorienting shift of perspective, the dark bank of clouds was now not far off. Directly in front of it was a magnificent oak tree, its limbs clothed in the russet of autumn—apart from a single branch, which seemed to be made of gold.

Standing beneath it, directly in their path, obviously armed and very much alive, was a large group of Severers. Nine of them, as far as Deina could see. They seemed to be having some sort of argument among themselves and were oblivious to the others' presence. So far.

"We're outnumbered," she murmured. As Aster opened his mouth, she forestalled him. "And no, we can't get into a battle with them; it's obvious from what happened to us and to the Mycenaeans that the . . . that those creatures will find us as soon as we spill any blood."

Deina could sense the gloom settling over her companions like ash after a forest fire, but no one disputed her words.

"What if we tell them the truth?" Dendris asked. "Explain that they've been tricked like the rest of us, that this is a competition, not just a quest. We could work together, find the queen, and leave together."

"But there are so many of them," Aster objected. "What if they don't believe us? What if they haven't met those creatures yet, and attack us? What if they don't want to work together? Even if they don't decide to take us out of the competition, if they already have the golden leaves, they can cross the Styx and leave us behind. There was nothing in the stories Neidius told us about how long we'd have to wait for the leaves to regrow."

An uncomfortable silence fell, until Drex cleared his throat.

"I—I have an idea. If they'd found the queen, they would have left already. We can't fight them, so perhaps—perhaps we should try to steal whatever token Orpheus gave them to bind the queen's soul. And if they've already taken the golden leaves to cross the Styx, we could steal those, too. It's cruel, because they'll never be able to leave the Underworld without the token, but . . ." He trailed off.

"You're right, Drex." Chryse took his hand. "You must make sure you—we—have a way out of here. It's them or us. And perhaps they don't deserve to win."

Deina glanced at Theron. He was nodding, but there was unease in his eyes. She felt the same. Competition back at the House—winning fights and races and trying to gain the most lucrative jobs—had been necessary, and even enjoyable. Coolly plotting a way to leave other Severers to die in the Underworld was different. But if they followed Dendris's suggestion, they might all end up dead. Deina realized everyone was looking at her.

"What?"

"Stealing . . ." Theron raised an eyebrow. "That's your area of expertise, isn't it?"

Deina spun away and began pacing up and down a little in the shadow of the ruin. Theron's tone irritated her, but he was right. "Well . . . it's not a straightforward theft. We'll need to trick them. But I think . . ." She paused, her mind working rapidly. "I think I know how."

14

Theron led their procession. As they moved briskly toward the oak tree, the ghosts of the unburied thinned and disappeared, unwilling or unable to come closer. Theron began singing a hymn to Hades; as Deina hoped, their competitors stopped arguing and stared rather than attacked. It gave her time to assess them. Two women, seven men—three of whom were at least as large and muscled as Aster. Three of them had pinned their cloaks with brooches marked with the image of a bull; they were from the House of Hades in Knossos, Crete. The necks of all of them bore the marks left by the torcs they'd had to wear.

As Deina's hand went to her own neck, Dendris murmured, "I still don't think it's right. We should be fighting the gods and the rulers who put us here, not each other."

Deina didn't answer; this wasn't the time for hesitation. As Theron's last note rang out, she stepped forward.

"Honored volunteers, we are so glad to have found you. His

Majesty sent us in pursuit of you not long after you entered the Underworld, but we feared we would be too late to reach you before you crossed the Styx."

One of the men, bull-necked and freckled, lumbered toward them, his eyes narrowed and a hand on the hilt of his knife.

"Orpheus sent you? For what purpose?"

"His Majesty received word from Delphi. The Oracle issued a prophecy concerning your quest. Behold, one of the acolytes of the Oracle." She made a low bow to Chryse. Standing there, imperious and aloof, her friend looked exactly like someone who might be privileged to hear the pronouncements of a god. Deina pointed next to Dendris. "And the acolyte's honored assistant, bearing a gift that His Majesty wishes you to offer to Lord Hades."

As instructed by Deina, Dendris held out both hands, displaying the jewel-studded gold chain Deina had stolen from Orpheus's ship. Most of the Cretans were staring, open-mouthed. But a couple, including the bull-necked man, looked dubious.

"The king told us to return as soon as we had found Queen Eurydice. He said nothing about us seeking to approach the god."

Drex stepped forward as Theron and Aster came to stand protectively on either side of Chryse.

"I am an elder of the Order of Hades. His Majesty's orders have changed, now that he has received instruction from the Oracle. The gift *is* to be presented to Hades. You would"—Drex glanced sideways at Deina and stood a little taller—"you would not do well to dispute me."

The man's eyes widened and he reached out to grasp the chain.

Drex held up a hand to stop him. "But first, we have been instructed by His Majesty to determine which of you is the chosen one."

"The chosen one?" the shorter of the two women asked.

"The Oracle vouchsafed that the one who presented the gift would be the recipient of a great honor. Therefore, we have been instructed to ascertain who among you is the least unworthy."

Deina was impressed. Drex was doing a good impression of a particularly pompous elder.

"Time is of the essence," Drex continued. "I see you already have the leaves you need to cross the Styx." The gleaming bough of the oak tree had been stripped bare. "I trust the token His Majesty gave you to bind the queen's ghost is also still secure?"

"The comb? Of course. Everything is safe." The answer came from the largest of the men, a flame-haired brute who looked as if he could crush Aster like a grape. He patted the strap of the bag hanging on his back.

Which told Deina exactly what she needed to know.

"So, what about this test?" the redhead continued. "And what's the reward?" He put his hands on his hips and scowled at his teammates. "Seems pretty obvious which one of us it should be."

Aster passed Drex the crystalline dagger. Drex murmured the words inscribed on the blade, and bright white light spilled across the dreary landscape, drawing gasps from the Cretans and making the golden bough blaze.

Drex gestured to the dagger. "This device was created by

Lord Aristaeus." The use of his name had the effect that Deina anticipated. All of the Cretans glanced about as if Aristaeus might suddenly appear out of thin air. "It will show us the two most worthy, who will then compete for the honor of bearing the gift. Line up and keep your eyes on me."

His tone commanded obedience, and the Cretans obeyed. As Drex, flanked by Chryse and Dendris, held the dagger in front of the woman who was first in line, Deina, Theron, and Aster went to stand close behind her. Theron and Aster each gripped one of the woman's shoulders. Theron covered her eyes with his free hand and began to loudly sing some nonsense words he'd made up as Aster tapped out the rhythm in the middle of her back with his other hand. Deina stood between them, so close behind the woman they were almost touching, chanting the word "Hades" over and over. A worry crept into her mind that their made-up ceremony was too outrageous to be convincing. But there was no time to change it.

They moved down the line together, performing the same actions. Deina had one of Drex's serpent fangs concealed in her palm. When they finally reached the red-haired man, she furtively pressed the tip against the side of his bag; the fang sliced through the leather as easily as her ceremonial knife had sliced through the wrists of the man condemned to the Punishment Rite. She nodded to the others. Theron sang even louder, and Aster tapped his back even harder as Deina rifled delicately through the bag. Within moments, her fingers found the shapes she was looking for. She extricated the leaves and the comb and slid them inside the pouch at her waist. Time for the decoy; she dropped one of the amethysts she'd stolen on the grass. She left the second amethyst in the grass behind the second largest of the men.

The "ritual" was over. Drex returned the dagger to Deina, and the light went out.

"Well?" demanded the redhead. "Nothing happened."

"On the contrary." Drex lifted his chin. "Two of you have been selected. Observe." He pointed dramatically to the two amethysts, glowing in the muddy grass. "Now, a competition. The first of you to hurl his stone into the Cocytus and return here will bear the gift to Hades. Are you ready?"

The two men looked at each other, dropped their bags, grabbed the polished stones, and started running.

Dendris put her hand on Chryse's forehead. The signal for the final part of the plan.

"Elder, I believe the acolyte is with prophecy . . ."

On cue, Chryse shrieked.

"Charon! I have a message for Charon . . ." She slumped dramatically into Aster's arms.

Drex took the stolen chain from Dendris and gave it to one of the women. "You must give this to whoever wins the race, do you understand? We must take the acolyte to deliver her message before we return to the mortal world."

The woman stared at the gold and gemstones that filled her hands, but didn't answer. The others were watching the figures of their teammates in the distance.

The Iolkosans, with Dendris in tow, hurried along the path—less muddy now—toward the bank of clouds. As they left the vicinity of the tree, the noise of the ghosts grew louder again, even louder than before. In Aster's arms, Chryse moaned and closed her eyes. Deina couldn't tell whether she was still acting or not, and sped up. It would take those two hulks long enough to race across the marsh, but the ruse would be quickly uncovered if someone else checked the redhead's bag in the meantime.

The dark clouds solidified into a tall fence of black tree trunks that ran at right angles across the path, blocking their way. In the middle of the fence was a gate of woven branches. Theron reached the gate first, but as hard as he tugged, it didn't move.

"The leaves?" he shouted, struggling to be heard over the inarticulate wailing of the ghosts.

Deina drew six of the delicate slivers of gold from her pouch and handed them out. They were beautiful; she held hers between finger and thumb and marveled at how the rib and veins were formed of a paler gold that contrasted with the lobed leaf blade.

Drex was peering at the gate, running his hands over its surface. Exclaiming, he slid his leaf into an almost invisible slit near the center of the gate and—

Disappeared.

"Drex?" Aster shouted, prodding the ground with his foot and then staring up at the sky. "Drex!"

Someone else was shouting. Deina looked back and saw the Cretans running toward them. The tall, muscular one who hadn't been sent off across the marsh outpaced the others and was almost upon them. Chryse pushed her leaf through the gate, vanishing instantly. Dendris quickly followed her.

"You next—"

Theron's hand was on her back, urging her forward. But

as she raised her arm to slip her leaf through the gap, the Cretan plowed into them, sending Theron flying and grabbing her wrist.

"Give me that, you—"

Aster brought his fist around and smacked it into the Cretan's jaw.

"Go!"

Deina nodded, slipped the leaf through the gap in the gate, and—

Quiet. Almost. Just the gentle wash of flowing water from the distance, and Chryse breathing shakily. She was leaning against Drex, and he had his arm around her. Dendris was kneeling nearby, running her fingers across the hunks of sea-smoothed driftwood that edged the path, things that might once have been the planks or masts of ships. Deina turned to look for the fence and the gate—but they weren't there. Instead, cracked paving stones beneath her feet, partly overgrown by silver-green moss, led away toward a sweep of trees, almost bare of leaves, that were silhouetted against a starless, dark gray sky. Beyond the path lay a flat expanse of black sand stretching into the distance. When she straightened up, Theron popped into existence, quickly followed by Aster, clutching his right hand and flexing his fingers. The beginning of what would probably be a huge bruise shadowed his cheekbone.

"You're hurt. I've got some salve in my bag—"

"Save it for when we really need it; this is nothing. Trust me, my opponent looks much worse."

Deina smiled at him. "Thank you."

Aster nodded stiffly. "You saved me from the wailing river. Repaying the favor was the honorable thing to do. And the deceit was clever—" The way Aster's eyes bulged, Deina was certain he was about to say *for a woman*, or *for a thief*. Whichever it was, he thought better of it, and just added, "Well done." His stomach growled. "We've not eaten since before we found the firefall. I think we should stop for a little while."

Without waiting for Deina to agree, Aster sat down, fished a flatbread from his provisions, and began tearing into it, giving little moans of enjoyment that a stale piece of bakery really didn't deserve.

"I'll give you some privacy," Deina murmured, half to herself. She wandered farther along the path, nearer to the sound of running water. Theron followed her.

"It was clever, your plan. Still, stealing all those things while we were on the ship, the gold chain and the amethysts as well as the dagger—did you not think about the danger you were putting us all in?"

"If I hadn't taken the risk, we wouldn't be here." It was too bad she'd had to give up the loose stones as well as the chain. The amethysts would have been easy to sell, and quite valuable. Her mind wandered back to her stash of stolen treasure at the House, and the potential cost of passage on a boat that might carry them away from Iolkos. She didn't immediately realize that Theron was holding something between his finger and thumb.

A gold ring. The one that had belonged to Leida. The one he'd taken from her room.

"I thought you'd traded it."

"I decided not to take the deal."

Deina held out her hand. But instead of dropping the ring into her palm, as she expected, Theron grasped her hand gently and slipped the ring onto one of her fingers.

"It fits." He jiggled the ring from side to side a little. "Almost." The smile he gave her—warm and slightly crooked, somehow full of the promise of excitement and adventure—was exactly the same smile that had drawn her to him all those years ago, when they were still children. Yet how could it be the same, when so much else had changed? Deina moved the ring to her forefinger.

"Thanks." She turned away, just slowly enough to catch the sudden hurt in Theron's eyes; he was expecting something more. Something in return.

Well, he could go on expecting. He wasn't the only one who knew how to wound.

No one apart from Aster seemed hungry. No one was that tired, either, despite the lack of rest and the endless walking, not to mention the running, fighting, and general terror. There was no night here; had they been traveling for one endless day or many? Either way, Deina reckoned she and the others should have been exhausted, but she wasn't, and even the thirst that had plagued her in the valley of the firefall had evaporated. Perhaps it was anxiety about the quest, or guilt about what they'd done to the Cretans. Or perhaps it was a sign that their bodies were becoming frozen in time, just like the flames of Aster's torch by the bank of Oceanus. The possibility worried her. Judging by the lack of conversation, it worried all of them.

Chryse was the first to get to her feet.

"We should go. I've had enough of this place. Of ghosts, and monsters"—she wrinkled her nose at the bespattered skin of her arms—"and dirt. I want to go back to the mortal world. To sunlight and baths and clean clothes and servants and jewels and feather-stuffed mattresses . . ."

Deina tugged on an earlobe, frowning. "You want to go back to the House?" Jewels and feather-stuffed mattresses weren't exactly a feature of their lives there.

"Not the House. I meant—" Chryse broke off. Blushed and shrugged. "I mean, I want to get out of here and be free. That's what you want, too, isn't it? Come on, Drex."

Chryse hurried ahead. Deina trailed behind her, doubtful, wondering about the nature of freedom. What it looked like to her was a ship and an open horizon. But what did Chryse see when she tried to dream of a better future?

The landscape around them shifted in one of those sudden changes of perspective that she was almost beginning to expect. The river, which had been in the distance, was now close at hand. The dull light revealed a wide ribbon of murky water, the broadest they'd yet encountered, flowing rapidly past the paving stones that ran right up to the river's edge. The surface was contorted into myriad swirls and eddies, so much so that the river seemed to writhe within its banks. Deina shivered. The temperature had been falling ever since they escaped from Cocytus and began to cross the marsh, but there was ice in the breeze that blew toward them across the Styx. Ice, and something sweet, as if the air were carrying the scent of some flower she didn't recognize. Whatever lay beyond, on the far side of the river, was concealed behind a tall hedge of holly.

Ahead, Drex, Chryse, and Dendris had come to a halt. Deina came to stand beside them. Chryse leaned closer. She lifted an arm, pointing at something up ahead, and murmured, "Charon?"

Deina looked where Chryse had indicated. For a moment, she couldn't see anything other than the river, but then she blinked, and what had been empty space was filled by a man and a large boat.

Not a man—a god. Hades's ferryman, responsible for carrying souls across the Styx. Deina clasped her hands together, half expecting to be struck with trembling awe, to be bowed down to the dust by this, their first physical encounter with the divine. And yet . . . and yet, Charon—if this was him—bore no resemblance to the god of her conjectures. He was long-limbed, tanned—how, Deina wondered, did anyone get a tan in the Underworld?—with deep lines across his forehead and around his eyes and long brown hair tied back in a loose ponytail. There was a circlet of bronze leaves on his head, and his tunic was of fine russet linen. He was leaning against the boat, tossing a coin up and down, and when she caught his eye, he winked at her.

Charon beckoned them nearer. "Hoping to cross the river, are you?"

"Yes, please," Aster answered.

The god chuckled. "Hope you're dead, then."

There was a long moment of silence. Deina looked at the others.

Dead?

"Perhaps," Drex began, scratching his head, "we could swim across. I might be able to teach you."

Before Deina could ask Drex exactly how long it was since he'd last swum anywhere, Charon interrupted.

"You're welcome to try. But it's a lot farther than it looks."

"How far?" Drex asked.

"Oh . . . about as far as life is from death."

Which could mean either very close or utterly distant. Deina folded her arms and began tapping her foot against the paving stone she stood on, trying to get rid of the tension crawling across her skin. Typical of a god to give a useless, deliberately deceitful answer.

"But, most honored ferryman of the Styx, surely, we don't have to be dead?" There was a forced calm to Theron's tone—he was clearly struggling to maintain his civility. "We know the living have been allowed to cross this river. We know the stories of the heroes and the ancient Songs. We made the correct sacrifice and were found worthy to cross Oceanus. We've passed the firefall of Phlegethon and have survived the river of blood. We plucked the leaves of the golden bough, too."

"Ah, but that's just it, isn't it?" Charon threw the coin into the air; it vanished. A cloth appeared in his hand as he turned away and began polishing the boat. "The tree with the golden bough is part of my domain, and I think perhaps that you didn't pluck those leaves so much as obtain them by deception." He glanced at Deina with a quick lift of his eyebrows that sent the blood rushing into her face. "I think perhaps I should send you to the back of the queue." He waved a hand vaguely toward the riverbank, and the empty black sands just beyond the path were suddenly covered by a snaking line of ghostly figures:

men, women, children—hundreds abreast, disappearing into the distance as far as the eye could see.

Deina recoiled. So did the others, gasping or looking away, or muttering a prayer in Aster's case. Only Drex was spared the full horror of the scene before them. The ghosts were silent, yet there was no mistaking the clutching, desperate anticipation that was rolling off them. Those at the front of the queue were leaning forward, arms stretched out toward the boat, fingers grasping, just waiting for the boatman to give the word. It made the hair on Deina's arms stand up. Although the ghosts were translucent and colorless, she could see every detail of those nearest to her. The garments they'd been buried in. The way their hair and the fabric of their clothes stirred in the breeze that came off the river. Even the injuries that had killed a few of them. Some had coins stuck to their mouths, others had coins covering their eyes. There were a few that clutched tablets covered with writing. But the faces of all of them were turned toward the Severers. Deina could almost hear their impotent anger—*Trespassers! Intruders!*—and it scared her.

"Hades tells me to ferry across the shades that have been properly buried, so that's what I do." Charon threw a glance back at the Severers. "I don't see any coins stopping your mouths or weighing down your eyelids. No coin, no crossing." Another glance at Deina. "And don't insult me by offering more stolen goods."

"Isn't this what normally happens when you ferry the living across?" Theron asked.

Charon gave a shout of laughter. "This is the Underworld, Severer." The ferryman leaned nearer. "There is no normal."

"But how else are we to get to the other side?" Theron said through gritted teeth. Deina decided to take over before he lost his temper completely. She stepped forward.

"Divine Charon, there must be something we can offer you."

"Oh, I doubt it." Charon shook his head. "I've been offered wealth, power, entire kingdoms of men." He paused. "Of course, mostly by people trying to escape the Underworld rather than get farther in." Leaning against his boat, with his arms crossed, the ferryman looked her up and down. "I've been expecting you, Soul Severer. The deep waters of the Styx call all things of the Underworld to themselves eventually."

Deina stiffened, suddenly very conscious of the others behind her; she could feel their surprise at Charon's words, their suspicion raking her back. But surely, if being a Soul Severer meant being a "thing of the Underworld," they were all in that category. The ferryman was just toying with them. Trying to keep them from their goal. She lifted her chin, challenging him, hoping she looked more confident than she felt.

"So you know of our quest." She glanced at the waiting ghosts. Perhaps they didn't need to go any farther. "Is the shade of Queen Eurydice here?"

"Eurydice, the poor lamenting queen . . . No. I bore her back to the Plains of Asphodel, not so very long ago. You'll need to look on the other side of the river. If you can get there." He tilted his head, studying her. "It's no concern of mine, though, this quest, or anything that humans choose to do with their brief allotment of time between birth and death. I had no particular interest in what brought Herakles here when he came seeking passage, even though he was what I'd call a proper hero, the genuine article. So I definitely don't care who they are, or what they're doing here." He waved a hand toward the other Severers. "But I will admit to some very slight curiosity about *you*." Behind her, Theron whispered something inaudible to Aster. Charon smiled. "I'd like to see what you're capable of. And what becomes of you."

An echo of Nat's words came back to her, almost as if he were standing beside her, murmuring into her ear: *I want to help you fulfill your potential. Your destiny.* Deina pressed one hand to her stomach as if she could crush out the uncertainty fluttering through her core.

"You're trying to trick us—hoping we turn on each other."

Charon chuckled and went back to polishing the boat. "Maybe. Maybe not."

Deina's jaw clenched. He *was* just playing games—

Was that the answer? Trying to swallow her anger, she edged closer.

"Well, what about a game? If we win, you take us—all of us, alive, just as we are—to the other side of the Styx. And allow us to go on our way."

Charon kept polishing. "I'm a god, Severer. Gods only play games that they're already certain to win. You know that. However"—the cloth became a coin once more, spinning and flashing as it leaped in Charon's palm—"a competition might be fun."

"A competition with you?" Deina wondered what that might look like. How many souls can you pack into a boat? Who can ferry them fastest?

But Charon was shaking his head. "No. A competition for

you." He waved a hand toward the rest of the Severers, still waiting behind her. "A choice first, and then a game."

"What's the choice?"

"You can choose to stay together, and I'll send you all back to where you started this little expedition. You won't be able to open the gate from this side, but you can try your luck against Cerberus a second time. Or you can choose to enter my competition. The first to successfully complete any one of three tasks of my choosing, I'll grant their wish and ferry them across the Styx." He held up one hand as Deina opened her mouth to argue. "Alive, unharmed. But the rest of you, or perhaps all of you, will lose."

"And then what?" Deina asked.

Charon shrugged. "I'm not sure yet. I might keep you here forever. I could do with some assistants." He laughed—the sound made Deina's blood run cold—and held out his hand. "So, Severer, do we have a deal?"

"That's a terrible idea." The comment came from Chryse. Deina had refused Charon's proffered hand—had persuaded the god that she should be allowed to consult, briefly, with the other Severers before entering into a contract that would potentially condemn all of them. Now they were huddled together while Charon surveyed them from a short distance away. "We should obviously stay together. He might be lying—if he sends us back to the start, perhaps we will be able to open the gate and escape. Or . . . or something else might turn up."

Drex was nodding in agreement. But Theron, Aster, and Dendris said nothing. Because, Deina realized, they all thought they might be the one to win. To have a chance, still, of gaining their freedom and Orpheus's gold. She didn't blame them; she felt the same. As the Cretans had proved, there weren't many Severers who could resist the lure of a prize or a competition. Even fewer who would turn down an opportunity to rub another Severer's face in his or her own inferiority.

Dendris, who had drawn out her ax, licked her finger and rubbed a spot of dirt from the ax head. "Nothing else is going to turn up. We don't have a choice, do we?"

"Hold on, though," Theron said. "If Deina or Aster win, they both have a token to bind the queen's ghost: the spindle and the comb taken from the Cretans. But what about the rest of us? There's no point crossing the Styx without one. Perhaps the two of you should give them to Charon before we start. For safekeeping."

As Aster started rumbling about honor, Deina stared down Theron.

"And you think Charon would give them back? If you win, I'll give you the comb. But I'm not giving it to you yet. Why should I? I stole it, and I've already proven you can trust me. I gave up my amethysts and my necklace to get us this far—"

"Interesting use of the word 'my,'" Theron interrupted. "Do we know we can trust you? It was you who suggested to Charon that we should play a game."

Was it Deina's imagination, or were the others edging away from her? She glared at Theron. "So?"

"So now that you've got a token, this could be a way for you to get rid of the rest of us. I haven't forgotten what you said, the night of the banquet. You told me you were going to win."

"And you told me you were going to put an arrow in me."

Theron's eyes shot open, as if she'd slapped him rather than just repeated his own words back to him. "I—"

"Quiet!" Drex snapped. In the shocked silence, he gestured toward the god, adding, "I—I may be wrong, but I don't think this is helping us."

Charon was laughing. And clapping. He strolled toward them.

"Oh, that was amusing. Nothing like watching a group of Severers throw each other to the lions. I take it that you will be participating in my competition?"

The question was directed at Deina. She hesitated, the whisper of an idea sizzling through her mind.

"Would you mind repeating your terms, most gracious shipper of souls, so that my associates might hear it again from your own lips? If you recall, you said you would grant the winner's wish and—"

"Yes, yes," Charon said testily. "The first one to successfully complete any of the three tasks will be the winner. I will grant their wish and ferry them alive and unharmed across the river to the Plains of Asphodel. The losers will stay here with me forever." He stuck out his hand. "And thus I swear upon the River Styx."

The only oath that would bind a god. Deina took his hand to repeat his words; his calloused grip was painfully tight.

"And thus I swear upon the River Styx."

Charon grinned.

"Let the games begin."

For the first test, Charon conducted them farther along the river, to a point where a wide net had been stretched from the nearest bank to the farthest. Behind the net, detritus had spread like scum across the surface of the water: barrels, shoes, broken pots, bits of statues, fragments of paintings, and a hundred more items that Deina couldn't begin to identify. The nearest stretch of bank was almost buried beneath variously sized heaps of similar trash: the ghostly resonances, the god claimed, of things lost or destroyed in the mortal world, surviving in the Underworld because each created thing contained some spark, some faint imprint, of its maker's soul. Charon handed them each what looked like a long-handled, long-tined rake.

"Pull one thing out of the river. Go."

The rakes were heavy and unwieldy. On her first attempt, Deina was almost tugged into the river; for supposedly ghostly objects, the stuff she was reaching for had an unusual amount of weight and resistance. It was as if the half-smashed amphora she'd hooked with her rake was actively opposing her attempt to pluck it from the cold waters of the Styx. A shouted curse from Theron drew her attention; he'd fallen backward, his rake flailing and almost knocking Dendris into the river. Deina turned back to her amphora, only to find it had escaped from her. She tried again, snagging it with the rake, drawing it carefully and slowly toward the shore. When it was close enough, she knelt down, stretching her arm out until she could just grasp the amphora's rim with her fingertips—

"Time's up!" Charon bellowed.

Deina lost her grip. The amphora splashed back into the river.

"So, how did we all do?" The god's voice, as he walked past them, was vibrant with ill-concealed glee. "Oh dear . . . not very well, it seems." He stopped in front of Aster, who was standing over the wooden statue of a veiled woman. "Apart from you."

Aster's grin was so wide it threatened to split his face. "I am honored, mighty god, to be—"

"Oh, but what's this?" Charon nudged the head of the statue

with his foot; it trundled away from the body and dropped back into the river. "I said one thing. You took two."

"But—but it's two parts of the same thing," Aster spluttered, "just broken, so I—"

"I'll have to disqualify you from this task, I'm afraid." The god sighed. "It wouldn't really be fair to the others not to."

Deina understood. The so-called competition was fixed—unwinnable. If only she'd pinned him down, made him specify what the competition would be and how it would be judged. Too late now. She ground her teeth, seething. She wanted to hurl the rake into the river. Actually, she wanted to smash it into Charon's complacently smiling face.

"Second task." The god gestured to the detritus that had been plucked from the river and gathered in ungainly heaps on the bank. "Pick a pile, any pile, and use the sacks next to it to transport the objects in the pile to my house." Charon waved a hand toward a long, low, crooked-roofed cottage that Deina could have sworn hadn't been there a moment ago.

She raised her hand.

"You have a question?" Charon asked.

"Yes. When you say 'to my house,' do you mean into the house, or—"

"No, just up to the wall. You can't see it, but you'll know when you've reached it. It keeps mortals out—the dead, as well as the living." He pulled a face. "I can't be having those queuing shades bothering me while I'm trying to rest. Ready? Go."

There was a scramble for the smallest piles. Deina saw Chryse trip Aster up as she raced Dendris for another of the more reasonably sized heaps. Each set of sacks was a different color. Deina grabbed a sack and began scooping the trash from her heap into it: bits of pottery, fragments of carved wood, broken but brightly colored tesserae from mosaics, rusted iron weapons. When the sack was as full as she could carry, she set off at a sprint. It was hard work; the sand shifted unpredictably beneath her feet, and with every step, the sack slammed into her back, knocking the breath out of her lungs and bruising her skin. But she couldn't slow down. She was nearly at the house, and Theron was just ahead of her—

He grunted and rebounded off something invisible, though Deina thought she could see a slight shimmer in the air, like late summer heat rising from parched earth. Theron had already struggled to his feet and was feeling ahead with his hand. As soon as he dropped his sack, Deina threw hers down next to it and ran back for the next load.

She passed the others—called out encouragement to Chryse—reached her pile, and began filling another sack with more of the same lost and broken items. Then it was back to the house again, stumbling across the sand, her fingers aching as the smooth fabric of the sack threatened to slip from her grasp. The line of sacks marking the boundary was just ahead. Overtaking Drex, she swung the sack off her back.

The movement unbalanced her. Deina tripped and went hurtling forward until she landed face down in the sand, spluttering. She rolled onto her back.

"Are you hurt?" Drex moved toward her. Or attempted to— each direction he tried, his way was blocked by Charon's invisible wall. And yet, somehow, she was on the other side of it . . .

They stared at each other. There was confusion in Drex's

eyes, but Deina could see a hint of distrust there, too. Distrust or something worse. Scrambling to her feet, ducking her head to avoid his gaze, she dragged her sack in line with the others and ran back toward Charon's heaped spoils. The god was playing games with her—that was all. He was watching them. He could easily have dissolved his so-called wall just so that she would fall through it. But she wasn't going to allow him to distract her. She'd moved most of her pile, and she was ahead of the others; one more sackful and she'd be done with this ridiculous competition. Deina reached her pile, grabbed another sack, and began to fill it. Any moment now, she'd move some bit of a smashed cup or a broken spear, and she'd uncover the black sand that would signal the end of her task . . . any moment now . . .

Except the pile was already lower than the level of the surrounding sand, and there was no end in sight.

No . . .

Deina sat back on her heels and dropped her sack as dismay, bitter in the back of her throat, drained her strength. These weren't heaps of objects piled up on the sand. They were the tips of enormous garbage dumps, the spewed excess from vast craters that had been filled to bursting with the debris caught by Charon's net. The task was impossible.

The ferryman's laugh rang out, as cold as the waters upon which he worked.

"Your time is up. And once again, we have no winner. Really"—he grinned at them—"I thought one of you might have succeeded. But no matter. You have one more chance."

No one spoke, but the others' expressions showed clearly

enough what they were all feeling: anger, exhaustion, despair.

"So . . ." Charon tossed his coin up into the air. It hung there, spinning slowly. "The last test. To pass, you just need to tell me what it says on this coin." He beckoned them forward. "That's all."

As his words sunk in, Deina laughed.

The easy humor vanished from Charon's face.

"You can read?"

"No." Deina pointed at Drex. "But he can."

Drex gulped. He approached the ferryman slowly, reached up, and plucked the coin from the air.

"It says, *To Charon from Herakles, with affection and eternal*—"

Charon snatched the coin back.

"That's enough. You've won." He grabbed Drex by the shoulder, ignoring his protests, and began to drag him toward the ferry. "Into the boat. The rest of you, get ready to start working."

"Wait," Deina called out. "What about his wish?"

Charon scowled at her. "I'm giving him his wish—I'm taking him across the Styx."

"But you swore to grant the winner's wish *and* take him across the Styx. Those were your exact words. He gets a wish in addition to his transport."

The god stopped trying to wrestle Drex into his boat. "What?"

"I'm merely pointing out, O gracious conveyor of the dead, that you swore by the Styx to—"

"I know what I said," Charon growled. He seized Drex's tunic in both hands, jerking him forward. "Well? What do you wish for, boy? I can send you anywhere. Back to some city of men that holds a place in your heart. I can give you fame, or riches, or women." The god let go of Drex. "What do you wish for, young one?" His voice was wheedling now. "Think carefully."

Deina held her breath. What would she wish for, if offered such temptation? The image of the ship pinned to her wall back at the House flashed into her mind. If offered instant freedom, even if saying yes would condemn every soul in Iolkos, every Severer next to whom she now stood—would she be strong enough to say no?

"I wish . . ." Drex was staring up at Charon, not looking at them—he was going to leave them here, she was certain. "I wish for you now to convey all six of us to the other bank of the Styx, alive and unharmed, not despoiled or altered in any way, and allow us to continue our quest."

Charon spat on the sand. "As you wish."

Deina's tense shoulders drooped as Aster huffed with relief. Dendris and Chryse were grinning. And Theron—Theron glanced at Deina and gave her a quick nod. Acknowledgment, perhaps, that although Drex's ability and generosity had played the major part in saving them, her trickery had at least helped. On the other side of the river lay the Plains of Asphodel. Charon had already told them Eurydice was there—the quest was nearly over. Deina, excitement fizzing through her core, began to hurry toward the boat.

"Not so fast," Charon snapped. "Only one of you can travel in the boat. No living things cross the Styx, not above the waterline." He held his hands up toward the sky. A cat appeared, falling through the air, twisting and mewling, until it landed in Charon's arms. He petted the animal for a moment, then hurled it across the river as Chryse cried out in protest. At about the halfway point came a flash of light. The cat dropped into the water as if it were made of lead. Its body, at least. The ghost of the cat continued its trajectory toward the opposite bank before fading from view.

No one spoke. Charon smiled, as if he was pleased at the way his casual cruelty had silenced them. He waved a hand at Drex. "You, lie down in the bottom of the boat. The rest of you will have to go in the boxes." He pointed to four narrow wooden boxes next to the boat. In shape, they were like the stone sarcophagi used for noble burials. A chain linked the boxes to one another and to the boat. "You three can take those." He directed Chryse, Aster, and Dendris toward the first three boxes. He turned to Deina and Theron, leering. "You appear to have some history, so you can share."

Deina decided not to push her luck any further by arguing. Theron had already pulled back the lid of the chest. She sat on the edge, swung her legs over, and lowered herself into the box. There wasn't enough room for them to lie shoulder to shoulder. There would barely be enough room for both of them whichever way they did it. She turned to face the wooden side of the box. Heard Theron mutter a curse. Felt him wriggle down and turn onto his side; he was trying to lie with his back to hers. His elbow jammed into her rib cage.

"Ow!"

"I'm sorry! There's not enough room—I've got nowhere to put my arms." More cursing. Theron shifted position and kicked her ankle in the process.

"Ow! Again!"

"It's not my fault! I'm going to have to put my arms around you."

"What? Absolutely not—"

"We're not going to fit otherwise. Believe me, I don't like this any more than you do. Raise your head a moment."

What choice did she have? Deina lifted her head, and Theron managed to wedge his arm so it fit beneath her neck. He slid his other arm around her waist.

"It feels like you're strangling me."

He shifted position a fraction. "Better?"

"A little."

A shadow fell across them. Charon was watching them. He laughed.

"Don't do anything I wouldn't."

The lid slammed shut, plunging them into darkness.

"Oh, Hades," Deina murmured. "I don't want my life to end like this. Drowning while crammed into a box with you."

"Believe me, it's not on the top of my list of ways to die, either. But he promised to grant Drex's wish, which included getting us to the other side alive."

The box began to move, creaking and grating across the sandy riverbank. Deina's pulse quickened. Charon had promised, but how trustworthy was a god? Especially a god you'd tricked into swearing a different oath to the one he thought he was swearing. She pressed her palm against the planks in front of her face and strained her ears, waiting for the first splash of water against the wood. There it was—the river, hitting the side of the box and then washing over it. Was it her imagination, or was the wood beneath her fingers growing damp? The far end of the box by their feet scraped over sand until, with a jerk, the box swung free and was caught by the current. It tipped and lurched. Theron gasped, tightening his arm around her waist. Deina gripped his hand without even thinking. She could feel his heart hammering against her back.

The box steadied. But neither of them moved. Deina closed her eyes, listening to the creak of the wood, the rush of the water, and Theron's breathing. How long would they have to stay in here? The width of the river was the distance between life and death, Charon had said. But though they were opposites, life could become death so very easily . . .

"Deina?"

"Yes?"

"Do you . . ." Theron exhaled slowly, and his breath was warm against her ear. "Do you remember that time we hid beneath the dais in the great hall?"

"Yes." She paused, recalling the tickle of dust in the back of her throat, the cold tiles against her cheek, the strange combination of excitement and fear building in the center of her chest until she'd shaken with suppressed laughter. The way Theron had grinned at her. They'd been hiding from Xantipe, one of the elders with a short temper and a fondness for inflicting corporal punishment on apprentices. "I remember."

"I really thought she was going to catch us. Though it would have been worth it. I can still remember the taste of that cake. Soft sponge coated with crystallized honey, infused with violet . . ."

Deina's mouth watered. But she didn't want to talk about cake.

"That was just before the solstice games." The competition held to complete a Severer's transition from apprentice to novice. It was more of a tradition than an actual requirement, and not every apprentice signed up for it—Chryse certainly hadn't. But most did, because the winners got two months wiped off their indentures. It was the last time that girls and boys were allowed to train and compete together.

Theron fell silent.

Deina waited. Had he nothing to say? Maybe he was merely a coward, after all. She moved her hand away from his.

"I—I didn't mean for it to happen." Theron's voice was hesitant. "I didn't mean for it to end the way it did. That last time we fought each other."

"We had an agreement. Or I thought we did." Neither of them had wanted to lose. Or to hurt each other. They were—had been—friends. Each the best in their class; the fastest, the strongest. Though Deina always seemed to have the edge. "You made me promise. You made me swear by Hades that I wouldn't beat you, that I'd pull my punches. And then you—"

"I know! I know. I remember."

So did she. Everything had been going as planned. She and Theron on equal points. Both landing blows but not hitting hard enough to truly hurt. And then the jeering had started—some of the other apprentices, the boys, sneering at Theron. Allowing himself to be fought to a draw by a girl? What was wrong with him? Maybe he should be held back a year or returned to the children's quarters! In her mind's eye, she saw Theron as he was then, the look of panic in his eyes, the way humiliation made him hunch his shoulders and sent the blood flaming into his cheeks. He'd begun hitting her harder. But she'd sworn to do no such thing. And besides, they'd had an agreement.

"You broke my ribs. You gave me a black eye. Just because the other boys were laughing at you." He hadn't even come to visit her in the infirmary. And the next time he walked past her, a full-fledged novice, he'd ignored her. She'd been held back from becoming a novice for six months as a penalty for losing. Six months when she could have started working off her indenture. Whereas Theron had reduced his indenture by two months—a prize that would have been split between them if they'd tied . . .

Theron's heart beat faster against her back. "I'm sorry, Deina. I regretted what I did, even as I was doing it. I just—I didn't know how to stop. I was scared. I didn't mean to hurt you."

Deina could still summon the image of his fist driving toward her face. Hard to believe he hadn't meant it.

Theron's hand sought hers. "Your fingers are cold."

"The river's cold."

Theron shifted even closer and wrapped his arms tighter around her. A droplet of icy water splashed from the leaky lid onto her cheek.

Deina sniffed. Sorry wasn't enough, not really. If Theron had wanted them to be friends again, why had he carried on being so obnoxious? Sorry couldn't make up for years of him actively trying to sabotage her attempts to get more work or accumulate a little capital. And this whole speech could be nothing more than an attempt to put her off her guard, to soften her up so that he could gain an advantage. There was nothing in Theron's behavior for the last six years to make her trust him. She thought about jamming her elbow into his ribs.

But, on the other hand, he was warm. And maybe . . . maybe sorry was a start.

"Sing something, will you?"

"What shall I sing?"

"I don't care. Something distracting." Another drop of water hit her temple and rolled across her forehead. "Something to make me forget."

"To forget what?" Theron murmured, his voice full of doubt.

"Everything," Deina replied. "That we're in the Underworld. That every creature we encounter wants to trap us or kill us." She paused, thinking of Nat. "Or trick us. That the chances of us all getting out of here alive are vanishingly small." She paused again, sorrow squeezing her throat and smothering her anger. "Argys and the way he died."

Silence for a moment. Then Theron's voice, low and soft, singing about summer in the mountains.

Deina let herself relax in his arms, imagining she was back in the pine forests outside the House, lulled by the warmth of the sun and the hypnotic hum of the cicadas.

The grate of solid land beneath them jerked her back to the present. Theron had fallen silent, his arm still wrapped around her waist, his forehead resting against the back of her head. His breathing was soft and even, like he'd fallen asleep.

"Theron?" No reply.

"Theron, wake up." She grabbed his hand and pushed his arm away from her just as the lid was lifted from above. Deina squinted and twisted her head around to get a better view. Aster was standing over the box, staring down at them. His eyebrows rose.

Theron was trying to change position, to disengage himself. He kicked her in the ankle again.

"Ow!" Deina kicked him back before stretching out her arm to Aster. "Help me up, will you?" Aster pulled her upright; she stepped over Theron and out of the box, wincing as her cold, cramped limbs achingly unbent. Dendris and Chryse were already hugging Drex, thanking him for his generosity; Chryse linked her arm in his. Aster strode up to Drex and clapped him on the shoulder.

"You're an honorable man, Drex. A better man than me."

"I agree," Theron said. "On both counts."

Aster groaned. "One of these days, Theron, I swear—"

"Please," Drex said, "if I've deserved your gratitude, then for Hades's sake, stop shouting at each other. I hate it." He spoke mildly enough, but there was real pain in his eyes. "My grandfather screamed and shouted at my mother for trying to hide me right up until the day he handed me over to the Order. I don't"—he lifted his hands to his ears, as if still hearing the echo of his grandfather's wrath—"I don't like it."

"I'm sorry, Drex," Theron murmured. "I'll try harder."

"As will I," Aster added.

"If we're all quite done here," Charon said sarcastically, unchaining the last of the boxes from his boat, "let me welcome you to the other side of the Styx. My oath is fulfilled, and I don't want to see any of you again until you're actually dead. Which, given that blood hunters are pursuing you, might be quite soon." He turned to face Deina. "As for you, Soul Severer, you'll find out soon enough that there is one down here who plays the game better than either of us. When the moment comes, I just hope I'm there to witness your defeat."

At Charon's words, Deina could feel the warmth of fellowship cool into the same old miasma of mistrust. She caught Chryse's puzzled, slightly fearful glance; she couldn't bring herself to look at any of the others.

Grinning, the god jumped into his boat, dropped the long pole into the water, and pushed off. He punted rapidly away from them, until it became difficult to distinguish the ferryman and his craft from the dark waters upon which he worked.

"Blood hunters?" Theron questioned.

"Those creatures that attacked us," Deina replied, adding quickly, "I guess that's what he meant."

"Well . . . we should carry on," Aster said. "We don't know if there are more Severers ahead of us. And if Charon is right, and the blood hunters are still pursuing us . . . I doubt even the Styx would prove an obstacle to them."

"At least we must be nearly there," Chryse replied. "The Plains of Asphodel lie on the other side of the Styx—that's what he said. All we have to do now is summon the queen's ghost, perform the binding, and we're done. We can go back." Though Deina could see the tension in her clenched fists, in the tight carriage of her shoulders, she sounded more excited than anything else.

"We'll be free." Drex smiled at her.

No one else shared their good mood. Theron looked as

exhausted as Deina had ever seen him. Even Aster seemed to have lost his earlier certainty.

Dendris hefted her ax over her shoulder. "As if it's going to be that easy."

No one mentioned that the last rite, the one that would send them back to Orpheus, only needed one person to perform it. Instead, they began toiling in silence up the steep slope that led away from the river. Even though she'd put her cloak on, Deina could feel the freezing damp seeping through her clothes and into her bones. Still, as she gained the top of the slope and stepped into the bank of fog, Theron's hand was warm on her back.

16

The mist was fracturing. By the time they'd covered a few more strides, a winter landscape lay before them. Deep, undisturbed snow covered the ground on either side of the path. The path itself was still visible—just—though the boundary markers had been reduced to drift-covered humps. Deina's feet sank into the snow nearly up to her ankles, and she could feel the moisture already seeping through her leather boots. More snow was tumbling lazily from the sky, the flakes large enough for her to admire their ornate symmetry as they landed on her dark clothing. Growing throughout the snowfield, especially close to the edges of the path, were what looked like large swathes of flowers creeping along the ground. Drex knelt to examine one of the blooms.

"There is beauty here, despite the barrenness. See?" He was addressing Chryse, but Deina leaned forward as he nudged one of the flowers with the edge of his little finger, sending a cloud of fine white pollen floating into the frozen air. "Entirely white, but every part a different shade. Silver-white petals, gold-white stamens, stem and leaves with just a hint of green." He plucked the flower, revealing fat gray roots, and held it out to Chryse. She drew his hand nearer to her and inhaled the flower's scent. Closed her eyes briefly and rewarded him with a smile that made him blush.

"It smells like the midwinter festival." She took the flower from Drex's fingers and held it up to her nose. "Spiced wine and woodsmoke. Even remembering it makes me feel warmer. Are these asphodel flowers?"

"I suppose so," replied Theron, scanning their surroundings. "But where are the ghosts? If these are the Plains of Asphodel, shouldn't Eurydice be here?"

Deina turned around slowly. Almost nothing but white snow and white flowers melting into the distance; the cold, and the brightness of it, despite the dull daylight—if what filtered through the clouds above them was daylight—made her eyes water. But in the distance, the path seemed to be leading toward an avenue of trees shrouded by a dark gray cloud. A fog bank, perhaps. Or, given where they were, something unimaginably worse.

"I think . . ." Aster began, also gazing at the avenue of trees, "I think we should stick close together. It may be beautiful, but I don't like these fields. It's too open."

"I agree," Dendris added. She poked at the exposed gray root of the asphodel plant with her toe. "There is something wrong about these flowers. A sweet scent may easily conceal a rotten core."

Deina remembered the aroma of Orpheus's perfume and

shivered, glancing at Chryse. But her friend was smiling at Drex and seemed unmoved by Drendris's words of caution. Seeing her happy made Deina smile, too. At least until she caught Drex's eye, and saw doubt pinch his brows together as he looked at her. But her falling through Charon's so-called anti-mortal wall—that was just another trick the god had played. She knew what she was, and she knew what she had to do: find the queen, return to the mortal world, claim her freedom and her gold. Or her share of it, at least. The idea of dividing it with the others didn't seem quite as terrible as it had before.

They walked in silence for a while, pushing themselves as fast as they could along the slightly rising path. Perhaps it was just the exertion, but it seemed to be getting warmer, even though the snow was still falling. Their pace gradually slowed. Theron was walking to one side of her; he yawned widely.

"Gods, I'm so sleepy . . ."

"Let's talk about something. It might help keep us awake."

"Like what?"

"Like . . ." Deina searched for a topic. "Like, if you'd never been a Severer, and you could be or do anything you wanted, what would it be?"

"Easy. I'd be a bard. I'd travel from city to city to sing the ancient poems, delighting archons in their palaces or performing in competitions for the entertainment of everyone else. I'd train my voice until I was the best in the Theban Dominion. Or the world. Until I could charm sea nymphs up from the depths of the oceans and the stars down from the sky."

"A modest ambition . . ."

Theron chuckled. "I already succeeded in sending Cerberus to sleep." He grimaced. "Almost. Drex," he called out, "what about you?"

"Me?" Drex glanced over his shoulder. "Well . . . I suppose I'd wish to be a craftsman. To have a workshop somewhere. To be able to carve scenes into stones, like the one I showed you, and give them settings of gold or finely wrought silver. Settings exquisite enough to grace even the most beautiful of wearers." He smiled shyly at Chryse. "And I'd like to travel. To see the work of other craftsmen and sell my own."

"You should work for the king," Chryse replied. "You're too talented for Iolkos. Maybe a workshop in the palace in Thebes . . ."

"I don't want to travel," Aster said.

"But I thought you wanted to be a commander in the army. Didn't you want to fight the Dominion's battles?" Deina asked.

"I would wish to have command over my own soldiers, but I want to protect Iolkos. I think"—he stopped walking and turned to face the others, his forehead creased—"I think I want to stay there and direct the palace guard and the garrison and keep the city safe." He flushed. "It's the only home I have. And the people"—his frown deepened—"the people have suffered much recently. Staying in Iolkos to help would be honorable."

Strange. Deina had always thought of Aster's "honor" as something self-serving. Shallow. But perhaps he was more selfless than she'd imagined. More selfless than her, at least.

Dendris said that if she wasn't a Severer, she would wish to be a gardener somewhere in the temperate north of the Dominion, and tend to an entire orchard of fruit trees.

Chryse, laughing, said she would wish for a life of comfort and luxury, to be a queen.

The word, an unwelcome reminder of their quest, echoed through the empty landscape.

Chryse blushed.

"But perhaps," she added, "I would not enjoy such a life after all."

The conversation dwindled into silence. Deina was too tired to try to revive it. The rich scent rising from the beds of flowers on either side of the path grew in intensity. The air became intoxicating. And so blissfully warm, despite the snow swirling through the sky and lying thickly between the white flowers. She could feel the summery breeze whispering across her skin and soothing her tense muscles until they slackened. Theron reached for her hand and slipped his fingers between hers, and instead of pushing him away, she moved closer to him so their arms were touching, too. They were merely strolling along the path now, all urgency gone, yet it didn't seem to matter. Ahead, Aster dawdled to a stop and shrugged his bag off his back. The flowers here spilled across the path, creeping over the boundary markers and clustering between the ragged edges of the paving stones. Aster sank to his knees and bent over the blooms.

Dendris prodded him in the shoulder. "What . . . what are you doing? Get . . . get . . ." She yawned and trailed off.

"Just resting, just for a moment. It's so warm here." He pitched forward into the flowers.

Dendris nodded, sighed, and slumped slowly to the ground next to him. Chryse, with Drex following her, wandered to the side of the path and sat down upon one of the snow-covered boundary stones. Drex lay down at her feet. Deina thought about calling out to them. Urging everyone to keep walking, but using her voice seemed like far too much effort.

Theron's grip on her hand loosened. He stumbled sideways, fell over, and dropped instantly into a deep sleep. Snow began to settle on him. Deina knelt and started to brush it off.

"Theron, wake up . . . It's . . . We've got to . . ." Something—there was something important they were meant to be doing. She was almost certain. But her eyelids, her limbs, her head—everything was so heavy. A little rest couldn't hurt. The powdery drifts of snow looked so inviting. Deina lay down next to Theron, smiling as the snowflakes began to settle on her hip and shoulder, covering her like a blanket. Oblivion enfolded her.

"Wake up, Deina."

The voice was coming from a long way away. Too far away. Easier to ignore it, and go on sleeping.

"Wake up. Now."

Something about the voice, some note of command, reached into her subconscious. Forced her eyes open even as her mind resisted.

Too bright. She blinked and squinted, trying to focus.

Nat. He was leaning over her, dark against the unrelenting whiteness of the snow-burdened sky, and somehow more solid; the landscape behind him seemed blurred in comparison, like a poorly painted piece of scenery. Deina tried to move, to roll away from him, but her legs were pinned in place. Shifting onto her elbows, she saw her entire lower body was wrapped

in the long, gray roots of the asphodel flowers. She let out a cry of revulsion and reached down to push them away.

Nat caught her arm. "Don't. They're far more dangerous than they seem." Drawing one of Deina's knives from her hip, he sliced off and speared a piece of root and held it up for her to see. The thing wriggled on the point of the blade; its surface was coated in minute thorns that looked as if they might be made of glass. Nat flicked it away and replaced the knife. "Please—allow me."

He held his hands flat above the gray tangle of roots. Nothing happened. Until a glimmering film of frost began to creep across the roots' surface, thickening as it went. Soon entirely encased, the roots blackened and shriveled beneath the onslaught of ice. The pressure on Deina's legs slackened and vanished as the roots crumbled into nothingness. She jumped up, keen to get farther away from the huge clumps of flowers. As Nat joined her, Deina cleared her throat.

"That was impressive. I have no idea how you did it, and the fact that you were able to—it scares me." Not a lie; fear prickled against the back of her neck. "But you saved me. Again. Thank you."

"You're welcome." He gave her one of his brilliant smiles. "Much as I'd like to stand here listening to you tell me how talented I am, I think your associates might need some assistance."

The others were still lying asleep, covered like she had been in tangled tendrils of asphodel roots. Drex and Chryse were almost entirely buried. As she watched, the gray web that was wrapped around them contracted, dragging their bodies toward the edge of the path.

Nat strode toward them, his hands already held out in front of him. As the roots began to shrivel, Deina brushed the snow away from Chryse's hair and lashes. She was so cold. No color left in her cheeks or lips. Pale enough that she might already be dead. Nat rose and turned toward Aster.

"Wait—aren't you going to wake her up?" Deina shook Chryse's shoulder. Shouted in her ear. But the other Severer didn't respond. Deina blinked away the tears that were clouding her vision. "What's wrong with her?"

"It's no ordinary sleep. The scent of the asphodel traps the minds of its victims in deep slumber. The roots drag their bodies from the path before the plant starts to digest them." Nat pointed to the mounds dotted across the snowfield beyond. "Not that many humans are stupid enough to wander down here, but each kill lasts a while, and the asphodel can go a long time between meals." He crouched next to her and touched Chryse's frozen cheek. "Mortals are born and they die. Between, life flickers within them for a brief moment, a faint flame too dim to do more than emphasize the darkness beyond. But she is not suffering. None of them are. If you leave them to the flowers, it will be an easy death, as deaths go. No more than a gradual fading into oblivion." There was a strange tenderness to his expression as he gazed down at Chryse. But in another moment, he'd shaken the mood off. "And yet, somehow I get the impression that isn't our plan. I'll deal with the roots, you wake them up. You can do it, you know." He placed the palm of one hand above her heart. "All you need is already within you."

As Nat got to his feet and hurried over to Aster, Deina squared her shoulders, placed her hands on either side of Chryse's face, and tried to remember exactly how Nat had called her back to consciousness. To summon that same suggestion of irresistible command.

"Wake up, Chryse. Wake up now." She held her breath, willing it to work. "Please . . ."

Chryse's eyelids fluttered open. "D-Deina?"

Deina sighed as the panic churning her stomach subsided. She helped Chryse sit up, then knelt next to Drex as Nat moved on to destroy the roots that were clinging to Dendris. Soon, everyone apart from Theron was awake. Deina hurried to crouch next to him and took his face in her hands. There was a waxy undertone to his skin. His flesh was so cold, so unyielding, it made her fingers ache. She took a deep breath and demanded that he wake up.

Nothing happened.

Aster was sitting in the snow, still dazed, and Chryse was lingering nearby—Deina could see Drex peering at her—but Dendris was regarding Nat warily; Deina was grateful for the confirmation that she wasn't hallucinating the blue-eyed stranger. Nat himself was standing just behind her.

"Perhaps it is too late for this one."

"No." Deina snarled the word through gritted teeth. She didn't know how she felt about Theron anymore. She wasn't sure, after what they'd been through, that she could hold on to the fierce hatred of him that had burned in her heart since he'd betrayed her. The doubt vexed her; it was so much easier to cling to her old, comfortable certainty. But whatever the truth of her feelings, she couldn't leave him to die like this.

She straddled him, moved one hand from his cheek to his chest, and bent so close that her face was almost touching his.

"Come, Theron. You must wake up. Now!"

A heartbeat, beneath her palm. Faint, but there. A flush of warmth crept back into Theron's flesh as his chest began to rise and fall again. His eyelids opened, and he stared into her eyes.

"Deina." As he breathed her name, he lifted one hand and placed his fingertips against the side of her face, almost mirroring her own posture. "Deina . . ."

"Well done," Nat said loudly. "I said you could do it."

Deina pulled away from Theron and stood up.

"Who's that?" Theron asked, pushing himself onto his elbows.

"That is an excellent question, son of Thebes," Nat replied.

Theron's eyes narrowed.

"I'm not from Thebes. I'm—"

Nat huffed with irritation and clicked his fingers. Theron, who had been getting to his feet, froze mid-action. Deina spun around. The others were similarly caught—unmoving, unseeing.

"What did you do?"

"Don't worry, they're fine. I've just suspended their perception of time." Nat gestured to their surroundings. "Time doesn't exist in the Underworld, not really. You, as living mortals, still feel you are moving through time, because you cannot conceive of any other way of being. Even for the dead, to disabuse themselves of the notion takes a long time." He grinned at his own joke. "The immense weight of eternity would crush your minds like empty walnut shells if you understood the true nature of this place."

"In other words, we're too stupid?" Deina waved a hand in front of Theron's face. There was no reaction. "Let them go!"

"I will. I just want to talk to you first." Nat tilted his head, one eyebrow raised. "I wouldn't have dealt with the asphodel roots if I meant them harm, would I?"

Deina shrugged, not trusting herself to answer. Whatever else he was, Nat was powerful.

"I just want to remind you: I stand ready to help you, Deina. Your fate lies along a different path from theirs. A path I can show you if you come with me. And you *should* come with me. Moreover"—he held up a finger as Deina opened her mouth—"consider this: You are not like them." He took her hands in his and drew her close; Deina's skin tingled at the cool strength of his touch. The chill in his eyes had melted away, but behind the warmth was something else—an echo of that burning want she had sensed before. "You must know by now that you are different. If they don't know it yet, they soon will. And they will not understand. Eventually, their confusion will sharpen into fear. They will turn on you."

Deina shook her head. "No. I know what I am. A Soul Severer. A thief and a trickster. Nothing more. Nothing less. And whatever this destiny is that you keep talking about, I refuse to accept it."

Nat's lips twitched briefly into a smile. "You already told me you're not a hero, but only heroes stand a chance of evading fate." He released her hands and stepped back. "You should hurry. The object of your quest is not far off, but the blood hunters never lost your trail. You don't have long." He raised his hand, thumb and middle finger pressed together as if about to click them.

"Wait—the blood hunters . . . what are they?"

"You really want to know?"

"One of them had a torc and a sigil. And the way they were stopped in the river, held close to the carcass of their vessel"—her stomach turned at the remembered horror of that pursuit through the bloody waters of the Cocytus—"it was almost as if they had once been Theodesmioi. Sea Singers."

"Really, Deina, there is so much that you don't yet know." Despite his phrasing, there was more pity than contempt in his tone. "They looked like Theodesmioi because that is what they once were." A click. Even as dread sent an icy flood across Deina's already cold skin, Nat vanished.

"—from Iolkos." Theron finally finished his sentence. He looked around. "Where did he go?"

"I don't know," Deina replied. "And before you ask, I don't know who he is or what he is. A daimon, I guess. I've never seen him before." Not true, but a lie felt safer. "I don't know why he saved us from being eaten by the asphodel, either." If the others hadn't noticed her role in waking them up, she wasn't about to call it to their attention. "But he told me"—she swallowed, trying to get the taste of fear out of her mouth—"he told me the blood hunters are following us again. We need to move. And we definitely need to get away from these flowers before they have another attempt at eating us." Everyone quickly shrank back from the edge of the path. Aster nodded, grabbed his bag, and began striding along the path. The others followed—apart from Theron, who was watching her, his face set and impassive. Nat's words echoed in her mind: *They will not understand.* She shook the memory away and walked after the others.

It didn't take as long as she had feared to reach the avenue of trees. Up close, they were stunted, leafless things, silver-gray bark blending into the gray of the sky. The pall of shadow into which the path led was revealed, too: not fog, or the swirling smoke and ash of a fire, but ghosts. Vast numbers of shades, milling around aimlessly, silently, seemingly oblivious to the Severers' presence.

Though the snow had thinned, the cold that clutched this bleak moor was, if anything, more intense. They came to a halt near a wind-twisted beech tree. Shriveled leaves still clung to the branches, rattling like teeth in the icy breeze. Dendris glanced around nervously—watching for the pursuing blood hunters.

Deina stamped her boots on the ground, trying to get some feeling back into her feet. "Charon told us Eurydice was here. Let's perform the rite and go home."

Theron caught Deina's eye. "Is this the point where we try to kill each other?"

A carelessly asked question, apparently. Yet the falling of silence across the winter-bound landscape was like the slamming shut of a tomb.

"Surely, after what Drex did for all of us . . ." Deina began. But perhaps that wasn't what he was asking. She tried again. "The Underworld has changed things. I want my freedom, and my share of the gold. I'd like more gold than Orpheus is offering, but I've no desire to kill the rest of our company to get it." Deina held his gaze. "Not even you."

His expression of distrust didn't alter. "One of us has to be the focal point of the rite. One of us takes control, and retains control, of the spindle. Or the comb. After that point, the rest of us might be considered expendable."

"*Fine.*" Deina flung the word back at him as she opened the pouch hanging from her belt. "If I'm so untrustworthy, you can have the comb.' She drew out the delicate carved ivory—only for it to fall apart in her hand. "Oh . . . Charon's race. I fell over."

"Unfortunate," Aster observed. "Luckily, I've been more careful than you." He began hunting in his bag. "I'm obviously not going to give the spindle up, but I have no intention of—I mean, it would be dishonorable to—" He turned on Deina. "It's gone. You've stolen it!"

Before Deina could deny the accusation, Chryse held something up: a pale wooden stick, thicker in the middle and tapered at both ends, with a ring of polished black rock fixed as a weight to one end. Eurydice's spindle.

"I took it, Aster." Chryse stood tall, defiant. "Just after you awoke from the asphodel. This needs to finish. Now. The quest is over. Or it soon will be." She gazed at the milling shades. "I can hear them, you know. Even here." For an instant, her voice cracked—Deina stepped forward instinctively. Chryse jumped back as if she thought Deina might try to seize the spindle. "They're talking to themselves. Worrying about things they left undone in the mortal world."

"This is ridiculous," Aster snapped. "You've no right. You didn't volunteer, and you weren't chosen." He held out his hand. "Give it back."

Chryse edged closer to Drex. Her knuckles whitened as she

clutched the spindle tightly to her chest. "No. I won't be left here."

"No one is going to—" Deina began, but Theron cut her off. "Why do you think we'd leave you? We're not leaving Dendris, and she's not even one of us." Theron glanced at the scowling Mycenaean. "No offense."

Deina scanned Chryse's face. This sudden desperation, and the theft of the spindle—it wasn't like her. But then, Aster was right: She *wasn't* supposed to be here. The stress had to be pushing her to breaking point.

"I have an idea," Drex offered. "The final rite, the one to get us back, it doesn't work without the spindle. So we're all worried that the one who has the spindle will strand the rest of us here. But Chryse"—he smiled at her—"doesn't know the incantations. If we allow her to bind the queen's ghost, it guarantees none of us will be left behind." He glanced around the group, squinting as he tried to read their expressions. "Well?"

After a moment's silence, Aster shrugged. "I suppose so." Theron and Dendris nodded.

Deina sighed. "Shall we proceed with the rite, then?"

According to the ancient Songs, the memories that had become part of the spindle from Eurydice's use of it would attract her ghost, which the rite would then bind to the spindle, allowing them to carry the ghost out of the Underworld with them. But first, preparations had to be made. The ground was frozen too hard for their blades to draw out the sacred circle or the sigil of Hades around its boundary.

Dendris picked up one of the twigs scattered thickly across

the ground. "We can use these to make the circle. And, Drex—I expect those serpent's teeth would be sharp enough to cut the sigil into the earth."

As the others worked, Deina selected a strand of Chryse's hair, cut it, and tied it around the spindle.

"Good luck, my friend."

Chryse shook her hair back from her shoulders. She took the slender wooden shape gently in her hands and stepped into the circle. Closing her eyes and breathing slowly, she held the spindle pressed against her sternum. The others spaced themselves evenly around the perimeter, though Deina noticed that Drex changed position so he wasn't standing next to her. Just as well they wouldn't be here for much longer.

"Shall I chant the incantation?" Theron asked. As they all joined hands, he began to sing, one line at a time. Chryse repeated each line after him, her voice wobbly with anxiety.

"With Hades's power, I pluck you from Death's embrace, Eurydice. With this circle of Severers, marked by the god's sigil, I summon your spirit. With your own spindle, I single you out and draw you near. Within its web of memories, I entangle you. With this strand of hair, I secure you. Come, beloved queen, turn away from Death's domain, that we may return you to the living lands . . ."

Over and over, Theron sang and Chryse repeated. Deina could hear the desperation and exhaustion creeping into both their voices. Her friend was trembling with the effort of it. Still, nothing happened.

Doubt gnawed at Deina's stomach—fear that some other Severers had gotten there first, had found the queen's ghost,

and left. She started repeating the words with Chryse, trying to match her intonation and cadence, to drown out her own misgivings. Slowly, Aster, Drex, and Dendris joined in, too. Deina closed her eyes. She could almost feel the power of Hades thrumming up through the soles of her feet and into her voice.

The chant rang out louder through the cold air.

Chryse gasped.

Deina's eyelids flew open.

Chryse was still there. But she wasn't alone.

17

Something was wrong. The ancient Songs said the queen's spirit should have been absorbed directly into the spindle. Instead, the ghost of Eurydice had enveloped Chryse, drawing solidity from her form. Chryse's golden hair was obscured by raven tresses, her features masked by darker eyes and fuller lips.

Drex made a grab for the spindle, but contact with the ghost sent him flying backward, and he landed heavily in a drift of snow.

Deina edged forward. "Chryse, can you hear me?"

The voice that issued from Chryse's mouth was low and musical, almost drowning out Chryse's own brighter tones, as if the ghost was near at hand and the Severer, speaking the same words, was somewhere far away.

"She hears you. But her body answers to me, for the time being."

"Release her!" Deina heard the sharp note of fear in her voice.

"No."

What has happened? She turned to Dendris.

"Did the elders in Mycenae warn you about this? Did they tell you how to—how to undo it?"

Dendris shook her head, worry creasing her brow. "They said nothing of this." She chewed her bottom lip. "Perhaps if we explain?"

Deina dropped to her knees, wishing her mouth wasn't so dry. "O great queen, we understand that you desire to live again, and that is why we are here. Don't be afraid. We are sent by King Orpheus to return you to the mortal world, and to your own body. There is no need for you to—to take over the form of this girl."

Deina expected some reaction—shock, or even joy, but Eurydice merely asked, "Did my lord Orpheus speak of his love for me? What did he tell you?"

Little enough, as far as Deina could remember from the three occasions she'd been in Orpheus's presence.

"He said . . . he said you were life itself to him. And—" Racking her brains, she looked to the others for assistance.

Theron bowed low before the ghost. "I was commanded to sing for His Majesty on our journey here. Afterward, he spoke to me of his great devotion, and his wish to be reunited with you. He described his unbearable grief when death claimed you. That is why he sent us into the dangers of the Underworld, to bring you back to life. By capturing your spirit within your spindle, we can—"

"Don't lie to me, boy," the ghost said calmly. "Orpheus cannot speak of love because he is not capable of love. And do not trouble yourself to explain to me what you seek to do. I understand the mechanics. I've been through this before."

Panic rippled through Deina's stomach. Leida's image swam before her eyes; Leida, who had been chosen to go to Thebes, who had believed she would soon be free . . .

"You mean, you have died before? And—and Orpheus has sent Soul Severers to call you back to life before?" She moistened her lips with her tongue, afraid of Eurydice's next answer. "How many times?"

"More than I can remember." Eurydice glanced down at the spindle that Chryse was still holding in her hands. "But until now, I had never found a Severer as responsive as this one to my power. She is the first I have been able to speak through."

"What power does a ghost have," Dendris asked, "even here?"

"My power comes from what I was. Not what I am. I was once a Soul Severer, just as you are. Yet I would live through a thousand years of the servitude I endured rather than return to the mortal world as Orpheus's wife. I would rather spend eternity in Tartarus."

"Surely," Aster murmured, "being the king's wife could not have been that bad . . ."

"I wasn't just his queen," Eurydice snapped. "I was his . . . collaborator." Her tone became venomous. "His willing accomplice. At least at the beginning." She looked from face to face. "Ah, you do not understand. You do not yet know the extent of his lies."

From the corner of her eye, Deina glanced at Aster, wondering whether he would rush out his standard defense of Orpheus as an honorable man. But he said nothing.

"Blessed by the gods, that's what people say," Eurydice

continued. "Orpheus is granted extraordinarily long life, is spared death, because the gods love him. But that is a lie: Orpheus lives because he cheats his way out of death. Over and over again. I thought he would stop, after the first one, or two, or three. I thought that he, like me, would sicken of draining the life from another, of watching some young body shrivel into an aged husk before our eyes so that he might add just a few more years to his life. But that time never came. However many we killed, it was never enough. Yet he could not act without my power. So I gave my life in an attempt to end his." She held out her arms; the flesh around her wrists was slashed into bloody ribbons. "It is a game we play, he and I. Alive, I have no memory of my previous incarnations. But it doesn't take long before the Tyrant reveals the truth of what he is and forces me to recommit the awful crime. Each time he brings me back. Each time I eventually attempt to stop him by ending my life. Each time he sends Severers to retrieve me, once again, from the Underworld. Around and around we go . . ." Eurydice's voice faded, and for a moment the image fluctuated, and all Deina could see was Chryse, pale and wide-eyed. "Orpheus does not love me. He wants me back because I am his instrument, nothing more."

So that was Orpheus's secret: He was draining the life force of others and adding it to his own, aiming for immortality. He wanted, in his blasphemous arrogance, to become a god. To live, to rule, to commit his cruelties forever. And Eurydice had been helping him. Deina pressed a hand to her mouth. She didn't want to believe it. How was it possible that the gods had allowed this crime to continue, had not struck him down, punished him for such unnatural murders? How many had he drained, how many—

"Wait." Deina forced herself to ask the question. "What of the Severers? What happens to those who are sent each time to summon you back to life?"

"Orpheus has them killed, of course. He does not care how much blood he spills to protect his secret. And if you return me to him, he will kill you, too. Just like the others. There is no freedom waiting for you. There is no gold. Just death."

"Then let him kill us," Dendris exclaimed, her hands clenched into fists. "Better to die without a torc around my neck than to return to the Order. Better to go to Elysium than return to the House of Hades in Mycenae."

Eurydice sighed, and it was like a winter breeze stirring the willow branches.

"There is no Elysium for you. Mortal forms are not meant to channel the immortal power of a god. When the human part of a Theodesmioi dies, something else lives on in the Underworld. Something miscreated. Accursed. You have already fled from them, I think."

Eurydice's claim was too terrible—that the reward for having your life taken from you, for being given over to the gods from childhood, was to become a monster. The worst of it was, Deina knew—from what she'd seen, from what Nat had said—that the ghost spoke the truth. She whispered the words. "Blood hunters."

Drex, Dendris—all of them cried out, denying, refusing to believe such a thing was possible.

"It can't be," Aster bellowed. "We were promised. Ever

since the kings of old struck the bargain with the gods, and the Theodesmioi were created—it can't be true. The Order promised us!" He advanced toward the ghost, drawing his sword. Theron and Drex threw themselves into his path, dragging him away from Chryse's possessed body, but he kept shouting. "You're lying! You claim to be Theodesmioi, and you're dead, and yet you are not one of those—those creatures—"

"Because I am more than just Theodesmioi," Eurydice replied. "I . . ." Her image faded, and Chryse moaned. "My time grows short. The girl is weakening. Save those whom Orpheus would use me to kill. Save yourselves." Eurydice held up her clasped hands, pleading. "I beg you, do not . . . do not deliver me to him . . ."

The image vanished. Chryse's eyes rolled back into her head. Drex ran to her side. She stood, swaying, then fell unconscious into his arms.

The spindle bounced and rolled across the ground to Deina's feet. She stooped to claim it. As her fingers brushed against the turned wood, a faint thrum of power shot up her arm and, for an instant, she was transported somewhere else: a curved room lit from above by starlight. She jerked her hand back. Took her veil from her bag, still trembling, and used that to stow the spindle safely before going to attend to Chryse.

Drex had lowered her to the ground and folded his cloak beneath her head.

"Chryse . . ." Deina knelt next to her.

"I'm here." Chryse's eyes blinked open. "It was like . . . like being underwater, in the baths. I could hear everything she was saying, but as hard as I tried, I couldn't get back to the surface. Someone was holding me down. Drowning me. I thought"—she groaned and covered her face with her hands—"I thought she was going to kill me."

"She's gone now. She's in the spindle."

Chryse closed her eyes again.

"Did you know that was going to happen? Is that why you let me perform the rite?"

"Of course not. We didn't know." *About that or about anything, as it turns out.* "We should . . ." Deina paused, uncertain of what to say. "We should move from here. The blood hunters—"

"What's the point in running?" Aster murmured. "Whether we die now or later, we know what horror lies in store for us."

"But we're not dead yet," Drex urged, "and we still have a choice to make." He leaned over to grasp Aster's shoulder. "We need to—to think. To decide what to do for the best."

Was Drex right? Or should they just save their energy and await their fate? Deina got to her feet, wondering what Dendris and Theron were feeling. The Mycenaean had her eyes closed and her arms wrapped around the trunk of one of the poor frostbitten trees, as if trying to draw some comfort from the rough bark. And Theron—

He tapped her on the shoulder, making her jump.

"You have the spindle."

"Yes." She paused, trying to read his intentions in his dark eyes. "Do you still think I'm going to leave you here? Or try to kill you?"

"I don't know why I said that. Habit, I suppose. Distrust has helped keep both of us alive so far." He arched one eyebrow and cast a pointed look at Deina's hands.

Deina glanced down. Her left hand had strayed automatically to the hilt of her knife. She forced herself to relax her stance.

"But after what we've just been told . . ." Theron sighed. "Our old certainties have gone, and it turns out they were lies anyway. What's left?"

"The truth, I suppose." Deina's gaze lingered on the leather cord Theron wore beneath his tunic; it had to be the butterfly pendant he'd made her. "However hard that might be."

"The truth?" Theron's voice sank as his hand grazed the back of hers. "I spent so long convincing myself that you were my enemy. Trying to make myself *hate* you, in the hope that I would hate myself less. Except it never really worked." They stood silent for a moment, as close as they had been the night of the banquet. "I've missed you, Deina. Did you know I used to watch you racing, after we both became novices?"

"Spying on the women's tournaments? That was a big risk."

"It was worth it. The exhilaration on your face as you outpaced the others and let the speed take you—it was like you were lit up inside by some secret fire. It was the closest I could get to spending time with you."

"You could have just told me you were sorry."

"I wanted to. But I was scared—of what the other men might think or say. Of looking weak. Of being punished by the elders for being too friendly with a woman. Of what might happen if I actually let myself—" He broke off, breathing hard, and brushed the fingers of one hand briefly against her cheek. "Excuses. I should have been brave enough. Then maybe everything could have been different."

Would *everything* have been enough? Separate halls every evening, separate training; their friendship would have been squeezed into stolen moments outside the House when they weren't working. And gods forbid they should have fallen in love . . .

The present had never belonged to them. Now they had no future, either.

Deina realized she was staring at Theron and dropped her gaze. Perhaps it had been for the best that they'd become enemies instead of staying friends. Still . . .

"I've missed you, too. That's just a statement, by the way. It doesn't mean I've forgiven you."

"I understand. But perhaps, before we die . . . perhaps you could think about forgiving me." Theron tried to summon a smile, even though Deina could see he had no heart for it. "What do you think—should we go back, give Eurydice to Orpheus, and die at his hands? Or stay here and wait for the blood hunters to catch up with us?" His eyebrows went up. "Or potentially those idiots from Knossos—they must at least be attempting to pursue us. There's nothing else they can do." He gulped. "I wonder—do we become blood hunters, if we're killed by blood hunters?"

"You've forgotten: There could be two other groups of Severers still wandering around," Deina replied. "If they find us, they might try to kill us and take the spindle. And they'll return it to Orpheus. No one who hadn't heard Eurydice speaking would believe what she told us."

"Do you believe it?"

Did she? Deina exhaled slowly, considering.

"Yes. I think I do. It explains lots of things: Orpheus's unnaturally long life, his seeming agelessness. We all knew the Tyrant was bad." She thought about the people starving in Iolkos because he'd taken the city's grain. About the young men conscripted into the Dominion's army who never returned. About the people she'd seen being enslaved. About those crushed beneath the keel of the Tyrant's ship, the tide red with their blood . . . Just a fraction of the lives he must have destroyed. "We just didn't know *how* bad."

"So what are we going to do?"

"I don't know, exactly. But we're not going sit here waiting to be slaughtered." Deina strode over to Aster and nudged him. "Get up. We've been lied to by Orpheus and the gods. You should be angry. Raging. Not moping, like a—a pathetic, mewling baby who—"

"No more!" Aster erupted upward and drove one of his spears into the ground. "I have fury enough burning through my veins. But we cannot defeat Aristaeus and his Iron Guards, and the rite we were given to return will deliver us straight into their hands."

"Then we don't use the rite. We—we do something else."

"But what?" Dendris asked, coming nearer. "What can we do that Orpheus won't have thought of? Seems like he's had a lot of practice at killing Severers. I'm assuming this is everyone's first time at trying to outwit a tyrant."

"Deina can do it," Drex observed. He was still crouching next to Chryse, one arm around her shoulder. "She was the one who got Charon to swear that oath."

"What about that"—Theron pulled a face—"that boy, with the pale scars on his arms?"

Would Nat help them? Maybe. But what would he want in return? Deina could guess—something about her promising to let him help her find her destiny. He still hadn't revealed his true nature or what he actually wanted, so she wasn't going to ask him unless the situation became desperate. Well—she corrected herself—even more desperate. She wandered a little farther along the path. In the distance was a break in the landscape that might be another river. Only two remained ahead of them: Lethe, the river of forgetfulness, and Acheron, the river of pain.

Maybe forgetting wouldn't be a bad choice. I could forget Chryse, forget Theron, forget Nat, forget I'd ever dreamed of being free.

There was only one path here. And there was only one decision to make: whether they should return to Orpheus or go on into the heart of the Underworld, where Hades sat like a spider, spinning his web of lies . . .

Deina gasped. "Hades."

"What about him?" Aster growled.

"What if . . . what if we don't leave the Underworld? We—we continue on the path and find the god whose sigil we bear on our foreheads. Hades has claimed our lives. It's time we reminded him of that. Let's respectfully point out to the god that Orpheus's refusal to die, and his murder of Soul Severers, show the Tyrant's utter contempt of Hades and his realm."

"What do you think Hades is going to do about it?" Theron swore and aimed a kick at the nearest tree, earning himself a sharp reproof and a slap on the arm from Dendris. "He might just slaughter us anyway. Or send us straight to Tartarus."

"He might. But he might not. Whereas Orpheus and the blood hunters definitely want to kill us." Deina turned slowly, addressing all of them. "We're Severers. We play the odds. Taking risks is what we do, even if it might mean we end up dead."

Theron stared at her for a moment, as if trying to work out whether she'd lost her mind, before letting out a shout of laughter. "Or, in your case, *especially* if it means you might end up dead."

Deina smiled grimly. "I'd also like to point out that I have the spindle. If any of you wants to take it back to that bastard Orpheus, you'll have to fight me."

"And maybe I will." Chryse was on her feet, fists and jaw clenched with anger. The smattering of laughter from the others died away. "Just because you've decided what you want, everyone else has to go along with it? You said you volunteered so we'd be free. Well, we have the queen's ghost now. Let's take it back to Orpheus and claim our reward."

Deina stared at her friend. "But . . . did you not hear what Eurydice said? He'll kill us. He kills all the Severers who take the queen back. And when he has her back, he'll use her to kill some other poor soul and steal his life so he can go on and do it again. Over and over and over, and it will never stop, unless we—" Deina broke off, breathing heavily. She hadn't wanted this. She stole, she lied—gods, she came to the Underworld—all so that she and Chryse could be free. So they could leave Iolkos, maybe even the Dominion, and never again have to look at or think about the other Theodesmioi or about what Orpheus was doing to the people he ruled. And yet, here was this . . . responsibility, like a mountain in her path. "It will never stop, Chryse. Unless we make it stop."

"What if Eurydice is lying? I think she's lying." Chryse's voice was cold.

Drex was shaking his head. "People want to live, Chryse. If she and Orpheus loved each other, and were happy, why would she not want to go back? Why would she make up something like that?" He reached for her hand. Chryse pulled away. Drex's face fell, but he squared his shoulders. "We should go to Hades, together. It's the right thing to do. I'll come with you, Deina."

"As will I," Aster said. "There's no honor in what the Tyrant is doing. And no honor in helping him do it. Perhaps Hades will at least send Eurydice beyond Orpheus's reach, even if he does kill us."

Theron clapped Aster on the shoulder. "There's the upside I was looking for." He inclined his head to Deina. "I'm with you."

Deina's heart swelled. "Thank you. And you, Dendris?"

The Mycenaean shouldered her bag. "According to the Songs, there are wonderful trees to be seen in the gardens of Hades's court, and an orchard that bears fruits unknown to the mortal world. A glimpse of those might be something worth dying for."

Deina turned to her friend. "Chryse, please. I know you didn't volunteer like the rest of us. That this is worse for you than anyone else, and that I'm deciding for you." Deina held out her hand. "But, please . . . I want you with me."

Chryse gazed down at her fingers, spread wide in front of her. The gold ring caught the light. She sighed and relaxed her hands, though it looked like an effort.

"I don't have a choice, do I? I can't leave without you." She sniffed. "Not that I would; you're my friend. But I think you're wrong. Remember that, Deina. Remember that I tried to persuade you to complete the task that you were sent here to undertake. I tried." Snatching her bag from Drex, Chryse started along the path.

"I'm trying, too," Deina called after her. "I'll think of something. Trust me."

"We're Severers, remember?" Chryse shouted over her shoulder, not breaking her stride. "We're not supposed to trust. You of all people should know that."

Theron gave Deina a sympathetic shrug. They set off after Chryse.

The Severers moved swiftly, but the journey seemed long; either the next river was farther off than it had appeared, or the Underworld was playing games with their perception. Deina, compelled by a creeping sense of dread to glance over her shoulder, saw both Dendris and Aster doing the same. The path behind them was empty. Still, the evidence of her eyes wasn't enough to dispel the unease that was clinging like a cold-clawed crab to the top of her spine. In silent agreement, the company sped up. Deina, walking just behind Chryse, stared at her friend's back. They hadn't spoken since their argument, but Deina couldn't stop turning everything over in her head.

She's being so unfair.

Because she's scared. She was always petted, back at the House. She always had it a little easier. She's not used to this.

And the rest of us are? It's Orpheus she should be blaming. He's the one murdering people. He's the one who embroiled her in this. She should have stayed at the House.

But what would you have done if the situation had been reversed? If you hadn't been chosen—you'd have done anything it took to get on that ship. You know you would . . .

On and on it went, with no resolution. Just a horrible feeling that something between them had broken, and Deina didn't know how to fix it. By the time the path finally dropped from a ridge down a wooded slope toward the river, she was overheated, fed up, and wincing with the pain of the blister forming on the back of her heel.

Although lying between precipitous banks, the river itself wasn't especially wide or deep. Along the top of the opposite bank, a high stone wall built of roughly squared-off stones ran in both directions as far as she could see. The path continued through a gap in the wall, flanked, sentinel-like, by two of the same dark-fronded cypress trees that grew on the near bank. The water itself ran clear across a bed of rough sand strewn with rocks, around which the river leaped and burbled.

Deina clambered down the steep bank to the water's edge. Lethe or Acheron? Oblivion or pain? Lethe was safe enough as long as you didn't drink it, if the ancient Songs were to be believed. Acheron, however . . . There was only one way to find out. Deina took a deep breath and readied herself to step into the river—but Aster forestalled her.

He stood ankle-deep in the water, apparently none the worse for the experience.

"It must be Lethe." He smiled. "And apart from climbing up the bank on the other side, easy enough to cross for once. Come on." Without waiting, he waded deeper into the river.

A roaring sound erupted. Deina spun toward the source of the noise: a wall of white water tearing downstream toward her and Aster, filling the river from bank to bank.

"Quickly," Theron yelled, "get back up here."

Deina began climbing. Behind her, Aster was splashing back toward the bank—but not quickly enough. Blinded by spray, he stumbled. The churning flood was almost upon him. As Dendris and Drex grabbed Deina's arms, hauling her back up to the safety of the path, a rope snaked through the air. Aster caught the end, clinging on tight as Deina and the others dragged him up the bank. The wild surge of water broke over his legs and he began to scream.

"Faster!" Theron urged. Finally, Aster collapsed over the lip of the bank. He was pleading, his gaze unfocused.

"No, no—not Melos! Please—stop hurting him—stop—"

"Aster!" Theron pulled him into a sitting position, one arm around the other man's shoulder. "Aster, can you hear me? You're with us—you're in the Underworld, not in Iolkos."

Aster, still breathing rapidly, blinked as if he were just waking up from sleep. He gazed at Theron. Recognition gradually dawned and he slumped forward, rubbing his hands across his face.

"When the water touched me—I thought I was back at the

House. The Iron Guards were there, and they were killing Severers. They were—they were holding heated swords to Melos's legs, and—and—" He broke off, whimpering. "I couldn't make them stop." Aster rubbed his eyes as if trying to dispel the image of his lover being tortured.

Deina glanced back at the river, now serene and shallow in its bed once more. Acheron, the river of pain. Just not the type of pain she had been expecting.

"Dendris—what about the trees? Could you make them sprout roots or branches that we could use to climb across?"

"No. I might get them to put out shoots, but they wouldn't bear our weight. Besides, these trees . . ." Dendris flattened her hand against the bark of the nearest cypress. "They are silent. Brooding. I'm not sure they'll listen to me."

Theron had gathered up the rope and was weighing it in his hands.

"Perhaps we can use the trees in a different way." He quickly outlined his plan: to pass the middle of the rope behind the tree nearest to the river on this side, then for Aster to tie both ends of the rope to his spears and hurl them into one of the trees opposite, at different heights. They could walk on the lower piece of rope and hang on to the higher one. Dendris wasn't happy about injuring the cypress. Drex wasn't confident about his ability to balance. But no one could think of an alternative.

Another moment, and Aster had secured the ends of the rope around his spears, tight enough that the spiked iron counterbalance that capped the end of each spear would stop the rope from slipping off. He hefted the first spear to his shoulder.

"You know, this is a spear, not a javelin. I can't promise that—"

Theron gripped Aster's shoulder. "Drex is right: You're the best in the House with a spear. If you can't make this work, no one could."

Aster nodded. Breathed in, nostrils flared, and blew out slowly. Took aim. Threw.

The first spear thudded into the base of the tree. Aster took up the second spear, frowned unhappily at the remaining coils of rope, and let fly. Deina held her breath as the spear arced through the air . . .

"Yes!" Aster—everyone—exclaimed with relief as the second spear sunk into the tree about six strides above the first. He tugged on both parts of the rope—it held. "I'll go first. I'm the heaviest, so if it's safe for me . . ." Aster trailed off, his gaze fixed on something behind them, his expression of relief draining away. He drew his sword, jaw clenched despite the fear Deina could see in his eyes. "Change of plan. Lightest first. Chryse, move. Now."

Chryse's instinctive complaint was cut short as the rest of them turned to look back up the path. There were figures crowded along the top of the slope, silhouetted against the sky. As Deina shielded her eyes with her hand, trying to see exactly what was facing them, a wordless shriek echoed across the frozen land.

The blood hunters had found them.

18

"Oh, Hades." Deina grabbed Chryse and pushed her toward the edge of the steep riverbank. "Move quickly. Don't look down." For once, despite the terror Deina could see on her face, Chryse didn't argue. "Drex, go with her. Help each other."

"But what about the rest of you? I can fight—"

"There're too many. Go!"

As soon as Chryse set foot on the rope, the blood hunters began to pour down the long, wooded slope. Their only chance was to get across the river before the creatures reached them. Dendris followed Drex as Chryse collapsed onto the far bank.

"Deina, you next." Aster was waving her toward the rope.

"No. Staying in the Underworld was my idea. You go."

Aster gave a quick nod. Dendris was still balancing on the far end of the rope; it sagged a little as Aster edged out over the river. Deina heard an ominous creak from the tree on the far bank. She jumped back as a spear sailed through the air and struck the ground only a few strides from her feet. Aster was halfway across. "Theron—"

"No. I won't leave you."

"We'll both be dead if you don't."

Theron dragged a shaking hand through his hair, cursed, and stepped onto the rope. Another creak. On the far side, the others were hanging on to the lower rope and the spear, attempting to keep the frail bridge in place. Two spears thudded into the tree next to Deina—the tree that had the rope around it. The blood hunters were trying to slice through it.

"Deina!" Aster, now on the far bank, was yelling at her. "Come on!" Theron was more than halfway across.

The blood hunters tore through the nearest belt of trees as Deina grabbed the upper rope and stepped out above the river, trying to find the calm balance in her center despite the terror behind her. One foot in front of the other, gripping the upper rope with her left hand. Ahead, she saw Theron leap onto the bank. Her foot slipped as the ropes twitched; she lunged and grabbed the upper rope with both hands, looked back—the creatures were pursuing her onto the bridge, clinging to both ropes, crawling like beetles, nearer and nearer.

"Deina!" Dendris tossed her ax through the air. As it spun toward her, Deina pulled herself up and hooked both legs around the upper rope. The ax handle smacked into her palm. Clinging on with her right hand, she reached back down and slashed through the lower rope. The blood hunters on it tumbled screaming toward the river. But those on the upper rope were almost upon her. She'd have to cut through that, too—trust that she could hold on, that she was high enough above the water. Twisting around, Deina brought the ax blade down on the rope as hard as she could, slicing through the raddled arm of the blood hunter that was reaching toward her.

Eyes closed, she dropped. The whistle of the air in her ears ended in an explosion of pain as her body slammed into the opposite bank. But she still had the rope—if she could just hang on a little longer . . .

Hands dragging her onto her back. Someone was trying to loosen her grip on the ax and the rope.

"You can let go now, Deina. We've got you. You're safe."

Chryse's voice. Deina opened her eyes. Her friend was kneeling above her, smiling through the tears that were gathered in her eyes.

"Chryse . . ." But even as Deina began to reach for her, to embrace her, the other woman's smile faded. Her whole expression altered. It was like being in a sunlit room the moment clouds descended.

"We're not safe." Aster was standing looking over the edge of the bank. Deina pushed herself to her feet and went to join him.

The blood hunters were fording the river.

"But where's the raging torrent?" Dendris asked. "Why aren't they in agony, or being swept away?"

"Too dead," Theron muttered. Directly below, a handful of the creatures were already climbing up the bank. "Through the wall, quickly."

Aster had already wrenched his spears out of the tree. Together they raced through the gap in the stone wall and on along the path. The blood hunters were soon on their heels, jostling one another in their haste to get past the wall. Deina scanned their surroundings. Nowhere obvious to hide, nowhere that was easily defensible. But a short distance ahead, the path split into three. The trail leading left wound toward a shadowy valley. There were ghosts drifting in that direction; some of the old Songs spoke of a place of judgment, presided over by three judges—Minos, Rhadamanthys, and Aeacus, three great kings of men. The rightmost trail continued over the bleak moorland, rising toward tumbled peaks in the distance. And the trail that went straight was a dead end, the way blocked by—

A wall. The only word that Deina could think of, but also entirely inadequate.

She and the others paused at the crossroads. Behind them, the blood hunters had slowed. They were spreading out, trying to surround the Severers. More and more of them poured like oil through the breach in the stone wall.

Deina swore. If they didn't make a decision quickly, the trails to the left and right would be cut off by the blood hunters. The dark structure that blocked the way directly ahead stretched higher than Deina could see and ran without an apparent end across the moor; it seemed to be built out of the night itself. A night unrelieved by any point of light. No stars, no moon. Just utter darkness. The darkness of the tomb. Of death. And it was calling to her: She wanted to run to it, to throw herself into it. "That way. We have to go that way."

"Are you joking?" Theron swung his sword, knocking to one side a spear that had been thrown toward them. "Even if it was safe, I don't think we're going to make it—"

The ranks of blood hunters were curving around them. If they stayed here any longer, they'd be encircled. But if they turned their backs and ran toward the—the . . . whatever it was, the creatures would fall on them. The Severers drew together.

"We're going to die here, aren't we?" Chryse's voice was tremulous. "Those things are going to eat us."

Guilt stabbed viciously through Deina's core, a precursor of what was about to come. There'd be no second chance. Whatever Nat demanded of her in repayment, it couldn't possibly be worse than this.

"Nat!" She yelled his name over the hissing and shrieking of the gathering blood hunters. "Please, if you can hear me, help us. Nat!"

The shrieks reached a crescendo, and the blood hunters charged. Theron's bow sang as he loosed his arrows into their midst. But even though he brought down his targets, there were too many. Deina gripped her knives tighter, raising them in front of her, her heart beating against her ribs as if it wanted to escape even more than she did. Nat wasn't going to help them. Another few breaths, and they'd be overwhelmed—

The shrieking cut off.

"I wondered when you'd finally realize this was getting out of hand." Nat—somehow, impossibly—was standing between the point of her knife and a mostly skeletal blood hunter that had been about to send a spear into her stomach but was now frozen in place, just like all the other blood hunters. Like all the other Severers, too. "Really, you're so unnecessarily stubborn." He winked at her. "Family trait, perhaps?"

Deina struggled for enough breath to reply, wincing at the violence of her heart. "How—how would I even know?" She lowered her knives. "You came."

"Of course I came."

"Because you want something."

"Yes." He pursed his lips, tilting his head from side to side. "But at least partly because you asked me to."

"And what is it you want?" Deina tried to steel herself—to be brave enough, for the sake of the others, to promise whatever Nat demanded of her.

He leaned forward, smiling gently, and whispered in her ear. "Your trust. I want you to believe that I want what's best."

Was that all? Deina realized she was trembling. From fear, exhaustion, and—maybe, just a tiny bit—from her proximity to Nat's sculpted lips and the chiseled planes of his face.

"I asked for your help, even though I still don't know exactly what kind of daimon you are. Doesn't that prove I trust you already?"

He gripped her shoulders. "You'll come with me, then? Let me show you what you've been missing?"

"No. I can't. Even if I wanted to, there's something I have to do." She winced at the sudden stab of regret; none of this was part of her plan. "I'm asking you to save all of us. We have to try to find Hades—"

"Hades?" Nat pulled a face and waved a hand dismissively. "No. Bad idea. Seriously bad. Hades is a liar. A cheat. No good will come of it."

"But we have to do something." A thought occurred to her. "Can you protect us? Can you stop Orpheus? He'll kill us if he can." Her gaze slipped from Nat's perfect features to the grotesque forms behind him. "We'll become just like them." Nausea turned her stomach.

"Orpheus's fate is fixed." Fate. Again. And was it truly her inescapable fate—the fate of all Theodesmioi—to become monsters? There was sympathy in Nat's eyes when she looked back at him. "I cannot protect you when you return to the mortal world." His fingers curled briefly around hers. "I wish I could."

"But Hades can?" Deina urged.

"Hades is one of the three greatest of the gods." Nat's tone became petulant. "Perhaps. If he chooses to."

"Then, please, if you want what's best, help us get there." She glanced at her unmoving teammates. "I won't leave them."

Perhaps it was just a trick of the light, but gold seemed to streak the intense blue of Nat's eyes. He nodded.

"I begin to understand, I think."

"So . . . you are offering to help?"

"I'm offering you the world." His mouth curved into a smile again. "But this will have to do, until you're ready to accept it." With a click of his fingers, the Severers suddenly returned to life. Theron's arrow continued its flight, and Aster's battle cry ended in a fit of coughing as he took in Nat's sudden appearance.

"Go." Nat pointed them toward the wall of night. "Through there. You'll be safe." Without waiting to be urged further, Aster began hurrying the others along the path. "I'll hold the blood hunters here for a little longer."

"Can't you hold them there until we're gone?" Deina asked.

"I could." Nat shot her one of his irrepressible grins. "But where would be the fun in that?"

On impulse, she reached up and kissed his cold cheek. "Thank you."

"Go!"

Deina took off, flying toward the darkness at the end of the path. Screams of rage behind her told her that Nat had released the blood hunters. She glanced back. Black flames, glowing purple at their hearts, were coruscating across Nat's open palms. He laughed and hurled a fireball into the middle of the cluster of blood hunters that had set off in pursuit of the Severers, sending a sheet of flame into the sky.

"Deina, why are you slowing down?" Theron, just ahead of her, was holding his hand out to her. Deina grasped it, and they plunged together into night.

Deina wondered if this was what it felt like to be blind. Even though her eyes were open, there was nothing but a suffocating absence of light, solid enough for her to sense its weight against her eyeballs. And though she could feel Theron's hand still clasping hers, his arm brushing hers, she couldn't hear him. She couldn't hear anyone. All was silence, apart from the rapid thrumming of her heart.

There was no time inside this lightless space. On and on they walked, for an hour, a day, or longer—she had no idea. On and on, holding fast to each other, until a bright point of light flared into existence. Followed by another and another, and Deina realized that the horrifying blankness was becoming the dark of an ordinary night. Instead of the featureless clouds that had formed what passed for the sky in the rest of the Underworld, there were stars glittering above them. Unfamiliar constellations, but constellations nonetheless. She'd never seen such starlight, until it was swallowed by bright silver, flooding the landscape as if a lamp had just been lit.

A full moon had burst into existence in the dark sky. Deina laughed from the sudden, surprising beauty of it.

"Deina? Is that you?" Drex called out to her. He and the others were huddled nearby. Theron relaxed his grip slightly as Drex stood to meet them. "We thought you were lost." He peered over Deina's shoulder. "What happened to that . . . ?"

"We left him fighting the blood hunters. I don't think we need to worry about him." Deina let go of Theron's hand to take in everything around her. The long night they'd walked through had disappeared. The space behind was now filled by two enormous bronze gates, seemingly set on their own in the middle of verdant, rolling countryside. Below her feet, the icy wasteland of the moor had vanished, too. They stood once again on the path, though here it was wide and laid with polished granite slabs, spaced to allow fragrant herbs to grow between them. On either side of the path were glades, lush with grass, trees, and flowers. Nightingales sang unseen among the foliage.

"What do we do now?" Aster demanded, anxiety sharpening his voice. "There's no path. Where's Hades? Where's his palace?"

"But the path's right here." Deina knelt and flattened her hand against the cool, smooth stone. It felt real enough. "Look, it leads on across the grass, between the trees."

"Trees?" Dendris turned in a circle. "Where? I don't see them."

"What do you see?"

"A desert. Black sand, stretching far into the distance." There were murmurs of agreement from the others. "Like the black

sand of the Styx, where the ghosts were waiting." She shook her fist at the sky. "Are we dead? Did that daimon trick us?"

Had Nat tricked them? Panic began to crawl up Deina's spine. How could they not see what she could see? Nat's voice, telling her she was different, whispered so loud through her head that she couldn't tell whether it was a memory or whether he was, somehow, there with them.

Shut up, Nat. I know what I am.

Even if it wasn't true, saying it to herself made her feel better. Somehow, she just had to help the rest of them see.

The flowers. She groped in the pouch hanging from her belt, searching for the purple flowers she'd pinched from the tree after her encounter with the Dream Children. Nat had crushed one and spread it on her eyelids to help her see what the Dream Children really were. Maybe she could use them in the same way.

"Dendris, close your eyes."

The Mycenaean scowled. "Why?"

"I'm going to try something. Just trust me." The way Dendris was gripping her ax handle didn't look very trusting, but she did close her eyes. Deina tore off a couple of the petals and rolled them between her fingertips, releasing the moisture inside. "I'm going to spread something on your eyelids . . ." It was done in an instant. "What about now? What can you see?"

Dendris blinked. Gasped. "It's beautiful." She bent to stroke the dark green grass, then hurried to the edge of the path, exclaiming. "An olive tree—but with golden leaves . . ."

"Where did you get those flowers, Deina?" Theron asked.

"He gave them to me. The daimon, I mean. When you were still asleep from the asphodel flowers." A lie. But then she'd already lied: She'd told the others that the first time she'd met Nat was at the Plains of Asphodel. Perhaps it was guilt that made Theron's tone seem so accusing.

"Why? Did he know we were going to need them?"

Deina sought refuge in anger. "I don't know, Theron. I didn't ask. Given we were trying to escape from plants that were planning on slowly eating us alive, it didn't seem like a particularly important question. Now, do you want me to help you see what's really here or not?"

"*Gods*, I was only asking . . ." Theron closed his eyes. At least the wonder that blossomed in his face as the flowers took effect distracted him from the question of where Deina had gotten them. Drex, Chryse, Aster—another few moments and they were all awestruck at the glories they could now see. It made Deina happy.

But it scared her, too. She wandered into one of the glades—not far enough to be out of sight of the path—and paused beneath a splay-leaved chestnut tree that bore long yellow catkins as well as the spiky green cases of the nuts. It seemed to be spring, summer, and autumn all at once here. "I'm just a Severer; nothing more, nothing less. I know what I am." She murmured the phrase to herself as she examined the tree. Told herself that any of the others, given the same purple flowers, would have been able to produce the same result. But Nat's insinuation, and Charon's hint, had seeded themselves in her mind and were growing like nettles, faster than she could root them out.

"What's wrong, Deina?" Theron had followed her into the glade.

"More questions? What makes you think something's wrong?"

"The way you're playing with your knife."

Deina glanced down. She hadn't even been aware of taking her knife out.

"You're worried about something." He brushed an escaped strand of hair away from her shoulder. "I remember how you used to do that when we were—"

"Of course I'm worried." She was in no mood for Theron to bring up their childhood again. "How many times have we almost died since we entered the Underworld? And now we're about to force ourselves into the presence of a god. If Hades knows anything about me, he'll know that I hate him." She toyed with the idea of relieving her feelings by driving her blade into the tree trunk, but Dendris might somehow find out. "The odds of us surviving this are not good."

"Weren't you the one telling us we should play the odds? And no one's trying to kill us right now." Theron's brow creased. "Did your brown eye always have a golden halo around the pupil? I thought I noticed it before, but it seems wider." He stared into her eyes for a moment longer, then his frown deepened. He looked down. "Your scars have gone. So have mine."

The change of subject threw her. Sliding her knife back into her belt, Deina lifted her fingertips to her cheeks. The skin was smooth, as if the pockmarks left by her illness had never been. She took hold of Theron's wrists and turned them over, examining both sides. The thick rings of scar tissue had vanished.

"My eye will go back to normal when we leave this place." She paused. "Normal for me. And I'm sure the scars will come back."

"Does it matter?" Theron cupped her cheek with one hand.

"You're beautiful. Without your scars, or with them. I've always thought so." He smiled, though there was sadness in his eyes. "Another thing I should have told you before and didn't." Pulling down the neck of his tunic, he revealed the rite-seals flowing across the top of his chest. "From the moment the sigil appears on our foreheads, we're all of us marked. Marked by the god. Marked by what we do."

Deina pointed to the leather cord around his neck. "Is the pendant you made for me hanging from that?"

In answer, Theron drew the pendant out from beneath his clothes. The delicately woven copper butterfly glinted in the moonlight; Deina hadn't seen it since he'd snatched it from her neck at the end of their last fight. Theron dropped his gaze. "After I took it—I was so angry with myself. So ashamed. I know I should have given it back—"

"I'd have thrown it in your face if you'd tried."

"—but I didn't want to." He slipped the pendant off. "It was the only bit of our friendship I had left." Gently, Theron placed the cord over Deina's head. His hands lingered for a moment, resting at the base of her neck, the cord still curled in his fingers. The sensation of his skin against hers, just there, made Deina shiver in a way that had nothing to do with the temperature. Her heart beat faster, her blood warmed by the heat spreading up from her core as she gazed into the deep brown of his eyes.

Theron moved his hands, and the spell was broken.

"Thank you." Deina's voice was hoarse. She tucked the butterfly beneath her tunic where she could feel it against her breastbone, sitting next to the charm Anteïs had given her.

"You're welcome." He paused, studying her, one eyebrow raised. "You'll tell me, won't you? If there's anything else you're worried about. Anything other than our impending extermination at the hands of a god, or whichever of our enemies catches up with us first. You can trust me."

He'd told her that before. Deina turned to study the flowers blooming on a nearby shrub—iridescent mother-of-pearl petals set around a central eye of hammered silver—and tried to imagine the conversation in her head. Her telling Theron exactly how long she'd really been aware of Nat, and what Nat had said about her. That she was scared. That perhaps, just perhaps, there was something different about her.

They will not understand . . .

She shook her head.

"No. There's nothing. We should probably carry on."

She walked back to where the others were resting, still aware of Theron's gaze boring into her back.

The path, easy to follow now, took them through a landscape that grew more gorgeous with every moment. The bright moonlight revealed rich, deep colors that glowed as if lit from within. Ruby-winged butterflies hovered around bushes of lavender that might have been made of polished amethyst. The amber petals of sea daisies sheltered tiny lizards with emerald scales. Deina felt the tension ebb from her shoulders, soothed by the sighing of the breeze through clumps of tall grasses and the chattering of a stream, out of sight but somewhere nearby. She felt she would have liked to stay here for a while. The others were silent, walking slowly and pausing every now and then to examine the details of the jeweled world that surrounded them.

Drex, ahead of the others, came to a halt as the path ran through a grove of small trees.

"What have you found?"

He lifted a glossy scarlet fruit from where it was half hidden among the leaves.

"Pomegranates. Looks good enough to eat if only we were allowed to." He frowned and let the fruit go. "Not that I'm hungry."

"There's no time here," Dendris reminded them. "Not really. No time in which to get hungry. My elder told us that if we stayed too long, we would end up stuck like insects in amber."

Yet another way to die. Everyone walked faster, hurrying through Hades's orchards, ignoring the russet-skinned apples, small scarlet strawberries, and purple plums that were growing, ripe for the taking, near the path. The distant lowing of cattle suggested the god's pastures were not far off. Finally, the path narrowed again, edged now by slender silver columns, about waist height, linked by a silver chain. The trees thinned a little, and the end of the path was visible for the first time.

A palace. White and glittering. Deina's eyes watered, and she rubbed them and blinked.

"Is that—" Her vision shifted again. The skulls she thought she had seen grinning at her from around the windows and doors were in fact ornately carved doorposts and window frames. White stone, not bone.

Together they climbed the steps to the towering double doors that swung open as they approached, admitting them into some sort of entrance hall. The stone floor was strewn with herbs. The air was sweetly scented. Dozens of gold and silver oil lamps hung from the ceiling on chains, revealing walls covered with alternating decorations of brightly colored tapestries and delicate frescoes. At the end of the room stood an archway, its graceful columns framing the entrance to another, much larger space. Deina gazed through the arch. There was a dais at the far end of the next room with two thrones set on it. A figure wrapped in a dark hooded cloak was standing next to one of them, one hand resting on the back of a throne, attention fixed on what seemed to be an enormous looking glass hanging on the far wall; it was reflecting the light from hundreds of floating, flame-filled globes that clustered in the vault above. Chryse came to stand next to her.

"Shall we go in?" Deina murmured, glancing at Chryse.

Chryse sighed. "We've come this far."

"Hold on," Aster whispered. "What's the plan?"

Deina rubbed her hands over her face. "Well, we ask to speak to Hades. If we get that far, we tell him the truth, I suppose. And . . ." She paused. They'd spoken to a god already, but Charon was different; a minor deity. Hades was *Hades*. One of the mightiest of the children of Cronos, brother to Zeus himself. Who knew what might happen if they displeased him? "We need to mind our language." She nudged Aster. "We're angry, but he doesn't need to know we're angry."

Together, the Severers made their way into the throne room. Their footsteps echoed across tiles of veined green marble. No guards—why would a god need them?—but alcoves in the walls contained massive statues of snakes carved from what looked like lapis lazuli, the rich blue stone speckled with gold. The snakes' heads were raised as if about to strike.

The Severers drew closer to the dais. The cloaked figure still didn't turn around.

Deina sank to one knee. Chryse and the others followed her example.

"May we know whether we address Lord Hades, mighty ruler of the realm of the dead? We are his servants, marked by his sigil, and we have come to humbly implore his aid."

The figure on the dais laughed. Turned and pushed back their hood.

A beautiful, voluptuous woman with jet-black hair and violet eyes was staring down at them.

"I am Hades." She smiled. "Welcome."

19

No one reacted. Deina turned her head a fraction, just enough so that she could see Chryse, that she could be sure the shock on her friend's face matched the disbelief and alarm that were pinning her in place and tightening around her chest. This could be a joke, or a trick, but how could they possibly find out? Because if it wasn't, and someone challenged this being who was actually a god—

"Is—is this a joke?" Aster asked.

Deina felt the blood drain from her face.

No, no, no—unsay it, for all our sakes, unsay it—

But he plowed on. "Hades is a god, not a goddess. He rules the Underworld as a king. He—he has his chariot drawn by a team of vicious, flesh-eating black horses. He got his queen by abducting her. He—he . . ." Aster trailed off. "Um . . ."

The woman on the dais was staring at Aster with the same focus as a cat watching a bird. Her smile had faded. "You don't believe me, Aster of Iolkos, Soul Severer of my Order, your forehead marked with my sigil?" Aster threw himself onto his face, trying to apologize, but the woman ignored his gesture. "I take it you expected someone different?" As the words left her mouth, the woman's voice deepened, and she morphed into a tall, broad-shouldered man with close-cropped dark hair. "Someone like this?" The god scowled and shifted back into her previous form. "Doubt yourself, Severer. Doubt your sanity, doubt your worth, doubt your very existence, but do not *ever* doubt me. I am a god." Hades's voice boomed as she grew larger, taking up the entire height of the chamber and leaning over the Severers. Deina threw up her arms, trying to shield her face, to make herself smaller so she might shrink beyond Hades's notice. "Do not think to confine me within the worn comfort of your narrow-minded definitions." The enormous figure shrank to human proportions. "You mortals are pathetic. So easily confused. So limited in your thinking, and your language." She clicked her fingers; the cloak disappeared. Now the god was clad in a draped gown of blue silk that exactly matched the color of the carved snakes in the alcoves, secured at the waist with a gem-encrusted belt. A matching diadem sat on top of her elaborately curled hair. She settled herself on the throne and crossed her legs. "Well?"

Deina opened her mouth—but she couldn't summon the words. What they'd just witnessed, the wholly unexpected nature and immensity of their encounter with this divinity—it had scattered her thoughts like autumn leaves stripped by the first winter gale. Surely one of the others would be able to speak?

The silence persisted. The god sighed.

"Come, now. You must want something, since you are here. You. Deina, as you call yourself."

Deina stayed on her knees. "We—we are Soul Severers, my lady, come from the House of Hades in the city of—"

"Iolkos. Yes, I know. Why are you here?"

"We were sent to the Underworld on a commission from Orpheus, Lord of the Theban Dominion. He wished us to find the ghost of Eurydice and—"

"I know." The god shifted impatiently on her throne. "But why are you *here*?"

Deina hesitated. "We hoped you might help us."

"Help you?" Hades examined her fingernails. "If gods spent all their time giving aid to humans who requested it, we'd never do anything else. Is that all? If so, you can move on."

The tone, the words—Deina remembered that hot and airless afternoon not so long ago, sitting with Chryse on the porch of the Temple of Poseidon, being shooed away by the temple servant. The same afternoon Orpheus had sailed into Iolkos harbor. She remembered her own thoughts: If gods could be killed, she'd hunt them down and slit their throats and smile while she was doing it . . .

Deina stood and looked Hades in the face, her plan to keep her temper evaporating. If she was about to be struck dead, she wasn't going to die groveling in the dirt. She was worth more than that. They all were.

"No. That isn't all. You may know that we were sent here to find the ghost of Queen Eurydice and to remove her from the Underworld. But she does not wish to return to the mortal realm. She told us that Orpheus keeps sending Severers after her so that he can use her powers to drain the life from those he chooses and add it to his own. He kills the Severers he sends on these expeditions—Severers serving their cities in your name, marked, as you pointed out, with your sigil. If we return to him, he's going to kill us. So, as your *faithful* servants, we seek your protection. And your counsel."

Leaning on the arm of the throne, her chin propped on one hand, Hades regarded Deina for what felt like an eternity. The god smiled slightly and sat up.

"I'm glad to find that your years as one of the Theodesmioi have not yet destroyed your spirit. Show me the spindle."

Deina fumbled in her bag for the slender wooden rod. As soon as she pulled the spindle out of the bag, it vanished from her grasp and reappeared, floating in the air above Hades's outstretched hand. The god gazed curiously at the unremarkable object.

"To me, mere moments of mortal time appear to have passed since I last saw Eurydice. For her, I suspect it may have seemed very much longer." Hades raised her other hand and touched the spindle with the tip of one long nail. "Long enough, I wonder, for her to have forgiven me?" As the god spoke, the spindle disintegrated into dust that trickled through her fingers, and Eurydice's ghost reappeared. She seemed frozen in position, yet more solid than she had been on the Plains of Asphodel; Deina felt she could have reached out and brushed her fingers across the folds of the other woman's pale gown. The god held out her palm and blew across it in Eurydice's direction. "I give you back your voice."

Eurydice stared at Hades. "I expected never to see you again." She turned, taking in her surroundings. Her gaze lingered

on Chryse, on the sigil scarring her forehead, before Hades reclaimed her attention by clearing her throat.

"I had thought the same. Yet I am glad you are here, Daughter."

Daughter? Was the god playing games? Deina studied the features of Eurydice and Hades, trying—failing—to see any family resemblance. If Eurydice was a demigod, it might explain why she hadn't become a blood hunter after her death, but—Deina's stomach heaved as she fought down a surge of panic—if the god had allowed her own daughter to aid Orpheus, what did that mean for them?

"I dare say your rescuers would like to hear more of your story." Hades clicked her fingers again, and Deina was no longer on her feet. Instead, she and the other Severers were sitting in chairs, forming a semicircle around Eurydice like an audience waiting for a bard to begin reciting one of the epic poems about fallen cities or impossible adventures. "You have the stage, Eurydice."

"As you wish." She turned to face the Severers. "I was a child, no more than four years old, when the sigil appeared on my forehead, and I was taken by the Order of Hades to their House in Thebes. I was placed in the children's dormitory, an initiate. In time, I progressed through the ranks: apprentice, novice, adept. I was skilled—strong—good at what I did. The best in the House. I could carry out every rite with ease, and without suffering. The Toll took no effect on me."

Deina sank down in her seat; she could feel the others looking at her. She was the only one in the House at Iolkos, so far as she knew, who seemed immune to the ravages of the Toll.

The ghost continued. "So far, my story is much the same as

yours, I imagine. But the elder who spent the most time with me did one thing differently. She broke the rules and told me my name. My true name. She told me my parents had called me Eurydice, after a great queen of Thebes. As well as feeling pride in my skill as a Severer, I now began to feel that I should have pride in my ancestry. Why was I named for a queen, if not to reflect some superiority in my bloodline, and therefore, I reasoned, in myself?"

No similarity there; Deina had no delusion that her parents had been anything other than ordinary. She was glad of it; as far as she could tell from Iolkos, the nobles based their claims to superiority on wealth—wealth that had been accumulated through their ancestors' acts of murder and theft. If she'd known Eurydice as a young woman, Deina suspected she wouldn't have liked her.

"I grew in pride," Eurydice continued, "and like all Theodesmioi, I longed for my freedom. So, when Orpheus, already king of Thebes, came to ask for my help and to offer me marriage in return, I said yes instantly. I didn't wait to ask what he wanted. Or why he wanted me in particular; I was beautiful, strong, of noble birth, or so I imagined." Eurydice gave a small, bitter smile. "In my own eyes, I was an obvious choice."

"But surely," Theron said, "when he told you what he was expecting, when he asked you to kill, to drain the life from someone—" He broke off. But Deina had heard the horror and disgust in his voice, and loved him for it.

"You know," Hades interrupted, pointing at Theron, "I like you. You're never afraid to ask the difficult questions. Brave, if not necessarily bright. So tell us, Eurydice. What did you say when Orpheus asked you to kill?"

The ghost looked at the floor. "I said yes. People die all the time. To die, to sacrifice oneself to extend the life of our mighty king—I convinced myself it was an honor. Just as being Theodesmioi is supposed to be an honor."

Aster was sitting to Deina's left. She saw his hands clench convulsively, gripping the arms of the chair. If Eurydice saw the movement, she gave no sign of it.

"Aristaeus had found an ancient rite in the archives at Mycenae. He and Orpheus had been searching for a Severer talented and strong enough to carry it out. They did not know that it was my divine heritage that gave me the power. They still don't. Neither did I, until later." She glanced at Hades. "Not until after my first death, when Hades told me the truth." Eurydice began pacing up and down in front of the dais, though her footsteps were soundless. "At first, all was well. Orpheus told me he loved me. He had concubines, but I alone was queen. Performing the rite served to slow my own aging as well as that of my king. I was . . . satisfied with my role. But then he began to call on me to use the rite more frequently. Each sacrifice adds only a handful of years to his span, and long life is no longer his aim. He wants immortality."

Hades growled, a low, guttural sound at odds with her polished appearance.

"The rest you know," Eurydice murmured. "I sickened of the slaughter. Of being Orpheus's instrument. The years brought some little wisdom, finally. I tried to end it. Orpheus sent Severers to bring me back. And each time they did, until now."

She turned to Hades. "You are aware of everything that takes place within the borders of your kingdom. You must have heard my pleas even when no one else could. But all you did was to tell me that you were my father, then abandon me."

The god drummed the ring-bedecked fingers of one hand on her thigh.

"Deina, why do you think I didn't help?"

The words spilled unbidden from Deina's tongue. "I think that gods play games with human lives. And they cheat. And that all you really care about is entertainment: anything to alleviate the terrible, mind-crushing boredom of immortality—" Too late, she clamped her hand over her mouth.

Hades threw her head back and laughed, a bell-like ripple of sound that set Deina's teeth on edge.

"Partly right. But if I'm being honest, as you humans claim to be, I did nothing because—honestly—I didn't care. I was fond of Eurydice's mother, in my own way. She was a Severer, too. I copied one of my brother Zeus's techniques and disguised myself as a mouse to get in and out of her room." Hades smiled as if at a pleasant memory. "We had a mutually enjoyable relationship, until she got pregnant and I grew bored. And at least I prevented the elders of her House from walling her up alive. She's dead now, of course." The god huffed impatiently. "More to the point, Eurydice is right. Human lives are short and full of grief. People kill each other all the time. Orpheus is hardly exceptional in that regard. That's why I ignored her cries for help."

"And now?" As Deina tried to stand, vine-like tendrils burst out of the chairs they were sitting on, looping tight around her legs, arms, and torso and pinning her to her seat. Almost like the Deathless Trees she'd summoned into the Threshold during the Punishment Rite. "Now that we're asking for help, too?" She strained her arms against the grip of the vines. "Does this mean you're going to punish us? That you're going to send her back again? What about Orpheus?"

"Enough questions," Hades snapped. "I must have silence. Even for a god, the weighing of an almost infinite number of possibilities requires a certain amount of focus." Hades sauntered up and down in front of the two thrones, her bracelets clinking softly. "If only my queen were here to advise me. Though, on the other hand, Persephone might not appreciate being reminded of my dalliance with Eurydice's mother. There was a certain amount of . . . unpleasantness." She turned and strode to the huge mirror that hung on the wall behind the thrones. With a wave of the god's hand, images began to appear. They flickered fast as thought across the polished surface, pausing occasionally, presumably in response to some unspoken command. Deina recognized or guessed at some: Iolkos, Orpheus in his golden mask, a city on a high peak encircled by massive walls—Thebes? But most she couldn't begin to identify, even if they moved slowly enough for her to see. Hades waved her hand again, and the mirror returned to being no more than a disk of polished obsidian, reflecting lamplight and their own shadowy forms.

The god returned to her throne.

"What was it you said, Eurydice? Orpheus no longer merely wants to spin out his years. He wants immortality . . ." She pursed her lips and frowned, shaking her head slowly. "You know, if there's one human trait the gods hate above all others, it's hubris. We don't care if one human thinks he's better than another, but if he should dare to even contemplate that he could, in any way, approach the ineffable glory of a god . . . Only the gods are immortal. Eurydice, you'll return no more to the mortal realm."

Surely, now, Chryse had to acknowledge that Deina had done the right thing? Deina glanced at the other woman. Her lips were pressed tightly together, but Deina couldn't make out her expression in the ruddy, flickering light.

The ghost had sunk to her knees. "Where will I go?"

"To the place of judgment, the place to which all human souls are eventually called."

"Judgment?"

"Did you think there would be no reckoning for your crimes? Still, take comfort, Daughter. What humans know of the true nature of the Underworld, or of the true nature of anything, might amount to a single grain of sand on an infinite beach. You may find it's not what you've been led to expect."

Hades extended her hand, as if in blessing. Eurydice's ghost rose into the air, spinning slowly as if being drawn upward into some invisible vortex. At the same time, she began to fade, her form becoming more translucent, more nebulous, until she was nothing more than a shimmering patch of light, like spring sunshine dancing on wind-rippled water. Then that, too, vanished.

"Hm." Hades returned her attention to the Severers. "As for you—how can I help you?" She smiled, sharp teeth white against red lips.

A request put to a god had to be carefully phrased. Polite. Deina hesitated.

Dendris didn't. "By destroying Orpheus and his Dominion and setting our cities free," she urged.

"By telling people the truth." Aster's voice was rough with anger.

"Shut up," Theron hissed.

Aster ignored him. "I want the Theodesmioi to know the fate that awaits them when they die. I want the world to know that gods are cheats and liars. That they have no honor."

"Oh, gods . . ." Drex closed his eyes in despair.

"You consider truth so important, do you?" Hades said brightly. "In that case, perhaps I should share some truths with you all." Rubbing her hands together, the god left the dais and came to stand in front of the Severers. "Aster, Orpheus gave you an extra commission, didn't he? He told you that Theron wasn't to leave the Underworld, and that if nothing else killed him, he wanted you to. And you were quite happy to acquiesce."

"What?" Theron stared at Aster, breathing hard. "You were going to *kill* me?" He began to struggle against the vines that bound him as the color drained from Aster's face. "Where's the honor in that?"

"He asked me to, he's the king, and—and—it was only at the beginning that I seriously thought about—" Aster looked desperately from one teammate to the other. "I didn't know that things would change, that we were going to—"

"Why?" Theron demanded. "Why was I to die? Did you even ask?"

"No, he didn't," Hades said. "But we'll get on to your truth in a moment, Theron. Drex first."

"No, thank you, my lady," Drex murmured.

"But you'll like it, I promise. It's a prophecy: When Iolkos battles Sparta, your life will fail, cut short by one of your own side. You're clever. I'm sure you'll work it out. Now it's Theron's turn." She pointed at Theron, who was still struggling to get at Aster. "Orpheus wants you dead because of another prophecy. Tiresias, mighty prophet of Thebes, told him that he would be slain by his own son. And you, marked by a very distinctive birthmark on the back of your neck, are the only son he has."

Chryse gasped. Theron stopped struggling. Hades began to laugh.

"No words, prince of Thebes? No smooth tongue to charm me?"

For what felt like ages, Theron said nothing. Just stared at the god. Deina's heart ached for him. She tugged uselessly against the vines, trying to free her hand so she could offer him some comfort. Perhaps the god was lying, but Deina had seen the birthmark.

"No." Theron forced the word out. "No, it's not true. It can't be true."

"You need more evidence?" Hades asked. "Have you never wondered about the scars around your wrists? Orpheus had you condemned to death when you were just old enough to walk. He feared the gods more at that time; to avoid the guilt of your murder, he had you tied to a stake on a mountainside in the expectation that a wolf would devour you. Instead, a shepherd found you and packed you off to his childless brother in Iolkos, where you lived quite happily, until I placed my sigil on your forehead and the Order came to take you away." She paused. "Neidius, the leader of your House—he told Orpheus about the birthmark and was well rewarded for it. When Orpheus arrived, wasn't Neidius the one who told you privately that the Tyrant might have a task he wanted undertaken? Wasn't he the one who suggested you should volunteer?"

Theron seemed too stunned to take in Neidius's betrayal.

"My—my mother?"

"One of Orpheus's many concubines. She did not survive your birth."

Theron groaned. His head was slumped down on his chest, as if the weight of this revelation was crushing him. In that instant, Deina saw the friend of her childhood more clearly than she had for years.

"Who shall we have next?" Hades asked. "Deina, Dendris, or Chryse?" There was a murmur of distress from Chryse, a muted cry of protest from Dendris.

"Enough," Deina begged. "Stop this."

"Really? But there are still delicious disclosures to be made. And would you all not rather know the reality of those with whom you've thrown in your lot?"

No one answered.

"Well. Perhaps there is such a thing as too much truth." Hades came to stand in front of Deina. "We will stop. But not before I've shown you your reality, Deina. Some things can no longer be concealed."

"I don't—" Deina began. *I don't understand.* But before she could complete the sentence, the god snapped her fingers, and the two of them were somewhere else.

* * *

A seashore, and not a tame one; this sea was a wild, brooding thing, smashing against the seaweed-clad rock just below where Deina was standing, spitting its wrath against her and the land that barred its path. She and Hades were standing alone. The wind howled past them, whipping the skirt of Deina's tunic up around her legs, forcing her back. Instinctively, she looked around for shelter. To one side was a low, one-room house, built of the same gray rock as the cliffs behind, windows shuttered against the storm. To the other—

Nothingness. A wall of pale mist.

"Where are we?" Deina tried to shout. The wind snatched her voice from her lips.

Hades, seemingly untouched by the gale, raised a hand. The wind evaporated. The dark swell of the sea set in place, frozen like a wall painting. The god smiled.

"Still in the Underworld. Still in my palace. This place is from your memory. The memory is fragmentary, so the place is, too. There's no need to be alarmed."

The little house drew Deina's gaze. She'd been outside, on a day like this, and someone had run to fetch her. To rescue her from the sea's fury. Her father.

There he was, standing on the rocks, gazing out to sea. Not a ghost—more substantial than that. But not real, either. No breath lifted his chest, no thought lent color to his expression.

Thick chestnut hair tied back. Darker skin and eyes than hers, but the same rounded oval face. Deina glanced at her hand, then at his. The same long fingers.

Time collapsed, and Deina could remember everything: him smiling down at her as she played among the wood shavings beneath his worktable; him comforting her and binding her knee when she fell and scraped it; him lifting her into his arms and holding her against his chest until the steady beat of his heart lulled her to sleep. And she remembered the night the Order had taken her—how they'd beaten him because he wouldn't surrender her.

"Father . . ." Weeping, Deina turned on the god. "Why are you showing me this? What is my childhood to you?" She wanted to hug the memories to her, to protect them from this cruel, violet-eyed divinity.

"Such a kind man, your father. One quality the gods invariably lack."

Dread began to wriggle like a parasite caught beneath Deina's ribs.

"You knew him?"

"Yes. One of the few humans I've taken the trouble to know well." Hades reached out and touched one of the tears rolling down Deina's cheek. "There was a nobility about him . . ."

"'Was'?" Deina breathed. "What do you mean 'was'?"

"After you were taken, he was conscripted into Orpheus's navy; they needed carpenters. He died in a fire at the timber yard. Many years ago now, as you would reckon it."

"No—" Deina ran to the image of her father and tried to embrace it. But her arms closed on emptiness. She sank to her knees and dug her nails into the damp turf. "Bring him back! Please . . ."

"Really, Deina, you barely knew him." Hades snapped her fingers, and the sea and the cottage disappeared, too. They were now in what seemed to be a garden cut into the side of a forested hill. Borders and trellises of vibrant flowers surrounded a large circular terrace of polished sandstone, rough beneath Deina's hands. But there were no sounds—no birdsong, no insects. "I've shown you your father. Aren't you going to ask about your other parent? Your mother?"

The dread grew into a serpent, crawling along Deina's spine. She searched her memory for any recollection of her mother. Nothing. Deep in her brain, the serpent hissed.

"No!" Deina clapped her hands over her ears. "I don't want to know. Take me back to the others."

Hades tsked. "So childish." Taking Deina's wrists, the god pulled her upright so they were face-to-face. "But I'm going to tell you, anyway. It's me, of course." She lifted her hand to Deina's cheek. "Welcome home, my child."

Revulsion turned Deina's stomach. She ran to the balustrade at the far end of the terrace and retched over the side. Clung to the cool stone and wondered what would happen if she threw herself into the crevasse below.

"I tell you you're a demigod, and this is how you react?" Hades sounded vexed. "Have you nothing to say to your mother, Khthonia? That was the name I gave you before I left you with your father."

Something deep in Deina's bones stirred at the name the god used—something ancient and inhuman—but she shook her head.

"No. You're lying—trying to deceive me. I hate the gods. I hate you," Deina yelled, jabbing a finger in Hades's direction, careless of the consequences. "I am *nothing* like you."

"Is that so? What, you don't lie or cheat or trick people?" Hades grinned. "I think Charon would beg to differ. I think we're more alike than you care to admit."

"That wasn't the same. And you are not my—my mother." Pots filled with deep purple lavender were set at intervals along the balustrade. Deina buried her nose in the nearest flowers and took a deep breath. "There's no scent. It doesn't smell of anything because it's not real." She grabbed the pot and hurled it toward Hades. It vanished. "None of this is real. It's all lies."

The god pinched the bridge of her nose. "You keep talking of truths and lies as if they are somehow completely different things and mutually incompatible—"

"Because they are!"

"—rather than just a matter of perspective. Did Charon not recognize you? Did you not summon your teammates back from the deadly sleep of the asphodel flowers? Were you not able to give them vision when their mortal eyes couldn't see the beauty of my realm?"

"I—" Deina bit off her words. She'd been able to do those things because Nat had showed her how—any of the others could have done the same, she was certain. Almost certain. Whatever Hades said, whatever Nat implied, whatever she'd done, however much like Eurydice she seemed to be—it couldn't be true. She despised the gods. She refused to believe that her existence—that any aspect of her—could be due to one of them . . .

A sob tore at Deina's throat and she drew one of her knives. "Tell me which parts of my body I owe to you, then. I'd rather cut them off now than be daughter to a god."

"So dramatic." Hades sighed. "Your father was, too. His least-appealing quality."

"What do you want from me?"

"You came to me, remember? You asked for my help. And"—the god shrugged—"I'm prepared to give it. If you'll give me something in return."

Deina didn't attempt to conceal her scorn. No such thing as a gift from a god.

"Orpheus's fate stands on a knife edge," Hades continued. "As does Theron's. Either the father slays the son, or the son slays the father. If the first, Theron and all your companions will be dead before the moon next renews itself. If the second, Theron, in retribution for his patricide, will be condemned to undergo the Punishment Rite. *If* he is caught by the Order of Hades. But the only way for you to gain him this extra time, this chance, and for you to save your friends, is for you to submit to me."

"If their fates are ordained, how can there be alternatives?"

"You make the mistake of thinking of time as linear. It isn't."

Deina hesitated. All dead, before the moon began to wax again . . .

"What would submitting to you involve?"

Hades tilted her head. "Your birth makes you a demigod. Stronger, a little more powerful, perhaps, but essentially human. But I want to elevate you to a god, as my brother once elevated Herakles. Then you will have the power to stop Orpheus.

In return, you'll give up your mortal life and stay here with me in the Underworld. Forever."

Forever. The word echoed in Deina's ears like the slamming shut of a door. Yet how could she leave Theron to such a fate? Fear squeezed her lungs. She didn't want to ask for help, not again. But Nat had seemed hostile to Hades. If there was any chance he could get her out of this . . .

"Nat, please, if you can hear me—"

Almost before the words had left her lips, Nat was standing next to her. Hades laughed.

"Nat? Is that what you've been calling yourself?"

Nat bared his teeth at the god.

Hades's smile faded. "I think you'd better tell her your real name. And who you are."

"What does she mean?" Deina asked. "Nat?"

"Now," Hades ordered, her voice bearing strange harmonics that rippled through Deina's core.

Nat stood up straighter. "My name is Thanatos. I'm the god of death."

20

A *god*? Deina stared at Nat, taking in details she hadn't noticed before. Or that hadn't been there before. The swirling patterns embroidered in black thread on his tunic. The black crystals studding the belt that was slung around his hips. The iridescent sheen to his hair. The tiny symbols forming the silvery scars that crisscrossed his arms. The way the dark shadows gathering around him fanned out from his shoulders like wings.

Deina slapped Nat as hard as she could across the face, the sound splitting the silence of the terrace. "You lied to me, you bastard!"

He held up his hands, placating. "I didn't lie, not technically. I didn't actually say I wasn't a god. I said I wasn't Hades or one of those who live on Olympus. And I'm not. I and my siblings—and my cousins the Titans—we existed before she was even thought of." He seemed to grow immensely tall, and the shadows that cloaked him became long black feathers, spread wide enough to sweep the stars from the sky. "I was there, on the Trojan plain, when Hector and Achilles breathed their last. I walked the streets of Troy as Hecuba and Andromache screamed out their grief for their slaughtered children." He diminished and became Nat again and gave Hades a derisive nod. "She and her siblings were just written into the story later."

"You *technically* didn't lie?" Deina's palm stung. She closed her hand into a fist.

"Before you hit me again, in my defense, I did tell you that coming to find Hades was a bad idea." He rubbed his cheek ruefully. "I did try to warn you."

"No, you didn't. Warning me would have been—it would have been—" Deina forced herself to speak through the tears that she could no longer restrain. "It would have been warning me what she was going to say. Warning me that she was going to tell me that—that—"

"That she was going to tell you the truth?" The pity in Nat's eyes was almost unbearable. Deina shook her head and closed her eyes, but his hand found hers. "It is the truth, Deina. You just weren't ready to hear it. Waking the others from the asphodel, using the flowers—I didn't give you any power that you didn't already have. I merely showed you how to use it." He paused. "You look beautiful, by the way. That color suits you."

"What?"

Deina's travel-stained tunic and cloak had gone. So had her bag and her knives. She was wearing a full-length, one-shouldered gown of diaphanous garnet-red silk. The hem and the neckline were studded with tiny rubies, and the gown was secured by a gold belt and a single gold shoulder brooch set with more rubies. Her boots had been replaced with delicate sandals made from a fine gold mesh. She could feel her hair loose against her back. Snatching her fingers from Nat's grasp, she turned on Hades.

"Change it back. I'm not a goddess. I don't want to dress like one."

"Oh, very well," Hades said irritably. "I merely wanted to show you that the Underworld isn't all ghosts and blood hunters. But if you're so determined . . ." The shift was instantaneous. Deina's hands went automatically to her knives—still there, still solid. Maybe solid enough to do some damage to a god, if she put enough belief behind the blow.

"Why do you even want to keep me here?" Deina asked. "You didn't care about Eurydice. Why do you care about me?"

"Perhaps I'm growing sentimental." Hades's violet eyes glittered dangerously. "I might ask why you are so indifferent to the great honor I am offering you. Most people would kill for immortality. Orpheus already does."

"Would it be so very impossible for you to be happy here?" Nat added. "Immortality and eternal youth don't seem like such a bad exchange. Plus, I'm here." He shrugged and spread his hands wide and smiled at her—the same confident, dazzling smile that she'd begun, somehow, to grow fond of.

Deina turned away and pressed the heels of her hands to her aching eyes. There it still was, dancing before her in the darkness: a crude sketch of a ship, sails bellied out by the wind, a single line across the cloth representing the wide, open horizon. What would be the use of youth or immortality? If she said yes to Hades, she would just be swapping one form of servitude for another; the scars left by the torc she'd worn for so many years might have temporarily vanished, but she could still feel the weight of the spell-cast bronze. She'd be shut up in the Underworld for eternity. Buried alive. The thought made it hard to breathe. If she said yes, she'd never again be able to feel the sun or the wind against her skin, or stand ankle-deep in a cold stream, or smell the aroma of baking bread. Worse—she wouldn't be human anymore. She might not even care. Could she make Nat understand?

"Can I ask you a question?"

He nodded.

"Well, then: Are *you* happy?"

Nat's eyes opened wide as he stared at her.

"Come now, Deina," Hades demanded. "What is it to be? I'm getting bored with your lack of proper filial devotion." She strolled up to Nat, raised her hand, and ran her long fingernails along his jaw; Nat jerked his head away. "And as for you, Thanatos, I'll be very interested to learn what game you've been playing by assisting Deina while she's been journeying through my realm. You may have existed before me, but I am ruler of the Underworld. You'd be wise to show a little more respect. Unless you *want* to end up in Tartarus with your cousins." Hades batted her eyelashes and smiled. "Or tied to a mountain with your liver being torn out by an eagle every day, forever."

The corded muscles of Nat's arms stood out as his hands curled into fists. "Don't threaten me, Hades. Without me, you'd be nothing. You need me."

"Perhaps not as much as you think. Deina?"

Games. That was what it all came down to. Orpheus had been playing them, and Charon had tried to trap them, and now Hades had some game of her own that she wanted Deina ensnared in. And Nat—Deina swallowed hard. He'd saved them more than once, but maybe that had been nothing more than a game, too. She sank to her knees. The thought of acknowledging any part of what Hades claimed sickened her, but she'd brought the others into Hades's palace. She had to get them out, too. So, if Hades wanted filial devotion . . .

"Mighty Hades, I cannot stay in the Underworld. Not *yet*." She emphasized the last word. "I beg you: Help my companions and me to find another way out of your realm. Give us a chance, at least, to escape from Orpheus." Deina saw her freedom, a bright feathered thing skimming away from her across the ocean. Hers, and Chryse's. Perhaps there was still a way she could seize it. "To live free, for at least a little while. That's all I want. That's all I've ever wanted." She clasped her hands together as if in prayer. "Please, Mother."

Hades pinched Deina's chin and lifted her head. The god's violet eyes bored into her as if trying to see inside her head. Inside her soul. Deina gazed back steadily until Hades released her.

"You may leave. I will set you on the right path to a different gate."

"How will we open it? Another rite, or—"

"Your own power will suffice—you will have to accept your birthright at least to that extent. But once you are outside my realm, remember: All of your companions are marked for death, and soon. If you decide you wish to take another path, you may call on me at any point until Orpheus kills his son. But at that moment, the die will have been cast, and it will be too late. Too late for all of you."

The scene around them changed; they were back in the throne room. Deina got to her feet. Nat was still hovering next to her. The vines binding the other Severers withered, and her companions scattered around the room, hastening to get away. From the imprisoning chairs, Deina wondered, or from one another? But though separated, they were all of them watching her. Trying to guess, no doubt, what Hades had told her, and why Nat was with her again.

All of them apart from Theron. He lingered nearby, but his attention was wholly focused on Hades. His eyes, as he looked at the god, burned with hatred.

Not that Hades cared. She turned away and ascended her throne.

"You are free to go. Follow the path beyond the palace and it will lead you to another gateway. You may have the chance to hide from Orpheus."

Nat tapped Deina on the shoulder. "I suppose this is farewell. For now, at least. Just try not to get yourself eaten between here and the exit." He winked at her and lowered his voice. "Congratulations, Hades's daughter. You've survived the Underworld." Judging by the smile he gave her, he was back to his normal, unquenchable self. Although . . . Deina tilted her head, frowning. Was there something different, some slight shadow lurking just behind his eyes?

Frustrated, she gave up. Whatever it was—if it was there—she couldn't pin it down.

"Will you be punished for helping me?"

Nat bent his head to murmur in her ear. "I'd like to see her try." He vanished, leaving Deina with the sensation of his lips just brushing against her skin, and the feeling that, despite all rational arguments to the contrary, she was going to miss him.

"Hades's daughter?" Theron mumbled. He looked . . . stricken—that was the only word Deina could think of. She could tell him he'd misheard, but he wouldn't believe her. Better to remind him, perhaps, that blood wasn't everything. She shrugged one shoulder unhappily. "Orpheus's son?"

Theron flinched and turned away from her. Deina tried to be glad that the others were too far off to have heard Nat's words.

Hades stood and clapped her hands. She was wearing her dark cloak again.

"This has been entertaining, Severers of Iolkos. But I warn you: Do not dare to trespass in my realm again." Her voice deepened and grew loud—a harsh, trumpeting roar that sounded as if it were coming from many throats, not one. "You might not find me in such a forgiving mood." She swept the cloak wide, shifting in one fluid movement from a woman into a huge black-and-blue-scaled snake that reared above them, long-fanged and hissing. Chryse cried out in alarm as Drex, trying to back away, tripped over some slight imperfection in the marble floor and fell. Dendris hauled him back to his feet.

"Look!" Aster's shout drew Deina's attention to the alcoves lining the walls of the throne room. The snake statues were pulsing and writhing as stone transformed into flesh and blue scales, mottled with gold. One by one the snakes, each longer than two men, slumped out of their alcoves and began slithering toward the Severers and the archway that led out of the throne room. "Run!"

Aster hurried Drex and Chryse toward the archway. Deina

saw him drive the wide-leafed blade of his spear into one snake, then pivot and stab the jaw of another with the iron spike. The snake opened its maw wider than Deina thought possible and vomited a stream of worms that began to swarm up the shaft of Aster's spear. He bellowed and leaped back. Dendris was hacking her way toward the arch.

"Deina—" Dendris yelled, pointing. A snake was diving toward her. Deina slashed both knives across its throat and kicked it away—too late to stop it spewing worms across her legs. She cried out—her skin was burning and blistering beneath their touch. Gritting her teeth, she swept the worms away with the side of her blade. Just in time, Theron grabbed her wrist and hauled her backward as Hades's giant fangs sliced through the air only a handspan from where she had been standing.

They turned and ran. Theron gasped and stumbled but quickly regained his balance and kept going. The others were already through the archway and had reached the far end of the antechamber. Together, Drex, Aster, Chryse, and Dendris were trying to drag the huge double doors open. Deina sped up, pulling Theron after her. The sudden stench and the way her boots crunched against the floor made her look down. She gagged; what had earlier appeared to be fragrant dried herbs were now countless small bones and teeth. The gold and silver oil lamps hanging from chains had become skulls, grinning in the light that spilled from empty eye sockets.

The doors were open just enough for them to slip through. Chryse, on the top step, screamed and pointed behind them. Deina risked a glance over her shoulder. A dark tide of nothingness, empty black space, was bearing down upon them. The snakes, the antechamber itself—the darkness was swallowing everything. With one last effort, Deina threw herself forward through the gap between the doors. Theron leaped through after her. The doors slammed shut and disappeared before he'd even hit the ground. Hades's palace and the parkland surrounding it had vanished as if they'd never been. They were alone on a desolate upland, surrounded by an endless vista of bare earth and jagged, rocky hills.

Deina sank to the ground, dragging air into her lungs, and examined her legs. The skin was red and weeping; the slightest touch set her nerve endings on fire. She found the jar of healing ointment Anteïs had given her—still intact, amazingly—and began spreading it across the injured flesh, wincing at each finger stroke. Finally it was done. As the pain began to ebb, something else crept in. Not happiness, not with Hades's revelation still fresh in her mind. (Could it have been a lie? She so desperately wanted it to be a lie.) What she felt instead was relief. They'd escaped. Everyone was still alive. They had a different way out; the rough slabs of the path Hades had promised them were hard and unforgiving beneath her. They'd be able to leave the Underworld and disappear. And as for Theron's fate—Hades herself said it could be altered. Orpheus couldn't kill Theron if he couldn't find him. Theron couldn't kill Orpheus if he never saw him again. She got to her feet as Theron himself pushed past her, head down, and began limping away along the path. Aster, his face etched with misery, hurried after him, calling to him.

"Theron, wait . . ."

A touch on her shoulder. "Deina?" Chryse was pale but uninjured. "Where did Hades take you? What did she tell you?"

"Little enough." A lie. "Nothing I wanted to know." That, at least, was the truth. "She showed me my father and told me how he died." Her father being beaten as they tore her from his arms—the resurrected memory brought tears to her eyes and drew a murmur of sympathy from Drex. "I suppose she wanted to punish me for daring to ask for her help. She summoned—" Deina hesitated. Nat's identity was another thing she didn't want to think about. "She summoned that daimon, too. I think it's in trouble for helping us."

"And yet Hades will allow Orpheus to go unpunished?" Dendris spat on the path. "So much for the justice of the gods. I'm sorry about your father, Deina." She shouldered her ax and started along the path after Aster and Theron.

"I'm sorry, too," Chryse said. Abruptly, she threw her arms around Deina's neck and hugged her tightly. "I'm sorry." Taking Drex's hand, she drew him along the path after Dendris.

Deina sighed as she heaved her bag onto her back and started walking. They just had to get to the gateway. How far off could it be?

Far enough that Deina began to wonder whether Hades had tricked them after all. The path seemed endless. There was no life of any sort in this part of the Underworld. The taste of the air reminded her of the crypts beneath the House where dead Severers were buried: stale and damp, with that aroma of decay that hinted at what was going on within the hollowed-out chambers lining the walls. She should have been grateful that it wasn't freezing; there was no asphodel here trying to lull them into its deadly embrace.

But at least there had been some beauty in the snowfields they'd trudged through. Here was nothing but bare stone, lit by the same dull gray sky that had been overhead since they crossed the Styx.

She was walking with Dendris. Drex and Chryse were side by side, hands still interlinked. Theron was now at the rear. His pace had been growing slower and slower and his limp more pronounced as the long upward climb continued. Deina kept glancing back, ready to help, but Theron locked his gaze on the path.

Aster, walking alone ahead of the others, came to a stop. Deina ran past Drex and Chryse to catch up with him. When she reached his side, he gestured toward the next section of the path. It dipped slightly and veered abruptly to the left, running around the base of the adjacent hill into what looked like a huge expanse of broken stone columns, wreathed in shadow and stretching into the distance. The closest stood no more than five strides away; one of them had fallen partly onto the path, as if drunkenly pointing out the way.

"I think we should rest before we tackle whatever that is," Deina suggested, nodding toward the columns. "Everyone's tired." The sound of voices carried clear through the still air—Theron and Dendris arguing. "What do you think, Aster?"

"Of course. Whatever you want." He seemed unwilling to meet her gaze. Guilt, Deina guessed, because of what Hades had told them about him.

"Deina." Drex approached her. "Theron's injured. Didn't Anteïs give you some healing ointment?"

"Oh—yes." Deina rummaged through her bag to retrieve

the ointment as Dendris and Theron, still bickering, reached the crest of the path.

"I saw you get swiped across the back by the tail of a giant magical snake, Theron. Why are you maintaining otherwise?" Dendris said gruffly.

"Because I want to be left alone." Theron spat out the words through gritted teeth.

"Too bad." Deina held up the ointment. "I'm sure someone said something to me once about what would happen to anyone who slowed the team down. Now take your bags off and sit. We're going to rest here."

Theron scowled at her. "So we're still a team, are we?" Grumbling beneath his breath, wincing, he dumped his gear on the ground and sat down. "Give the ointment to me. I can do it."

"Don't be ridiculous. If the injury's on your back, you won't be able to see."

Theron grunted and leaned forward, wrapping his arms around his knees. The thick scars around his wrists had reappeared; whatever magic had removed them in Hades's garden had vanished along with the garden itself. Deina didn't bother to check her face. She knew the pockmarks would be back, too, and the sudden realization of what Theron must have gone through when his scars were inflicted—a small child, terrified and alone in the dark and the cold—was making her hands shake. She rolled Theron's tunic up. The skin was unbroken, thankfully, but dark bruises were already visible across his whole lower back. Deina bit her lip. When she'd been an apprentice, following Anteïs as she'd attended the dying, the elder had taught her about how people would sometimes bleed inside after a violent blow, how such an injury might kill them slowly even when no blood had been spilled. But Deina didn't have the skill to tell whether that had happened here. And even if she did, what could be done about it? She scooped some of the ointment onto her fingers and began smoothing it over Theron's skin.

He flinched and pulled away, and gasped a little with the pain of the sudden movement.

"Try to stay still," Deina urged. "I'm being as gentle as I can."

"Which is not gentle at all," Theron retorted. "But do carry on. Perhaps you'll do Aster's job for him." He laughed—if that was the right name to give such a bitter sound. "You claim to be a man of honor, Aster. Yet you didn't even ask Orpheus why I was to die."

Aster shrank into himself, flinching away from the scrutiny of five pairs of eyes.

"I . . . He . . ." For a moment, Aster dropped his head into his hands. "Orpheus told me you had committed some great treason, and I didn't question it. I didn't dare. He's the ruler of the entire Theban Dominion. The king. And I thought—I thought that meant he had the honor that should belong to that great office." He cursed. "I'm sorry. I should have told you."

"There." Deina drew Theron's tunic down. "Hopefully, that will help."

"Thank you." Theron shifted position, wincing. "The only treason I'd committed, Aster, was to be born. Were you happy with your commission?"

Aster shook his head slowly. "I hoped I wouldn't have to

act—that the Underworld would do the task for me. I certainly wasn't fantasizing about thrusting a spear between your ribs, if that's what you're imagining. And the more we've journeyed together, the more I've tried not to think about it. It was almost a relief when I finally understood the true extent of Orpheus's evil. Though I already knew I couldn't do it. I couldn't murder my comrade." Aster got to his feet, hesitated, then came to kneel in front of Theron. "You—all of you—have shown me where honor truly lies. Not in rank or wealth or bodily strength but in friendship. I hope you can forgive me, eventually."

"I'll think about it." Theron turned his head just fractionally toward Deina. "I've done things I should wish to see forgiven."

There was a sigh of relief from Drex.

"I'm so glad you're friends again."

"I said I'd think about it," murmured Theron. He nodded at Drex. "Have you worked out your prophecy yet?"

"What's to work out?" Drex raised his eyebrows. "If it's true, I can apparently avoid dying altogether as long as I don't get caught up in a battle between Sparta and Iolkos, and that should be easy enough." He grinned at Chryse. "Given my eyesight, I somehow doubt the city guard or the Dominion's hoplites will try to recruit me."

Chryse pulled his hand into her lap. "It might not be true. The gods lied to us about our place in Elysium. Perhaps everything Hades and Eurydice said was lies. What is truth in the mouth of a god?"

You don't know, Deina thought, *how much I hope you're right.*

"But one thing is certain," Chryse added warmly, smiling at Drex. "No one of any sense would make you be a soldier;

you're too great an artist. You'll end up working for the king, I'm sure of it." She grew very still. "For *a* king, I mean. Or a prince." Her gaze drifted to Theron. "I can't believe Orpheus is your father . . ."

"I don't want to talk about it. I don't even want to think about it." Theron drew the dagger from his belt. "Unless Hades's prediction comes true, and I have the pleasure of cutting out my father's heart"—he drove his blade into the ground next to him—"and holding it, pulsing, in front of his eyes, until he's dead."

Deina placed her hand on his arm.

"You won't have to kill him. You won't have to see or think about him ever again. We just need to get out of here." She glanced at the others. "We should keep going."

Dendris grabbed her ax and her bag and got to her feet, signaling her agreement. "I'm glad Hades told me no truths." She gave Deina a tight smile. "I believe in the truth of my ax, and that is enough for me."

The others got ready to depart. Theron reached for his bags and his quiver, but Deina got there first.

"Drex and I will carry these. Aster, stay next to Theron?"

"Seriously?" Theron growled. "He was planning to murder me."

"No, I was *asked* to murder you," Aster replied. "I didn't get as far as planning it." He held out a hand to pull Theron to his feet. "Come, let me help you."

"So you can make yourself feel better by playing the hero?" Theron retorted, though there was humor lurking in the lines of his face. "I'm not some princess chained to a rock waiting to be rescued."

Aster sighed, crouched next to Theron, slipped an arm around his waist, and carefully pulled him upright.

"If you were, you'd be on your own. You're definitely not my type."

Theron gave a reluctant chuckle.

"Can you walk?" Deina asked. "I wish we had something you could lean on."

Aster slid out his one remaining spear from where it was strapped to his back.

"He can lean on this."

Theron looked the spear up and down. "But no one touches your spears. You said so."

Aster thrust the weapon into Theron's hands. "I think, under the circumstances, I'm going to make an exception."

Together, they headed down the path and into the midst of the stone columns. They all rose high above Aster's head, but their height and their color—the same dull gray as everything else here—were the only ways in which they were identical. Size and shape varied, surfaces were rough and cracked, and the columns had unusual splayed bases and random jagged protrusions. Ahead of them, Dendris drew to one side and rapped her knuckles on one of the nearest columns before running her hands across its surface, shaking her head and muttering something in a tone of despair. She called over her shoulder.

"Stone now. But I think they were once trees."

Deina, at the rear of the group, gazed up at the branchless trunks. What had these trees done, what god had they offended, to be punished like this? Everyone felt the silent menace of the stone forest. They drew together, sticking to the center of the path as it began to slope upward once again. The taint of stagnant water—a nearby lake, perhaps—soured the air briefly. The shadows ahead grew deeper. The strip of sky, such as it was, had narrowed; the valley of the dead forest was becoming a chasm as the hills on either side rose into cliffs that jutted out above the path. Deina remembered the stolen dagger and retrieved it from her bag.

As she stared at the words carved into the weapon, she was conscious of a pang of disappointment; she still struggled to make sense of the incised symbols, despite Drex's patient attempts to teach her. But she could remember what they said.

"I am death and I am light, taking life and giving sight." Light blazed from the crystal blade, illuminating the path well ahead.

"Deina," Chryse called, "come up to the front." Once Deina had obeyed the summons, she pointed to one side of the path. "Running water, I think."

Deina walked to the edge of the path and held the shining knife high. Chryse was right. A stream, purling along the path's rocky margin. They'd found the last river of the Underworld.

21

Up and up the path wound. There was vegetation here. Delicate gray-green ferns were scattered along the banks of the river, while tall rushes with fluffy seed heads grew at the water's margin. There were trees, too. Living ones: brooding, dark-fronded cypresses. Poppies glowed scarlet among their roots. After the bleak desolation they'd been walking through, the vibrant color was shocking. Pleasing, though. Especially combined with the breeze whispering through the rushes, and the way the water splashed melodiously over the rocky riverbed. It looked inviting and delicious; good enough to drink. For the first time in as long as Deina could remember, she felt thirsty.

"Can you hear it?" Chryse asked, staring at the water. "The river speaks the memories it has taken. It carries the words of the dead."

Deina listened. It was impossible to distinguish what the voices were actually saying, but the tumult of conflicting emotions—fear, rage, joy, grief—made her pulse race wildly. If she really concentrated, the rushing of the stream sounded like singing: countless overlapping voices woven into complex, heartrending harmonies. A tear spilled onto her cheek.

No. This was Lethe, the river of forgetfulness. A single drop of its waters would wash her mind blank. Dendris had knelt beside her. Deina pulled her away from the river and retraced her steps up the bank—steps she barely remembered taking.

"Stay away from the water. We need to move faster. Theron—"

"I can keep up."

"Don't worry. I've got him," Aster said firmly. Theron sighed heavily.

They pressed on. The tops of the cliffs on either side met to form an enormous, high-ceilinged cavern. The path disappeared into shadow as it continued upward, curving away from the river and leading them through a thicket of elm trees. Withered, yellowed leaves formed a pale carpet that covered the ground on either side of the path. The noise of the water faded. In its place was a dense, watchful silence that seemed to fill the spaces between the dusky trees like cobwebs. Only the occasional crunch, when one of them trod on some dead twig, disturbed the peace. Deina strode out as swiftly as she could, tempering her pace for the others. Left to herself, she would have run; her feet felt like they had wings. Somehow, she knew the gateway wasn't much farther. The trees thinned, revealing the honeycombed rock that lay beyond them, dark tunnel entrances covering the whole interior of the cavern. She could sense the boundary between the realm of the dead and the realm of the living, and it was just out of reach.

If only Theron could move a little faster. There were shadows lingering beneath the last few trees that not even her torch could entirely dispel. Perhaps Aster could carry him?

She looked over her shoulder, the question forming on her lips as a yell and the sounds of a scuffle came from behind. Someone screamed.

Drex, who'd been bringing up the rear, was struggling with a figure in dark clothes. Aster grabbed his spear from Theron and raced back toward them. Deina followed. But before she reached them, the attacker gained the advantage. He got one arm around Drex's neck and pressed his knife against his abdomen.

"Stay back! Stay back or I'll kill him!"

Deina skidded to a halt. The man was another Severer, the sigil clear on his forehead.

"You're outnumbered. Let him go, and we can try to help you."

"Tell me who I am!" the man bellowed. He glanced from side to side, still holding fast to Drex. "Tell me what this place is, and—and what you've done to me!" Fear twisted his features. "Tell me!"

Drex gasped as the blade was pushed harder against his flesh.

Deina raised her empty hand, palm facing out, and tried to speak slowly—calmly—despite the urgency that made her want to spit her words.

"You're a Severer. One of the Theodesmioi of the Order of Hades. Sent by Orpheus into the Underworld. Do you remember which House you're from? Which city?"

The man looked blank.

"The Theodesmioi," Deina repeated. "Those marked by the

gods." She gestured to her own sigil. Took a deep breath to stifle the frustration and panic building in her guts. "We're the same as you. Do you understand?" From the corner of her eye, she saw Theron reaching slowly toward the bow and arrows Aster had just laid down. Chryse had her knife in her hand, Dendris was slowly hefting her ax, and Aster's spear was already aimed toward Drex's attacker. Maybe, if she just distracted him, got him to focus purely on her, one of the others could strike.

"Here, I'm going to lay down my weapons." He wouldn't know the light she bore was also a blade. Keeping the torch high, she pulled the knives from her belt, one at a time. Then she slowly knelt to place them on the path, edging slightly away from the others as she did so, never taking her eyes from the man's face. His gaze followed her. "You're from one of the cities of the Theban Dominion. I don't know which one. But I think you drank the waters of Lethe, and that took your memory."

Silently, Theron fitted an arrow to the string of his bow. The man groaned.

"No. You're lying. Making up words to—to confuse me. You've done something to me. Taken away my—my—" The man tightened his grip. Drex began to choke and grabbed at his arm.

"You're killing him!" Deina shouted. "Let him go and we can get you out of here—"

Theron's arrow whistled through the air as Drex collapsed, dragging the man down and out of its path. Aster leaped forward. Spotting him, the man raised his arm to drive his knife into Drex's side. His back was to Deina. She shifted her grip on the light-filled dagger and hurled it toward him. He cried out as the crystal blade tore into his back.

They were plunged into darkness. Someone was whimpering in pain.

"Drex?" Chryse whispered. "Drex!"

White fire seared Deina's vision. The man, on his knees with his arms opened wide, was outlined in loops of brilliant light that fanned out from the blade of the knife and coruscated across the surface of his body. He threw his head back and screamed.

The light got brighter, encasing the man in brilliance. Deina started forward as lightning arced upward from his body and hit the roof of the cavern, knocking her off her feet and propelling her backward. Her head spun from the impact. A horrible, high-pitched shriek echoed through the air as the lightning crackled around her. She flung her arms over her face, trying to shield her eyes from the painfully intense glare.

The lightning vanished as suddenly as it had appeared, fading into the glow of ordinary fire. The afterimage of the bright white streaks clouded Deina's vision, but she could see flames beginning to flicker among the elm trees behind them. Smoke filled her nose and made her cough. Smoke and, worse, the stench of burned flesh. Motes of ash were drifting through the air, settling on skin, clothes, hair. There was no other remnant of the unknown Severer.

Next to her, Chryse was breathing rapidly. Farther off, someone was groaning.

Deina stumbled to her feet. By the firelight, she could see Aster crouching next to Theron, examining his back. Dendris was clinging to one of the elm trees, eyes closed, head resting against the bark. And Drex—Drex was still lying face down where he had fallen, half on the path, half on a scattering of golden leaves. He wasn't moving. Chryse limped hurriedly forward. Deina followed.

"Oh, Hades . . ." Chryse, her hand to her mouth, turned away. Drex was covered in burns: the backs of his hands, his scalp, his forehead, and the entire side of his face. Hades's sigil was no longer visible. The burned skin of Drex's back was showing through the clinging scraps of still-smoldering fabric. He was still breathing—shallow, wheezing breaths that reminded Deina of too many deaths she'd attended back in Iolkos.

What had she done?

Chryse sniffed, straightened her shoulders, and came to kneel by Drex's head. She was trembling. "Help me."

Together, she and Deina lifted Drex slowly and turned him onto his front. The left side of his face was uninjured. His eyelid fluttered open.

"Who . . ."

"It's me, Deina. And Chryse's here. All of us. I'm so sorry, Drex. I used the crystal dagger, but I didn't know. I didn't—" The words choked her. "I was trying to save you."

The uninjured side of Drex's mouth quirked up. "So much for . . . for Hades's pre"—he swallowed painfully—"predictions. Supposed to die in—in battle."

Deina shook her head. "You're not going to die. Not here. We're going to get you out, and then—"

"No." Drex paused. "No. Let . . . let me go. But promise . . ." His eye closed.

"Drex? Promise what?"

"Promise me . . . burial. Chryse . . ."

Chryse leaned closer, resting her hand above Drex's heart. "I'm here."

"I wish . . . I wish . . . time."

Her tears splashed onto Drex's face. "So do I. I wish we had more time, too."

One more rasping, drawn-out breath. Another. And then—Silence. Drex's head fell to one side.

"Drex?" Chryse whispered. "Please, Drex . . ."

There was no answer.

"No." Deina pushed herself to her feet. "No—he can't be dead. Nat!" Turning, she searched the shadows for his dark form. "Thanatos! If you're truly a god, do something!"

Theron caught hold of her wrist. Tears streaked his face, cleaving tracks through the ash that clung to his skin.

"The creature that helped us is a god?" When Deina didn't answer, he pulled her closer. "And what are you? Why didn't you stop this, Hades's daughter?"

Deina could sense the slow unfolding of fear.

"Hades's daughter?" Aster questioned.

"That's what he called her," Theron replied. "The daimon—god—whatever he is."

Fear tinged with anger.

Deina wrenched her arm free from Theron's grasp.

"I'm sorry. I didn't tell you because I didn't think you'd understand. I didn't want you to think I'd made the wrong choice. Hades—she said I was her daughter. She wanted me to stay there with her. To become a god. But I said no." Deina shook her head, unable to tear her gaze away from Drex's mangled corpse. "Even if Hades told me the truth, it doesn't change anything. I don't have any power. I couldn't have done anything."

"Why?" Chryse turned her head. "Why would you say no? If you'd said yes, you could have saved Drex. You could save all of us."

"If I'd said yes, I'd have to stay trapped in the Underworld forever. I'd have become something I hated and I—I—" She took a step toward Theron, her hand half lifted, trembling, willing him to believe her. "I don't want to stop caring. To be less than human. That's why I said no."

Chryse began coughing; the smoke was getting thicker.

"Please, we have to get out of here. Hades said"—Deina forced herself to finish—"she said I'd be able to open the gate. I don't think it's much farther."

"Wait." Dendris gulped. "There's something hanging in the branches up there." She dashed back to the trees and returned a moment or two later with something in her hands: a cloak, the same as the rest of them had been given. Shaking the garment out, she examined a brooch pinned to the fabric. Swore softly. "A swan. Symbol of Queen Leda. He was Spartan."

Aster, still weeping, bellowed with rage, then snatched the cloak from Dendris and ripped it apart.

"When Iolkos battles Sparta, your life will fail," Theron murmured. The prophecy Hades had given to Drex.

"Cut short by one of your own side." Chryse completed the prophecy. "You did this, Deina." Her voice was raw with distress. "I told you that dagger you stole was dangerous. So did Theron. But you wouldn't listen."

"It was fated, Chryse," Theron began. "There was nothing anyone could have done."

"That's not true—she could have said yes to Hades." Chryse picked up what was left of Drex's bag and folded it into her own. "But she didn't want to, so Drex is dead. You're selfish, Deina. Selfish." The word dissolved into a sob. Dendris put her arm around Chryse's shoulder and began to hurry her away from the burning trees.

Aster passed his gear to Theron and knelt, scooping Drex's body gently into his arms.

Deina trailed after them along the path, its slabs just visible in the light from the spreading fire. The others were weeping. Their grief echoed around the high cavern. She could see Drex's body ahead of her, frail as a feather in Aster's strong arms. She could hear his last words to Chryse whispering through the shadows like a thread being drawn out of a tapestry. So why wasn't she crying, too? Curling her right hand into a fist, she slammed it into the center of her chest, driving the two pendants that hung there—the image of Hecate that Anteïs had given her, and Theron's butterfly—hard into her skin. With each blow, she hoped the pain would force tears into her eyes. That it would force her to feel *something*. But the blankness inside her, like a piece of the pearlescent Underworld sky broken off and plunged deep into her soul, was stubborn.

Deina murmured a prayer, asking Hecate for the strength to get the others out of this accursed place. To save her friends. Perhaps if she could see the sky again, she'd be able to grieve.

"Deina." Dendris was calling her. She hurried forward. Dendris and Chryse were standing in front of a sheer wall of rock. A dead end. Dendris smacked the butt of her ax handle against the stone. "Solid. How do we get out? You said you could open it."

Deina could hear the panic underlying the gruff accusation. Stepping back, she allowed her gaze to roam over the rock face, searching for some clue that might be revealed by the dim light of the fire still burning behind them.

There.

Hades's sigil, no larger than her palm. She traced her fingers over the familiar outline, a smaller echo of the sigil that they'd found when they'd crossed Oceanus to enter the Underworld. A lifetime ago, or so it seemed. They'd slaughtered the sacred animals on the beach outside the entrance to the caves and had smeared the blood and ash on their foreheads, and that had opened the gateway.

Blood she had; blood tainted by Hades, running in her own veins. As for ashes . . . there were no animals here to be killed and burned. But they'd already sacrificed something far more precious.

Hades had known all along.

Deina found the small white poplar bowl and ceremonial knife in the bottom of her bag. She drew the blade of her knife across the soft flesh inside her arm, held up her arm, and let the blood drip into the bowl. Finally, she turned to Aster and reached with the knife toward Drex's burned cheek.

"What are you doing?" Aster pulled away, horror and disgust twisting his features. "Leave him alone."

"I'm getting us out of here." Deina couldn't bring herself to explain. "Please—"

Aster didn't answer, but he stood still, gaze averted, as Deina forced herself to scrape the side of the knife against Drex's ravaged face, to swallow the bile that was rising in the back of her throat as she gathered fragments of his charred skin into the bowl.

Oh, gods, what are you making me do . . .

Screeches reverberated around the cavern. Deina flinched and spun around. Blood hunters were crawling out of the honeycomb of tunnels that opened into the cavern, swarming down the walls toward them, weapons and bones and teeth rattling in anticipation. There was no time left for reluctance. As Dendris readied her ax and Theron fitted one of his few remaining arrows to the string of his bow, Deina ran to the wall, smeared the mixture in the bowl across the sigil on her forehead, and pressed her forehead hard against the corresponding symbol carved into the cool surface of the stone.

Nothing, and the blood hunters were already upon them—

The crack was loud enough to knock Deina backward. A jagged, diamond-shaped opening had appeared, as if someone had sunk their hands into the rock face, just where the sigil had been, and wrenched the stone apart. It was barely big enough for a person to wriggle through. But on the other side was daylight.

Next to her, Aster was crouched over Drex's body, blade flashing as he tried to protect it from the encroaching tide of monsters.

"Aster!" Agony erupted in Deina's leg, and she fell to the ground—a blood hunter had sunk its teeth into her thigh. Deina grappled with the creature. "Aster—go!"

He obeyed, crawling backward through the opening and dragging Drex's body after him as Deina jammed her fingers into the shriveled remnants of the blood hunter's eyes and forced its head back, grunting with effort, until the skull snapped off the spine. The creature's grip slackened enough for Deina to kick it away. She got to her feet, knives out, breathing hard. Chryse had followed Aster through. Theron had abandoned his bow and was fighting with Aster's spear. As Deina watched, Dendris—right in front of the opening—brought her ax down and sliced one of the creatures in half. But there was another behind her, its huge hammer raised above Dendris's head. Deina launched herself at the creature, ignoring the burst of agony from her injured leg, slammed into it, and pinned it to the ground. She raised both knives and slashed their blades through the putrefying flesh of the creature's neck.

"Deina." Theron held out his hand and pulled her to her feet. His tunic was ripped, and blood was running down the side of his face. He pushed her toward the opening.

"You first. Don't argue." A blood hunter lunged toward them with a spear; she brought her knife up, just managing to deflect the blow, but the action tore the blade from her grasp. Theron swore, shoved Aster's spear into her hand, and scrambled into the opening.

Deina was alone, surrounded by blood hunters. If she turned away to climb into the opening, the creatures would attack her from behind. How far would they be able to pursue her? She swung the spear, jabbing with it, trying to use its length to keep the creatures at bay. But they kept edging nearer. She could see their sigils, still visible in decayed flesh or yellowed bone. She could see the desiccated remains of organs poking through exposed ribs. The blood hunters' rotting, skeletal faces grinned at her.

Theron was calling her name.

Come on, Deina. Now or never.

She shoved her remaining dagger back into her belt and felt for the edge of the opening—perhaps she could clamber into it backward. As she glanced down fleetingly to check her footing, the creatures surged forward.

Deina dropped the spear and scrambled into the narrow gap. A blood hunter caught hold of her foot, but she kicked it away and struggled toward the daylight.

There were hands reaching for her. Aster and Theron grabbed her arms and hauled her out of the opening in the rock.

With a thunderous crash, the gateway into the Underworld slammed shut behind her.

It was over.

Dendris led them to a stream—a deep-channeled, fast-flowing brook that tumbled through a sunlit hollow in the middle of steep woodland. Deina, exhausted and numb, scooped the clear, cold water over the bloody bite marks on her thigh, gritting her teeth against the pain. Nearby, Theron was singing softly: a threnody, a Song of lamentation. Grief broke his voice every other line. She moved on to her hands and her face, splashing the water over the sigil on her forehead, scrubbing until every last trace of blood and ash was gone. Dendris emerged from the trees and shrubs lining the bank, her eyes red and swollen, her arms full of foraged food: olives, figs, plums. As Deina watched, she offered some of the fruit to Aster, slumped on the ground next to Drex's body. When he pushed it away, Dendris sat next to him and put her arms around him, and he wept against her shoulder. Deina left the stream and looked around for Chryse. She found her on her own, huddled beneath an ancient oak tree, her head buried in her arms. Deina settled in the grass next to her.

Time passed. They bathed their wounds and drank, quenching the voracious thirst that had returned as soon as they'd left the Underworld. They shared what was left of Anteïs's healing ointment; everyone had some injury inflicted by the blood hunters' teeth or weapons. The wound on Theron's head had stopped bleeding, but there was a gray undertone to his skin that made Deina's brows draw together whenever she looked at him. No one seemed hungry. No one seemed inclined to talk.

"We should bury Drex," Aster said eventually, breaking the silence. "We should wash his body, then bury him."

"We've no spades to dig a grave," Dendris observed. "I suppose if we collect enough stones, we can make a burial mound."

"Let's do it quickly, then," Theron replied. "We should move on from here as soon as we can."

"But we need to do it properly," Chryse muttered. "Besides, it's quiet here." She paused, and Deina listened to the faint thrum of insects and the call of a bird some way off. The warmth of the sun was making her drowsy. "There's no rush, surely?" Chryse continued. "We've already escaped. And we don't know where we are or where to go."

Deina cleared her throat.

"But Orpheus will come looking for us eventually, and he'll

start at the gateways. We don't know how much time has passed in the mortal world while we were in the Underworld." She gazed upward, though there was nothing to see—just a circle of cloudless blue sky, fringed with trees. "It's *too* quiet here." She shivered and wrapped her arms around her torso. "Quiet as a tomb."

Aster groaned, pressing the heels of his hands into his eyes. "You've spent too long in the Underworld. It's peaceful, that's all. And I for one wouldn't mind a rest. Let's stay here tonight with Drex and move on in the morning."

"I'd like that," Dendris murmured. "I'd like to sleep properly, for as long as I want." She patted the root of the tree she was leaning against. "These are good trees."

Deina glanced at Theron. He shrugged slightly. She couldn't tell whether the stiffness in his posture was due to unease or discomfort. Either way, the other three wanted to stay, and she didn't want to make any more decisions than she had to. Not after choosing to use the crystal dagger had gone so terribly, horribly wrong.

"If that's what everyone wants."

"Thank you, Deina." Chryse smiled at her. She smiled back. Or tried to; it didn't feel right, not with Drex's body still lying at the edge of the clearing.

"I'm going to start looking for stones for the tomb." Pushing herself to her feet, Deina limped away from the stream, inspecting the ground for suitable stones as she went. There was a narrow path, of the sort made by goat herders, rising through the trees toward the ridge that formed one edge of the hollow. Deina followed it. With luck, she might feel a breeze there; perhaps she'd even get some sense of where they were. Not that she'd recognize the geography. Drex was the only one who could read a map. As she toiled up the slope, she tried to remember some of the letters and words he had taught her, but her fragmentary knowledge seemed to trickle away like sand even as she groped for it. A sharp stroke of grief brought tears to her eyes.

She knew what she would have asked Drex to do, if he'd lived: to find a way of telling the leaders of the four Orders of Theodesmioi the truth about what Orpheus had been doing. What had happened to Leida and to all the others. How they had died and what happened to all Theodesmioi after their deaths. Drex could have sent each of the leaders a clay tablet, or something. He was clever. He'd have found a way of letting them know. Deina plucked one of last year's dead leaves still clinging to a nearby tree. There was barely anything of it left, just the stem and the veins and the outermost margin. At her touch, it crumbled away entirely. Perhaps she would have to try to find a way, even if it took years. She wanted to do more than just hide from Orpheus and hope that he would die before he found her. If other people knew what the Tyrant really was, it might change things. It might make Drex's death count for something.

With a last effort—feet slipping on the dusty surface of the path, using overhanging branches to pull herself up—Deina gained the summit of the ridge. It wasn't what she'd expected. Instead of another wooded plain, the sea lay before her, glimmering in the bright sunshine, crashing against the bottom of the cliffs far below. Too far for her to hear the roar of the waves above the whistle of the wind. Spreading her arms wide, she closed her eyes for a moment, buffeted by the breeze that blew inland from the sea, breathing the salt-laden air deeply. She was still some way back from the edge of the cliff. Dropping onto her knees, she crawled forward cautiously, curious to see exactly how far above the sea the cliffs rose.

Deina stuck her head over the edge of the cliff. Drew it back quickly and rolled away, her heart racing.

Ships. Black-sailed ships, anchored in the bay directly below. Orpheus.

22

She had to warn the others. They had to hide. Deina flung herself back down the path, half sprinting, half sliding. She saw Dendris first, wandering among the trees.

"Orpheus—he's here. I saw his ships."

Dendris gasped and ran toward the hollow. Deina followed. She didn't dare shout in case Orpheus's Iron Guards were already nearby. The Tyrant didn't know they were here; the ships must be collecting tribute, or waiting for one of the other teams of Severers to return. If they could just get farther away and find somewhere to hide, deep in the woods—

Together, Deina and Dendris burst into the hollow.

Theron, Aster, and Chryse were standing back to back in the center of the hollow. Their weapons were on the ground at their feet. More than two dozen Iron Guards, maces in their hands, surrounded them.

Deina drew her knife and charged at the nearest guard. A pointless gesture. The guard stuck one arm out and grabbed the front of her tunic, lifting her off the ground and holding her there, impervious to her attempts to stab him; the blade of the knife shattered against the iron casing of the guard's arm. Dendris started shouting, the same language she'd used on the boat when they were fleeing the blood hunters along the River Cocytus. The ground rippled and split as tree roots broke through the earth, knocking two of the guards off their feet.

But there were too many of them. One of the guards lunged forward and seized Dendris in its arms, clamping one hand around her mouth, silencing her. The tree roots quivered once and stilled.

"Well . . . the Severers from Iolkos, what's left of them. Plus a stowaway from Mycenae. His Majesty has been anxiously expecting your return."

Aristaeus. He came to stand next to the guard who was still holding Deina aloft.

"Put her down, but keep hold of her." The guard obeyed, dropping Deina to the ground, then dragging her upright and pinning her wrists behind her back in one of its ironclad hands.

Aristaeus swung to face Theron, thrusting the point of his sword against his chest. "You're still alive."

"Still," Theron snarled. "My father should have chosen a less honorable man to carry out his orders. Someone like you."

Aristaeus laughed. "A wit, as well as a bard. Too bad His Majesty isn't in need of a buffoon to entertain him. But as it is, he had already conceived an alternative use for you, should you have survived. Now tell me, Chryse, who has the spindle?"

"Leave her alone," Deina yelled. "She wasn't even meant to be part of this—"

"You think I'm going to hurt her?" Aristaeus laughed. "Why would I do that? She is His Majesty's honored and trusted servant." He held out his hand to Chryse. "Come, my dear. What report do you have to make?"

Chryse stepped between the guards, walked past Aster and Theron, their eyes wide with disbelief, and knelt briefly before Aristaeus.

"Chryse, what are you doing?" Deina couldn't breathe properly, couldn't make her voice rise above a murmur. Aristaeus was lying, or he was forcing her somehow. Chryse wouldn't betray them. She wouldn't betray her. "Please, Chryse—look at me."

Chryse ignored her. "Eurydice—she was able to speak to them, Lord. Through me. She told them about"—Chryse ran her tongue over her lips—"she told them what she had been doing to assist His Majesty. They believed her. Deina persuaded them not to use the rite to return but to seek out Hades—even though I told them not to, even though I tried to convince them to carry out their orders. The god"—Chryse gulped, twisting her hands together—"the god released Eurydice and destroyed the spindle."

"Eurydice is gone? How did you allow this to happen?" Aristaeus's voice was vibrating with barely controlled fury. He grabbed Chryse's arm, pulling her closer. "How?"

"But, Lord, there is another way." Chryse's gaze darted toward Deina, a mixture of triumph and misery in her eyes.

"No, Chryse," Deina begged. "Please don't."

She pointed at Deina. "She has the same powers as Eurydice."

Theron tried to push Aristaeus's blade away. "Chryse, I swear to the gods I'll—"

"Be still!" Aristaeus shifted the sword to bring the edge

against Theron's neck; a trickle of blood ran across his skin. "Such touching concern." He nodded at Chryse. "Continue."

"Hades's blood runs through her veins. That is what gave Eurydice her power, too. Deina can perform whatever task His Majesty requires just as well."

Aristaeus let go of Chryse's arm. "You've done well, Chryse. I'm glad to see His Majesty's trust was not misplaced."

"Why, Chryse?" Aster demanded. "What did we do to you in the Underworld other than keep you safe?"

"I think the more interesting question is when, not why," Aristaeus replied. "This plan was laid before you even went into the Underworld." He took Chryse's hand and held it up. "You must have noticed the beautiful ring gracing your companion's finger. Spell-cast gold, the fruits of a collaboration between the Theodesmioi of Hephaestus and the priests of the Anemoi, the gods of the winds. Chryse could have chosen to be whisked from the Underworld at any point. As it was, she was true to her commission, and stayed with you. All she had to do then was to whisper the correct words when she emerged from the Underworld to lead us straight to you."

That was why she'd wanted them to linger. To give Orpheus's ships time to reach the right spot.

Deina struggled against the rigid grip of the Iron Guard. "What did he do to you, Chryse? How did he force you to betray us?"

Chryse swung to face her. "I told you, Deina: His Majesty did nothing. He made me an offer, and I accepted it. I chose what was right for me." She waved a hand, as if dismissing all the years of friendship that had gone before. "I'm sorry."

Aristaeus placed a hand on her shoulder.

"Well done, Chryse. I'm sure His Majesty will be anxious to reward you once we reach Thebes. I will have a cabin prepared for you." He began to steer her away. "Bring the rest of them."

The remnants of Deina's knife were still lying on the grass. The instant the Iron Guard let go of her wrists, she ducked, snatched up the broken blade, and lunged toward Aristaeus. Not quickly enough; another Iron Guard grabbed her and threw her to the ground. Within moments, her arms and feet were bound. The same thing was happening to the others, and Dendris was gagged for good measure. Each of them was picked up by a guard and thrown over its shoulder.

"Wait." Aster's voice. "What about our fallen comrade? Surely you will allow us to complete the burial rites before—"

"This one?" Aristaeus asked. "The thinker, wasn't he? Well, his ghost will have eternity to ponder the mysteries of the universe. Traitors do not deserve burial. And we have no more room for dead weights"—he chuckled at his own joke—"on board the ship. Throw the corpse into the sea."

"Chryse," Deina screamed, writhing to be free of the Iron Guard's grip, "don't let them do this! You've got to stop them!"

No answer.

Craning her neck, the last glimpse Deina got of the hollow was of one of the guards dragging Drex's body up the slope toward the ridge as if it were nothing more than the carcass of some animal that had been sacrificed to the gods. The guard who was carrying her plunged into the trees, jolting her painfully against its iron body as they descended to the shore. The motion, and her head being upside down, made her sick and dizzy. She closed her eyes, trying to breathe steadily, trying not to think about what might be coming next. The rush of waves and the crying of gulls grew louder. Her guard crunched across the sand and dropped her into the bottom of a boat before settling on one of the benches that spanned the vessel. Deina tried to push herself up, to look for the others, but was instantly shoved back down again. The guard placed a foot on her back. There was nothing to do but lie there, twisted uncomfortably against the damp timbers, until they came alongside the ship. The guard dragged her upright and threw her into a net that had been let down from above on top of Theron, Aster, and Dendris.

"Deina . . ." Theron whispered. "I'm sorry. If I'd known what Chryse was going to do, I'd never have mentioned what I heard. But when Drex died . . . I'm sorry."

The net closed up around them. She couldn't move. Couldn't turn her head to try to see him. But somehow, she found his bound hands. Managed to interlace two of her fingers with his.

The net was dumped onto the deck and cut open, spilling them across the sanded planks. A guard—a human guard, not one of the iron creatures—undid the rope that bound Deina's ankles, leveling a blade at her chest.

"On your feet."

At knifepoint they were herded down the ladders that led to the bowels of the ship. Aristaeus followed. In the lamplit gloom far below the water's surface, they stopped.

"Those three in there." Aristaeus pointed toward a hatch in the floor that opened onto a dark space stinking of damp. "This one"—he tugged Deina away—"is to be kept separately."

"No!" Theron pulled free from his guard, reaching for Deina.

The guard dragged him back and pushed him through the open hatch. Deina heard him cry out in pain. Aster and Dendris were pushed in after him.

"Deina! Don't let them—" Theron yelled. Too late. The hatch slammed shut, silencing him.

Deina turned on Aristaeus. "You can't leave them in there."

"Oh, but I can." He smiled, revealing the sharply pointed teeth she remembered. "Another word from you, and you'll be joining them. His Majesty will want you alive, but your condition, otherwise, is of no concern. Unless . . ." Aristaeus hesitated. "Unless you'd rather spend the journey in my quarters." He lifted his fingers toward Deina's face and ran one nail down her neck, from jaw to collarbone. "You'd be considerably more comfortable." He cupped her breast with his hand.

Deina froze, until fury freed her. She spat her rage in his face. "I'd rather be thrown into the darkest hole you can find."

Aristaeus snarled. He struck her hard across the cheek, sending her stumbling against the nearest guard. Her cheek hurt so much, it brought tears to her eyes. She fought them back. If she cried now, he would think he'd won. That he'd broken her. At least the smile had faded from the man's narrow face. He was red with anger.

"Fortunately for you, you're too valuable for me to have you dragged behind the ship on a rope. Put her in the storage space over there." He stalked away and began to climb up the ladder. One of the guards drew back the heavy bolts securing a nearby door. Deina was thrust through it, and the door slammed shut behind her. She turned and kicked the door and beat her bound hands against the wood. Pointless; the scrape of the bolts being pushed home again told her she was trapped. There wasn't even a handle on this side of the door. No window, either. The guard's footsteps faded away, and the lantern light, too.

Deina sank to the floor, stunned, the airless darkness hemming her in just as effectively as an iron cage. They'd been through so much: fighting the horrors of the Underworld, facing a god, enduring Drex's death. Yet they'd still ended up trapped. Betrayed by Chryse. It felt like someone was flaying her body and her soul, sharp nails raking across her, over and over—and she didn't know how to make it stop. All she could do was scream and rage and weep, until exhaustion took her.

The pitching of the ship woke her. Disoriented, it took a few moments for her to remember where she was, to recall the crushing blow of Chryse's betrayal. At least her vision had adjusted. She could detect the faint daylight filtering around the edges of an uneven plank near the ceiling. A little light crept beneath the ill-fitting door, too, secondhand sunshine drifting down from the deck above. Not much. But more than Theron and the others had.

Were they still alive? All she could do was act as if they were. Make a plan or do something that might help them. She sniffed and rubbed her nose on her arm. There was no point sitting here doing nothing, waiting for Aristaeus or Orpheus himself to pronounce her doom. She'd escaped the Underworld. She ought to be able to escape Thebes. She just had to be ready when the opportunity presented itself.

Her fingers were tingling; the Iron Guard who tied her

wrists had done its job well. Lifting her hands, Deina tried to undo the knot with her teeth, but the rope was too thick. She looked around, searching for an alternative.

The storage space was mostly taken up with large sacks. She prodded one with her foot; it yielded a little. Barley, probably. The wall to her left was lined with shelves bearing clay amphorae, most likely full of wine or olive oil. The amphorae were kept in place by a light wooden lattice pinned over the front of the shelves, but they still might serve her purpose.

She got as close as she could, leaning over the sacks, peering into the shadows. A brief glow of satisfaction warmed her: Two of the amphorae had broken handles. One of them might be just what she needed. If she could get close enough.

She returned to the doorway and dropped to her knees, pressing the side of her face against the floor and peering beneath the door. No feet, as far as she could see; no one on guard immediately outside. Hopefully no one would notice if she made a little noise. Back on her feet, she stretched as much as she was able, loosening her muscles, and set herself to drag as many of the sacks out of the way as she could to get to the shelves. It was hot work; the sacks were heavy and awkward, and her hands and shoulders began to ache from the effort. Her injured leg was throbbing. She pushed away the fear that the wounds might be infected; there was nothing she could do about it if they were. The rise and fall of the ship threw off her balance and slowed her down, but eventually it was done. She reached through the lattice to feel the broken handles. One of them had snapped in such a way as to leave a sharp, jagged ridge on the side of the amphora. Bracing herself against the shelves, Deina began to rub the rope around her wrists against the broken edge. She had to be careful. Every so often the ship pitched wildly enough to throw her across the room and back again. And the fired clay wasn't that strong; too much pressure and she might break the entire thing, leaving her with nothing but shards of pottery that she couldn't pick up and use. But there was no rush—she hoped. It might take days to reach the port nearest to Thebes. And the steady work, the concentration, made it easier not to think about other things. About her friends, abandoned in the darkness. About Chryse.

Was she on this ship, Deina wondered, or on one of the other vessels that made up the little fleet?

A surge of mingled grief and fury made Deina catch her breath. She blinked away the tears that had clouded her vision and carried on with her task.

The daylight, such as it was, had faded to nothing by the time Deina finally cut through the last of the threads that still pinned her wrists together. She felt, rather than saw, the rope slip away from her arms. Her chafed skin was too sore to touch. She flexed her fingers until the pain and stiffness in her hands had eased. The darkness—soothing, seductive—weighted her eyelids. She was exhausted again, but she couldn't rest quite yet. Crouching down, Deina felt around until she found the rope. Then she groped her way across to the sacks that lay piled against the ship's side and sank down with a sigh. Working as quickly as she could in the dark, she tied a loop at each end of the rope and slipped her hands into them. It wouldn't pass close inspection. Still, she hoped a casual observer might be fooled into thinking she was still bound. Finally, she allowed herself to stretch out on the sacks. Body and soul, she was too tired for even fear and grief to trouble her as they might otherwise have done. Sleep came quickly.

The sea voyage dragged on. The days, a constant twilight, passed slowly; the nights were almost endless. At intervals, one of the human guards would open the door a little and push a platter of stale, weevil-infested bread and a cup of water through the gap. Each time, Deina tried to ask whether her friends were being fed, too. The guards ignored her, bolting the door shut again before she'd even finished her question. Other than these brief interruptions, she was left entirely alone, penned up in the suffocating gloom, with nothing to do but worry about her friends and brood on Chryse's betrayal. Deina tried to work out whether she'd done something to prompt it or whether Chryse had never cared for her as much as she'd believed. Tried to pinpoint the exact moment when Chryse's choice became inevitable. Wondered what would happen if she could go back to that moment and do things differently.

The guards didn't even let her go on deck to relieve herself. Before long, the storage room stank. Deina couldn't bring herself to eat. The tainted air made her nauseous and induced continual, pounding headaches. The pain in her leg had faded to a constant dull ache. The only event to enliven the monotony was a storm one afternoon. The thunder and the shouts of the sailors and the trundle of a loose barrel rolling across the deck above gave Deina an idea. She lay with her feet against the wooden lattice that kept the amphorae in place. At the next crack of thunder, she kicked the nearest crossbar as hard as she could, right in the center. It snapped. Deina rolled out of the way as the ship crested a wave and began its descent into a trough. The loose amphorae slid through the damaged lattice, tumbled across the floor, and smashed against the opposite wall. Wine puddled on the planks and started to soak into the nearest sack of grain. Deina hurried to inspect the damage. As she'd hoped, the amphorae had broken into shards, a couple of which wouldn't be a bad approximation of a small dagger. She selected the sharpest, wrapped a fold of her tunic around the end, and tested it on the ruined grain sack. It sliced through the rough fabric easily. Encouraged, Deina cut away a long strip of the sackcloth and tied it around the shard to form a sort of handle. Another square served to wrap the whole thing in. Reaching into her tunic, she pushed the makeshift weapon beneath the band that encircled her chest, between her breasts. If Aristaeus touched her again, she would be ready.

The storm blew itself out. Night fell. In the darkness, dizzy with thirst, Deina lay on her side on the grain sacks, tracing her fingers across a knot in the wood, over and over. Her mind drifted, lulled by the rocking of the ship. Drifted to Iolkos, where Anteïs was perhaps working by lamplight at her table in the herbarium, grinding herbs or brewing distillations, still hoping she and the others would return. Drifted to Thebes, where she imagined Orpheus decked in gold and waiting for their arrival. To Chryse—

No. She couldn't think about her. Not yet. Nor about Drex's body, abandoned on the seabed. To the hold below, then, where Theron and Aster and Dendris were immured, perhaps injured, perhaps dying of thirst.

Theron—he had to be alive still. He had to be.

As if in answer to her unspoken plea, the faint sound of singing whispered up through the ship's creaking joints. So faint, a mere trace of resonance, that Deina couldn't be sure she wasn't imagining it. She sat up. Pressed her hands and her ear hard against the timbers.

It *was* him. He was singing a lullaby, the same song he'd sung to calm Cerberus. The music wound its way into her bones and blood. It was beautiful enough to break her heart. To break anyone's heart. She caught her breath. Swallowed painfully.

"I can hear you, Theron." She whispered her message to the plank beneath her hands, her voice frail from thirst and disuse. "I can hear you. I'm here. I'm still alive." Theron wouldn't be able to hear her. But Dendris—with the blood of dryads flowing through her veins, able to recall the dead wood of a boat to some recollection of its living past—she might. The music faded. Deina leaned her forehead against the ship's side.

"They're still alive, Deina. All three of them."

Nat. The god of death was seated, legs planted wide, on another pile of sacks—though with him on top of them, they could have passed for a throne. A glow of silvery light surrounded him, bright enough to make Deina squint.

"Am I dreaming?"

Nat smiled. "You know better than most that there is a thin line between the realms of the mortal and the immortal, between life and death, between death and sleep."

"I'm too tired for riddles, Nat." Deina sat up, wincing as sickening pain lanced through her head. "What are you doing here? You didn't come when I called you. When Drex was dying."

"I was prevented." He conjured one of the black, purple-hearted flames Deina had seen before. It danced on his palm for a moment until he curled his fingers closed and extinguished it. "I'm sorry. Hades and fate acting together can be difficult to resist. As for why I'm here now . . ." His nose wrinkled. "This place smells almost as bad as Tartarus." Nat snapped his fingers, and the inside of the tiny space was smothered with deep white blooms. They trailed over the sacks of barley and climbed up the wooden walls. Deina sniffed the nearest flower. It was cold as ice to the touch, and its perfume was like the wind that carried the first snows of winter. Her headache lifted a little.

"I've never seen flowers so—" Deina's throat closed up, and she started to cough. Another click of the god's fingers, and a large cup of water appeared in her hand. She drained it gratefully. "Thank you."

"You're welcome. As I was saying, I'm here now because my offer still stands. Let me take you back to the Underworld. We can explore your destiny together." He raised his eyebrows. "It might be enjoyable."

Nat's idea of enjoyment was bizarre.

"Isn't my destiny bound up with me becoming a god? I don't even want to be a demigod. If I could change my parentage, I would."

Nat sighed. "It's hard to escape the fact of what you are, Deina. Believe me, I've tried. Whether you like it or not, half of your heritage is divine."

"I've already said no."

"Hear me out." Nat came to sit next to her, wriggling back onto the sacks to get comfortable. "It's not that simple, not anymore. Half of you is bound to the Underworld, just as I am. Your visit to the Underworld has awoken your heritage. You can't"—he paused, looking upward as if searching for a word—"you can't *unawaken* it." Nat's gaze roamed her face. "It's left its imprint in your appearance." He gestured to her left eye. "That ring of gold around your pupil will never disappear. And I know you've felt the tension—the pull, in two different directions. Part of you didn't want to leave Hades's gardens, isn't that right?"

Deina didn't answer.

"I know I'm right," Nat continued. "And I'm right about this, too: That tug will tear you apart, eventually. The duality of your nature will destroy your mind, even if, somehow, you escape from Orpheus without calling on Hades and accepting her offer. Did you never wonder why demigods tend to die young?"

Deina hurled the empty cup at the wall. The freedom she'd dreamed of for so long was slipping away from her.

"Can't you just click your fingers and get us off this ship?"

"Your friends are entirely mortal—I can't do anything for them. Or at least nothing they'd thank me for. You, I can help—if you'll just come with me."

"Why, Nat?" Deina scowled. "You keep asking me the same thing, over and over. Why are you so interested in me? What do you really want?"

He didn't answer—just stared down at his clenched hands.

Exhaustion drained Deina's anger. "I'm tired. If taking me to the Underworld is all you're offering, then go. Leave me alone." Nat began drumming his fingers on his thighs. Such a human action; could it really help a god to think, or was it just copied?

"There is," he murmured, "one other possibility." He opened his palm to reveal a tiny square pouch made of a linen so fine it was almost transparent. There were seeds inside it. "If you eat these, they will give you the power to save your friends. To allow Theron to fulfill the prophecy rather than be slain by Orpheus."

Deina poked the seeds with her little finger. "And what's the downside? You're a god, offering me a gift. There has to be a downside."

Nat hesitated, staring at the little square of linen. Shrugged. "They might well destroy you, too."

23

"They'll destroy me?" Deina pushed his hand away. "I don't actually want to die. All I've been doing ever since I said yes to Orpheus is trying to avoid dying."

"I understand. And I don't—" He stopped short.

Deina heard him swallow. Another human affectation? If it had been Theron sitting next to her, she'd have said he was nervous.

"I don't want you to eat these seeds unless you really have no other choice. But at least take them. Just in case." He looked into her eyes. "Your fate, and that of your friends, is already in motion. Only calling on Hades or eating the seeds will change that."

"Fate." Deina didn't try to keep the bitterness from her voice.

"We're all bound to it. It is my fate to gather in the souls of mortals. I have no choice in the matter." He smiled, though by Nat's standard it was a sad smile, and there was only resignation in his eyes. "For humans, I am as inevitable as the dawn."

A tear escaped down Deina's cheek.

Nat raised his eyebrows and put his arm around her shoulders. "You're weeping for your friends?"

She nodded. For Theron. For Drex. For all of them. Even for Chryse. More than that, she wept for the death of her dreams. Did gods dream? She dashed the tear away, angry with herself.

"It doesn't matter. And you wouldn't understand."

"I might. If you'd only let me try."

The artistry of Nat's face struck Deina anew: the perfection of his proportions, the intense deep blue of his eyes, the curve of his lips. She reached across and pressed one palm to his chest. He felt solid. Real. As real as Theron . . . apart from one thing.

He had no heartbeat.

She could feel her own pulse racing, but there was no answering thud from within his muscled chest.

Deina let her hand drop. "I'm not going to take the seeds. Or call on Hades. And I'm not going to go with you to explore my destiny."

Nat's expression reminded her of a spurned puppy. "Because you don't like me?"

"No. Because of this." Deina tapped her fingers against his heart. Or where his heart should have been. "I won't leave my friends. I have to stay the course. To try to save them, if I can. Them, and myself." She lifted her hand to his cheek. "If I didn't, I wouldn't be properly human."

Nat bowed his head. Took her hand and kissed the palm and tucked the bag of seeds inside it. "Until we meet again, then."

He vanished, plunging her back into the fetid darkness. For a moment, Deina thought about dropping the seeds somewhere among the sacks of barley. She didn't want anything to do with the gods. She certainly didn't want their gifts. But having them gave her another choice. Of sorts. She unpinned one of the shoulder brooches that secured her tunic and repinned it with the linen bag held between the pieces of fabric.

Until we meet again . . . When she called upon Hades and chose divinity. Or when she ate the seeds and died. Or when Orpheus killed her. Deina sank back on the sacks and lay there, eyes open, wondering to which end her fate would lead her.

Lamplight, shining on her face. Deina frowned and blinked, screwed her eyes almost shut. The light was too bright for her to see who was standing behind it.

"On your feet. Quickly, now."

A rush of relief warmed her—one of the human guards, not Aristaeus. The man lingered at the doorway. Deina checked the rope looped around her wrists and caught the loose end between her hands before swinging her feet to the floor and stepping across the threshold. The makeshift knife was still in place between her breasts.

The guard grabbed her upper arm and jerked her forward toward the ladder leading to the upper part of the ship. Deina began to climb. Not easy, with the rope still around her wrists, but at least now she could move her fingers enough to grip the flat rungs. The air, chill after the close confinement of the storage room, raised goose bumps across the exposed flesh of her arms. Another two ladders took her and her guard up past the double bank of rowing benches. One of the oarsmen, a grizzled, one-eyed lump of a man, called out to her.

"If you want a rest, there's plenty of room here for you to

lie on your back and spread your legs." He laughed, and his companions laughed with him.

Ignoring the gruff orders of her guard, Deina stopped climbing and turned to look at him. Watched as his gaze found the sigil on her forehead, as the laughter died in his throat and blood drained from his ruddy cheeks.

"Pray that I forget your face," she hissed, "you misbegotten sack of filth."

A second prod in the back from the blunt end of her guard's spear drove her up the final few rungs onto the deck. Aristaeus was standing with his back to her, looking out across a high, rocky promontory. A town sprawled from the rugged heights all the way down the steep slope to the sandy beach that formed the harbor, buildings and houses clinging to their stony foundations like limpets. The very top of the promontory was hidden by low clouds. A fine drizzle quickly misted Deina's hair and clothes with tiny crystalline raindrops.

"Where are we? Where are the others?"

Aristaeus turned to the human guard standing at her shoulder. There were two Iron Guards waiting silently nearby.

"Give her some bread and water, then put her in the cart." He looked Deina up and down, his face twisted into a sneer. "I advise you to eat. It's a day's journey from Aulis to Thebes, and we won't be stopping."

Her human guard took her arm again and pulled her aside to sit in a space by the bulwarks. He barked an order to another man, who returned with a waterskin and a small hunk of bread. Fresh bread—perhaps they'd already taken on supplies from the town. Deina tore at the bread wolfishly, but she only allowed herself a few sips of water before tucking the mouth of the waterskin into her belt, hoping the guard—busy issuing a list of requests to one of his comrades who was going ashore—wouldn't notice. He didn't. Or he chose not to. When he turned back, it was to order one of the Iron Guards to take her to the carts drawn up on the beach. The creature approached Deina, its heavy tread loud against the deck. She stood before it reached her.

"I can climb down myself."

The guard stared at her. There was the merest flicker of something in the human eyes set deep within the metal face. Recognition, perhaps. Or regret. It couldn't answer her, but it understood. It jerked one arm toward the rope ladder that led from the deck to the surf below.

Deina inclined her head. "Thank you."

It was difficult. The ladder swung in the breeze, and Deina's arms were aching by the time she jumped down into the water. The ache in her thigh had grown worse, too, but it was better than being carried like a carcass. More Iron Guards were waiting for her. She splashed up the beach between them. No witnesses, at least. The townspeople were keeping out of the way, just as they had at Iolkos. The Iron Guards stayed away from the carriages and carts—Deina guessed they made the horses nervous—but there were plenty of heavily armed human guards, including some Battle Wagers marked with the sigil of Zeus. Too many for her to think of escaping. One of them manhandled her into the back of a large cart. No windows here, either. But it was light and airy compared to the storage room on the ship.

As Deina waited, she crouched with her eye against a gap between the slats that made up the body of the cart. There was a fine chariot being piled with baskets of delicacies—for Orpheus, presumably. Other than that, four more carts. They were being loaded with chests, like those she'd seen on the voyage from Iolkos. More tribute for the Tyrant. With a jolt, she recognized their things being thrown in on top of the chests. The bags she and the others had carried. Dendris's ax.

But where was Dendris herself?

The tide crept farther up the beach toward the carts. Aristaeus appeared. He climbed into the carriage. Behind him was a guard carrying Chryse, dressed in a fine gown of creamy linen, through the water.

Too important to get her feet wet now, was she? Deina banged her fists against the wooden slats.

"Chryse!"

Chryse's head turned slightly, but that was the only response Deina got. Chryse was lifted into the carriage, and Deina lost sight of her. It looked as if they were nearly ready to set off. Had her friends been left to die in the hold?

The cart rocked slightly as its driver clambered up to his seat.

Gods, no—

The back of the cart was let down again. Three figures stumbled inside and collapsed onto the rough, straw-strewn floor.

Deina sank back, pressing one hand to her chest. Her heart hammered beneath her palm. Theron, Aster, and Dendris. And all three of them still alive. Nat had been right.

The cart jolted into motion. Deina shuffled over to Theron.

He looked terrible: haggard and hollow-cheeked, with blood caking his face. It looked as if the wound on his temple had reopened somehow—had he struck his head on something? She smoothed his hair back from his face.

"Theron, can you hear me?" She pulled the makeshift knife from beneath her tunic and sliced through the ropes cutting into his wrists, retying them loosely for the look of it. "Theron?"

He was trying to open his eyes, but his eyelids were gummed up with dirt and blood. Deina cut a strip of fabric from her tunic, poured a little of the water onto it, and rubbed Theron's eyes gently.

"Try now."

Theron blinked. Flinched—the daylight must have hurt his eyes after so long in the dark.

"Deina?" A whisper, no more.

She slipped an arm behind his neck, lifted his head, and pressed the filched waterskin to his lips. He drank greedily, but she soon pulled the skin away.

"More."

"I have to save some for the others. We don't have much."

He nodded. Smiled slightly in acknowledgment.

Deina kissed his forehead. "Rest. We'll be in Thebes soon."

Theron closed his eyes and slipped back into sleep.

Quickly, Deina moved to help Dendris. The Mycenaean was as gaunt and grimy as Theron but uninjured. After slicing through the ropes that bound her wrists and Aster's, Deina gave Dendris the makeshift knife. Deina was needed by Orpheus; she hoped that meant it was less likely she'd be harmed. But Dendris, as strong and gifted as she was, might well be considered expendable. Deina didn't need the old stories to tell her the usual fate of women captured and enslaved by men. It had always been the same.

At the moment, though, Aster worried her the most. When Deina pressed her hand to his forehead, the heat radiating from his skin shocked her. He was burning up from the inside. She managed to get him to drink and poured the rest of the water over his head, hoping to cool him down a little. It wasn't enough, but all she could do was wait for the fever to run its course.

"Deina . . ."

Theron was calling her. She finished making the others as comfortable as she could, piling up the straw into makeshift pillows, and returned to him. There was no water left to clean the wound on his head. Nothing to bind it with, either.

"I'm . . . afraid," he whispered. "Stay."

"Don't worry. I'm not going anywhere." Deina shifted position so that she could sit with Theron's head in her lap and attempted to sing him some of the lullaby she'd heard him singing on the ship. She didn't remember the words, but he was soon asleep again. Asleep and dreaming, maybe, of somewhere better. She closed her eyes and tried to follow him there.

It was dark by the time the cart drew to a halt. They'd stopped once—to rest the horses, Deina guessed—but Aristaeus was otherwise true to his word. No one had given them any more food or water. Whatever Orpheus had planned for Theron, Aster, and Dendris, she wondered if it needed them to be alive.

The back of the cart opened. Torchlight bathed the interior of the cart in a ruddy glow. Hands reached in to pull Aster, who was nearest the rear, out of the vehicle. He stumbled, but Deina was relieved to see that he stood on his own feet; the fever had dropped the last time she'd pressed her hand to his forehead. Soon they were all standing, shivering, in the courtyard of Orpheus's citadel.

As the guards were given their orders, Deina studied her surroundings, or what she could see of them in the uncertain, flickering glimmer from the guards' torches. To one side of the courtyard stood a pair of massive gates, still open; the last carts from their convoy were just being driven beneath the rampart that surmounted the gates. Beyond the gates, the land seemed to drop away steeply. The slopes of the hill below were thickly scattered with points of lamplight. More light glinted from the plain beyond. The scale of it stunned her. She'd heard rumors of the might of Thebes, but she'd never conceived of a city this enormous, housing so many people. So many potential warriors. No wonder the Tyrant's armies were believed to be invincible. On the opposite side of the gates loomed the massive bulk of the Cadmea, the fortified pinnacle of the city, dark and menacing against the star-scattered sky.

The iron spike of a spear end in her back prodded her into motion. Their guards, human and iron, led them forward and forced them through an opening in the rock face that looked more natural than human-made. It turned out to be the entrance to a narrow tunnel carved into the rock of the hillside. The tunnel climbed, steeply in places, its uneven floor winding up toward the Cadmea, the citadel perched on top. Aster stumbled and was jerked upright again by the Iron Guard who walked between him and Dendris. The walls shrank together. The ceiling lowered until the heads of the Iron Guards were scraping across the rock face in places. The air grew thick and heavy with smoke from the burning torches. Deina's head began to swim. She was about to discard the rope she still had around her wrists so she could use her hands to steady herself when a draft of cooler air revived her. Echoes told her they were moving into a large chamber, and within moments, she was stepping out into a wide hall, lit by oil lamps suspended from chains attached to the ceiling. They were still within the mountain—there was solid rock above them—but openings had been made at the top of the wall on the left-hand side, and the floor had been paved with stone slabs, rough-hewn, but smoother underfoot than the chiseled-out floor of the tunnel. Directly opposite, a wide staircase, also lit by oil lamps, led upward. One of the human guards grabbed Deina's arm and began to pull her toward the staircase. Theron, Aster, and Dendris were herded off to the right, toward a passage that looked as if it led farther into the heart of the mountain.

Deina pulled away from her guard. "Wait—what's happening to them?"

The only answer she got was another jab from his spear that sent her sprawling to the stone floor. Pain shot through her knees. By the time she'd struggled back to her feet, the others had disappeared from view.

There were four human guards around her. The Iron Guards came no farther, but they flanked all the exits from the hall. If she ran after her friends right now, she wouldn't get far. Deina took a deep breath and began to climb the staircase.

It ended in a long, well-lit corridor that intersected with other corridors. The walls were pierced at intervals with doorways. Deina counted doors and turnings, building a sketchy map in her mind. If she could escape this way and find the route back to the courtyard, she might be able to lose anyone pursuing her in the city beyond. Some of the doors were open, allowing her a glimpse of the spaces beyond. Storage rooms, bedrooms, workrooms. They were in the lower level of the citadel, below the megaron, temples, and courtyards that lay within its walls. Despite the hour, a few servants still hurried past. Men bearing amphorae, women carrying baskets of food or linen. They cast frightened glances at the guards but were careful to pay no attention to Deina. She wondered how many other prisoners they'd seen escorted along these paths. How many of those had escaped? How many had survived?

Few. None, more likely.

The guard ahead came to a halt outside a pair of double doors. He knocked, and one of the doors was opened. From the corner of her eye, Deina saw the guard behind, the one who'd pushed her before, raise his spear to do it again. She twisted away. His momentum carried him forward, and she stuck her leg out to trip him. As he stumbled past her into the wall, she snagged the hilt of his dagger, pulled the weapon from his belt, and held it against the back of his neck.

The other guards had their spears leveled at her, but none of them attacked; too scared of what Orpheus might do to someone who injured his prize, no doubt.

"There's nowhere to run," one of them said. "You can't escape."

"This isn't about escape. This is about reminding you who I am: Theodesmioi, a Soul Severer of the Order of Hades." Deina pushed the point of the knife farther into the folds of the man's flesh; she heard him moan as a trickle of blood escaped across the skin. "Touch me again, and you'll regret it." She dropped the knife and walked through the door.

It was shut behind her. Not by another guard, but by a middle-aged woman. A servant, judging by her dress. There was more comfort in this large room than Deina had expected: rushes strewn on the floor, and windows that, while they were barred and still too high to see out of, were at least wide enough to give a glimpse of the sky. From somewhere nearby came the sound of running water.

"Come. Follow me. You must be hungry." The woman began walking.

"Who are you?"

To her surprise, Deina got an answer. The woman glanced back over her shoulder.

"My name is Bacchis."

"And what is this place?"

"Your quarters. There's food and drink prepared for you."

Deina's stomach turned. So Orpheus had already had word from Aristaeus—he knew what she was. And what he believed he could make her do.

There were only two exits as far as she could see: the double doors she'd come through, set beneath the row of high windows, and another door in the corner accessed by a short flight of steps. And only three servingwomen, Bacchis and two younger maids, in here with her.

As if reading her mind, Bacchis murmured, "There will be Iron Guards outside both doorways by now."

That didn't necessarily matter. If she had to, Deina was sure she could overpower the three servants. If she took the clothes from one of them and wore the veil low over her forehead, she could walk through the citadel freely. She could start with Bacchis. The rope was still looped about Deina's wrists. It would be the work of a moment to slip it around the other woman's neck—

But Bacchis was probably trapped here just as much as she was. She'd done nothing so far to deserve Deina's ire. Perhaps Deina could persuade her or one of the others to help her. That, or find a way to climb up to the windows. None of it was impossible. She just needed time.

Though time might be the one thing her friends didn't have.

The sound of running water grew louder. Bacchis led her through an archway. A spring was gushing from a crack in the rock wall; the water ran into a gutter that channeled it away into a small hole in the floor.

"It's cold." Bacchis shrugged. "But at least you'll be clean. We're forbidden to untie your wrists." The woman reached for the brooch pinning the shoulder of Deina's tunic.

"Wait—a cup of water first, please. I feel . . ." Deina sank to her knees, doubling over. As Bacchis ordered one of the other servingwomen to fetch the water, Deina quickly yanked the bag of seeds free from the brooch and concealed it between her hands.

The faintness was an act, but the cup of water was welcome nonetheless. Once she'd drunk it, the women quickly stripped away the torn and stained tunic and her other clothes. At least they left her the two pendants still hanging around her neck. One of them brought a stool for Deina to sit on while they combed out her hair and massaged olive oil into her scalp and skin. She had to stand beneath the icy cascade of spring water while Bacchis scraped and rinsed off the oil—the water was cold enough to take her breath away, and she was trembling by the time the servants wrapped her in warmed linen cloths and made her sit next to the fire. But she still had the seeds.

Clean clothes were brought. A robe of black linen with the familiar sigil of Hades embroidered in red around the hem. Correct dress for a Soul Severer adept about to perform a ritual, right down to the pouch for the ceremonial tools hanging from the belt, though the tools themselves were missing. For a moment, as Bacchis dried and dressed her hair, Deina closed her eyes. Pretended she was back at the House in Iolkos. That she'd returned to the only home she'd ever known, with Aster and Drex and Theron. That Anteïs was the one combing her hair, and that Chryse was waiting for her in the women's hall.

The slam of a door woke her from the dream. Bacchis flinched and bowed to someone behind her.

"My lord . . ."

Aristaeus, flanked by an Iron Guard and—Deina studied the sigil on the man's forehead—a Theodesmioi of the Order of Hephaestus. A Spell Caster. The man was carrying a bronze torc in his hands.

"No—" Deina tried to stand, to get away, but the Iron Guard pushed her back onto the stool, its hands heavy on her shoulders.

"Yes," Aristaeus said. "You are Theodesmioi. The torc will remind you of that, as well as keep you in your place. The spell bound into this particular torc will limit your movements to this room and those directly above in this part of the Cadmea." He gave her a thin-lipped smile. "I hope you enjoyed your last taste of the outside. You'll never see it again. Lift her hair."

Bacchis obeyed. The Spell Caster moved forward, but Aristaeus held up his hand.

"Wait." He closed one fist around the leather cords that hung from Deina's neck and yanked them away; Deina had to clamp her lips together to keep from crying out. Aristaeus dangled the two pendants in front of her eyes. "Hecate and a butterfly, symbol of Psyche, the soul." He gave a soft, scornful exclamation. "You'll have no need of them now. The gods won't help you. And your soul belongs to Lord Orpheus. Continue."

The two halves of the torc were slipped around Deina's neck, the bulbous terminals resting uncomfortably on her collarbone, leaving just the small dip at the base of her throat uncovered. Just enough space for someone to drive a knife, Anteïs used to say. A pin was driven into the join at the back by the Spell Caster, who clutched the metal tightly as he mumbled the words of the spell to seal the joint, to make the torc as permanent as if it had been forged as one almost complete circle. It was the same ceremony Deina had gone through before, several times, but the weight of this new torc was almost unbearable.

Eurydice had been Orpheus's queen. But Deina—apart from her abilities, she was nothing. There was no reason for Orpheus to treat her as anything other than a valued slave.

This was to be her prison.

"Good." Aristaeus looked her up and down. "His Majesty will summon you soon. Be ready. And be obedient. Any attempt at resistance would not end well, either for you or your friends."

As Aristaeus, the guard, and the priest left, Bacchis removed the rope from Deina's wrists; there was no need of it now. If the servingwoman noticed that the rope had been cut, she didn't say anything. Just put it to one side and gestured to a table that had been set out with some food. Smoked fish, bread, cheese, fruit—the sight made Deina's mouth water and reminded her just how long it had been since she'd had a proper meal. As she walked to the table she slipped the seeds into the pouch hanging from her belt, then began eating as fast as she could, not caring how it might look to Bacchis and the others. It felt as if she'd barely gotten started when the door at the top of the steps opened. To her surprise, it was not Orpheus, or another guard.

It was Chryse.

24

She was dressed in a fine gown of pleated green silk, the color of young beech leaves. There were golden bangles stacked up her arms; they jangled slightly as she trod down the steps, followed by a spear-bearing human guard. As Chryse drew nearer, Deina saw other adornments. A heavy gold chain around her neck, and on her finger, a delicately engraved gold ring set with a carved agate. Chryse stopped next to the table where Deina was seated. Deina took her hand and examined the ring

The ring had been set with Drex's agate: the one he'd been carving. Its minute, intricate details just as fresh and vivid as when he'd first shown it to her in the Underworld, before they entered the cavern of the firefall. But complete now. Almost as if predicting his own death, he'd carved a fallen warrior at the feet of the two antagonists. "He finished it. When did he have time?" Deina asked.

"I'm not sure. When we first arrived in Hades's garden, perhaps. It was in his bag."

"And you took it."

Chryse pulled her hand away. "I didn't come here to argue with you."

"Then why did you come?"

"To explain."

Deina turned back to her food. "What's to explain? You could have told us what Orpheus wanted you to do, just like Aster did. You could have told us about the spell-cast ring he'd given you. Instead, you chose to betray us."

"I did what I thought was best." Chryse's eyes flashed with anger. "You told me often enough that I needed to stand up for myself. The night before we left Iolkos, you reminded me: If you see an opportunity, take it. Orpheus offered me an opportunity. A way that I might get what I wanted—"

"But I was going to look after you!" Deina pushed herself to her feet, knocking the stool she'd been sitting on to the floor, ignoring the way Chryse's guard shifted his grip on his spear. "I had a plan—"

"*Your* plan. Not our plan. You never even told me the details, but I can guess. You'd be happy spending our days on one ship after another, just trying to get as far away as possible from Iolkos, or settling on some gods-forsaken, unpeopled island in the middle of nowhere to scratch out a living on the soil, all in the name of freedom. That was *your* dream, Deina. It was never mine."

"And what was your dream? To be the servant of a monster?" Deina raised her hands to the torc that had been placed around her neck. Chryse stared at the spell-cast bronze. "Didn't you even want to be free?"

Chryse seemed unable to tear her gaze from the torc. "Of course I did. But the freedom I wanted was a—a comfortable life. A life with luxuries. With a husband, and children to care for. A family and a home of my own—I didn't even know how much I wanted that, until His Majesty held it out as a possibility. Perhaps, in time, I'll have all I desire. Or more. He has no queen now."

Deina stared at Chryse's face. A face she knew as well as her own, every curve and dimple familiar. And she would have sworn she knew her friend's mind just as intimately.

But she was wrong.

"Why didn't you tell me?"

Chryse shrugged. "You didn't ask."

Why hadn't she asked? Now, too late, Deina finally knew the answer. She hadn't asked Chryse what she'd wanted because she'd been afraid to. Deina had long known that Chryse didn't—couldn't—return her love in the same way. Still, she'd been unwilling to see the truth. Unwilling to accept that, once she'd freed Chryse, she would have to let her go. Deina's image of her entire life, the landscape she'd moved and lived in, fractured and scattered like a mountain blown apart by a volcano. When the ash began to settle, it was across a world she no longer recognized.

They stared at each other. Chryse half lifted one hand toward Deina. "When I said yes to Orpheus on the ship, I didn't think it would matter. I thought we'd find the queen and return her, that he'd give us the gold and our freedom, and I could go to Thebes and you could . . . you could do whatever you wanted. But then Eurydice convinced you to disobey. And even at the end, if Drex had lived, then maybe—" She dropped her arm. "But he didn't. I made my choice. I did what I had to do, Deina."

Deina moved away from the table, not wanting to look at her friend anymore. "And what you had to do includes condemning the rest of us to death?"

"You volunteered to undertake Orpheus's quest," Chryse shot back. "Death was always the most likely outcome." She took a deep breath. "His Majesty needs you. He won't harm you. Your life here won't be so very different to what it would be if you were still in Iolkos."

"How can you say that? I'm never to be allowed outside again. I'm to be forced to murder so that Orpheus might gain immortality. And what about the others, who counted you as a friend? What of Drex's unburied body?"

"I didn't know what Aristaeus was going to do. You saw how angry he became when I told him about Eurydice. I was too afraid to ask that Drex be buried. I wish . . . I wish I'd been braver." She sniffed and looked down at Drex's agate. "I know he would have been. As for the others, I'll beg His Majesty for mercy—"

"Even you can't believe the Tyrant is capable of mercy," Deina interrupted. "They were locked in the hold on the way here. They almost died. Didn't you see what state they were in when we arrived?"

Chryse's hand fluttered to her chest.

"I didn't know. And I couldn't—we arrived before you, but I'm sure that now . . ." She trailed off, twirling a lock of golden hair between her fingers the same way she always did when she was anxious. "It would never have worked, Deina. Your plan. Even if it had been what I wanted, too. If Orpheus hadn't arrived and changed everything, you wouldn't have been able to free yourself, or me. We both saw a chance to change our destiny. We both took it."

Deina's anger drained away, leaving nothing behind. Not even sorrow. She was too exhausted to feel, let alone fight with Chryse.

"You don't know your destiny, Chryse. Remember? I made Hades stop before she told you what your truth was."

Chryse shrugged. "Then perhaps this was my destiny all along. To serve the king and live in a palace. We have one life—that's what you used to say, Deina." Chryse spread her hands wide in a gesture of helplessness. "What else was I to do?"

Deina thought about saying, *You could have talked to me. You could have told me what Orpheus asked you to do, and why you were tempted to do it.* But it was too late for that. Much too late.

"You've made your choice, Chryse. I hope you'll be happy in it. Orpheus is probably planning a second try at murdering his own son, and Aristaeus threw Drex's body into the ocean, but still—I hope you can be happy with the masters you've chosen."

Chryse's eyes filled with tears, but Deina resisted the urge to run to her. To put her arms around her, to pull her close and comfort her.

Chryse dropped her gaze. She took off Drex's ring, placed it on the table. Two Iron Guards, impassive, indistinguishable, had appeared at the top of the steps.

"You're to go with them," Chryse said. "His Majesty requires you now." Her human guard followed her out of the room.

Deina moved toward the stairs. She picked up Drex's ring as she passed the table and slid it onto her finger. Aristaeus's torc may have destroyed her dreams of freedom, but he hadn't won, not yet. She didn't plan on returning to this room if she could help it.

Up and up the Iron Guards led her, until they reached a point where there were no more steps to climb. Two figures waited outside the double doors at the top of the stairs. Just more Iron Guards, Deina thought, but as she drew closer, she realized she was wrong.

These guards were unlike any she had seen before. The armor that entombed them was more closely fitted to their bodies, and it shone with the warmth of bronze. The sigil of Zeus was carved into the mouthless metal plates that covered their faces. A fresh wave of horror turned Deina's stomach. Once, these guards had been Theodesmioi, Battle Wagers of the Order of Zeus. But if they'd been created in the same way as the Iron Guards, she guessed they were little more now than walking weapons, half alive and spellbound. Deina wondered whether Aristaeus or Orpheus controlled them, whether they spent their entire existence confined here within the secret heart of the Cadmea. She was surprised, when she gazed up into the eyes of the nearest of them, to see such depths of pain there. Surprised, and filled with pity.

The Bronze Guards dismissed their iron brethren and opened the doors. On the other side lay a circular room lined entirely with white marble, apart from the white granite hexagonal floor tiles that were bordered with red. The stone sparkled in the light of the torches set around the curving wall and the fire that was burning in the sunken central hearth. The smoke from the fire rose up, escaping by way of a wide hole in the roof above; cold moonlight streamed down through the same opening. Deina caught a glimpse of faint stars, and with their subtle beauty came sudden recollection. She'd seen this room before. It was the vision she'd had when she'd touched Eurydice's spindle, after the ghost had been confined within it. Deina's heart beat erratically as fear clawed its way up her throat. She hadn't thought that Orpheus would try to force her to kill so soon, but this had to be the space where the rite had been conducted, where Eurydice had drawn the life out of so many innocents and transferred it into Orpheus. The entire room looked as if it was built for magic: the large aperture to harness the power of the moon; the circle with a triangle inside it drawn on the floor; the tripod set over the fire with a steaming cauldron hanging below; what looked like words painted in a flowing line around the wall. At one point of the triangle was an altar, and at the second point a stone table. The third was empty, for now. Iron manacles had been fixed into one section of the wall, and Bronze Guards were stationed around the entire perimeter—ten of them, including the two standing on either side of her.

As well as the door she'd entered through, there were three other doors, evenly spaced around the circular wall. Between two of them was a large stone chair draped with furs, with a table next to it. As her guards forced her toward the altar, the fourth door opened and another two Bronze Guards entered with Theron, Aster, and Dendris between them.

"Theron—" Deina stretched out her hand toward her friends. She saw Theron's shock, the dismay on all their faces, as they recognized her and took in the Severer's robes and the torc around her neck. Still, they were all three of them alive and standing; Deina relaxed, fractionally. Until the door to the right of the chair opened and another figure emerged. One who glittered so brightly it hurt Deina's eyes.

Orpheus.

The Tyrant was clad entirely in gold. As well as the gold mask and the golden armor on his forearms and hands that Deina remembered, he was wearing a robe entirely covered in tiny disks of beaten gold. The crown on his head and the belt around his waist were both thickly covered in precious gems. An empire's ransom, let alone a king's, while throughout the Dominion people were starving . . . Deina saw Aster clench his fists. She could guess what he was thinking: There was no honor in the accumulation and display of such wealth.

Orpheus sank down upon the fur-covered chair, his shoulders sagging. He clapped his hands; servingwomen appeared through the door to the left of the chair. All of them had torcs around their necks, even though they were not Theodesmioi—there was no sigil on their foreheads. Deina wondered if they were spellbound in some other way. As one of the women poured Orpheus some wine, another two unclasped the gold mask from Orpheus's head and lifted it away.

If Deina hadn't known it was the same man, she wouldn't have recognized him. The features that were revealed were so much older than that of the man they'd seen on the ship before entering the Underworld. Orpheus's skin hung loose and wrinkled from the bones of his face and was marked with the spots of age. His eyes were rheumy, his teeth yellowed. He looked like a man whose allotted span of life had almost come to its end. Orpheus noticed her watching him.

"Do not be concerned for me, Severer. I will soon regain all my youth and vigor." He smiled, revealing red, shrunken gums. "And you will help me do it. Bring him."

Two Bronze Guards dragged Theron forward to stand in front of his father.

"Well," Orpheus murmured after he'd drained a cup of wine, "you seem to have a knack for survival, my son, even if you have few other worthy skills. If I'd ever given you another thought after I had you tied to that stake on the mountainside, and if things had been different, I suppose I might have hoped for you to have grown into a warrior. Instead, when Neidius alerted me to your existence, I found a boy who, if left to his own devices, would prefer to sing for his supper."

Theron spat on the floor in front of Orpheus's feet. "Fine words from such a mighty king. I would rather be the son of the most scurrilous villain in Iolkos's prison than share the same blood as you."

Orpheus laughed. "Mighty? Yes. Too mighty now to worry whether the gods will care about your death. Mighty enough that even Fate has no hold over me. Because you *are* going to die."

"Then I'll die killing you." Theron lunged forward, his hands reaching for Orpheus's throat. His guards stopped him before he even got close.

"No," Orpheus said, "you'll do exactly what I say. I may need

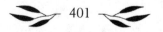

you alive and unharmed, but the same doesn't go for your friends." He pointed at Aster. "Break his arm."

"Stop, please—" Deina tried to push past her guards as Theron struggled and raged at Orpheus. Dendris stepped in front of Aster and was shoved out of the way. The Bronze Guard grabbed Aster's forearm—in vain Aster yelled, hitting and kicking the metal body—and snapped the bone in two.

Aster screamed; the sound went through Deina like a knife. The guard released him and he dropped to his knees, cradling his injured limb, moaning, retching over and over. There was no blood as far as she could see, but the arm was unnaturally bent, bulging where the shattered end of the bone was sticking up beneath his skin.

Theron was hanging limp in his guards' hands, his head bowed.

"You wicked, accursed—" Dendris began.

"Hold your tongue," Orpheus snapped. "Unless you want it ripped out. Chain those two up." One Bronze Guard shackled Dendris to the wall. Another took hold of Aster's wrists and jerked him upright. Too hard—with a spattering of blood, the broken bone ripped through the skin of his forearm.

Aster fainted. Yet still the guard persisted in its orders, fixing Aster's unconscious body into the manacles. Blood began splashing onto the floor, dark against the white stone.

Deina was held fast by her own guards, but she could still scream at Orpheus. "You're going to kill him—he'll die—"

"Apart from me, all men die. Though I hope he will survive. He may be useful hereafter; if I choose to absorb his life, he will give me the strength of a warrior. I'm not expecting so much from my son's contribution, but perhaps my songs will become famous, and history will speak of Orpheus the musician, who charmed the gods themselves with the beauty of his voice." He nodded toward Theron. "Prepare the boy."

Deina was forced to watch as Theron's arms were bound behind him, as he was gagged and made to kneel at the third, empty point of the triangle. There were tears in his eyes. As she caught his gaze, he shook his head a little. She understood. He believed it was over. That they'd lost.

Deina dug her fingernails into her palms as rage and grief welled up inside her, so much that she trembled from keeping it all locked inside. The temptation to cry out to Hades was growing harder and harder to resist. The words were on the tip of her tongue: *I'll promise to stay in the Underworld—I'll promise you anything—if you'll turn me into a god and give me the powers you claim could be mine.* If she was a god, she could stop Orpheus from killing Theron. She could take her friends away from all this.

Except the gods didn't care about what Orpheus was doing, or about the fate of the Theodesmioi, or about any human suffering. Once she was a god, she might not care about such things, either. She had a sudden image of her turning her back on Theron and the others, walking away and leaving them to die . . .

Better to eat the seeds. Eat the seeds, save her friends, and die. Not much of a choice. But at least it would be hers.

Aristaeus entered the room, followed by Chryse. Her old friend threw one frightened glance at Orpheus, then fixed her gaze on the ground. If she'd seen Deina standing there, or

Theron kneeling, or Dendris and Aster chained to the walls, she didn't show it.

"Well, my faithful servant? Your message said you had something to show me?" Orpheus asked.

"Yes, Majesty. Something of great value, I believe." Aristaeus held out a small gold box. "Serpent's teeth. Collected in the Underworld by one of the Severers. Chryse alerted me to their existence."

Yet another betrayal. Deina hissed at her old friend as Orpheus stretched out his fingers toward the fangs that Drex had gathered.

"Could they be? The legendary heirloom of the House of Cadmus? Well done, Chryse. Your loyalty will shortly be rewarded with the highest of honors." Orpheus picked up one of the fangs and held it between thumb and forefinger. "Worth losing Eurydice for, especially since I have found a—" A fit of coughing racked the Tyrant's body. When he'd recovered, he tapped the table that had been placed next to the chair. "Set the box down there for now. We will investigate the truth of the legend in due course, but we must carry out the rite first. I feel myself weakening." Orpheus beckoned to his servingwomen. They began unfastening the golden armor that covered his hands and arms and body, removing his gaudy outer clothes until he was wearing just a linen tunic. "Good. It is time."

The servants were dismissed. The Bronze Guards released Deina and stepped back, out of the sacred circle. Deina ran to Theron and knelt to throw her arms around him. He was shaking.

"I'll never help you, Orpheus. Never."

"Oh, I think you will. Otherwise, rather than keeping your friend there alive"—he nodded to Aster—"I'll hand him over to Aristaeus, to be made into another one of his Iron Guards; he bears the wrong sigil to wear the bronze armor of my guards, and I will have only the best and strongest to answer to my will. And instead of a quick death for her"—Orpheus jabbed a finger toward Dendris—"she can become one of my silent handmaidens."

He must have meant the women who had removed his golden coverings. Deina wondered if their torcs contained spells that had taken their voices.

Orpheus smiled. "You can't bargain with me, Deina. Accept your fate. I don't intend to lose you as I lost Eurydice."

"Then let me at least say goodbye to him."

Orpheus regarded her for a moment, then nodded. "Since he is my son." He smiled. "And to sweeten his final moments of life, so that he might curse the losing of it even more."

The Tyrant rose from the chair, made his way to the stone slab, and lay down upon it. Deina turned to face Theron. Kneeling in front of him, she whispered hurriedly into his ear as she slid the seeds from her pouch.

"Don't grieve for me. If I succeed, at least I'll have died for something." She caressed his face, staring into his dark eyes. No doubt Drex could have written an entire scroll about what she saw there. Sorrow, regret, and fear, but also affection, friendship, love. Deina threw an arm around Theron's neck and hugged him, holding her breath as if somehow it might stop this moment from ending.

"Enough. It is time for the rite." Aristaeus dragged Deina

roughly to her feet and pushed her toward the altar. "I will tell you what to say this time; you will have between a few months and a year to memorize the rite before it is required again. You will perform the ritual to drain the boy's life, but there is a preliminary sacrifice required, which I will deal with. His Majesty and the chosen one"—he gestured to Theron—"will both drink the blood of the sacrificial victim, mixed with certain potent herbs. By this means, they will enter the trance that is necessary to extract the life force from one and place it within another. Are you ready to begin?"

Deina nodded; while the unfortunate animal was brought into the room, she'd have time to eat the seeds.

But no animal appeared.

Instead, two of the Bronze Guards seized Chryse's arms and began to drag her toward the altar.

"Wait, you can't do this—" Deina cried out, stunned with the sudden realization of what Aristaeus planned.

Chryse began to plead and shriek. "Lord Aristaeus, no! You said you'd help me—that you'd take care of me!" She twisted her head around, trying to appeal to Orpheus as she struggled to get away from the altar. "There's been a mistake! I did everything you asked—"

Deina shook the seeds out of their linen wrapping. There was no more time for hesitation—whatever Chryse had done, Deina couldn't let it end like this.

Orpheus sighed. "I'm afraid you know too much, my dear. Besides, to die for your king is the highest honor. Silence her, Aristaeus."

Deina crammed the seeds into her mouth and began chewing

the bitter kernels. She darted toward Chryse, but Aristaeus kicked her in the stomach and knocked her to the floor. The Bronze Guards forced Chryse onto her back across the altar. Deina, still clutching her stomach, looked up into her friend's inverted face as Aristaeus pulled a knife from his belt.

"Deina," Chryse whimpered, "help me—"

Deina's mouth was dry as dust. She forced herself to swallow the seeds and flung up her arm. "Stop!"

Any hope she had that her command would have some effect—turn Aristaeus to stone or somehow force him to hold his hand—withered. Even as Deina's voice rang out, even as she threw herself forward again in a futile attempt to reach him, he raised the knife and slashed Chryse's throat.

"No—no!"

Blood gushed from the widening gash across Chryse's neck, ran across her pale skin and down into her golden hair. Her body convulsed once and was still. Her blue eyes were wide open. Sightless. The blood dripping from her neck began to gather in the grooves of the triangle cut into the floor below the altar.

No. Deina tried to form the word. Tried to reach her friend's murderer, to claw away his face. But intense, sudden agony, worse even than the hallucination of burning Aristaeus's scorpion had induced in Iolkos, ripped through her core and crawled across skin, nails, teeth, eyeballs, everywhere, forcing her onto her hands and knees. She could hear herself moaning in pain. She could see her hands beneath her, nails trying to dig into the unyielding stone floor. Her veins were becoming visible, spreading like a dark web of marbling across her skin, stinging as if some acidic venom was running through them.

Had Nat lied to her? The seeds were supposed to give her the power to save her friends, and then destroy her, but this . . . Her stomach heaved, and blood gushed from her mouth across the white granite.

"Aristaeus," Orpheus demanded, "what is happening?"

Deina felt Aristaeus grip her arm and haul her up onto her knees. His other hand seized her face and forced her to look at him. She could see him staring at her, horror-struck, through a red film that was clouding her vision.

"Poison, Your Majesty—it has to be. I know of several that induce these symptoms—weeping blood, vomiting blood—though not usually together. One of the attendants must have given her something. They will be punished. I will—"

"I don't care what caused it," Orpheus roared. "Just stop it. Stop her from dying."

"Of course. I'll find an antidote."

The first convulsion was strong enough to jerk Deina out of Aristaeus's grasp. Her back arched uncontrollably, forcing a scream from her throat. In the distance, she could hear Dendris praying, gabbling the words out as fast as she could. But the only god Deina wanted to see was Nat.

Please let this end—

Another convulsion, but smaller. As the pain built unbearably, her body was becoming rigid. She wanted to curl into a ball, to hide away from the agony, but her contorted limbs were fixed, splayed into unnatural positions. Another scream, on and on, until her lower ribs seized up, crushing her lungs. Was this what Nat had meant by destruction? If she died, it would stop Orpheus. He couldn't use her power to drain any more victims.

But what about her friends? More of her rib cage solidified, forcing her to fight for every tiny breath. Her heart was slowing, stuttering, losing the race against the all-consuming pain. The paralysis crept farther, ossifying shoulders, throat, face, eyelids, until she was entombed in her own body, suffocating, and still the agony went on.

Please, Nat, just let me die. Let me—

25

Deina was weightless, wrapped in the soft warmth of early summer . . .

Was this what death felt like? The pain had gone away. Her heart had stopped beating. She wasn't fighting for breath anymore. She was weightless, then, because she was free of her ruined body—that made sense. Thanatos had claimed her soul, and Orpheus could no longer touch her.

Strange, then, that she could still hear his voice, thick with rage . . .

"Aristaeus, what have you done? She's dead!"

Dead. I'm dead. I don't need to stay here. It's over.

Deina waited for the voices to fade. But if anything, only the weightlessness faded, as she became aware of the hard surface beneath her body. Of warmth loosening the petrified fibers of her muscles. The voices grew louder.

"Surely, Your Majesty, you do not doubt my loyalty?" Aristaeus, a note of pleading in his tone.

"How can I not when you have failed me so abysmally—"

Deina stopped paying attention—an argument between Orpheus and Aristaeus had little to do with her. Other things seemed more important. She was dead—she knew she was. She'd felt her heart spasm and solidify, caught into immobility as the agony reached its climax. Whatever blood was left in her body should be still now, freed from the insistent pulse that had driven it through her veins while she was alive. And yet, she could feel *something* running beneath her skin. Something stronger than the dull ache that seemed to be resurfacing in every part of her. The sensation reminded her of the raw, crackling energy that had filled the crystal-bladed dagger she'd stolen from Orpheus's ship. The power of it scared her.

It's time, Deina. If you're going to save your friends, you need to do it now. You can, you know.

Nat's voice, inside her head.

Deina understood. She was dead. The seeds had killed her. But they'd also given her, at least temporarily, the strength to save Theron and Aster and Dendris. To give them a chance to live. If she was brave enough to take it.

She flexed her hand cautiously. The movement hurt a little. But the other thing—the power—she could feel that, too, sliding between skin and sinew, sharp as a blade.

Deina?

I don't know. I'm afraid. The pain—

The worst is over. Trust me, Deina, you can do this. Fight harder.

Fight harder. The words echoed through her memory. A hot night, and the scent of rosemary—

"Your Majesty, I think she's alive—" Aristaeus's boots rang on the stone floor. No more time for hesitation. Deina opened her eyes as Aristaeus reached her. Sword in hand, he bared his teeth.

"You will pay for this attempt at defiance. You, and your friends, and all those who helped you." He drew his leg back and kicked.

Deina caught his ankle in one hand and squeezed. Aristaeus fell, shrieking as the bone shattered beneath the pressure of her grip. She rolled and jumped to her feet, stooping to snatch Aristaeus's sword.

"Guards!" Orpheus bellowed. "Disarm her! Capture her!"

He was still hoping to keep her alive. The twelve Bronze Guards began to close in on her. They had been Theodesmioi once, stronger than the ordinary men that Aristaeus used for his Iron Guards. That sorrow she'd seen in the guard's eyes—maybe that strength had helped them to hold on to some of their humanity, despite what Orpheus had done to them.

The nearest guard lunged, trying to catch hold of her arms, but the power burning through her body gave her more speed, more agility than ever before. Deina used the guard's outstretched arm to swing herself up onto its shoulders. She reached for the mouthless faceplate, hooking the very tips of her fingers into the eyeholes, and wrenched it from the guard's face. Maybe it would die, but better death than such a life as these creatures had. As it stumbled to its knees, she jumped clear, spun, and ducked beneath the drawn blade of another guard to reach up and pull its faceplate off, too. A woman's features were revealed. Orpheus began screaming.

"Kill her! Kill her!"

A bronze arm circled her neck and started to choke her. As

Deina groped for her attacker's faceplate, a shadow fell across her. Another guard—but she could see his face, pallid from lack of light. He smiled at her—uncertain, as if he couldn't quite remember how—reached behind her, and tore the other guard's faceplate away. Its grip slackened. Deina nodded to her rescuer.

"Save the others." A moan of pain drew her attention. She saw Aristaeus dragging himself through an open door. He screamed for his Iron Guards. "Destroy them! Destroy them all!"

Orpheus was shuffling toward the same door.

"Stop him!" Deina yelled. "Bar the doors!"

One of the freed guards heard her and raced for the open door, ramming it shut and bracing himself against it as the fists of the Iron Guards began to beat against the other side. Another guard, faceplate intact, attacked him. Deina ran and leaped onto the guard's shoulders and ripped the faceplate away. In another few moments, the faces of all the Bronze Guards were visible. As three of them freed Theron, Dendris, and Aster—still unconscious, thankfully—the others held the doors closed. The Iron Guards had already gathered on the other side and were trying to force their way through. Aristaeus had escaped. But Orpheus . . .

Orpheus, cowering behind the fur-draped chair, was hers.

Deina turned to the altar. Chryse's lifeless body was still draped across it. Aristaeus had just left her there, discarded like the scraps set aside to be tossed to the dogs after a feast.

"Chryse . . ." Deina lifted the body down from the altar, shut her eyes, and pressed her lips against Chryse's cold forehead. She didn't dare risk more; a plan had formed in her mind, a way to truly save Theron. If only the power of the seeds allowed her enough time to carry it out. "Rest, my dearest friend. Dendris, you must make sure she's buried. Do you understand?" Rage surged through her, making the power the seeds had given her blaze even brighter.

Dendris, Theron next to her, was kneeling by Aster's side. She looked confused but nodded all the same.

Deina picked up Aristaeus's sword and strode across to where Orpheus was hiding. She thrust the chair out of the way. Orpheus whimpered as Deina leveled the blade of the sword at his chest.

"There will be no more evading death for you, Tyrant. No more stealing other people's lives. No more sending Severers to their deaths. No more starving your people, no more sending them into pointless wars, and no more tribute. Whatever happens to your empire, for you, this is the end." Deina smiled at him. "And I am going to be the one to kill you, not your son. Theron will live. He'll have his freedom, finally, and the Order of Hades will not pursue him."

"What about you?" Orpheus spat. "I wear the crown of Thebes and her Dominion. Killing me is treason. They will tie you to the Deathless Trees forever."

Deina laughed.

"They won't have the chance. I'll be dead and gone before they even know I've killed you." The thought buoyed her. She raised the sword higher. She was going to execute Orpheus now. And then—

She'd finally have her freedom. Even if it was only the freedom of death.

Deina thrust the blade forward—

And missed. The point of the sword grazed the wall to one side. She tried again. Missed again. She seized a spear from one of the Bronze Guards and ran at Orpheus, aiming to drive the leaf-shaped blade into his chest. Again, the spear slipped sideways, twisting out of her grasp.

Orpheus began to cackle. "Perhaps the gods don't want me to die, Soul Severer."

"Perhaps, but I don't particularly care what they want."

She snatched the spear up again, spun it around as she stood over Orpheus, and plunged the iron spike down toward his belly. But it hit the stone floor instead. Deina screamed with frustration.

A hand gripped her wrist. She jerked free and swung around.

Theron. He laid his hand on her shoulder. His eyes were glistening with unshed tears. "Hades was right, Deina. I can't avoid my fate. Drex couldn't."

"No! You don't understand—"

Theron raised one hand to Deina's cheek. "I do. I know what you're trying to do. And why. But I have to be the one to kill him." He walked forward and picked up Aristaeus's sword from where it lay. Knelt and held the blade against Orpheus's throat. The sword's edge was sharp; a trickle of blood ran across the Tyrant's neck. "I want to be the one to put an end to this monster. I *need* to be the one to kill him. As for the Order of Hades—they'll have to find me before they can tie me to the Deathless Trees." He smiled slightly, though Deina could see the effort it was costing him. "You're not the only one who can be devious, you know that. I'll take my chances. I know it will mean a lifetime alone; I'm not going to ask anyone to share the risk and the running with me. But if they do find me"—he pressed the sword deeper into his father's skin, making Orpheus writhe with pain—"eternity watching myself slit this fiend's throat might not be all that bad."

Theron gripped Orpheus's hair with his free hand, forcing the Tyrant's head back. "I'm sorry, Deina. For everything." His voice was raw with grief; at any moment, Deina thought, he might break beneath the weight of it. "You don't know how much I wish things could have been different." He raised the sword, ready to strike the final blow. "Better the Deathless Trees than an eternity in Tartarus, Father, which is where you're going."

Eternity. The Deathless Trees.

The man who'd undergone the Punishment Rite back in Iolkos—she and Anteïs had left his soul there, in the Threshold, imprisoned for all time in the boundary between life and death. Not alive, but not dead, either . . .

Deina gasped.

"Stop!" With a burst of strength, she knocked the sword from Theron's hand and seized both him and Orpheus, dragging them upright. "There's another way."

Theron looked startled at her sudden excitement.

"What are you talking about?"

"We're Severers, aren't we?"

He nodded, doubtful. "Yes, but—"

"Then let's act like Severers. Bring him." Deina couldn't repress a grin. "Finally, we can end this. Together." She started murmuring the words of the Punishment Rite as she hurried to where Chryse's body lay in a pool of blood. Chryse had been

Orpheus's victim just as surely as if he'd wielded the knife himself. Theron forced Orpheus onto his knees and held his arms wide. Deina dipped her fingers into her friend's blood and daubed it onto Orpheus's forehead, palms, and chest, even as the Tyrant raged and spat at her. She marked Theron and herself in the same way, chanting all the time. Not the full rite, not as it should be done, but hopefully the power of the seeds would supply what was missing. The air inside the sacred circle began to grow cold.

"Deina, what are you doing?"

Thanatos.

The god of death began striding toward her, but she wasn't finished yet. And she couldn't allow Nat to interfere. Deina gabbled through the last lines of the rite as he reached out to take her—

Nat, the Cadmea, and everything in it fell away.

The Threshold, as Deina had constructed it with the Punishment Rite, looked very similar to that version of it she had summoned for the man in Iolkos. Just as bleak, just as cruel and unforgiving. But there were some oddities, things she'd never witnessed before. A rotting fur was crumpled upon the floor. A broken chest with gems spilling out of it lay among the roots of the Deathless Trees. And over by the boundary was what looked like a throne with a broken leg, butted up against piles of rusting swords. It was almost as if something from Orpheus's own mind had spilled into the Threshold as Deina was building it—perhaps because she hadn't exactly followed the rite to the letter. Anteïs would find it interesting. When she got back to Iolkos, she could tell Anteïs about it . . .

Deina stiffened. She wouldn't be going back to Iolkos. She'd never see Anteïs again.

"Theron, if you make it back to the House—tell Anteïs—tell Anteïs—" Deina shook her head. "Tell her, thank you. For everything."

"What do you mean? Why would I be going back to the House without you? I don't understand any of this." He gestured to Orpheus, who was staring around, bewildered. The Tyrant hadn't noticed the silver lifeline looped around his waist and around the waists of Deina and Theron. As they watched him, he began running around the boundary, desperately looking for a way to escape, just like Dionys had back in Iolkos.

Deina turned her back on him. Let him run. Orpheus wasn't going anywhere.

Theron gripped her shoulders. "Why didn't you just let me kill him?"

"Because I want you to be free—finally free, of all of this. And because we don't need to." She lifted her hands to Theron's face. "Whatever else we are, you and I are Soul Severers. It's perhaps the most important part of what we are. And it's time we remembered that. The Threshold is a place that our kind created, that only we can call into existence. It lies in the boundary between life and death, but is separate from both the mortal world and the Underworld. 'Who wields power over this place? Not gods. Not men. Only us.'" A line from one of the first Songs she'd had to learn. "You know this. You learned it, too, when you were an initiate." Theron nodded. "So now that we've brought your father here, we're going to leave him here. Forever. Alone. To spend an eternity reliving the wickedness of all the lifetimes he's lived." She glanced at Orpheus, hurling himself against the unyielding boundary. "He'll suffer the pain he has inflicted over and over. It's the least he deserves. But . . . we're not actually going to kill him."

Comprehension dawned in Theron's eyes. He caught hold of her hands.

"The Order of Hades—"

"—will have no reason to pursue you."

He grinned at her, one of those smiles that always made her stomach flip, no matter how hard she tried to resist. But his smile quickly faded.

"What about you? I watched you die in agony, or I thought I did." He swung away and rubbed his hands over his face. When he turned to her again, she could see the distress lingering in his eyes. "And then you jumped up and freed the guards and—" Theron's mouth rounded as he blew out a long breath. "You've always been fast, but this was different, wasn't it?" He brushed his fingers against her cheek. "Your scars have gone. You said yes to Hades, didn't you?"

"No. I didn't."

Theron's grin returned. "Then we're both free. All we have to do is escape Thebes and we can be together." He put his hands on her waist as if he were about to lift her into the air. "Deina—"

"Theron . . . it's not that simple."

"What do you mean?"

"Nat—the god of death—he gave me an alternative. Some

seeds. Eating them would give me the ability to save my friends, but they'd also destroy me." Deina swallowed the lump in her throat. "That was what you saw. The power of the seeds. But after I leave the Threshold . . ."

"No." Theron's fingers tightened against her flesh. "No, I won't let him take you—I'll find a way. Some way of protecting you. Of stopping him."

"I don't think we can stop him." She took Theron's wrist and pressed his palm against the silence of her heart. Or where her heart used to be. "I think I'm already dead."

Theron gazed down at his hand. Lines of horror etched his face. Deina closed her eyes, waiting for him to draw away from her. For something that no longer existed, her heart ached more than she could possibly have imagined.

But instead of pulling away, Theron slid his arms around her and held her tightly against him. She laid her head on his chest, listening to the steady beat of his heart.

"What are we going to do?" Theron murmured.

"Nothing. Unless I stay here forever, there's nothing to be done." Deina looked up into his face. There were tears running down his cheeks. She brushed them away with her thumbs. "Don't weep for me. I chose this. Just as I chose to volunteer for Orpheus's quest, just as I chose to seek out Hades, just as I chose to throw the dagger that killed Drex. At least I'll be at peace, knowing that I've given you and Aster and Dendris a real chance to escape. To live. Knowing that I've done something worth remembering." She smiled at him. "Maybe even worthy of a song."

Theron groaned. "But there has to be a way." He clung to

her all the more tightly, as if somehow he alone could stop the Underworld claiming her. "I wanted to tell you before, when we were in Hades's garden. My feelings toward you . . . I . . . I can't stop thinking about you, Deina. I went into the Underworld just wanting freedom for myself. But before we were halfway done, I realized that my freedom would be worthless without you. Unless you were there to share it with me." He drew back a little to look at her, to trace his fingers gently along the line of her jaw, his dark eyes so full of desire and affection that longing coursed like wildfire through Deina's body, even though she didn't understand how it was still possible. "I know I don't deserve it, but I want more than your friendship, Deina. I want you. All of you. Every stubborn, unscrupulous, fierce, glorious fragment. Because I—"

Deina put her fingers to his lips. Her hand was trembling.

"No more, please. Don't say any more." Tears spilled across her cheeks. "It will only make things worse." Deina allowed her forehead to rest against his for a moment longer. "You have to let me go, Theron. There is no other way." She disengaged his hands and stepped back. "Come, my old friend. Let's perform the rest of the rite and leave this place."

Theron pressed the heels of his hands into his eyes, sniffed and nodded.

Orpheus was hammering his fists against the barrier. He didn't pay attention to either Deina or his son.

"Theron, you should be the one to complete the rite. I'll make sure we sever the lifeline at the end."

Theron began to chant the ancient words of binding. As he did so, the sigil on his forehead began to glow. Just as before, the roots and branches of the Deathless Trees seemed to come to life, slithering toward Orpheus, crawling over the ground until they reached him. Orpheus screamed in terror when he realized what was happening. He tried desperately to peel them off him, until the skin of his fingers was bloodied and split, but it did no good. Soon they were woven all around him and he was caught fast, like a fly in a web.

Theron's voice grew louder and louder, as if he was determined to drown out the shrieks of terror from his father. The sigil of Hades burned upon Orpheus's forehead, but this time there were two marks instead of one—one for her and one for Theron, Deina assumed. Although Theron was carrying out the rite, she was the one who had brought Orpheus here. As Theron continued to chant the incantation, smoke poured from the marks, the clouds growing larger and larger, until finally Deina could see images in it. Quickly, she averted her eyes. She couldn't bear to look. So much suffering, so much death. The screams of Orpheus's victims filled the air.

And then there was silence. It was finally over.

"Theron?" Deina questioned.

"I'm fine," he replied. A trickle of blood ran from his nose. Grimacing, he wiped it away with the back of his hand. "Mostly."

Together they made their way over to where Orpheus hung motionless, suspended between the trees. Theron stood there, glaring into the blank, unresponsive eyes of his father, while Deina picked up the glittering silver thread of his life and secured it firmly onto one of the branches. She had no knife with which to sever the thread, but it didn't matter. She simply ripped it apart with her hands. As the Threshold tumbled away from them, she glanced at Theron's shoulder. A fresh rite-seal was forming in his flesh—a year off his indenture. Not that it mattered anymore. He was free.

Deina opened her eyes. They were back in the room at the top of the Cadmea, Theron beside her, Orpheus's body slumped on the ground. No sign of Nat, though he couldn't be far away. The Bronze Guards were straining to keep the metal doors shut against the battering rams of the Iron Guards on the other side. She could hear the doors shaking in their frames. A crack had appeared in the wall, and dust was drifting down from the ceiling. Theron dragged Orpheus's body toward the hearth in the center of the room and threw it onto the fire. Deina hurried to Aster and Dendris.

"How is he?"

"I don't know." Dendris's face was pinched with worry. "He's lost so much blood, and I don't know how to help him. It might be too late." She glanced at the doors. "How are we going to get out of here?"

"There's another way." The shout came from one of the Bronze Guards, who was bracing his shoulders against the nearest door—the same guard who had helped Deina before. "We can show you."

Deina knelt next to Aster. His arm was mottled, his hand below the break unnaturally pale.

"If we can get him out of here, perhaps we can—"

"Deina." Nat's voice behind her, echoing across the granite dome above them.

As Dendris gasped and jumped to her feet to stand

protectively over Aster and some of the Bronze Guards exclaimed in fear, Deina rose to meet him. Dark wings flaring out from his shoulders, ice crystallizing across the stone floor beneath his feet, he looked as he had on the terrace conjured by Hades in the Underworld. Not Nat, but Thanatos, god of death. When he reached her, Thanatos touched the bronze torc she wore with one finger. The metal shattered instantly, its fragments scattering.

"Please, help him." Deina gestured to Aster. "You told me if I ate the seeds I'd save my friends, but he's going to die . . ."

The god hesitated, but only for a moment. He knelt briefly and laid his hand above Aster's heart. The gaping wound on the Severer's arm began to knit itself together, and even before Thanatos had straightened up, Aster's eyes fluttered open.

"It is done, Deina." As close as he was, Thanatos seemed remote. "As is your time here."

Sorrow rippled through Deina's core. She would have to leave her friends, and go on alone, and never see them again.

I thought I was ready. But I'm not.

"I wish I could have known you better, Dendris." She hugged the other woman tightly, then crouched next to Aster, squeezing his hand. "It's been an honor."

"I don't understand," Aster murmured.

"The gods are cruel," Theron replied. "This one has claimed Deina's life as the price for saving ours. She's to die. She's already dead." He gasped a little and pain flickered across his face, as if saying the words aloud somehow made them real. "He's come to take her to the Underworld, to join the shades."

"To the Underworld, yes," Thanatos confirmed. "But not as a shade."

"What?" Deina demanded.

"I said the seeds might destroy you. Not that they would kill you."

More trickery? Deina's hand fluttered to her chest. "My heart no longer beats." She held out her arm to Nat. "I'm dead. I have no pulse."

Nat gently laid his cold fingers across Deina's wrist. "I know, but not because you've died. Your heart's rhythm has stilled because you belong to the Underworld now. And there is no time there in which it might beat."

Deina remembered Hades's offered bargain, and the god's unexplained desire for her to stay in the Underworld. The word *No* formed on her lips, but horror took her voice.

Nat gazed at her, his expression unreadable.

"It is time, Hades's daughter. I must take you to the Underworld, and there you will remain. You will never be allowed to leave."

Fury broke through Deina's silence. She shoved Nat with such force that he stumbled backward, eyes wide with surprise.

"Who gave you the seeds, Thanatos? Who told you to give them to me?"

"Hades, of course." Anger flared into his voice and eyes, though Deina couldn't tell at whom it was directed. "And it is into her presence I must now conduct you. Orpheus is neither dead nor alive, and you've managed to turn aside that one's destiny." He scowled, flinging a hand out and pointing at Theron. "My sisters the Fates are already petitioning Zeus for your punishment. There is clamor in the halls of Olympus." Nat's wings grew until they seemed to fill the entire room—black, iridescent, glittering with points of light that might have been the stars themselves. Yet his expression softened. "You must come with me, Deina. You have no choice in the matter. Neither do I." A doorway appeared on the far side of the room, standing alone, detached from its surroundings, almost floating above the white stone floor, but somehow more solid than anything else. Beyond the doorway lay the wall of night they'd walked through to reach Hades's palace. Deina rocked back on her heels. Facing this immense, impenetrable blackness, she was more terrified than she'd ever been.

Thanatos seized her wrist and started to drag her toward the doorway.

"No. Wait!" Deina struggled against Nat's grasp. "I didn't get to say goodbye to Theron. Just a little longer, Nat. Please . . ."

The god of death kept walking, either unable or unwilling to respond to her plea. Deina used all her weight to try to slow him down, but he was already stepping through the doorway. Disappearing. "Theron—"

Theron raced toward her. He grabbed hold of her outstretched hand and caught her in his arms. Deina lifted her mouth, and Theron crushed his lips against hers, kissing her urgently, desperately, until the pull of the doorway became too much for her to resist. She pushed him to safety.

Deina kept her eyes fixed on Theron's face, trying to etch every feature into her memory, until the darkness swallowed her.

Epilogue

"Deina, no—"

She was fading from view. Theron flung himself forward, trying to reach her fingertips, to touch her one last time.

Too late. The doorway vanished, Deina with it. Theron sank to his knees.

All those years they'd spent at each other's throats, only for him to realize too late that he loved her.

And now he'd lost her.

A crash reverberated through the room as a hand gripped his shoulder. He glanced up. Aster—pale, but in one piece. His arm bore no trace of the awful trauma apart from a long scar that looked as if it had healed many years ago.

"The Bronze Guards are with us, but they are only twelve in number, and the Iron Guards are breaking through. We've not got much longer."

Theron shook his head. "I don't care. Let them in."

"Theron . . ." There was a note of chiding in Aster's voice. "Deina gave up the life she wanted so we could survive. So that you could survive. Do you want her sacrifice to have been in vain?"

The blood rushed to Theron's face. Aster was right. He'd have time later to grieve. To work out some sort of revenge against the gods, if that was even possible. What mattered now was to get out of here. He pushed himself to his feet.

Dendris and one of the Bronze Guards were over where Orpheus's chair stood, bracing themselves against the massive piece of marble to push it out of the way. He and Aster hurried to help.

"What are we doing?"

"There's another way out, a trapdoor," the guard answered, pointing to the floor.

Theron studied the large hexagonal tiles; they all looked the same.

"Are you sure?"

"Quite sure." His voice was frail and raspy; Theron shuddered, wondering how many years had passed since these guards had been sealed within their bronze armor. Still, the man was grinning despite the fact that the hinges of the nearby doors were beginning to give under the Iron Guards' onslaught. He bent, hooked his fingertips beneath one of the red-edged tiles, and grunted. The entire hexagon lifted away to reveal a spiral staircase descending into the dark depths of the Cadmea. "Half of us will come with you. The other half will stay to protect our retreat. Four will stay at the doors until the last minute while two replace the chair above the trapdoor." His smile faded. "I don't know how much time this will buy you. Aristaeus knows about this door, even though the Iron Guards do not."

Theron grasped the man's shoulder. "But the ones who stay will be killed."

"We are Battle Wagers of Zeus, and you are the true king of Thebes. And even if you were not, it is better to die fighting than to live any longer in this long, slow suffocation." The guard gritted his teeth, grabbed the rest of his helmet, tore it away from the body armor, and hurled it into the corner of the room. His grin returned. "My name is—was—Critos."

"Open! Open in the name of King Aristaeus!" It sounded as if human guards had joined the fray outside the circular room. So much for loyalty—Aristaeus hadn't even waited to check that Orpheus was dead before claiming the throne. Theron glanced toward the burning remains of his father, his mouth twisting in grim satisfaction. There was a yell from a Bronze Guard—a spear was thrust through the widening gap at the edge of one of the doors.

"We can't hold them much longer!"

Dendris darted to the side table and snatched up the gold box containing the teeth Drex had collected.

"We should bring these. And Chryse's body." When Theron hesitated, she added, "Deina asked me to make sure she received burial."

Theron nodded. They would have to do what they could.

"Aster—"

He'd already scooped Chryse's body into his arms. They were ready.

Critos put his hands to his mouth, yelling over the groans from the door hinges.

"The true king's guard—be ready."

Aster and Dendris, with Critos ahead of them bearing a torch, began descending the spiral stair. As the guards who

were to join them raced toward the trapdoor, Theron took a last quick glance at the circular room. This place should have been his home. His birthright. The ancient hearth gods of Thebes should have been his protectors.

So much for that. The gods were of little value to humans. Unless it was perhaps to swear by. He hurried after the others.

Theron dragged his fingernails against the sides of the stairwell, gouging some of the earth wall into his hand, and murmured an oath to himself.

"By the gods and by Thebes, if it's the last thing I do, I swear I'll find a way to save Deina and to destroy Aristaeus. Or I will die trying."

To be continued . . .

Authors' Note

Daughter of the Underworld is a work of fantasy inspired by two questions. The first was this: What would have happened if the Mycenaean civilization of Bronze Age Greece had never collapsed? (A bit of context: The Mycenaean civilization existed from approximately 1400 BCE to 1100 BCE, and its kingdoms are thought by some historians to have inspired Homer's *Iliad*. No one knows for certain why the cities were abandoned.) What if, we wondered, the rulers of those kingdoms had tried to save themselves from approaching destruction by striking a bargain with the gods? Protection, in return for a tithe of children each year to be given up to the gods' service, marked by the gods and drawing a little of their power. The Mycenaean kingdoms would endure, and in return the gods would get some *serious* belief. The marked children became our Theodesmioi, their freedom of choice sacrificed for the good of their communities, their rulers, and their divinities.

Our other question arose from the story of Orpheus and Eurydice. (In the myth, they get married, she promptly dies, then he enters the Underworld and sings so beautifully that he convinces Hades to restore her to life. At the last moment he fails by breaking the god's condition and looking at Eurydice before they both regain the mortal world.) We wondered whether Eurydice was as keen to return from the Underworld as Orpheus was to retrieve her. We decided perhaps she wasn't, and set about creating an Orpheus whose behavior would give her good reason to want to escape. Our Orpheus is loosely inspired by Alexander the Great (in reality, about eight hundred years after the end of the Mycenaeans), perhaps combined with any of the more extreme Roman emperors. The past is littered with megalomaniacs, and the present seems to be no different. Let's hope there will also always be people who stand up to them.

We've taken a number of liberties with the history that inspired this story, including assuming that the Mycenaean cities, had they survived, would have developed an alphabet similar to that used in ancient Greek. We've also given them coinage and much larger ships. In reality, quinqueremes were not in use until several centuries later. Deina's ceremonial outfit in the banquet scene is drawn from Bronze Age frescoes in Mycenae and Knossos depicting priestesses or possibly goddesses. The agate that Drex carves is closely based on the Pylos Combat Agate, discovered by archaeologists Sharon Stocker and Jack Davis in a Mycenaean-era tomb. Do look it up; it is an artifact of astonishing beauty.

The city of Iolkos was mentioned in the *Iliad* and the *Odyssey*, and its archaeological remains are near the modern port of Volos in Greece. The Thebes in the book is the one in Greece, not the one in Egypt; it is still a thriving city today. The Caves of Diros, one of the legendary entrances to Hades's realm, are on the west coast of the Mani region of the Peloponnese in southern Greece. You can take a boat trip through the caves, though we can't promise you'll reach the Underworld.

We really hope you've enjoyed reading *Daughter of the Underworld* as much as we've loved writing it. Deina and Theron's story will continue in *Queen of the Gods*, book two of the duology. Nat and Hades will be back, too, with more gods, more myths, and possibly a trip to the ancient city of Mycenae itself . . .

Acknowledgments

If it takes a village to raise a child, it takes at least a large hamlet to produce a book. Huge thanks and appreciation go from us to everyone who has helped transform *Daughter of the Underworld* from an idea into the novel you're holding in your hands.

At RCW, our agent Claire Wilson, ably assisted by Safae El-Ouahabi.

At Hot Key Books, our editors old and new, Carla Hutchinson and Ruth Bennett. It's been an absolute joy working with both of you! Also Emma Matthewson, Tia Albert, Talya Baker, Melissa Hyder, Jane Burnard, our tireless publicist Molly Holt, and everyone else at Bonnier who has worked so hard to get *Daughter of the Underworld* into the world.

Micaela Alcaino for our gorgeous, gorgeous cover. We are still in awe.

Georgie Penney for wrangling our epigraph into ancient Greek.

All our friends in the bookish community. Publishing is often a bumpy ride, and sharing it makes everything so much easier. Particular shout-outs to Perdita Cargill, Holly Race, Bex Hogan, Mary Watson, Josh Winning, Kristina Pérez, Vic James, Lexi Casale, Chris Moore, everyone in the UKYA Author Support Group, and the mighty women of Fem 2.0.

All the lovely readers and bloggers who have helped spread the word about our books over the years—we appreciate you more than we can say!

Finally, to our families, for putting up with the obsessive editing and the deadline panics. We love you all.

Coming in summer 2026,

the stunning sequel to *Daughter of the Underworld*:

Deina has only just found what matters most to her in the world—and now lost it. Bound to the Underworld, her future seems as endless and dark as the shadowy depths of Hades.

But her sacrifice isn't enough. Can Deina destroy their world's tyrants and the gods altogether?

In a game with the gods, the rewards are infinite . . . but the punishments are eternal.

Turn the page for an excerpt . . .

An excerpt from *Queen of the Gods*

Prologue

Sing, Goddess, of rage . . .

That is the poet's request. Yet whose ire shall I make the subject of my song?

The wrath of Deina? Soul Severer, daughter of Hades, demigod, thief. Tricked, as others have been, by Thanatos, god of death. The seeds he gave her, the seeds she ate that night in Thebes, allowed her to defeat the tyrant Orpheus and save her friends. They also bound her to the Underworld. Now she makes her way through the darkness to Hades's realm, her heart silenced by the grip of eternity, forced to obey the summons of her divine parent, and fearing that she will never see the sun again.

Or the anger of Theron, true prince of Thebes? Another Soul Severer, son of Orpheus. Slaying his father would have left him lawful prey of the implacable Furies. Instead, he trapped his father's blood-soaked soul forever in the Threshold. He and Deina, Hades's daughter. Only as he lost her did her realize that he loved her. Now he lingers with his companions, hidden in the forest outside Thebes. Listen: He sings a threnody, a song of lamentation, as flames take the body of the betrayer, Chryse. Within, Theron burns with frustration. He wishes to reclaim Deina from the Underworld, but he knows his duty. He must reveal the truth to the Theodesmioi, the god-marked servants of Zeus, Poseidon, Hades, and Hephaestus—the truth of what awaits them after death. Not the joy of Elysium but the eternal nightmare of becoming a blood hunter. Theron and his friends have evaded their pursuers thus far, and their sights are set on Iolkos, city of broad streets in the Gulf of Pagasae—if they can survive long enough to get there.

Perhaps I shall sing the fury of Aristaeus. He is nursing his spite and his injuries in the sumptuous marble and gold surroundings of the Cadmea, the citadel of Thebes, the mighty city of which he now claims to be king. Alone in his chambers, Aristaeus plots his enemies' destruction, sending his spies to hunt them out.

Or shall I tell of the rage of my sisters, the Fates? For this is not how the story should have gone. That night in the Cadmea, Orpheus was to have destroyed his son, or Theron was to have slain his father. Either way, Aster and Dendris were to have died. Deina, having watched her friends suffer, was to have been imprisoned in the Cadmea to serve Orpheus or Aristaeus for the rest of her days. This was what the Fates had planned. This is what would have happened—if I hadn't stepped in so many years ago. If I hadn't ensured Deina caught the plague and brought her to the point of death. If I hadn't nudged Thanatos into sparing her life. If he hadn't seen the gold bloom around her iris. If he hadn't dared to hope. Shall I tell my sisters for how long their plans have been unraveling and reveal Thanatos's role? I think I should. Even now, the cloud-capped halls of Olympus ring with the clamor of their

An excerpt from *Queen of the Gods*

protests. Once they know the full story, their resentment and bitterness will be beyond all measure.

Yes, that shall be my song. I will even give the poet his opening line.

Sing, Goddess, of the impotent fury of the Fates.

For I am Tyche, goddess of fortune.

And fate means nothing if you have luck on your side.

An excerpt from *Queen of the Gods*

1

The darkness was suffocating, and Deina felt the weight of it. Like a too-tight second skin, it squeezed her body, stealing speech as well as sight.

Thanatos's fingers still gripped her left wrist. With every step, he took her farther from her friends, further from the future she'd dared to dream of, and nearer to the perpetual imprisonment that awaited her. His touch was so cold it felt like fire. Yet she'd stopped pulling against his grasp. She was terrified that if he let go, she'd wander here forever.

On and on they walked until the darkness was displaced by a flaring brilliance that made Deina throw up her right arm to shield her eyes. That, too, faded into the ordinary glow of oil lamps.

If you could call anything about Hades's court ordinary.

Deina blinked, looking around as her vision adjusted. Thanatos was next to her, his face impassive; he'd released his grip on her arm. They were back in Hades's throne room. There was the huge obsidian looking glass on the wall, the

An excerpt from *Queen of the Gods*

sweep of its polished black disk offering Deina a shadowy reflection of herself and her surroundings. There were the two empty thrones, lofty on their dais. There, the lapis lazuli snakes that had attacked her and Theron and the others, ossified and confined to alcoves once more. So much the same—but Deina herself was different. To her dismay, her Severer's robes had gone. Instead, she was wearing the clothes that Hades had conjured her into—briefly—the last time they'd met. A full-length, one-shouldered gown of diaphanous garnet-red silk, secured by a gold belt and a single gold shoulder brooch set with rubies. There were more rubies scattered across the hem. She was shod with delicate sandals made from a fine gold mesh, and—Deina lifted one hand to her head—the dark waves of her hair were confined by what felt like more of the same material.

She turned on Thanatos.

"Is this your doing?"

"No." Hades's voice echoed through the immense room. "It's mine."

Deina spun to see one of the empty thrones now occupied. The god of the Underworld—the god who claimed to be Deina's mother—was wearing the same rich blue gown as at their last encounter. She crossed her legs and grinned. "Don't you like your new clothes, Deina? I think the color suits you. And Thanatos approves. Don't you, Thanatos?"

Thanatos blinked at Deina as though just becoming aware of her presence. His eyes widened as he took in her appearance, and a faint flush warmed his pale cheeks. Hades laughed. The sound was chilling.

An excerpt from *Queen of the Gods*

Deina wrapped her arms tightly around herself. "Why are you doing this?" she demanded.

The god tilted her head.

"Because I can." Some invisible force seized Deina's limbs and forced her onto her knees. "And because you have displeased me," Hades continued. "Either Orpheus or Theron was fated to die. One of them should have been down here by now, pursuing the desolate paths of the Underworld toward the place of judgment." Her voice began to vibrate with anger. "Instead, what do I find? Theron still alive, free, and Orpheus neither dead nor alive but trapped in the Threshold—in a place of your making." She flung out her arm, pointing at Deina accusingly.

Deina couldn't get up; her body was no longer under her control. But she could still speak.

"And I would do it all again."

"Deina"—Thanatos murmured from behind her—"you mustn't."

Deina paid no attention—she would not, could not, conceal her loathing of the being lounging on the throne. If she tried to swallow her hate, it would choke her. "I'd do all of it, and more. I do not fear the wrath of the gods. And I do not fear you."

For a moment Hades stared at her. The god's violet eyes glittered dangerously.

"You should be afraid." She gestured in Deina's direction: one languid flick of her long, beringed fingers. Deina found she could no longer move her mouth, tongue, or throat. "You should be absolutely terrified. You are bound to this realm and to me now, Daughter. And I can make you do anything. Even tear out your own hair, should it amuse me."

An excerpt from *Queen of the Gods*

Deina's fingers immediately wound themselves in her hair and began tugging against her scalp. The pain brought tears into her eyes. She would have cried out if she hadn't been silenced.

"Or . . ." Hades mulled as Deina's hands went slack. "Or I could give you a pin and command you to blind yourself." A long brooch pin appeared in Deina's left palm. Unbidden—unable to resist despite the terror turning her stomach—she lifted the pin so that the point hovered just in front of her eyeball. The muscles in her arm tensed as she tightened her grip on the sliver of sharp metal, ready to plunge it into her eye.

"Hades, you have to stop this!" Thanatos demanded.

Hades's head snapped around to stare at the god of death as Deina's arm dropped to her side; she felt faint with relief. The pin rolled away across the marble tiles.

"Have to?" The god raised an eyebrow. "You dare issue orders to me?"

Whatever spell was restraining Deina's body vanished; if she hadn't put out her hands to brace herself, she would have pitched headfirst onto the stone floor. Quickly, she forced herself to scramble upright; whatever Hades was planning next, better to meet it on her feet. The god's attention switched back to her.

"Tell me. How do you feel about Thanatos right now?" Hades questioned.

Deina gritted her teeth. "I despise him. He gave me the seeds to eat. He told me they'd make me strong enough to defeat Orpheus, made me think that they'd at least kill me, too. But instead, they bound me to the Underworld, and to you." She turned and glared at Thanatos. "He claimed to be my friend.

An excerpt from *Queen of the Gods*

He said he wanted to help me, but all the time he was working for you." Her voice sank to almost a whisper. "He betrayed me."

Thanatos shook his head, the word no forming silently on his lips.

A long-bladed knife appeared in Deina's hand.

"Well, then." Hades smiled. "Here is a chance to take your revenge. Thanatos may have carried out my orders on this occasion, but I grow tired of his insolence and mischief-making. So do my siblings on Olympus. He interferes and constantly oversteps his authority. If you want to hurt him, I won't stop you."

The knife was heavy in Deina's palm. Part of her—a large part—wanted to make Nat suffer. She'd thrown a knife at him once before, and he'd just plucked the spinning blade straight out of the air; what if, this time, Hades prevented him from defending himself? The idea of Thanatos writhing in pain at her feet was attractive. Yet Hades *wanted* her to attack the god of death. That alone seemed like a good enough reason not to. Instead, Deina lifted the knife and threw herself at Hades, allowing her rage to drive her forward, bringing up her arm to strike—

The blade slashed through nothing more than air. At the last moment, moving too quickly for her to see, Hades had stepped out of the way and was standing, instead, beside her.

"Don't test me, Daughter," the god warned.

Deina ignored her. Pivoting, she plunged the dagger toward Hades's chest. Again the god moved. Deina snarled. "Fight me, damn you!" She lunged, slashing the knife through already empty space. "You—you coward!"

An excerpt from *Queen of the Gods*

Hades raised her hand and dealt Deina a stinging backhanded blow, splitting Deina's cheek open with one of her rings and knocking her to the floor. Blood dripped from Deina's face. With a scream of rage, Deina drove the knife against the green marble, cracking the tile in two and shattering the blade.

Hades was watching her coldly.

"The seeds have made you strong, Daughter. But you can still suffer. You can still die. And you can still be forced into obedience."

Deina felt Hades seize control of her body again. She got up and began to walk toward Thanatos, coming to a halt no more than a hair's breadth away from him. Even while her mind yelled at her to stop, her arms reached up to embrace his neck. She felt herself rising onto tiptoe. Felt her lips curving into a seductive smile—despite the ripple of pain from the wound on her cheek—as her mouth lifted to his and she pressed herself against his muscled torso.

Perhaps Thanatos could see in Deina's eyes the emotions that she couldn't express any other way: horror, despair, fury. Gripping her wrists, he forced her away from him, holding her at arm's length.

"Please, Hades," he said. "You've proved your point."

"Which is?"

Thanatos gazed at Deina sadly. "That she is not a god."

"Precisely." Before Hades even finished speaking the word, Deina was freed again. Thanatos released her and backed away. "But," the god continued, "she could be."

The statement hung in the air like warm breath on a winter's day.

An excerpt from *Queen of the Gods*